'CASTING THE RUNES'
AND OTHER GHOST STORIES

MONTAGUE RHODES JAMES, author of some of the finest ghost stories in English and one of the most accomplished scholars of his generation, was born in 1862 at Goodnestone next Wingham in Kent, where his father was then Perpetual Curate, though the family moved soon afterwards to Livermere, Suffolk. He was educated at Temple Grove preparatory school, the setting of 'A School Story', and from 1876 to 1882 at Eton. At King's College, Cambridge, he took a First and became in due course Fellow, Dean, Tutor, and, in 1905, Provost. In 1895, the year he was awarded his D.Litt. degree, he published the first of his pioneering descriptive catalogues of manuscripts; the same year also saw the magazine publication of the two earliest ghost stories—'Canon Alberic's Scrap-book' and 'Lost Hearts'. *Ghost Stories of an Antiquary*, a collection of eight stories including these first two, appeared in 1904 after the death of his friend and illustrator James McBryde. This was followed by *More Ghost Stories of an Antiquary* (1911), *A Thin Ghost and Others* (1919), and *A Warning to the Curious* (1925). *His Collected Ghost Stories* were published in 1931 and have remained in print ever since. In addition to the ghost stories and his many scholarly publications, James also wrote two popular architectural and historical guidebooks (*Abbeys*, 1925 and *Suffolk and Norfolk*, 1930) and a children's fantasy (*The Five Jars*, 1922), as well as publishing a volume of recollections (*Eton and King's*, 1926) and a translation of forty Hans Andersen stories (1930). In 1918 he accepted the Provostship of Eton, the place closest to his heart, and in 1930 received the Order of Merit. He died unmarried, a much-loved and revered figure, in the Provost's Lodge at Eton in 1936.

MICHAEL COX is a graduate of St Catharine's College, Cambridge, and works in publishing. His long interest in M. R. James resulted in a widely praised bibliography, *M. R. James: An Informal Portrait* (Oxford, 1983; Oxford Paperbacks, 1986). He is also co-editor, with R. A. Gilbert, of *The Oxford Book of English Ghost Stories*.

OXFORD WORLD'S CLASSICS

*For over 100 years Oxford World's Classics have brought
readers closer to the world's great literature. Now with over 700
titles—from the 4,000-year-old myths of Mesopotamia to the
twentieth century's greatest novels—the series makes available
lesser-known as well as celebrated writing.*

*The pocket-sized hardbacks of the early years contained
introductions by Virginia Woolf, T. S. Eliot, Graham Greene,
and other literary figures which enriched the experience of reading.
Today the series is recognized for its fine scholarship and
reliability in texts that span world literature, drama and poetry,
religion, philosophy and politics. Each edition includes perceptive
commentary and essential background information to meet the
changing needs of readers.*

OXFORD WORLD'S CLASSICS

M. R. JAMES

'Casting the Runes'
and Other Ghost Stories

Edited with an Introduction and Notes by
MICHAEL COX

OXFORD
UNIVERSITY PRESS

OXFORD
UNIVERSITY PRESS

Great Clarendon Street, Oxford OX2 6DP

Oxford University Press is a department of the University of Oxford.
It furthers the University's objective of excellence in research, scholarship,
and education by publishing worldwide in

Oxford New York

Athens Auckland Bangkok Bogotá Buenos Aires Calcutta
Cape Town Chennai Dar es Salaam Delhi Florence Hong Kong Istanbul
Karachi Kuala Lumpur Madrid Melbourne Mexico City Mumbai
Nairobi Paris São Paulo Singapore Taipei Tokyo Toronto Warsaw

with associated companies in Berlin Ibadan

Oxford is a registered trade mark of Oxford University Press
in the UK and in certain other countries

Published in the United States
by Oxford University Press Inc., New York

Introduction, Note on the Text, Select Bibliography,
Chronology, and Notes © Michael Cox 1987

First issued as a World's Classics paperback 1987
Reissued as an Oxford World's Classics paperback 1999

British Library Cataloguing in Publication Data

Data available

Library of Congress Cataloging in Publication Data

James, M. R. (Montague Rhodes), 1862–1936.
Casting the runes, and other ghost stories.
(Oxford world's classics)
1. Ghost stories, English.
I. Cox, Michael, 1948– . II. Title.
PR6019.A565A6 1987 823'.912 86–23636

ISBN 0–19–283773–7

3 5 7 9 10 8 6 4

Printed in Great Britain by
Cox & Wyman Ltd.
Reading, Berkshire

CONTENTS

Contents

ACKNOWLEDGEMENTS

I AM grateful to the following for their help and advice during the preparation of this edition: Michael Halls, R. A. Gilbert, Warwick Gould, Paul Quarrie, Patrick Strong, Rosemary Pardoe, Richard Dalby, Glen Cavaliero, Roger Johnson, the late C. E. Wrangham, Nicholas Rhodes James.

For permission to quote from material in their possession I wish to thank: the Provost and Fellows, King's College, Cambridge; the Provost and Fellows, Eton College, Windsor; the Syndics of the Cambridge University Library; the Master and Fellows, Magdalene College, Cambridge; the British Library.

For
EMILY

INTRODUCTION

I

ONE writer dominates the modern English ghost story: M. R. James, without whom no anthology of supernatural fiction would be complete. Few authors in this small but fertile corner of English fiction have had James's ability to please both critics and enthusiasts. He continues to be packaged for popular consumption, mythologized as one of those 'masters of the macabre' like Edgar Allan Poe or Bram Stoker, his stories having been adapted, usually unsatisfactorily, for television and the cinema and popularized, more successfully, through radio readings and recordings. All this would have amused—and probably surprised—him; for, somewhat like the fantasies of Lewis Carroll, Tolkien, or C. S. Lewis, James's stories were written in the interstices of a busy academic life, and for James himself were incidental to more important work.

Montague Rhodes James was the youngest child and third son of Herbert James, a scholarly and genial Evangelical clergyman, and his wife Mary Emily (née Horton), the daughter of a distinguished naval officer. In 1865, when Montague was 3, the family moved from his birthplace at Goodnestone next Wingham in Kent to the Suffolk village of Great Livermere, near Bury St Edmunds. The white-walled, slate-roofed rectory on the edge of Livermere Park appears in James's posthumously published ghost story 'A Vignette', whilst East Anglia in general provided settings for some of his most memorable tales—for instance, Burnstow (based on Felixstowe) in ' "Oh, Whistle, and I'll Come to You, My Lad" ', or the fond evocation of Aldeburgh (called Seaburgh), where his grandmother had lived, in 'A Warning to the Curious'. The four children—Sydney, Herbert ('Ber'), Grace, and Montague—were brought up in what Sydney James called a 'devotional' atmosphere, which meant morning and evening prayers, a daily psalm and hymns, Bible study, and above all a respect for the ideals of Christian living. Yet it was not an oppressive regime: though he was strong for pastoral labour and scriptural authority, the rector was no Theobald Pontifex, and 'Monty' passed a placid and contented childhood under the wide Suffolk skies: a clever, sensitive boy with a rich sense of humour and a lively imagination; sociable, dutiful, and marvellously self-contained.

Early and effective Christian training, however, left its mark, though Monty never fulfilled his father's dearest wish that he should take Holy Orders (unlike Sydney, who ended his life as Archdeacon of Dudley). When the rector traced what he termed 'the anarchy of belief' in the 1880s to a rejection of dogma, claiming that people were hampered by error because they had not been taught what to believe, and when he advanced the antidote of 'wholesome restraint' against 'ill-regulated speculation', he was expressing the kind of intellectual conservatism for which his youngest son was later to be criticized at Cambridge. Monty's religious upbringing also fed his imagination. In 1933, in a sermon preached at Eton, he recalled how as a boy he had transformed the imagery of the Apocalypse into a personal vision of judgement:

There was a time in my childhood when I thought that some night as I lay in bed I should be suddenly roused by a great sound of a trumpet, that I should run to the window and look out and see the whole sky split across and lit up with glaring flame: and next moment I and everyone else in the house would be caught up into the air and made to stand with countless other people before a judge seated on a throne with great books open before him: and he would ask me questions out of what was written in those books—whether I had done this or that; and then I should be told to take my place either on the right hand or the left.[1]

Such stark Old Testament concepts of accountability and retribution were familiar to him by the age of 9, and at 71 he was 'as clear as ever I was, that I shall be judged for what I have done and what I have been'. No surprise, then, that the theme of being called to account

[1] Sermon preached in Lower Chapel, Eton, 3 December 1933 (James Papers, Cambridge University Library).

surfaces in his ghost stories, twisted though it is to include the apparently innocent like Mr Wraxall in 'Count Magnus' as well as the plainly culpable like Poschwitz (interestingly, the only unmistakably Jewish character James created) in 'The Uncommon Prayer-book'. The retributive imagery of the Middle Ages—the remorseless demons and gaping hell mouths—fascinated him intellectually and imaginatively, as did the eschatology of New Testament apocrypha, on which the medieval imagery was largely based. He recognized that his lifelong fascination with these subjects was out of the common, even describing it in the language of psychoanalysis as 'a complex'.

The boy was in nearly every respect father to the man. At his preparatory school—Temple Grove, near East Sheen, the setting of 'A School Story'—he was already precociously accumulating recondite information in what he loosely called 'the bookish line', which for him included obscure biblical legends, Church history and archictecture, and the martyr-doms of saints ('the more atrocious the better'). As in the ghost stories, detail was all. 'Nothing', he said of his school-boy forays into the margins of historical and biblical research, 'could be more inspiriting than to discover that St Livinus had his tongue cut out and was beheaded, or that David's mother was called Nitzeneth.' From Temple Grove, in the autumn of 1876, he passed on with a scholarship to Eton, which became for him 'the hub of the universe' and remained one of the main focuses of his emotional life. At Eton he showed an interest in the supernatural and the occult, and became familiar with such works as de Plancy's *Dictionnaire infernal* and Walter Map's *De Nugis Curialium*, in which he found 'some extraordinary stories about Ghosts, Vampires, Wood-nymphs, etc.'. To the *Eton Rambler* in 1880 he con-tributed an essay on ghost stories and an anecdote, claimed to be veridical but more likely his own invention—perhaps the first ghost story of his to appear in print. He did bril-liantly at Eton, securing a Newcastle Scholarship, Eton's highest academic award, and a scholarship to the college's sister foundation at Cambridge, King's, thereby realizing his father's high academic expectations of him and those of his

Eton tutor H. E. Luxmoore, who became something of a second father-figure to him. He remained at King's—from undergraduate to Provost—until 1918, when he returned to Eton as *its* Provost. He thus passed virtually his entire adult life within the confines of the two royal colleges and appropriately wrote his recollections, *Eton and King's* (1926), 'to show cause for the gratitude which I feel for the two great foundations of King Henry the Sixth'.

As an undergraduate he had collected a string of glittering prizes, culminating in a Fellowship at King's in 1887 for his dissertation on the apocryphal Apocalypse of Peter. Even before this he had taken preliminary steps towards his grand ambition of cataloguing all the Cambridge manuscript collections—a stupendous undertaking that was eventually completed in 1925. Throughout his life he published extensively and regularly—reviews, editions, translations, monographs, catalogues, articles—in the fields of palaeography, biblical and apocryphal studies, bibliography, medieval art and iconography, and antiquarianism in general. As well as his international reputation as a scholar, he was also widely known for his accessibility to undergraduates, and many fell under the spell of his charm, humour, and what we would now call charisma. Even those who regarded him as a negative influence intellectually, such as E. M. Forster's mentor Nathaniel Wedd, paid tribute to him as a civilizing and stabilizing force within both the college and the university, a link with the best of the past.

In 1905 he was elected to the Provostship of King's, a post which, though he filled it with distinction, cut him off somewhat from the undergraduates and involved him in uncongenial administrative duties. By the end of the First World War Cambridge, drained of its youth, had become a lonely place, made worse by the inevitable and debilitating losses of friends. He was tied to King's by affection and loyalty, but —as he admitted—all his sentiment was given to Eton. When he returned there as Provost he felt he had come home: and when he was installed on Michaelmas Day 1918 his old tutor, Luxmoore, was there to welcome him back. Ever a loyal Anglican and steadfast in the Christian principles of his

Victorian childhood, he had little time for the post-war world. He loathed James Joyce, Aldous Huxley, and modern art, and never had any patience with politics (one of the few issues he felt strongly about was Irish Home Rule, which he opposed). He never married. As he remarked in the stately Epilogue of *Eton and King's*, all his temporal needs had been supplied by King Henry's two colleges. After eighteen contented and productive years at Eton he died in 1936, peacefully in the Provost's Lodge on 12 June (the same day as his father) just as the *Nunc dimittis* was being sung in Chapel.

II

'Do I believe in ghosts? I am prepared to consider evidence and accept it if it satisfies me.'[2]

There, with typical reticence, spoke Dr M. R. James, O.M., Provost of Eton, and world authority on the manuscripts of Western Christendom, whose reputation as a scholar had been achieved by an enormous capacity for industry and a rare skill in making sense of disparate fragments of information. Though the careful consideration of evidence was thus second nature to him he was never prepared to discuss publicly what exactly constituted evidence for the supernatural, or on what side of the argument for the existence of ghosts he felt the balance of probability tipped. Natural caution, together with a desire not to compromise his public position, encouraged an evasion of the obvious questions about his stories.

But there was a private side to the scholar who was only prepared to consider the evidence for ghosts impartially. The voice of this man—of the much loved Monty James, who enjoyed pantomimes and writing Dodgsonian letters to young female friends (and receiving replies addressed to 'Dear Dr Apple Pie'), who devoured detective fiction, relished P. G. Wodehouse, and mimicked friends and colleagues uncannily to the life—can be caught at many points in the ghost stories. This side of him almost certainly felt the truth of Hamlet's

2 Preface to *Collected Ghost Stories* (1931).

celebrated admonition to Horatio (alluded to at the end of 'The Diary of Mr Poynter'): 'There are more things in heaven and earth . . . / Than are dreamt of in your philosophy.' In the context of his Christian faith he was unshakable in his belief that human relationships are not irrevocably sundered by death. Writing to his friend James McBryde, whose father had recently died, he spoke of his 'strong belief that instead of being cut off and separated from you by an immeasurable distance, he has as living an interest in you and your doings as ever'.[3] Though he had no interest at all in either psychical research or Spiritualism (how glad he was that J. S. Le Fanu, his favourite writer of ghost stories, had been a 'decided foe' to 'spirit rapping') he had firm views on the question of the survival of bodily death, which he discussed with his sceptical friend Arthur Benson in 1905: '[James] showed a petulant and childish mind,' Benson tartly recorded in his compulsively kept diary, 'confusing a scientific certainty with an inherited prejudice. He showed himself to be of the school . . . who when they say that they *believe* that a thing will happen only mean that they will be much annoyed if it does not.'[4]

But were there other ways in which the living and the dead could interact, apart from the 'living interest' James had spoken of to McBryde? At Eton in 1881 he had publicly maintained that something like 10 per cent of ghost stories had a basis of truth in them, but were dismissed simply because people did not like the idea of such things happening. As for himself, in private he was far more inclined to believe in supernatural possibilities than his few public pronouncements suggested. Commenting to his parents in 1891, when he was a young Fellow of King's, on a tale attaching to a wood near Livermere, he admitted that 'These things always give me *an impression of truth*. I should be very unwilling to spend a night there, and heaven send I may not have to walk that way at six o'clock in November.' (My emphasis.) M. R. James, it seems, could never quite *disbelieve* in the

[3] MRJ to James McBryde, 9 December 1898 (M. R. James Papers, King's College, Cambridge).

[4] Manuscript diary of A. C. Benson, Saturday, 6 May 1905 (Magdalene College, Cambridge).

supernatural. Late in life he wrote to McBryde's widow Gwendolen—half playfully, but also surely half seriously: 'Just now as I re-entered my room what should I see but a toad hopping across the floor . . . It has retired behind the curtain near the door. Will it clasp my leg as I go out? and what does it portend?' This same receptive core is uncovered in a story recounted by Nathaniel Wedd, who for some years had rooms below James in King's. Every night Wedd would knock out his pipe on the mantelpiece before going to bed: 'Monty told me how often and often when in bed he heard the tap, tap, tap he used to lie shivering with horror. He couldn't believe it wasn't a ghost in his outer room, though he knew all the time exactly how the sounds were produced.'[5] We may distrust that 'shivering with horror' and yet agree with Wedd that James possessed the 'Celtic sense of the unseen', exemplified in 1917 when, at two o'clock in the morning, James heard taps at his window, 'which may well have been the magnolia outside—and then for several seconds an appearance of a curtain being pulled aside from the window again and again. I lighted up at once and watched, but there was no one: I could make nothing of it.'[6] Even the great considerer of evidence could occasionally drop his guard slightly, as when he recorded reading 'with horrified interest De Lancre's *Tableau de l'Inconstance des Mauvais Anges*, 1612—chiefly confessions of witches, very carefully recorded, and I quite think with a good deal of fact at the back of them'.

James's object in writing ghost stories was to give 'pleasure of a certain sort'—what the American writer Edith Wharton called 'the fun of the shudder'. He had always enjoyed frightening others—and himself. As a boy at Eton he reported being 'engaged for a "dark seance", i.e. a telling of ghost stories, in which capacity I am rather popular just now.' The social context of his stories was to remain an essential catalyst. Their scholarly trappings—the footnotes, Latin phrases, and bibliographical references—are more

---

5 Nathaniel Wedd, unpublished Memoirs (King's College).
6 MRJ to Gordon Carey, 31 July 1917 (King's College).

than technical devices, innovative though they were for the English ghost story, to suspend the reader's disbelief: they also present a faintly ironical, at times almost self-mocking, image of himself as a scholar and antiquary that was more apparent to his first audience of *listeners* than to later readers. (The dedication of *Ghost Stories of an Antiquary* was, appropriately, 'To all those who at various times have listened to them.') More than this, the stories reflect the enclosed and privileged world in which James—and many of his friends— lived, a world bounded in his case by Cambridge and Eton, country houses and cathedral closes, museums and libraries, and by the holiday points of call—East Anglian inns, comfortable continental hotels, country railway stations—that this bachelor don regularly encountered during the palmy quarter century before the First World War.

The first of his ghost stories to be published, 'Canon Alberic's Scrap-book', was written some time after April 1892, when James visited S. Bertrand de Comminges (where the story is set), and before October 1893, when it was read at the 601st meeting of the Chitchat Society, a select and convivial weekly gathering at Cambridge which James had joined as an undergraduate in 1883 and to which he gave several papers. Early in 1894 James sent the story, then called 'A Curious Book', to his friend Leo Maxse, owner and editor of the *National Review*, who eventually published it in March 1895. 'Lost Hearts', first published in the *Pall Mall Magazine* in December that year, was written at about the same time as 'Canon Alberic', with which it was read to the Chitchat in October 1893.

The Chitchat readings coincided with the arrival in King's of James McBryde, who came up from Shrewsbury in the autumn of 1893. Despite his non-Etonian background McBryde soon found a place in Monty James's rather exclusive inner circle and for eleven years, until his early death in 1904, provided Monty with what was perhaps the most significant friendship of his life. McBryde accompanied him on several continental holidays, including the Scandinavian trips that inspired 'Number 13', 'Count Magnus', and McBryde's own illustrated comic fantasy, *The Story of a Troll-*

hunt. By the turn of the century the ghost stories had become part of a yearly ritual enjoyed by a gathering of James's close friends at King's over Christmas. The party varied from year to year, but amongst the regulars were McBryde, Luxmoore, Walter Morley Fletcher, E. G. Swain (Chaplain of King's and himself the author of Jamesian ghost stories), Arthur Benson, Owen Hugh Smith (who purchased several of the manuscripts of the ghost stories after James's death), and S. G. Lubbock, author of the 1939 *Memoir* of James. The story was often composed at 'fever heat'; as one listener recalled: 'Monty emerged from the bedroom, manuscript in hand, at last, and blew out all the candles but one, by which he seated himself. He then began to read, with more confidence than anyone else could have mustered, his wellnigh illegible script in the dim light.'[7]

Early in 1904 McBryde, then studying art at the Slade, was laid up in bed with appendicitis and to pass the time he suggested to James that he should illustrate some of his stories, with a view to publication. James responded enthusiastically and sent a list of six stories he considered suitable: 'Canon Alberic', 'The Mezzotint', 'The Ash-tree', 'Number 13', 'Count Magnus', and ' "Oh, Whistle, and I'll Come to You, My Lad" '. By the beginning of May McBryde had made good progress with several drawings; but in June, following an operation, he died, leaving only four pictures completed (two each for 'Canon Alberic' and ' "Oh, Whistle" '), two unfinished illustrations for 'Count Magnus' (the interior of the De la Gardie mausoleum, and Mr Wraxall's meeting with his pursuers at the crossroads), and a preliminary sketch for 'Number 13'. A drawing had also been planned for 'The Ash-tree' based on a real tree at Ingmanthorpe Hall in Yorkshire, the family home of McBryde's wife Gwendolen.

Ghost Stories of an Antiquary, published by Edward Arnold in November 1904, was seen by James principally as a memorial to McBryde. To fill up the volume he decided to include 'Lost Hearts' (which he said he didn't care for) and wrote a new story, 'The Treasure of Abbot Thomas', suggested by some stained glass he had examined that summer

7 Oliffe Richmond, unpublished Reminiscences (King's College).

at Ashridge Park, Hertfordshire. The book was neither widely nor particularly enthusiastically reviewed, but in due course Arnold asked James for more stories and was confident enough to offer improved terms. *More Ghost Stories of an Antiquary*, containing seven tales, duly appeared in 1911, followed by *A Thin Ghost and Others* (five stories) in 1919, and *A Warning to the Curious* (six stories) in 1925. All twenty-six stories were gathered together in 1931 as the *Collected Ghost Stories of M. R. James*, together with 'There Was a Man Dwelt by a Churchyard', 'Rats', 'After Dark in the Playing Fields', and 'Wailing Well'. The latter, written for the Eton Boy Scouts and read to them at Worbarrow Bay in Dorset by James himself in the summer of 1927, was published in a limited edition of 157 copies (seven signed by the author) by Robert Gathorne-Hardy and Kyrle Leng at the Mill House Press in 1928. The *Collected Ghost Stories* concluded with 'Stories I Have tried to Write' (first published in 1929), in which James briefly described ideas that had failed to ripen. Three stories are missing from the collected edition: 'The Experiment' (1931), 'The Malice of Inanimate Objects' (1933), and 'A Vignette' (posthumously published in 1936). All three are reprinted herein.

Enthusiastic early readers of James's stories included Arthur Machen, S. M. Ellis (who with James was responsible for establishing the canon of J. S. Le Fanu's ghost stories), Montague Summers, Theodore Roosevelt, A. E. Housman, and Thomas Hardy. In 1913 Housman sent Hardy *Ghost Stories of an Antiquary* and *More Ghost Stories*, recommending in particular ' "Oh, Whistle" ' and 'Count Magnus'. In his letter of thanks Hardy wrote that 'Two or three of them have been read aloud in this house [i.e. Max Gate, Dorchester], and I was agreeably sensible of their eeriness, even though the precaution was taken of keeping them at a safe distance from bed-time. There is much invention shown in their construction, especially in those you mention.'[8] The inventiveness of the stories is indeed one of their chief

[8] Thomas Hardy to A. E. Housman, 15 November 1913: *The Collected Letters of Thomas Hardy*, ed. Richard Little Purdy and Michael Millgate, vol. 4, 1909–13 (Oxford, 1984), 320–1.

delights and emphasizes James's freshness of approach to a literary form which by 1904 was well worked. Already in the first collection James's characteristic narrative method is highly developed and confidently applied. In 'Canon Alberic', for instance, the cardinal points of Dennistoun's character are quickly established with a few deft strokes—such as the passing indication of his well-bred pretence of not noticing the sacristan's fervent supplications to the painting of St Bernard (which Dennistoun—no familiarizing Christian name is given—loftily dismisses as a 'daub'): for him it is clearly bad form both to give way to emotion and to notice such failure in others. Though he himself comes to feel the intensest terror, the fundamentals of his 'North British character' remain unviolated: ' "I had no notion they came so dear" ', he remarks when arranging a Mass to be said for the soul of the unprincipled Canon Alberic.

In the same way it is easy for the reader, who as always in James's best stories quickly becomes engrossed in the atmosphere and the working out of the plot, to overlook the subtle shifts of perspective in the narrative. The narrator/author—for there is little practical distinction between the two—is both distanced from the action and part of it: it is he who shows the drawing of the demon to a 'Lecturer in Morphology', and the description of the drawing is the narrator's own, not Dennistoun's in report. But when the climax is reached a brief paragraph sets the reader for a moment in *Dennistoun's* place; past tense changes to present as we see through his eyes when he becomes aware of the menacing object lying at his left elbow. The viewpoint then reverts to the narrator's: 'The lower jaw was thin—what can I call it? —shallow, like a beast's . . .'. Though James always implicitly denied that his stories were anything more than the products of idle moments, such control of narrative dynamics indicates an instinctive artistry.

III

'Canon Alberic' is in many ways the quintessential M. R. James ghost story. Here, as elsewhere, James dramatizes with great skill—and with touches of characteristic humour—the unlooked-for revelation of an alien order of things, of a wholly malevolent Beyond, linked to our world by a perplexing and dangerous logic: a chance word, an unthinking action, curiosity, or simply being in the wrong place at the right time, can all spring the trap. This thematic continuity is matched by a consistent, almost formulaic technical approach:

Let us, then, be introduced to the actors in a placid way; let us see them going about their ordinary business, undisturbed by forebodings, pleased with their surroundings; and into this calm environment let the ominous thing put out its head, unobtrusively at first, and then more insistently, until it holds the stage.[9]

In 'Canon Alberic' James also puts his scholarly expertise to effective use, creating convincing background details that anchor the seemingly impossible to apparent fact and establishing an instantly recognizable style. Though the use of documentation and antiquarian detail had been used to some extent before, James may be said to have originated a new narrative mode for the English ghost story. It was for him a natural reflex: even as an Eton schoolboy he had put his specialist knowledge to mildly deceptive purposes (he once forged 'sixteenth-century' instructions for finding buried gold which, he claimed, had deceived both his tutor and the Master in College), whilst his mimetic gift showed itself in contributions to the *Eton College Chronicle*, including extracts purporting to come from a fifteenth-century Etonian's diary.

Dennistoun himself defines the typical protagonist of an M. R. James story, a bachelor scholar of independent means whose 'ordinary business' involves quiet delvings into history and antiquities. Such is Mr Williams in 'The Mezzotint' who is engaged in enlarging the Ashleian Museum's collection of topographical drawings; yet 'even a department so homely and familiar as this may have its dark corners, and to one of these Mr Williams was unexpectedly introduced.' Mr

[9] Introduction to V. H. Collins, *Ghosts and Marvels* (Oxford, 1924), vi.

Williams is only a passive observer of a supernatural event
and survives the experience. Mr Wraxall in 'Count Magnus'
is less fortunate. Wraxall is intelligent and cultivated, a
Fellow of Brasenose, Oxford, whose only fault—pardonable
in a traveller, as the narrator remarks—is over-inquisitiveness.
His fate is sealed by articulating the seemingly trivial desire
to see the long-dead Count Magnus. Once expressed, the wish
is fulfilled. On the other hand, scepticism, not scholarly
curiosity, is Professor Parkins's flaw in ' "Oh, Whistle, and
I'll Come to You, My Lad" '. Parkins is a keen golfer (not
something James means us to admire), precise of speech,
humourless, a modern Sadducee dismissive of 'antiquarian
pursuits'. Like Mr Williams he survives his experience,
though he has to come face to face—literally—with one of
James's most celebrated agents of vengeance.

The final story in the first collection, 'The Treasure of
Abbot Thomas', which begins audaciously with a whole page
of Latin, introduces elements of the Holmesian detective
story in the ingenious unravelling by the clerical antiquary
Mr Somerton of the clues that lead him to the gold hidden
by the unscrupulous Abbot Thomas in the sixteenth century.
Like Parkins, he disregards a warning (*'Gare à qui la touche'*)
and by this point in the collection we expect the worst. What
awaits Mr Somerton in the well at Steinfeld is a truly night-
marish encounter with something that cannot strictly be
called a ghost (the same is true of several other Jamesian
entities) but whose very lack of definition intensifies the
shock and revulsion Somerton experiences: ' "I was conscious
of a most horrible smell of mould, and of a cold kind of face
pressed against my own, and moving slowly over it . . ." ' The
post-Freudian reader may speculate that this repulsive
moment of intimacy perhaps exteriorizes a fear of sexual
contact in James himself; at any rate it is one of the most
disturbing moments in his fiction, matched only by the violation of Mr Dunning's bed—the one place where he *ought*
to feel safe—in 'Casting the Runes'.

In the world of M. R. James's antiquaries, passions are
aroused not by human contact, or even money or power, but
by intellectual endeavour and discovery. Dennistoun again is

typical: 'All at once Dennistoun's cherished dreams of finding
priceless manuscripts in untrodden corners of France flashed
up . . .'. The same cerebral pleasure is shared by Mr Somerton,
by Mr Anderson in 'Number 13', by Paxton in 'A Warning
to the Curious'; even the amateur Mr Humphreys, in 'Mr
Humphreys and his Inheritance', anticipates the drawing up
of a *catalogue raisonné* as being 'a delicious occupation for
winter'. Women figure rarely in James's stories, for this is a
world where sex is not. The sacristan's daughter in 'Canon
Alberic' is merely 'a handsome girl enough', whilst the married state as depicted in 'The Rose Garden' is one of petty
domestic tyranny on the part of Mrs Anstruther and a
perpetual pining for the golf links on the part of her husband.
Garrett in 'The Tractate Middoth' does feel the pull of sexual
attraction; but it hardly impinges on the story. Only the
tragic mock-wooing of Ann Clark in 'Martin's Close' (*More
Ghost Stories*, 1911)—one of a handful of stories with historical settings, this one drawing on the State Trials of the late
seventeenth century—has sexual overtones; and here, unusually for James, the female ghost is as much a victim as her
imagined lover and murderer George Martin, sentenced to
hang by the implacable Judge Jefferies. James linked sex with
needless physical horror as things to be avoided by the ghost
story writer: 'Reticence may be an elderly doctrine to preach,'
he wrote, 'yet from the artistic point of view I am sure it is a
sound one . . . sex is tiresome enough in the novels; in a ghost
story, or as the backbone of a ghost story, I have no patience
with it.'[10]

The sexlessness of James's fiction reflects a social structure
that faces neither disruption nor tension. His characters move
in an unthreatened world—until, that is, 'the ominous thing'
puts out its head. Order and custom prevail, with social
distinctions, expressed through standard and non-standard
language, quietly taken for granted. Though James's treatment of his minor characters—the servants, housekeepers,
gardeners, tradesmen, bus conductors, and various factotums
—may now seem occasionally patronizing, his delight in the

---

[10] 'Some Remarks on Ghost Stories', *The Bookman* (Dec. 1929), 171.

vigour of vernacular idiom was genuine and is evident, for instance, in the loquacious Mr Cooper in 'Mr Humphreys and his Inheritance', or in the narrative of the admirable Mr Worby in 'An Episode of Cathedral History'.

It is not people, however, but places and landscapes that sharpen the focus of James's prose. (Places, he once said, had been 'prolific in suggestion'.) It is landscape that draws forth a rare passage of carefully modulated lyricism in 'Canon Alberic':

It was time to ring the *Angelus*: a few pulls at the reluctant rope, and the great bell *Bertrande* high in the tower began to speak, and swung her voice up among the pines and down to the valleys loud with mountain-streams, calling the dwellers on those lonely hills to remember and repeat the Salutation of the angel to her whom he called Blessed among women.

Landscape, again, turns description into meditation in 'A Neighbour's Landmark':

The sun was down behind the hill, and the light was off the fields, and when the clock bell in the Church tower struck seven, I thought no longer of kind mellow evening hours of rest, and scents of flowers and woods on evening air . . . but instead images came to me of dusty beams and creeping spiders and savage owls up in the tower, and forgotten graves and their ugly contents below, and of flying Time and all it had taken out of my life.

Set in the landscapes of James's stories are the small country houses (often East Anglian) he loved so much. It is M. R. James *in propria persona* who writes in the opening paragraph of 'The Ash-tree' (1904) of the

grey paling of split oak, the noble trees, the meres with their reed beds, and the line of distant woods. Then, I like the pillared portico . . . the hall inside . . . I like the library, too, where you may find anything from a Psalter of the thirteenth century to a Shakespeare quarto . . . I wish to have one of these houses, and enough money to keep it together and entertain my friends in it modestly.

James's sensitivity to place and to the living presence of

the past gives his stories a resonance and edge that more than compensate for the occasional flatness or stereotypicality of his characters. For the kind of ghost story James wrote, atmosphere and incident are more important than subtle character delineation, for we need to feel that there is nothing peculiar to the protagonists that singles them out for supernatural violation. As Mr Somerton remarks plaintively in 'The Treasure of Abbot Thomas': ' "Well, what would any human being have been tempted to do . . . in my place?" ' In James's fictional world we are meant to feel the capriciousness of supernatural malevolence *and* realize that rules exist of which we have no knowledge—as indicated by a stone or a prayer-book that must not be removed, a whistle that ought not to be blown, a wish that should not be spoken, a crown that must not be dug up. Though we are shown wrongdoers who receive their just deserts, such as Karswell or John Eldred, many of James's characters are baffled victims, the most baffled of all being Mr Wraxall: 'His constant cry is "What has he done?" . . . What can he do but lock his door and cry to God?'

The 'ghosts' themselves are various in form but united in their malevolence and palpability. They are all fearfully present to the physical senses. James is especially adept at conveying tactile horror:

He put his hand into the well-known nook under the pillow: only, it did not get so far. What he touched was . . . a mouth, with teeth, and with hair about it, and, he declares, not the mouth of a human being.   ('Casting the Runes')

I was resting my hand on one of the carved figures . . . the wood seemed to become chilly and soft as if made of wet linen.
                    ('The Stalls of Barchester Cathedral')

James's facility for tapping natural sources of revulsion can be seen in the brilliantly executed climax of 'Mr Humphreys and his Inheritance'. Combined with this is an unerring eye for the telling detail that makes his ghosts so unsettling:

It was not a mask. It was a face—large, smooth, and pink. She remembers the minute drops of perspiration which were starting from its forehead: she remembers how the jaws were clean-

shaven and the eyes shut. She remembers also, and with an
accuracy which makes the thought intolerable to her, how the
mouth was open and a single tooth appeared below the upper
lip.   ('The Rose Garden')

Though few of James's executors of unappeasable malice
have a specific *literary* lineage, he was contributing to a form
that by 1895, when the first of his stories were published,
was well established. We encounter ghosts in Homer,
Chaucer, the ballads; in Shakespeare and Jacobean tragedy;
and in the melodramatic spooks of Gothic romance. But it is
not until the 1820s that the short literary ghost story began
to mature into genuine art, with Sir Walter Scott's 'Wandering Willie's Tale' (from *Redgauntlet*, 1824) and 'The
Tapestried Chamber' (from *The Keepsake*, 1829). A decade
later the first ghost stories of Joseph Sheridan Le Fanu (1814–
73) began to appear in the *Dublin University Magazine*. In
James's estimation (and his opinion carries weight) the best
ghost stories in English were all by Le Fanu, who succeeded
in inspiring 'a mysterious terror' better than any other writer.
James observed in Le Fanu the necessity to pace a ghost story:
'The gradual removal of one safeguard after another, the
victim's dim forebodings of what is to happen gradually growing clearer; these are the processes which generally increase
the strain of excitement.' He took note too of the effect of
'unexplained hints': 'The reader is never allowed to know the
full theory which underlies any of [Le Fanu's] ghost stories,
but this Le Fanu has in common with many inferior artists.
Only you feel that he has a complete explanation to give if
he would only vouchsafe it.' The most complete of Le Fanu's
'unexplained hints' occurs in 'The Familiar' (first published
as 'The Watcher', 1851), a story James rated highly. Captain
Barton, like Professor Parkins in ' "Oh, Whistle" ', starts out
by being 'an utter disbeliever in what are usually termed
preternatural agencies'; but he becomes convinced by his
experiences that

there does exist beyond this a spiritual world—a system whose
workings are generally in mercy hidden from us—a system which
may be, and which is sometimes, partially and terribly revealed.

I am sure—I know . . . that there is a God—a dreadful God—and that retribution follows guilt, in ways the most mysterious and stupendous—by agencies the most inexplicable and terrible . . .

We might perhaps deduce some such 'system' at work in James's stories, but none of his victims ever experiences Captain Barton's epiphanic certitude. The narrator's comment on the aftermath of Parkins's adventure at the Globe Inn is merely that 'the Professor's views on certain points are less clear cut than they used to be'. Even more than Le Fanu, the power of omission (a feature, too, of many traditional ballads with a supernatural theme) is apparent throughout James's work, so that the gulf between action and reaction is never satisfactorily bridged. 'The reading of many ghost stories', he concluded, 'has shown me that the greatest successes have been scored by the authors who can make us envisage a definite time and place, and give us plenty of clear-cut detail, but who, when the climax is reached, allow us to be just a little in the dark as to the workings of their machinery.'[11]

Though James's stories owe much to his keen enjoyment of Le Fanu over many years (he had, he said, lost count of how many times he had read *The House by the Churchyard*) they are far from being blatantly Le Fanuesque in either theme or treatment. Superficially more controlled than Le Fanu's, James's stories are actually more anarchic in their implications. Their cumulative effect is to suggest an ineradicable perplexity in the mind of their creator which pulls against the humour, against the consoling anchorage of historical detail, and against the pose of narrational detachment. According to James, in the 1931 Preface to the collected edition, only one incident in his tales derived from his own experience (in ' "Oh, Whistle" '); but did his last ghost story, 'A Vignette', set at Livermere and narrated, unusually for James, in the first person, perhaps refer to another—an inexplicable childhood incident that (as the story puts it) 'had some formidable power of clinging through many years to my imagination', making adult scepticism about the super-

---

[11] *The Bookman* (Dec. 1929), 172.

natural (whatever he maintained publicly) impossible? an experience, to borrow words from 'A Neighbour's Landmark', which he could neither explain away nor fit into the scheme of his life? Though 'A Vignette' must not be read as unadorned autobiography its tone is quite unlike any of James's other stories and suggests a strong personal element— not just in the actuality of the setting, but more particularly in the confessional mood of the piece (appropriate at this point in his life). The narrator remarks: 'That I was upset by something I had seen must have been pretty clear, but I am very sure that I fought off all attempts to describe it.' Such reticence is wholly in keeping with James's disinclination to place his obvious fascination with the supernatural in a personal context. It also has the ring of psychological truth, for as another of James's narrators (in 'Rats') noted: 'I have not had other experiences of the kind which are called super-natural, or -normal, or -physical, but, though I knew very well I must speak of this one before long, I was not at all anxious to do so; and I think I have read that this is a common case.' On the other hand, 'A Vignette' may be nothing more than an embellishment of what James identified as the definite source of his interest in ghosts: a cardboard Ghost in a toy Punch and Judy set—'a tall figure habited in white with an unnaturally long and narrow head . . . and a dismal visage. Upon this my conceptions of a ghost were based, and for years it permeated my dreams.'[12]

When all is said and done, though, we do not read the ghost stories of M. R. James—or indeed any ghost story worthy of the name—for biographical revelations or enlightenment on the mysteries of life and death but for the supplying of that 'pleasure of a certain sort' to which he himself referred. Even if we are not frightened by the stories (and some people are not) there remains much to admire and enjoy: their inventiveness and quiet humour; the controlling presence of a learned and humane intelligence; the allusive texts; the evocation of place and time. James's method of creating a convincing reality into which the supernatural can

12 'Ghosts—Treat Them Gently!', *Evening News* (17 Apr. 1931).

be intruded has its own fascination and inspired others to write antiquarian ghost stories, beginning with his colleague at King's Edmund Gill Swain, whose *Stoneground Ghost Tales* (dedicated to James) appeared in 1912. By 1919 Arthur Gray, Master of Jesus College, Cambridge, had taken the deadpan antiquarian approach to its limits in *Tedious Brief Tales of Granta and Gramarye*, and the 1940s saw two accomplished collections (both associated with King's) that continued the Jamesian style: R. H. Malden's *Nine Ghosts* (1943, though the earliest story first appeared in 1912) and A. N. L. Munby's *The Alabaster Hand* (1949), with its Latin dedication to James. But these form only the tip of a considerable iceberg, and it is probable that M. R. James has generated more imitators than any other English ghost story writer.

The English ghost story is a vigorous and varied form and deserves more critical attention than it currently enjoys. Happily, it has never lacked enthusiastic readers, for whom the tales of M. R. James remain as entertaining, and as implausibly plausible, as ever. The secret of their success is at once obvious and impenetrable; but perhaps a quatrain by W. F. Harvey, himself a respected writer of ghost stories, comes as close to definition as we need:

> I will tell you what always has frightened me most
> In reading or writing the tale of a ghost:
> Not details, however grotesque or uncouth,
> But the lurking belief that the story's the truth.

MICHAEL COX

NOTE ON THE TEXT

The Collected Ghost Stories of M. R. James (CGS, 1931) has formed the basis of nearly every subsequent edition or selection. James wrote to Gwendolen McBryde on 4 February 1931 that 'Proofs of the Collected Ghost Stories come in almost daily—we are at p. 448 and I think it should run to nearly 600, which seems a lot.' To the extent that James corrected and presumably approved the proofs we might suppose CGS to represent his final textual intentions. But James was not a particularly good proof-reader; as he went on to tell Gwendolen: 'It's very hard to nail the mistakes: if the words are real words, everything looks all right.' More importantly, he never looked upon the texts of his stories with a possessive or a fastidious eye, and a study of the available manuscripts suggests that he submitted happily to an imposed house style, especially in the matter of punctuation and paragraphing.

There is thus a case to be argued against duplicating CGS uncritically where manuscripts are available for comparison. In the end, this is largely a matter of removing redundant accidentals (commas, semicolons, and so on) and reverting to the freer use of punctuation apparent in the manuscript texts. Though such changes may appear trivial in isolation their cumulative effect can be significant for the narrative energy of a particular story. This is the first edition of James's stories to draw on manuscript readings in this way, though I have refrained from reproducing an exact transcript of existing manuscripts, which would have been a rather pointless exercise in pedantry.

Substantive discrepancies between CGS and manuscript are another matter and I have assumed that, on the whole, these were instigated, or at least approved, by James at proof stage. However, in one or two cases, indicated in the Explanatory Notes, manuscript readings seem worth reinstating: for instance, the wholly M. R. Jamesian aside about the quality of Vin de Limoux in 'Canon Alberic's Scrap-book' (see p. 9).

The paragraphing of CGS has been generally followed, since James seems to have paid little attention to this in the heat of composition; but, again, I have tried to retain a flexible attitude and have reverted to the manuscript where this seemed dramatically appropriate or more in line with current practice. In minor details—such as layout of quoted material—the texts have been silently brought up to date.

The result is a number of syncretic texts that combine the best (in the present editor's view) of manuscript and printed versions. For those stories where manuscripts are unavailable I have followed *CGS* or, in the case of the last three stories, the earliest printed versions. The choice of text for each story is indicated in the Explanatory Notes.

SELECT BIBLIOGRAPHY

BIOGRAPHY AND BIBLIOGRAPHY

The two main sources for M. R. James's life and work are R. W. Pfaff, *Montague Rhodes James* (1980) and my own *M. R. James: An Informal Portrait* (Oxford, 1983; Oxford Paperbacks, 1986). The latter focuses on James's private life and personal characteristics and contains a chapter on the genesis and development of the ghost stories; Pfaff's book concentrates on James's scholarship and includes a valuable chronological bibliography of his scholarly writings. For James's other published work A. F. Scholfield's bibliography *Elenchus Scriptorum Montacutii Rhodes James* (1935), based on a list prepared by James, is adequate but not definitive. Also of interest are J. Randolph Cox, 'Montague Rhodes James: An Annotated Bibliography of Writings About Him', *English Literature in Transition*, 12 (1969), 203–10, and Richard Dalby, 'The Ghost Stories of M. R. James', *Book and Magazine Collector*, 16 (June 1985), 46–53.

S. G. Lubbock's *A Memoir of Montague Rhodes James* (Cambridge, 1939), which reprints Scholfield's *Elenchus*, is a brief but charming portrait of James by a close friend. Other biographical sources of interest include: *Montague Rhodes James . . . Three Tributes* (by J. H. Clapham, A. B. Ramsay, and from *The Times*) (1936); Sibyl Cropper, 'Letters to a Child' (i.e. to her from James), *Cornhill Magazine*, 160 (Nov. 1939), 639–51; *Eton College Chronicle*, 18 June 1936 (various obituary notices); Sir Stephen Gaselee, 'Montague Rhodes James 1862–1936', *Proceedings of the British Academy*, 22 (1936), 418–33; M. R. James, *Eton and King's: Recollections, Mostly Trivial* (1926); Shane Leslie, 'Montague Rhodes James', *Quarterly Review*, 304 (1966), 45–56; Gwendolen McBryde (ed.), *Montague Rhodes James: Letters to a Friend* (1956); Norman Scarfe, 'The Strangeness Present. M. R. James's Suffolk', *Country Life* (6 Nov. 1986), 1416–19. See also the *Dictionary of National Biography* (1931–40), 471–3 (article by A. F. Scholfield). For a résumé of unpublished biographical sources see my *M. R. James* (above), pp. 236–7.

M. R. JAMES'S GHOST STORIES

A. *Magazine publication*

'Canon Alberic's Scrap-book', *National Review*, XXV, 145 (Mar. 1895), 132–41; 'Lost Hearts', *Pall Mall Magazine*, VII, 32 (Dec. 1895), 639–47; 'The Stalls of Barchester Cathedral', *Contemporary Review*, XCVII, 35 (1910), 449–60; 'The Story of a Disappearance and an Appearance', *Cambridge Review* (4 June 1913), 535–40; 'An Episode of Cathedral History', *Cambridge Review* (10 June 1914), 533–8; 'The Uncommon Prayer-book', *Atlantic Monthly*, 127, 6 (June 1921), 756–65; 'The Haunted Doll's House', *Empire Review*, XXXVIII, 265 (Feb. 1923), 91–101; 'A Neighbour's Landmark', *The Eton Chronic* (17 Mar. 1924), 4–10; 'After Dark in the Playing Fields', *College Days*, 10 (28 June 1924), 311–12, 314; 'There Was a Man Dwelt by a Churchyard', *Snapdragon* (6 Dec. 1924), 4–5; 'A View from a Hill', *London Mercury*, XII, 67 (May 1925), 17–30; 'A Warning to the Curious', *London Mercury*, XII, 70 (Aug. 1925), 354–65; 'Rats', *At Random* (23 Mar. 1929), 12–14; 'The Experiment', *Morning Post* (31 Dec. 1930), 8; 'The Malice of Inanimate Objects', *The Masquerade*, I, 1 (June 1933), 29–32; 'A Vignette', *London Mercury*, 35 (Nov. 1936), 18–22.

B. *Volume publication*

Ghost Stories of an Antiquary (1904); *More Ghost Stories of an Antiquary* (1911); *A Thin Ghost and Others* (1919); *A Warning to the Curious* (1925); *Wailing Well* (1928) (limited edition of this story by Robert Gathorne-Hardy and Kyrle Leng, Mill House Press, Stanford Dingley); *Collected Ghost Stories* (1931) (stories from the four individual collections plus 'An Evening's Entertainment', 'There Was a Man Dwelt by a Churchyard', 'Rats', 'After Dark in the Playing Fields', 'Wailing Well', and 'Stories I Have Tried to Write').

   Thirteen Ghost Stories (Albatross, 1935) (first paperback selection); *Ghost Stories of an Antiquary* (Penguin, 1937) (*More Ghost Stories*, Penguin 1959; combined edition, 1974; *Collected Ghost Stories*, 1985); *Ghost Stories of an Antiquary*, introduction by E. F. Bleiler (Dover paperback, 1971); *Ghost Stories of M. R. James*, introduction by Nigel Kneale (Folio Society, 1973); *The Ghost Stories of M. R. James*, selected and introduced by Michael Cox, illustrations by Rosalind Caldecott (Oxford, 1986).

C. James on Ghost Stories

V. H. Collins (ed.), *Ghosts and Marvels: A Selection of Uncanny Tales* (Oxford, 1924), introduction by MRJ; [J. S. Le Fanu], *Madam Crowl's Ghost*, ed., with a bibliography of Le Fanu's novels and tales, by MRJ (1923); 'The Novels and Stories of J. S. Le Fanu' (abstract of a lecture), *Proceedings of the Royal Institution*, 24 (1923–4), 79–80 (for an edited version of MRJ's notes for this lecture, now at King's College, Cambridge, see Rosemary Pardoe, 'M. R. James on J. S. Le Fanu', *Ghosts and Scholars*, 7 (1985), 24–7); MRJ, 'Some Remarks on Ghost Stories', *The Bookman* (Dec. 1929), 169–72; [J. S. Le Fanu], *Uncle Silas*, introduction by MRJ (1926); 'Stories I Have Tried to Write', *The Touchstone*, 2 (30 Nov. 1929), 46–7; 'Ghost Story Competition', *Spectator* (27 Dec. 1930) (comments on a competition run by the *Spectator* and judged by MRJ); 'Ghosts—Treat Them Gently!', *Evening News* (17 April 1931).

CRITICISM

There is no full-length study of James's ghost stories, but the following have material of interest: Julia Briggs, in *Night Visitors: The Rise and Fall of the English Ghost Story* (1977); Mary Butts, 'The Art of M. R. James', *London Mercury*, 29 (1934), 306–17 (apparently the first critical appraisal of MRJ's ghost stories and which he dismissed as 'fulsome'); J. R. Cox, 'Ghostly Antiquary: The Stories of M. R. James', *English Literature in Transition*, 12 (1969), 197–202; Michael Cox, 'The Malice of Inanimate Objects', *Ghosts and Scholars*, 6 (1984), 1–5; Peter Fleming, 'The Stuff of Nightmares', *Spectator Literary Supplement*, 18 (Apr. 1931), 633; Michael Halls, 'A Night in King's College Chapel', *Ghosts and Scholars*, 7 (1985), 1–5, 23; Richard Holmes, 'Of Ghosts and King's', *The Times* (23 Nov. 1974); H. P. Lovecraft, in *Supernatural Horror in Literature* (1945); Peter Penzoldt, in *The Supernatural in Fiction* (1952); Jack Sullivan, in *Elegant Nightmares: The English Ghost Story From Le Fanu to Blackwood* (1978); Austin Warren, 'The Marvels of M. R. James, Antiquary', in *Connections* (1970), 86–107, 194–5. For the English ghost story tradition as a whole see the introduction to Michael Cox and R. A. Gilbert (eds.), *The Oxford Book of English Ghost Stories* (1986).

A CHRONOLOGY OF M. R. JAMES

1862   M. R. James born on 1 August at Goodnestone next Wingham, Kent, third son and fourth child of the Revd Herbert James and Mary Emily (*née* Horton).

1865   James family moves to Livermere, near Bury St Edmunds, Suffolk.

1873–6   MRJ at Temple Grove preparatory school, East Sheen (setting of 'A School Story'). Meets A. C. Benson.

1876–82   MRJ at Eton (King's Scholar). Newcastle Scholar 1882.

1882–5   Undergraduate scholar at King's College, Cambridge. Takes Firsts in both Parts of the Classical Tripos.

1886   Appointed Assistant Director of the Fitzwilliam Museum.

1887   Awarded Fellowship at King's for dissertation on the Apocalypse of Peter.

1887–8   Excavating in Cyprus and considering classical archaeology as a career. 'Excavations in Cyprus, 1887–8' (with D. G. Hogarth *et al.*) published in the *Journal of Hellenic Studies* for 1888.

1889   Becomes Dean of King's.

1892   In the spring, holidays in France with J. A. Robinson and Arthur Shipley and visits S. Bertrand de Comminges. July: visits Ireland and sees the preserved corpses in St Michan's, Dublin, mentioned in 'Lost Hearts'.

1893   Autumn: James McBryde comes up to King's from Shrewsbury. MRJ appointed Director of the Fitzwilliam Museum. 28 October: 'Canon Alberic' and 'Lost Hearts' read to the Chitchat Society.

1895   Awarded D.Litt. degree. The first of MRJ's descriptive catalogues of MSS published. March: 'Canon Alberic's Scrap-book' published in the *National Review*; December: 'Lost Hearts' published in the *Pall Mall Magazine*.

1898   September: Mary Emily James dies at Livermere.

1899   Holiday in Denmark with James McBryde and Will Stone.

1900   Becomes Tutor of King's. Second Danish holiday with McBryde and Stone.

1901   Holiday in Sweden, which provides background for 'Count Magnus'.

1902   Christmas: MRJ visits his friend Walter Morley Fletcher's fiancée, Maisie Cropper, and her family at Ellergreen in Westmorland.

1903   James McBryde marries Gwendolen Grotrian.

1904   5 June: McBryde dies. MRJ becomes guardian to Jane McBryde. McBryde's *The Story of a Troll-hunt* published by subscription. November: *Ghost Stories of an Antiquary*, illustrated by James McBryde, published by Edward Arnold.

1905   13 May: MRJ elected Provost of King's. November/December: 'The Edwin Drood Syndicate' published in the *Cambridge Review*.

1909   12 June: Herbert James dies at Livermere.

1910   'The Stalls of Barchester Cathedral' published in the *Contemporary Review*.

1911   *More Ghost Stories of an Antiquary* published by Edward Arnold.

1913   June: 'The Story of a Disappearance and an Appearance' published in the *Cambridge Review*. October: MRJ becomes Vice-Chancellor of Cambridge.

1914   June: 'An Episode of Cathedral History' published in the *Cambridge Review*.

1918   29 September: MRJ installed as Provost of Eton.

1919   *A Thin Ghost and Others* published by Edward Arnold.

1921   June: 'The Uncommon Prayer-book' published in the *Atlantic Monthly*.

1922   *The Five Jars* published by Arnold, with illustrations by Gilbert James (no relation).

1923   February: 'The Haunted Doll's House' appears in the *Empire Review*. 16 March: MRJ lectures on Le Fanu at the Royal Institution. Le Fanu's *Madam Crowl's Ghost*, edited and introduced by MRJ.

1924   March: 'A Neighbour's Landmark' published in the *Eton Chronic*. 'After Dark in the Playing Fields' appears in *College Days* (June) and 'There Was a Man Dwelt by a Churchyard' in *Snapdragon* (December). *The Apocryphal*

New Testament published by Oxford University Press. Introduction to V. H. Collins (ed.), *Ghosts and Marvels*.

1925   *Abbeys* (for the Great Western Railway) published. MRJ appointed a Trustee of the British Museum. 'A View from a Hill' and 'A Warning to the Curious' appear in the *London Mercury* (May and August), reprinted later this year in *A Warning to the Curious*. Arthur Benson dies (17 June).

1926   *Eton and King's* published by Williams and Norgate. November: H. E. Luxmoore, MRJ's Eton tutor, dies. Le Fanu's *Uncle Silas*, published with an introduction by MRJ.

1927   Summer: 'Wailing Well' read to Eton Scout Troop at Worbarrow Bay, Dorset.

1928   Limited edition of *Wailing Well* published by Robert Gathorne-Hardy and Kyrle Leng at the Mill House Press.

1929   March: 'Rats' published in *At Random* (reprinted this year in Lady Cynthia Asquith's anthology *Shudders*). November: 'Stories I Have Tried to Write' published in *The Touchstone*. 'Some Remarks on Ghost Stories' published in *The Bookman* (December).

1930   MRJ awarded the Order of Merit. *Suffolk and Norfolk* and *Hans Andersen: Forty Stories* published.

1931   April: *The Collected Ghost Stories of M. R. James* published by Arnold. 31 December: 'The Experiment: A New Year's Eve Ghost Story' appears in the *Morning Post*.

1933   June: 'The Malice of Inanimate Objects' published in *The Masquerade*.

1934   Sydney Rhodes James, Archdeacon of Dudley and MRJ's eldest brother, dies.

1936   Friday 12 June: MRJ dies peacefully at Eton. Monday, 5 June: MRJ buried in Eton town cemetery. November: 'A Vignette' published posthumously in the *London Mercury*. 9 November: sale of MRJ's books and some of the ghost story manuscripts at Sotheby's.

'Casting the Runes'

and Other Ghost Stories

CANON ALBERIC'S SCRAP-BOOK

S. BERTRAND DE COMMINGES* is a decayed town on the spurs of the Pyrenees, not very far from Toulouse, and still nearer to Bagnères-de-Luchon. It was the site of a bishopric until the Revolution, and has a cathedral which is visited by a certain number of tourists. In the spring of 1883 an Englishman arrived at this old-world place—I can hardly dignify it with the name of city, for there are not a thousand inhabitants. He was a Cambridge man, who had come specially from Toulouse to see S. Bertrand's Church, and had left two friends who were less keen archaeologists than himself in their hotel at Toulouse under promise to join him on the following morning. Half an hour at the church would satisfy *them*, and all three could then pursue their journey in the direction of Auch. But our Englishman had come early on the day in question, and proposed to himself to fill a note-book* and to use several dozens of plates in the process of describing and photographing every corner of the wonderful church that dominates the little hill of Comminges. In order to carry out this design satisfactorily, it was necessary to monopolize the verger of the church for the day. The verger or sacristan (I prefer the latter appellation, inaccurate as it may be) was accordingly sent for by the somewhat brusque lady who keeps the inn of the *Chapeau Rouge;** and when he came, the Englishman found him an unexpectedly interesting object of study. It was not in the personal appearance of the little, dry, weazened* old man that the interest lay, for he was precisely like dozens of other church-guardians in France, but in a curious furtive, or rather hunted and oppressed air which he had. He was perpetually half-glancing behind him; the muscles of his back and shoulders seemed to be hunched in a continual nervous contraction, as if he were expecting every moment to find himself in the clutch of an enemy. The Englishman hardly knew whether to put him down as a man haunted by a fixed delusion, or as one oppressed by a guilty conscience, or as an unbearably henpecked husband. The probabilities when reckoned up certainly pointed to the last idea; but still, the impression conveyed was that of a more formidable persecutor even than a termagant wife.

However, the Englishman (let us call him Dennistoun*) was soon too deep in his notebook and too busy with his camera to give more than an occasional glance to the sacristan.* Whenever he did look at him, he found him at no great distance, either huddling himself back against the wall or crouching in one of the gorgeous stalls. Dennistoun became rather fidgety after a time. Mingled suspicions—that he was keeping the old man from his *déjeuner*—that he was regarded as likely to make away with S. Bertrand's ivory crozier or with the dusty stuffed crocodile that hangs over the font—began to torment him. 'Won't you go home?' he said at last; 'I'm quite well able to finish my notes alone: you can lock me in, if you like. I shall want at least two hours more here, and it must be cold for you, isn't it?'

'Good heavens!' said the little man, whom the suggestion seemed to throw into a state of unaccountable terror, 'such a thing cannot be thought of for a moment. Leave monsieur alone in the church? No, no! Two hours, three hours, all will be the same to me. I have breakfasted, I am not at all cold, with many thanks to monsieur.' 'Very well, my little man,' quoth Dennistoun to himself: 'you have been warned, and you must take the consequences.'

Before the expiration of the two hours, the stalls, the enormous dilapidated organ, the choir-screen of Bishop John de Mauléon, the remnants of glass and tapestry, and the objects in the treasure-chamber, had been well and truly examined; the sacristan still keeping at Dennistoun's heels and every now and then whipping round as if he had been stung when one or other of the strange noises that trouble a large empty building fell on his ear. Curious noises they were sometimes. 'Once,' Dennistoun said to me, 'I could have sworn I heard a thin metallic voice laughing high up in the tower. I darted an inquiring glance at my sacristan. He was white to the lips. "It is he—that is, it is no one: the door is locked" was all he said, and we looked at each other for a full minute.'

Another little incident puzzled Dennistoun a good deal. He was examining a large dark picture that hangs behind the altar, one of a series illustrating the miracles of S. Bertrand. The composition of the picture is wellnigh indecipherable, but there is a Latin legend below, which runs thus: 'Qualiter S. Bertrandus liberavit hominem quem diabolus diu volebat strangulare.'[1] Dennistoun was turning to the sacristan with a smile and a jocular remark of some sort on his lips, but he was confounded to see the old man on his knees, gazing at the picture with the eye of a suppliant in agony, his hands tightly clasped, and a rain of tears on his cheeks. Dennistoun naturally pretended to have noticed nothing, but the question would not away from him, Why should a daub of this kind affect anyone so strongly? He seemed to himself to be getting some sort of clue to the reason of the strange look that had been puzzling him all the day: the man must be a monomaniac; but what was his monomania?

It was nearly five o'clock; the short day was drawing in, and the church began to fill with shadows, while the curious noises, the muffled footfalls and distant talking voices that had been perceptible all day seemed—no doubt because of the fading light and the consequently quickened sense of hearing—to become more frequent and insistent. The sacristan began for the first time to show signs of hurry and impatience. He heaved a sigh of relief when camera and notebook were finally packed up and stowed away, and hurriedly beckoned Dennistoun to the western door of the church, under the tower. It was time to ring the *Angelus*:* a few pulls at the reluctant rope, and the great bell *Bertrande* high in the tower began to speak, and swung her voice up among the pines and down to the valleys loud with mountain-streams, calling the dwellers on those lonely hills to remember and repeat the Salutation of the angel to her whom he called Blessed among women. With that a profound quiet seemed to fall for the

1 How S. Bertrand delivered a man whom the Devil long sought to strangle.

first time that day upon the little town, and Dennistoun and the sacristan went out of the church.

On the doorstep they fell into conversation.

'Monsieur seemed to interest himself in the old choir-books in the sacristy.'

'Undoubtedly. I was going to ask you if there were a library in the town.'

'No, monsieur—perhaps there used to be one belonging to the Chapter, but it is now such a small place——' Here came a strange pause of irresolution, as it seemed. Then, with a sort of plunge he went on: 'But if monsieur is *amateur des vieux livres*, I have at home something that might interest him. It is not a hundred yards.' At once all Dennistoun's cherished dreams of finding priceless manuscripts in untrodden corners of France flashed up,* to die down again the next moment. It was probably a stupid missal of Plantin's printing,* about 1580: where was the likelihood that a place so near Toulouse would not have been ransacked long ago by collectors? However, it would be foolish not to go: he would reproach himself for ever after if he refused. So they set off.

On the way the curious irresolution and sudden determination of the sacristan recurred to Dennistoun, and he wondered in a shamefaced way whether he was being decoyed into some purlieu to be made away with as a supposed rich Englishman. He contrived, therefore, to begin talking with his guide and to drag in, in a rather clumsy fashion, the fact that he expected two friends to join him early the next morning. To his surprise, the announcement seemed to relieve the sacristan at once of some of the anxiety that oppressed him. 'That is well,' he said quite brightly, 'that is very well. Monsieur will travel in company with his friends; they will be always near him. It is a good thing to travel thus in company—sometimes.' The last word appeared to be added as an afterthought, and to bring with it a relapse into gloom for the poor little man.

They were soon at the house; one rather larger than its neighbours—stone-built, with a shield carved over the door, the shield of Alberic de Mauléon, a collateral descendant, Dennistoun tells me, of Bishop John de Mauléon. This

Alberic was a Canon of Comminges from 1680 to 1701. The upper windows of the mansion were boarded up, and the whole place bore, like the rest of Comminges, the aspect of decaying age.

Arrived on his doorstep, the sacristan paused a moment. 'Perhaps,' he said, 'perhaps after all monsieur has not the time?'

'Not at all—lots of time—nothing to do till tomorrow. Let us see what it is you have got.'

The door was opened at this point, and a face looked out, a face far younger than the sacristan's, but bearing something of the same distressing look: only here it seemed to be the mark, not so much of fear for personal safety as of acute anxiety on behalf of another. Plainly the owner of the face was the sacristan's daughter; and but for the expression I have described she was a handsome girl enough. She brightened up considerably on seeing her father accompanied by an able-bodied stranger. A few remarks passed between father and daughter, of which Dennistoun only caught these words, said by the sacristan, 'He was laughing in the church,' words which were answered only by a look of terror from the girl.

But in another minute they were in the sitting-room of the house, a small high chamber with a stone floor, full of moving shadows cast by a wood-fire that flickered on a great hearth. Something of the character of an oratory was imparted to it by a tall crucifix which reached almost to the ceiling on one side: the figure was painted of the natural colours, the cross was black. Under this stood a chest of some age and solidity, and when a lamp had been brought, and chairs set, the sacristan went to this chest and produced therefrom, with growing excitement and nervousness as Dennistoun thought, a large book wrapped in a white cloth, on which cloth a cross was rudely embroidered in red thread. Even before the wrapping had been removed, Dennistoun began to be interested by the size and shape of the volume. 'Too large for a missal,' he thought, 'and not the shape of an antiphoner;* perhaps it may be something good after all.' The next moment the book was open, and Dennistoun felt that

he had at last lit upon something better than good. Before
him lay a large folio, bound perhaps late in the seventeenth
century, with the arms of Canon Alberic de Mauléon stamped
in gold on the sides. There may have been a hundred and
fifty leaves of paper in the book and on almost every one
of them was fastened a leaf from an illuminated manuscript.
Such a collection Dennistoun had hardly dreamed of in his
wildest moments. Here were ten leaves from a copy of
Genesis illustrated with pictures, which could not be later
than AD 700. Further on was a complete set of pictures from
a Psalter of English execution, of the very finest kind that
the thirteenth century could produce; and perhaps best of all,
there were twenty leaves of uncial writing* in Latin, which,
as a few words seen here and there told him at once, must
belong to some very early unknown patristic treatise. Could
it possibly be a fragment of the copy of Papias *On the Words
of Our Lord** which was known to have existed as late as the
twelfth century at Nîmes?[1] In any case, his mind was made
up: that book must return to Cambridge with him, even if
he had to draw the whole of his balance from the bank and
stay at S. Bertrand till the money came. He glanced up at the
sacristan to see if his face yielded any hint that the book was
for sale. The sacristan was pale, and his lips were working.

'If monsieur will turn on to the end,' he said.

So monsieur turned on, meeting new treasures at every rise
of a leaf; and at the end of the book he came upon two sheets
of paper, of much more recent date than anything he had
yet seen, which puzzled him considerably. They must be
contemporary, he decided, with the unprincipled Canon
Alberic, who had doubtless plundered the Chapter library of
S. Bertrand to form this priceless scrap-book.* On the first
of the paper sheets was a plan, carefully drawn and instantly
recognizable by a person who knew the ground, of the south
aisle and cloisters of S. Bertrand's. There were curious signs
looking like planetary symbols, and a few Hebrew words in
the corners; and in the north-west angle of the cloister was
a cross drawn in gold paint. Below the plan were some lines

[1] We now know that these leaves did contain a considerable
fragment of that work, if not of that actual copy of it.

of writing in Latin which ran thus: *Responsa* 12*mi Dec.* 1694. *Interrogatum est: Inveniamne? Responsum est: Invenies. Fiamne dives? Fies. Vivamne invidendus? Vives. Moriarne in lecto meo? Ita.*[1]*

'A good specimen of the treasure-hunter's record: quite reminds one of Mr Minor Canon Quatremain in Old St Paul's,'* was Dennistoun's comment: and he turned the leaf.

What he then saw impressed him, as he has often told me, more than he could have conceived any drawing or picture capable of impressing him. And, though the drawing he saw is no longer in existence, there is a photograph of it (which I possess) which fully bears out Dennistoun's statement. The picture in question was a sepia drawing of the end of the seventeenth century representing, one would say at first sight, a biblical scene; for the architecture (the picture represented an interior) and the figures had that semi-classical flavour about them which the artists of two hundred years ago thought appropriate to illustrations of the Bible. On the right was a king on his throne, the throne elevated on twelve steps, a canopy overhead, lions on either side—evidently King Solomon. He was bending forward with outstretched sceptre, in attitude of command: his face expressed horror and disgust, yet there was in it also the mark of imperious will and confident power. The left half of the picture was the strangest, however. The interest plainly centred there. On the pavement before the throne were grouped four soldiers surrounding a crouching figure which must be described in a moment. A fifth soldier lay dead on the pavement, his neck distorted and his eyeballs starting from his head. The four surrounding guards were looking at the king. In their faces the sentiment of horror was intensified: they seemed, in fact, only restrained from flight by their implicit trust in their master.* All this terror was plainly excited by the being that crouched in their midst. I entirely despair of conveying by any words the impression which this figure makes upon any one who looks at it. I recollect once showing the photograph of the drawing

[1] Answers of the 12th of December 1694. It was asked: Shall I find it? Answer: Thou shalt. Shall I become rich? Thou wilt. Shall I live an object of envy? Thou wilt. Shall I die in my bed? Thou wilt.

to a Lecturer in Morphology*—a person of, I was going to
say, abnormally sane and unimaginative habits of mind. He
absolutely refused to be alone for the rest of that evening,
and he told me afterwards that for many nights he had not
dared to put out his light before going to sleep. However, the
main traits of the figure I can at least indicate. At first, you
saw only a mass of coarse matted black hair: presently it was
seen that this covered a body of fearful thinness—almost a
skeleton, but with the muscles standing out like wires. The
hands were of a dusk pallor, covered like the body with
long coarse hairs, and hideously taloned. The eyes, touched
in with a burning yellow, had intensely black pupils, and
were fixed upon the throned king with a look of beast-like
hate. Imagine one of the awful bird-catching spiders of South
America translated into human form and endowed with
intelligence just less than human, and you will have some
faint conception of the terror inspired by this appalling effigy.
One remark is universally made by those to whom I have
shown the picture: 'It was drawn from the life.'

As soon as the first shock of his irresistible fright had
subsided, Dennistoun stole a look at his hosts. The sacristan's
hands were pressed upon his eyes; his daughter, looking up
at the cross on the wall, was telling her beads feverishly.

At last the question was asked. 'Is this book for sale?'
There was the same hesitation, the same plunge of determination that he had noticed before, and then came the welcome
answer 'If monsieur pleases.'

'How much do you ask for it?'

'I will take two hundred and fifty francs.'

This was confounding. Even a collector's conscience is
sometimes stirred, and Dennistoun's conscience was tenderer
than a collector's.

'My good man!' he said again and again, 'your book is
worth far more than two hundred and fifty francs, I assure
you, far more.'

But the answer did not vary: 'I will take two hundred and
fifty francs, not more.'

There was really no possibility of refusing such a chance.
The money was paid, the receipt signed, a glass of wine (Vin

de Limoux, not to be recommended) drunk* over the transaction, and then the sacristan seemed to become a new man.
He stood upright, he ceased to throw those suspicious glances
behind him, he actually laughed or tried to laugh. Dennistoun rose to go.

'I shall have the honour of accompanying monsieur to his
hotel?' said the sacristan.

'Oh no, thanks! it isn't a hundred yards. I know the way
perfectly, and there is a moon.'

The offer was pressed three or four times, and refused as
often.

'Then monsieur will summon me if—if he finds occasion?
he will keep the middle of the road, the sides are so rough.'

'Certainly, certainly,' said Dennistoun, who was impatient
to examine his prize by himself; and he stepped out into the
passage with his book under his arm. Here he was met by
the daughter; she, it appeared, was anxious to do a little
business on her own account; perhaps, like Gehazi, to 'take
somewhat' from the foreigner whom her father had spared.*

'A silver crucifix and chain for the neck: monsieur would
perhaps be good enough to accept it?'

Well, really, Dennistoun hadn't much use for these things;
what did mademoiselle want for it?

'Nothing, nothing in the world. Monsieur is more than
welcome to it.'

The tone in which this and much more was said was
unmistakably genuine, so that Dennistoun was reduced to
profuse thanks, and submitted to have the chain put round
his neck. It really seemed as if he had rendered the father
and daughter some service which they hardly knew how to
repay. As he set off with his book they stood at the door
looking after him; and they were still looking when he waved
them a last good night from the steps of the *Chapeau Rouge*.

Dinner was over, and Dennistoun was in his bedroom, shut
up alone with his acquisition. The landlady had manifested
a particular interest in him since he had told her that he had
paid a visit to the sacristan and bought an old book from
him. He thought, too, that he had heard a hurried dialogue

between her and the said sacristan in the passage outside the *salle à manger*: some words to the effect that 'Pierre and Bertrand would be sleeping in the house' had closed the conversation.

All this time a growing feeling of discomfort had been creeping over him: nervous reaction, perhaps, after the delight of his discovery. Whatever it was, it resulted in a conviction that there was someone behind him, and that he was far more comfortable with his back to the wall. All this, of course, weighed light in the balance as against the obvious value of the collection he had acquired. And now, as I said, he was alone in his bedroom taking stock of Canon Alberic's treasures, in which every moment revealed something more charming.

'Bless Canon Alberic!' said Dennistoun, who had an inveterate habit of talking to himself. 'I wonder where he is now! . . . . Dear me! I wish that landlady would learn to laugh in a more cheering manner. It makes one feel as if there was someone dead in the house. Half a pipe more, did you say? I think perhaps you are right. I wonder what that crucifix is that the young woman insisted on giving me. Last century, I suppose. . . . . Yes, probably. It's rather a nuisance of a thing to have round one's neck: just too heavy. Most likely her father has been wearing it for years. I think I might give it a clean up before I put it away.'

He had taken the crucifix off, and laid it on the table, when his attention was caught by an object lying on the red cloth just by his left elbow. Two or three ideas of what it might be flitted through his brain with their own incalculable quickness. 'A penwiper? No, no such thing in the house. A rat? No, too black. A large spider?* I trust to goodness not: no. Good God! a hand like the hand in that picture!'*

In another infinitesimal flash he had taken it in. Pale dusky skin covering nothing but bones and tendons of appalling strength; coarse black hairs, longer than ever grew on a human hand; nails rising from the ends of the fingers and curving sharply down and forward, grey, horny, and wrinkled. He flew out of his chair with deadly inconceivable terror clutching at his heart. The shape whose left hand rested on the table was rising to a standing posture behind his seat, its right hand crooked above his scalp. There was black and tattered drapery about it; the coarse hair covered it as in the drawing. The lower jaw was thin—what can I call it?—shallow, like a beast's; teeth showed behind the black lips. There was no nose: the eyes of fiery yellow against which the pupils showed black and intense, and the exulting hate and thirst to destroy life which shone there, were the most horrifying features in the whole vision. There was intelligence of a kind in them, intelligence beyond that of a beast, below that of a man.

The feelings which this horror stirred in Dennistoun were the intensest physical fear and the most profound mental loathing. What did he do? What could he do? He has never been quite certain what words he said, but he knows that he spoke, that he grasped blindly at the silver crucifix, that he was conscious of a movement towards him on the part of the demon, and that he screamed with the voice of an animal in hideous pain.

Pierre and Bertrand, the two sturdy little serving-men who rushed in, saw nothing but felt themselves thrust aside by something that passed out between them, and found Dennistoun in a swoon. They sat up with him that night; and his two friends were at S. Bertrand by nine o'clock next morning. Dennistoun, though still shaken and nervous, was almost himself by that time, and his story found credence with them—though not until they had seen the drawing and talked with the sacristan. Almost at dawn the little man had come to the inn on some pretence and had listened with the deepest interest to the story retailed by the landlady. He showed no surprise. 'It is he: it is he! I have seen him myself,' was his only comment; and to all questionings but one reply was vouchsafed: 'Deux fois je l'ai vu: mille fois je l'ai senti.' He would tell them nothing of the provenance of the book, nor any details of his experiences. 'I shall soon sleep, and my rest will be sweet. Why should you trouble me?' he said.[1]

[1] He died that summer; his daughter married, and settled at S. Papoul. She never understood the circumstances of her father's 'obsession'.

We shall never know what he or Canon Alberic de
Mauléon suffered. At the back of that fateful drawing were
some lines of writing which may be supposed to throw light
on the situation:

Contradictio Salomonis cum demonio nocturno.
Albericus de Mauleone delineavit.
V. Deus in adiutorium. Ps. Qui habitat.
Sancte Bertrande demoniorum effugator intercede pro me
miserrimo.
Primum uidi nocte 12mi Dec. 1694: uidebo mox
ultimum. Peccaui et passus sum, plura adhuc
passurus. Dec. 29, 1701.[1]*

I have never quite understood what was Dennistoun's
view of the events I have narrated. He quoted to me once a
text from Ecclesiasticus:* 'Some spirits there be that are
created for vengeance, and in their fury lay on sore strokes.'
On another occasion he said: 'Isaiah* was a very sensible
man; doesn't he say something about night-monsters living
in the ruins of Babylon? These things are rather beyond us
at present.'

Another confidence of his impressed me rather, and I
sympathized with it. We had been, last year, to Comminges,
to see Canon Alberic's tomb. It is a great marble erection
with an effigy of the Canon in a large wig and *soutane*,* and
an elaborate eulogy of his learning below. I saw Dennistoun
talking for some time with the Vicar of S. Bertrand's, and
as we drove away he said to me: 'I hope it isn't wrong: you
know I am a Presbyterian—but—I have just ordered a trental
of masses for Alberic de Mauléon's rest.'* Then he added,

---

[1] i.e., The Dispute of Solomon with a demon of the night. Drawn
by Alberic de Mauléon. *Versicle*. O Lord, make haste to help me.
Psalm. Whoso dwelleth (xci.).*

Saint Bertrand, who puttest devils to flight, pray for me most
unhappy. I saw it first on the night of Dec. 12, 1694: soon I shall see
it for the last time. I have sinned and suffered, and have more to
suffer yet. Dec. 29, 1701.

The *Gallia Christiana* gives the date of the Canon's death as
December 31, 1701, 'in bed, of a sudden seizure'. Details of this kind
are not common in the great work of the Sammarthani.*

with a touch of the Northern British in his tone, 'I had no notion they came so dear.'

The book is in the Wentworth Collection* at Cambridge. The drawing was photographed and then burnt by Dennistoun on the day when he left Comminges on the occasion of his first visit.

THE MEZZOTINT

SOME time ago I believe I had the pleasure of telling you the story of an adventure which happened to a friend of mine by the name of Dennistoun* during his pursuit of objects of art for the museum at Cambridge.

He did not publish his experiences very widely upon his return to England; but they could not fail to become known to a good many of his friends: and among others to the gentleman who at that time presided over an art museum at another University.* It was to be expected that the story should make a considerable impression on the mind of a man whose vocation lay in lines similar to Dennistoun's, and that he should be eager to catch at any explanation of the matter which tended to make it seem improbable that he should ever be called upon to deal with so agitating an emergency. It was indeed somewhat consoling to him to reflect that he was not expected to acquire ancient MSS for his institution: that was the business of the Shelburnian Library.* The authorities of that might if they pleased ransack obscure corners of the Continent for such matters: he was glad to be obliged at the moment to confine his attention to enlarging the already unsurpassed collection of English topographical drawings and engravings possessed by his museum.* Yet, as it turned out, even a department so homely and familiar as this may have its dark corners, and to one of these Mr Williams was unexpectedly introduced.

Those who have taken even the most limited interest in the acquisition of topographical pictures are aware that there is one London dealer whose aid is indispensable to their researches. Mr J. W. Britnell* publishes at short intervals very admirable catalogues of a large and constantly changing stock of engravings, plans, and old sketches of mansions, churches, and towns in England and Wales. These catalogues were of course the ABC of his subject to Mr Williams: but as his museum already contained an enormous accumulation of topographical pictures, he was a regular rather than a copious buyer; and he rather looked to Mr Britnell to fill up gaps in the rank and file of his collection than to supply him with rarities.

Now in February of last year there appeared upon Mr Williams's desk at the museum a catalogue from Mr Britnell's emporium, and accompanying it was a typewritten communication from the dealer himself. This latter ran as follows:

Dear Sir,

We beg to call your attention to No. 978 in our accompanying catalogue, which we shall be glad to send on approval.

Yours faithfully,

J. W. BRITNELL.

To turn to No. 978 in the accompanying catalogue was with Mr Williams (as he observed to himself) the work of a moment, and in the place indicated he found the following entry:

978. *Unknown.* Interesting mezzotint.* View of a manor-house: early part of the century. 15 by 10 inches; black frame. £2 2s.

It was not specially exciting, and the price seemed high. However, as Mr Britnell, who knew his business and his customer, seemed to set some store by it, Mr Williams wrote a postcard asking for the article to be sent on approval, along with some other engravings and sketches which appeared in the same catalogue. And so he passed without much excitement of anticipation to the ordinary labours of the day.

A parcel of any kind always arrives a day later than you expect it, and that of Mr Britnell proved, as I believe the right phrase goes, no exception to the rule. It was delivered at the museum by the afternoon post of Saturday, after Mr Williams had left his work, and it was accordingly brought round to his rooms in college by the attendant, in order that he might not have to wait over Sunday before looking through it and returning such of the contents as he did not propose to keep; and here he found it when he came in to tea, with a friend.

The only item with which I am concerned was the rather large, black-framed mezzotint of which I have already quoted the short description given in Mr Britnell's catalogue. Some more details of it will have to be given, though I cannot hope to put before you the look of the picture as clearly as it is present to my own eye. Very nearly the exact duplicate of it may be seen in a good many old inn parlours, or in the passages of undisturbed country mansions at the present moment. It was a rather indifferent mezzotint, and an indifferent mezzotint is perhaps the worst form of engraving known. It presented a full-face view of a not very large manor-house of the last century,* with three rows of plain sashed windows with rusticated masonry about them, a parapet with balls or vases at the angles, and a small portico in the centre. On either side were trees, and in front a considerable expanse of lawn. The legend 'A. W. F. sculpsit'* was engraved on the narrow margin and there was no further inscription. The whole thing gave the impression that it was the work of an amateur. What in the world Mr Britnell could mean by affixing the price of £2 2s. to such an object was more than Mr Williams could imagine. He turned it over with a good deal of contempt; upon the back was a paper label, the left-hand half of which had been torn off. All that remained were the ends of two lines of writing: the first had the letters —*ngley Hall*; the second, —*ssex*.

It would perhaps be just worth while to identify the place represented, which he could easily do with the help of a gazetteer, and then he would send it back to Mr Britnell, with some remarks reflecting upon the judgment of that gentleman.

He lighted the candles, for it was now dark, made the tea, and supplied the friend with whom he had been playing golf (for I believe the authorities of the University I write of indulge in that pursuit by way of relaxation); and tea was taken to the accompaniment of a discussion which golfing persons can imagine for themselves, but which the conscientious writer has no right to inflict upon any non-golfing persons. The conclusion arrived at was that certain strokes might have been better, and that in certain emergencies neither player had experienced that amount of luck which a human being has a right to expect. It was now that the friend—let us call him Professor Binks*—took up the framed engraving, and said: 'What's this place, Williams?'

'Just what I am going to try to find out,' said Williams, going to the shelf for a gazetteer. 'Look at the back, Somethingley Hall, either in Sussex or Essex. Half the name's gone, you see. You don't happen to know it, I suppose?'

'It's from that man Britnell, I suppose, isn't it?' said Binks. 'Is it for the museum?'

'Well, I think I should buy it if the price was five shillings,' said Williams; 'but for some unearthly reason he wants two guineas for it. I can't conceive why. It's a wretched engraving and there aren't even any figures to give it life.'

'It's not worth two guineas, I should think,' said Binks; 'but I don't think it's so badly done. The moonlight seems rather good to me; and I should have thought there *were* figures, or at least a figure, just on the edge in front.'

'Let's look,' said Williams. 'Well, it's true the light is rather cleverly given. Where's your figure? Oh yes, just the head in the very front of the picture.'

And indeed there was—hardly more than a black blot on the extreme edge of the engraving—the head of a man or woman, a good deal muffled up, the back turned to the spectator, and looking towards the house.

Williams had not noticed it before. 'Still,' he said, 'though it's a cleverer thing than I thought, I can't spend two guineas of museum money on a picture of a place I don't know.'

Professor Binks had his work to do, and soon went; and very nearly up to Hall time Williams was engaged in a vain attempt to identify the subject of his picture. 'If the vowel before the *ng* had only been left it would have been easy enough,' he thought; 'but as it is, the name may be anything from Guestingley to Langley; and there are many more names ending like this than I thought; and this rotten book has no index of terminations.'

Hall in Mr Williams's college was at seven. It need not be dwelt upon—the less so as he met there colleagues who had been playing golf during the afternoon, and words with which we have no concern were freely bandied across the table—merely golfing words, I would hasten to explain.

I suppose an hour or more to have been spent in what is called Common-room after dinner. Later in the evening some few retired to Williams's rooms and I have little doubt that whist was played and tobacco smoked.* During a lull in these operations Williams picked up the mezzotint from the table without looking at it and handed it to a person mildly interested in art, telling him where it had come from, and the other particulars which we already know.

The gentleman took it carelessly, looked at it, then said, in a tone of some interest: 'It's really a very good piece of work, Williams; it has quite a feeling of the romantic period. The light is admirably managed, it seems to me, and the figure, though it's rather too grotesque, is somehow very impressive.'

'Yes, isn't it?' said Williams, who was just then busy giving whisky and soda to others of the company, and was unable to come across the room to look at the view again.

It was by this time rather late in the evening, and the visitors were on the move. After they went, Williams was obliged to write a letter or two and clear up some odd bits of work. At last, some time past midnight, he was disposed to turn in, and he put out his lamp after lighting his bedroom candle. The picture lay face upwards on the table where the last man who looked at it had put it, and it caught his eye as he turned the lamp down. What he saw made him very nearly drop the candle on the floor, and he declares now that if he had been left in the dark at that moment he would have had a fit. But as that did not happen he was able to put down the light on the table and take a good look at the picture. It was indubitable—rankly impossible, no doubt, but absolutely certain. In the middle of the lawn in front of the unknown house there was a figure where no figure had been at five o'clock that afternoon. It was crawling on all-fours towards the house, and it was muffled in a strange black garment with a white cross on the back.

I do not know what is the ideal course to pursue in a situation of this kind. I can only tell you what Mr Williams did. He took the picture by one corner and carried it across the passage to a second set of rooms which he possessed.

There he locked it up in a drawer, sported* the doors of both sets of rooms, and retired to bed: but first he wrote out and signed an account of the extraordinary changes which the picture had undergone since it had come into his possession.

Sleep visited him rather late: but it was consoling to reflect that the behaviour of the picture did not depend upon his own unsupported testimony. Evidently the man who had looked at it the night before had seen something of the same kind as he had, otherwise he might have been tempted to think that something gravely wrong was happening either to his eyes or his mind. This possibility being fortunately precluded, two matters awaited him on the morrow. He must take stock of the picture very carefully, and call in a witness for the purpose, and he must make a determined effort to ascertain what house it was that was represented. He would therefore ask his neighbour Nisbet to breakfast with him, and he would subsequently spend a morning over the gazetteer.

Nisbet was disengaged and arrived about 9.30. His host was not quite dressed, I am sorry to say, even at this late hour.* During breakfast nothing was said about the mezzotint by Williams, save that he had a picture on which he wished for Nisbet's opinion. But those who are familiar with University life can picture for themselves the wide and delightful range of subjects over which the conversation of two Fellows of Canterbury College* is likely to extend during a Sunday morning breakfast. Hardly a topic was left unchallenged, from golf to lawn-tennis. Yet I am bound to say that Williams was rather distraught: for his interest naturally centred in that very strange picture which was now reposing, face downwards, in the drawer in the room opposite.

The morning pipe* was at last lighted, and the moment had arrived for which he looked. With very considerable—almost tremulous—excitement, he ran across, unlocked the drawer, and, extracting the picture—still face downwards—ran back and put it into Nisbet's hands.

'Now,' he said, 'Nisbet, I want you to tell me exactly what you see in that picture. Describe it, if you don't mind, rather minutely. I'll tell you why afterwards.'

'Well,' said Nisbet, 'I have here a view of a country house
—English, I presume—by moonlight.'

'Moonlight? You're sure of that?'

'Certainly. The moon appears to be on the wane, if you
wish for details, and there are clouds in the sky.'

'All right. Go on. I'll swear,' added Williams in an aside,
'there was no moon when I saw it first.'

'Well, there's not much more to be said,' Nisbet continued.
'The house has one—two—three rows of windows, five in
each row, except at the bottom, where there's a porch instead
of the middle one, and——'

'But what about figures?' said Williams, with marked
interest.

'There aren't any,' said Nisbet; 'but——'

'What! No figure on the grass in front?'

'Not a thing.'

'You'll swear to that?'

'Certainly I will. But there's just one other thing.'

'What?'

'Why, one of the windows on the ground-floor—left of
the door—is open.'

'Is it really? My goodness! he must have got in,' said
Williams, with great excitement; and he hurried to the back
of the sofa on which Nisbet was sitting, and, catching the
picture from him, verified the matter for himself.

It was quite true. There was no figure, and there was the
open window. Williams, after a moment of speechless surprise, went to the writing-table and scribbled for a short time.
Then he brought two papers to Nisbet, and asked him first
to sign one—it was his own description of the picture, which
you have just heard—and then to read the other, which was
Williams's statement written the night before.

'What can it all mean?' said Nisbet.

'Exactly,' said Williams. 'Well, one thing I must do—or
three things, now I think of it. I must find out from Garwood
(this was his last night's visitor) what he saw, and then I
must get the thing photographed before it goes further, and
then I must find out what the place is.'

'I can do the photographing myself,' said Nisbet, 'and I

will. But, you know, it looks very much as if we were assisting at the working out of a tragedy somewhere. The question is, Has it happened already or is it going to come off? You must find out what the place is. Yes,' he said, looking at the picture again, 'I expect you're right: he *has* got in. And if I don't mistake there'll be the devil to pay in one of the rooms upstairs.'

'I'll tell you what,' said Williams: 'I'll take the picture across to old Green' (this was the senior Fellow of the College, who had been Bursar* for many years). 'It's quite likely he'll know it. We have property in Essex and Sussex and he must have been over the two counties a lot in his time.'

'Quite likely he will,' said Nisbet; 'but just let me take my photograph first. But look here, I rather think Green isn't up today. He wasn't in Hall last night, and I think I heard him say he was going down for the Sunday.'

'That's true, too,' said Williams. 'I know he's gone to Brighton. Well if you'll photograph it now I'll go across to Garwood and get his statement and you keep an eye on it while I'm gone. I'm beginning to think two guineas is not a very exorbitant price for it now.'

In a short time he had returned and brought Mr Garwood with him. Garwood's statement was to the effect that the figure, when he had seen it, was clear of the edge of the picture, but had not got far across the lawn. He remembered a white mark on the back of its drapery, but could not have been sure it was a cross. A document to this effect was then drawn up and signed, and Nisbet proceeded to photograph the picture.

'Now what do you mean to do?' he said. 'Are you going to sit and watch it all day?'

'Well, no, I think not,' said Williams. 'I rather imagine we're meant to see the whole thing. You see between the time I saw it last night and this morning there was time for lots of things to happen, but the creature only got into the house. It could easily have got through its business in the time and gone to its own place again: but the fact of the window being open I think must mean that it's in there now. So I feel quite easy about leaving it. And besides, I have a kind of idea that it wouldn't change much if at all in the daytime. We might go out for a walk this afternoon and come in to tea or whenever it gets dark. I shall leave it out on the table here and sport the door. My skip can get in, but no one else.'

The three agreed that this would be a good plan; and further that if they spent the afternoon together they would be less likely to talk about the business to other people: for any rumour of such a transaction as was going on would bring the whole of the Phasmatological Society* about their ears.

We may give them a respite until five o'clock.

At or near that hour the three were entering Williams's staircase. They were at first slightly annoyed to see that the door of his rooms was unsported: but in a moment it was remembered that on Sunday the skips came for orders an hour or so earlier than on week-days. However, a surprise was awaiting them. The first thing they saw was the picture leaning up against a pile of books on the table, as it had been left, and the next thing was Williams's skip seated on a chair opposite, gazing at it with undisguised horror. How was this? Mr Filcher (the name is not my own invention) was a servant of considerable standing and set the standard of etiquette to all his own college and to several neighbouring ones, and nothing could be more alien to his practice than to be found sitting on his master's chair or appearing to take any particular notice of his master's furniture or pictures. Indeed he seemed to feel this himself. He started violently when the three men came into the room, and got up with a marked effort. Then he said:

'I ask your pardon, sir, for taking such a freedom as to set down.'

'Not at all, Robert,' interposed Mr Williams. 'I was meaning to ask you sometime what you thought of that picture.'

'Well, sir, of course I don't set up my opinion again yours, but it ain't the pictur I should 'ang where my little girl could see it, sir.'

'Wouldn't you, Robert? Why not?'

'No, sir. Why, the pore child, I recollect once she see a

Door Bible,* with pictures not 'alf what that is, and we 'ad to set up with her three or four nights afterwards, if you'll believe me; and if she was to ketch a sight of this skelinton here, or whatever it is, carrying off the pore baby she would be in a taking. You know 'ow it is with children; 'ow nervish they git with a little thing and all. But what I should say, it don't seem a right pictur to be laying about, sir, not where anyone that's liable to be startled could come on it. Should you be wanting anything this evening, sir? Thank you, sir.'

With these words the excellent man went to continue the round of his masters: and you may be sure the gentlemen whom he left lost no time in gathering round the engraving. There was the house as before, under the waning moon and the drifting clouds. The window that had been open was shut, and the figure was once more on the lawn. But not this time crawling cautiously on hands and knees. Now it was erect and stepping swiftly with long strides towards the front of the picture. The moon was behind it and the black drapery hung down over its face so that only hints of that could be seen, and what was visible made the spectators profoundly thankful that they could see no more than a white dome-like forehead and a few straggling hairs. The head was bent down, and the arms were tightly clasped over an object which could be dimly seen and identified as a child—whether dead or living it was not possible to say. The legs of the appearance alone could be plainly discerned, and they were horribly thin.

From five to seven the three companions sat and watched the picture by turns. But it never changed. They agreed at last that it would be safe to leave it, and that they would return after Hall and await further developments.

When they assembled again, at the earliest possible moment, the engraving was there: but the figure was gone, and the house was quiet under the moonbeams. There was nothing for it but to spend the evening over gazetteers and guide-books. Williams was the lucky one at last, and perhaps he deserved it. At 11.30 p.m. he read from Murray's *Guide to Essex** the following lines:

16½ miles, Anningley. The church has been an interesting building of Norman date but was extensively classicized in the last
century. It contains the tombs of the family of Francis, whose
mansion, Anningley Hall, a solid Queen Anne house, stands
immediately beyond the churchyard in a park of about 80 acres.
The family is now extinct, the last heir having disappeared
mysteriously in infancy in the year 1802. The father, Mr Arthur
Francis, was locally known as a talented amateur engraver in
mezzotint. After his son's disappearance he lived in complete
retirement at the Hall and was found dead in his studio on the
third anniversary of the disaster, having just completed an
engraving of the house, impressions of which are of considerable
rarity.

This looked like business; and indeed Mr Green on his
return at once identified the house as Anningley Hall.

'Is there any kind of explanation of the figure, Green?' was
the question which Williams naturally asked.

'I don't know, I'm sure, Williams. What used to be said in
the place when I first knew it, which was before I came up
here, was just this. Old Francis was always very much down
on these poaching fellows and whenever he got a chance he
used to get a man whom he suspected of it turned off the
estate, and by degrees he got rid of them all but one. Squires
could do a lot of things then that they daren't think of now.
Well this man that was left was what you find pretty often
in that country—the last remains of a very old family. I
believe they were lords of the manor at one time. I recollect
just the same thing in my own parish.'

'What, like the man in *Tess of the D'Urbervilles?*'*
Williams put in.

'Yes, I dare say: it's not a book I could ever read myself.
But this fellow could show a row of tombs in the church
there that belonged to his ancestors, and all that went to sour
him a bit: but Francis, they said, could never get at him—he
always kept just on the right side of the law—until one night
the keepers found him at it in a wood right at the end of the
estate. I could show you the place now: it marches with some
land that used to belong to an uncle of mine. And you can
imagine there was a row; and this man Gawdy* (that was the

name, to be sure—Gawdy; I thought I should get it—Gawdy),
he was unlucky enough, poor chap, to shoot a keeper. Well
that was what Francis wanted; and grand juries—you know
what they would have been then—and poor Gawdy was
strung up in double-quick time; and I've been shown the
place he was buried in, on the north side of the church*—you
know the way in that part of the world: anyone that's been
hanged or made away with themselves, they bury them that
side. And the idea was that some friend of Gawdy's—not a
relation, because he had none, poor devil! he was the last
of his line: kind of *spes ultima gentis**—must have planned
to get hold of Francis's boy and put an end to *his* line too.
I don't know—it's rather an out-of-the-way thing for an Essex
poacher to think of. But, you know, I should say now it looks
more as if old Gawdy had managed the job himself. Booh! I
hate to think of it. Have some whisky, Williams.'

The facts were communicated by Williams to Dennistoun,
and by him to a mixed company of which I was one and the
Sadducean Professor of Ophiology* another. I am sorry to say
that the latter, when asked what he thought of it, only
remarked: 'Oh, those Bridgeford* people will say anything'—
a sentiment which met with the reception it deserved.

I have only to add that the picture is now in the Ashleian
Museum; that it has been treated with a view to discovering
whether sympathetic ink has been used in it but without
effect; that Mr Britnell knew nothing of it save that he was
sure it was uncommon; and that, though carefully watched,
it has never been known to change again.

NUMBER 13

AMONG the towns of Jutland Viborg* justly holds a high
place. It is the seat of a bishopric; it has a handsome but
almost entirely new cathedral, a charming garden, a lake of
great beauty, and many storks. Near it is Hald, accounted
one of the prettiest things in Denmark; and hard by is
Finderup, where Marsk Stig murdered King Erik Glipping
on St Cecilia's Day, in the year 1286. Fifty-six blows of
square-headed iron maces were traced on Erik's skull when
his tomb was opened in the seventeenth century: but I am
not writing a guidebook.

There are good hotels in Viborg. Preisler's and the Phoenix
are all that can be desired. But my cousin, whose experiences
I have to tell you now, went to the Golden Lion* the first
time that he visited Viborg. He has not been there since, and
the following pages will perhaps explain the reason of his
abstention.

The Golden Lion is one of the very few houses in the town
that were not destroyed in the great fire of 1726, which
practically demolished the cathedral, the Sognekirke, the
Raadhuus, and so much else that was old and interesting. It
is a great red-brick house; that is, the front is of brick, with
corbie steps on the gables and a text over the door; but the
courtyard into which the omnibus drives is of black and
white 'cage-work' in wood and plaster. The sun was declining
in the heavens when my cousin walked up to the door, and
the light smote full upon the imposing façade of the house.
He was delighted with the old-fashioned aspect of the place
and promised himself a thoroughly satisfactory and amusing
stay in an inn so typical of old Jutland.

It was not business in the ordinary sense of the word that
had brought Mr Anderson to Viborg. He was engaged upon
some researches into the Church history of Denmark and it
had come to his knowledge that in the Rigsarkiv of Viborg
there were papers—saved from the fire—relating to the last
days of Roman Catholicism* in the country. He proposed

therefore to spend a considerable time—perhaps as much as a fortnight or three weeks—in examining and copying these, and he hoped that the Golden Lion would be able to give him a room of sufficient size to serve alike as a bedroom and a study. His wishes were explained to the landlord, and after a certain amount of thought the latter suggested that perhaps it might be the best way for the gentleman to look at one or two of the larger rooms and pick one for himself. It seemed a good idea.

The top floor was soon rejected as entailing too much getting upstairs after the day's work. The second floor contained no room of exactly the dimensions required. But on the first floor there was a choice of two or three rooms which would, so far as size went, suit admirably. The landlord was strongly in favour of Number 17, but Mr Anderson pointed out that its windows commanded only the blank wall of the next house, and that it would be very dark in the afternoon. Either Number 12 or Number 14 would be better, for both of them looked on the street and the bright evening light and the pretty view would more than compensate him for the additional amount of noise.

Eventually Number 12 was selected. Like its neighbours it had three windows all on one side of the room. It was fairly high and unusually long. There was of course no fireplace, but the stove was handsome and rather old—a cast-iron erection on the side of which was a representation of Abraham sacrificing Isaac, and the inscription '1 Bog Mose, Cap. 22'* above. Nothing else in the room was remarkable. The only interesting picture was an old coloured print of the town—date about 1820.

Supper time was approaching, but when Anderson, refreshed by the ordinary ablutions, descended the staircase there were still a few minutes before the bell rang. He devoted them to examining the list of his fellow lodgers. As is usual in Denmark their names were displayed on a large blackboard divided into columns and lines, the numbers of the rooms being painted in at the beginning of each line. The list was not exciting. There was an advocate or Sagförer, a German, and some bagmen* from Copenhagen. The one and only point which suggested any food for thought was the absence of any Number 13 from the tale of the rooms, and even this was a thing which Anderson had already noticed half a dozen times in his experience of Danish hotels. He could not help wondering whether the objection to that particular number, common as it is, was so widespread and so strong as to make it difficult to let a room so ticketed and he resolved to ask the landlord if he and his colleagues in the profession had actually met with many clients who refused to be accommodated in the thirteenth room.

He had nothing to tell me (I am giving the story as I heard it from him) about what passed at supper, and the evening, which was spent in unpacking and arranging his clothes, books, and papers, was not more eventful. Towards eleven o'clock he resolved to go to bed; but with him, as with a good many other people nowadays, an almost necessary preliminary to bed if he meant to sleep was the reading of a few pages of print, and he now remembered that the particular book which he had been reading in the train and which alone would satisfy him at that present moment was in the pocket of his greatcoat—then hanging on a peg outside the dining-room.

To run down and secure it was the work of a moment, and, as the passages were by no means dark, it was not difficult for him to find his way back to his own door. So at least he thought; but when he arrived there and turned the handle, the door entirely refused to open, and he caught the sound of a hasty movement towards it from within. He had tried the wrong door, of course. Was his own room to the right or to the left? He glanced at the number. It was 13. His room would be on the left: and so it was. And not before he had been in bed for some minutes, had read his wonted three or four pages of his book, blown out his light, and turned over to go to sleep, did it occur to him that whereas on the blackboard of the hotel there had been no Number 13, there was undoubtedly a room numbered 13 in the hotel. He felt rather sorry he had not chosen it for his own. Perhaps he might have done the landlord a little service by occupying it and giving him the chance of saying that a well-born

English gentleman had lived in it for three weeks and liked it very much. But probably it was used as a servant's room or something of the kind. After all it was most likely not so large or good a room as his own, and he looked drowsily about the room, which was fairly perceptible in the half-light from the street-lamp. It was a curious effect, he thought. Rooms usually look larger in a dim light than a full one but this seemed to have contracted in length and grown proportionately higher. Well, well, sleep was more important than these vague ruminations: and to sleep he went.

On the day after his arrival Anderson attacked the Rigsarkiv of Viborg. He was, as one might expect in Denmark, kindly received and access to all that he wished to see was made as easy for him as possible. The documents laid before him were far more numerous and interesting than he had at all anticipated. Besides official papers there was a large bundle of correspondence relating to Bishop Jörgen Friis,* the last Roman Catholic who held the see, and in these there cropped up many amusing and what are called 'intimate' details of private life and individual character. There was much talk of a house owned by the Bishop—but not inhabited by him—in the town. Its tenant was apparently somewhat of a scandal and a stumbling-block to the Reforming party. He was a disgrace, they wrote, to the city: he practised secret and wicked arts and had sold his soul to the Enemy. It was of a piece with the gross corruption and superstition of the Babylonish Church that such a viper and blood-sucking *Troldmand** should be patronized and harboured by the Bishop. The Bishop met these reproaches boldly: he protested his own abhorrence of all such things as secret arts and required his antagonists to bring the matter before the proper court—of course the spiritual court—and sift it to the bottom. No one could be more ready and willing than himself to condemn Mag. Nicolas Francken if the evidence showed him to have been guilty of any of the crimes informally alleged against him.

Anderson had not time to do more than glance at the next letter of the Protestant leader Rasmus Nielsen before the record office was closed for the day, but he gathered its general tenor, which was to the effect that Christian men were now no longer bound by the decisions of Bishops of Rome and that the Bishop's court was not and could not be a fit or competent tribunal to judge so grave and weighty a cause.

On leaving the office Mr Anderson was accompanied by the old gentleman who presided over it; and as they walked the conversation very naturally turned to the papers of which I have just been speaking. Herr Scavenius, the Archivist of Viborg, though very well informed as to the general run of the documents under his charge, was not a specialist in those of the Reformation period. He was much interested in what Anderson had to tell him about them. He looked forward with great pleasure he said to seeing the publication in which Mr Anderson spoke of embodying their contents. 'This house of the Bishop Friis,' he added, 'it is a great puzzle to me where it can have stood. I have studied carefully the topography of old Viborg, but it is most unlucky—of the old terrier* of the Bishop's property which was made in 1560, and of which we have the greater part in the Arkiv, just the piece which had the list of the town property is missing. Never mind. Perhaps I shall some day succeed to find him.'

After taking some exercise—I forget exactly how or where —Anderson went back to the Golden Lion, his supper, his game of patience,* and his bed. On the way to his room it occurred to him that he had forgotten to talk to the landlord about the omission of Number 13 from the hotel board, and also that he might as well make sure that Number 13 did actually exist before he made any reference to the matter.

The decision was not difficult to arrive at. There was the door with its number as plain as could be, and work of some kind was evidently going on inside it, for as he neared the door he could hear footsteps and voices or a voice within. During the few seconds in which he halted to make sure of the number the footsteps ceased, seemingly very near the door, and he was a little startled at hearing a quick hissing breathing as of a person in strong excitement. He went on to his own room and again he was surprised to find how much smaller it seemed now than it had when he selected it. It was a slight disappointment, but only slight. If he found it really not large enough he could very easily shift to another. In the meantime he wanted something—as far as I remember it was a pocket-handkerchief—out of his portmanteau, which had been placed by the porter on a very inadequate trestle or stool against the wall at the farthest end of the room from his bed. Here was a very curious thing. The portmanteau was not to be seen. It had been moved by officious servants; doubtless the contents had been put in the drawers and wardrobe.* No, none of them were there. This was vexatious. The idea of a theft he dismissed at once. Such things rarely happen in Denmark, but some piece of stupidity had certainly been performed (which is not so uncommon), and the *stuepige** must be severely spoken to! Whatever it was that he wanted, it was not so necessary to his comfort that he could not wait till the morning for it, and he therefore settled not to ring the bell and disturb the servants. He went to the window—the right-hand window, it was—and looked out on the quiet street. There was a tall building opposite with large spaces of dead wall; no passers-by; a dark night; and very little to be seen of any kind.

The light was behind him and he could see his own shadow clearly cast on the wall opposite. Also the shadow of the bearded man in Number 11 on the left, who passed to and fro in shirtsleeves once or twice, and was seen first brushing his hair, and later on in a nightgown. Also the shadow of the occupant of Number 13 on the right. This might be more interesting. Number 13 was like himself leaning on his elbows on the window-sill looking out into the street. He seemed to be a tall thin man—or was it by any chance a woman?—at least it was someone who covered his or her head with some kind of drapery before going to bed, and, he thought, must be possessed of a red lamp-shade— and the lamp must be flickering very much. There was a distinct playing up and down of a dull red light on the opposite wall. He craned out a little to see if he could make any more of the figure: but beyond a fold of some light, perhaps white, material on the window-sill, he could see nothing.

Now came a distant step in the street and its approach seemed to recall Number 13 to a sense of his exposed position, for very swiftly and suddenly he swept aside from the window, and his red light went out. Anderson, who had been smoking a cigarette, laid the end of it on the window-sill and went to bed.

Next morning he was woke by the *stuepige* with hot water, etc. He roused himself and after thinking out the correct Danish words, said as distinctly as he could: 'You must not move my portmanteau. Where is it?'

As is not uncommon, the maid laughed, and went away without making any distinct answer.

Anderson, rather irritated, sat up in bed, intending to call her back; but he remained sitting up, staring straight in front of him. There was his portmanteau on its trestle, exactly where he had seen the porter put it when he first arrived. This was a rude shock for a man who prided himself on his accuracy of observation. How it could possibly have escaped him the night before he did not pretend to understand; at any rate, there it was now.

The daylight showed more than the portmanteau: it let the true proportions of the room, with its three windows, appear and satisfied its tenant that his choice after all had not been a bad one. When he was almost dressed he walked to the middle one of the three windows to look out at the weather. Another shock awaited him. Strangely unobservant he must have been last night. He could have sworn ten times over that he had been smoking at the right-hand window the last thing before he went to bed, and here was his cigarette-end on the sill of the middle window.

He started to go down to breakfast. Rather late, but Number 13 was later: here were his boots still outside his door—a gentleman's boots. So then Number 13 was a man not a woman. Just then he caught sight of the number on the door. It was 14. He thought he must have passed Number 13 without noticing it. Three stupid mistakes in twelve hours were too much for a methodical accurate-minded man, so he turned back to make sure. The next number to 14 was number 12, his own room. There was no Number 13 at all.*

After some minutes devoted to a careful consideration of everything he had had to eat and drink during the last twenty-four hours, Anderson decided to give the question up. If his sight or his brain were giving way he would have plenty of opportunities for ascertaining that fact. If not, then he was evidently being treated to a very interesting experience. In either case the development of events would certainly be worth watching.

During the day he continued his examination of the episcopal correspondence which I have already summarized. To his disappointment it was incomplete. Only one other letter could be found which referred to the affair of Mag. Nicolas Francken. It was from the Bishop Jörgen Friis to Rasmus Nielsen. He said:

'Although we are not in the least degree inclined to assent to your judgment concerning our Court and shall be prepared if need be to withstand you to the uttermost in that behalf, yet forasmuch as our trusty and well-beloved Mag. Nicolas Francken, against whom you have dared to allege certain false and malicious charges, hath been suddenly removed from among us, it is apparent that the question for this time falls. But forasmuch as you further allege that the Apostle and Evangelist St John in his heavenly Apocalypse describes the Holy Roman Church under the guise and symbol of the Scarlet Woman, be it known to you,' etc., etc.

Search as he might, Anderson could find no sequel to this letter nor any clue to the cause or manner of the 'removal' of the *casus belli*.* He could only suppose that Francken had died suddenly; and as there were only two days between the date of Nielsen's last letter (when Francken was evidently still in being) and that of the Bishop's letter, the death must have been completely unexpected.

In the afternoon he paid a short visit to Hald and took his tea at Baekkelund; nor could he notice—though he was in a somewhat nervous frame of mind—that there was any indication of such a failure of eye or brain as his experiences of the morning had led him to fear.

At supper he found himself next to the landlord.

'What,' he asked him, after some indifferent conversation,

'is the reason why in most of the hotels one visits in this country the number thirteen is left out of the list of rooms? I see you have none here.'

The landlord seemed amused.

'To think that you should have noticed a thing like that! I've thought about it once or twice myself, to tell the truth. An educated man, I've said, has no business with these superstitious notions. I was brought up myself here in the High School of Viborg, and our old master was always a man to set his face against anything of that kind. He's been dead now this many years: a fine upstanding man he was, and ready with his hands as well as his head. I recollect us boys one snowy day——'

Here he plunged into reminiscence.

'Then you don't think there is any particular objection to having a Number 13?' said Anderson.

'Ah, to be sure. Well, you understand I was brought up to the business by my poor old father. He kept a hotel in Aarhuus first, and then when we were born he moved to Viborg here, which was his native place, and had the Phoenix here until he died. That was in 1876. Then I started business in Silkeborg, and only the year before last I moved into this house.'

Then followed more details as to the state of the house and business when first taken over.

'And when you came here, was there a Number 13?'

'No, no. I was going to tell you about that. You see in a place like this the commercial class—the travellers—are what we have to provide for in general. And put them in Number 13? Why they'd as soon sleep in the street, or sooner. As far as I'm concerned myself it wouldn't make a penny difference to me what the number of my room was, and so I've often said to them. But they stick to it that it brings them bad luck. Quantities of stories they have among them of men that have slept in a Number 13 and never been the same again, or lost their best customers, or—one thing and another,' said the landlord, after searching for a more graphic phrase.

'Then, what do you use your Number 13 for?' said

Anderson, conscious, as he said the words, of a curious anxiety quite disproportionate to the importance of the question.

'My Number 13? Why, don't I tell you that there isn't such a thing in the house? I thought you might have noticed that. If there was it would be next door to your own room.'

'Well, yes, only I happened to think—that is, I fancied last night that I had seen a door numbered 13 in that passage, and really I am almost certain I must have been right for I saw it the night before as well.'

Of course Herr Kristensen laughed this notion to scorn, as Anderson had expected, and emphasized with much iteration the fact that no Number 13 existed or had existed before him in that hotel.

Anderson was in some ways relieved by his certainty, but still puzzled, and he began to think that the best way to make sure whether he had indeed been subject to an illusion or not was to invite the landlord to his room to smoke a cigar later on in the evening. Some photographs of English towns which he had with him formed a sufficiently good excuse.

Herr Kristensen was flattered by the invitation and most willingly accepted it. At about ten o'clock he was to make his appearance; but before that Anderson had some letters to write, and retired for the purpose of writing them. He almost blushed to himself at confessing it, but he could not deny that it was the fact that he was becoming quite nervous about the question of the existence of Number 13; so much so that he approached his room by way of Number 11, in order that he might not be obliged to pass the door, or the place where the door ought to be. He looked quickly and suspiciously about the room when he entered it, but there was nothing—beyond that indefinable air of being smaller than usual—to warrant any misgivings. There was no question of the presence or absence of his portmanteau tonight. He had himself emptied it of its contents and lodged it under his bed. With a certain effort he dismissed the thought of Number 13 from his mind and sat down to his writing.

His neighbours were quiet enough. Occasionally a door opened in the passage and a pair of boots was thrown out, or a bagman walked past humming to himself, and outside, from time to time, a cart thundered over the atrocious cobble-stones or a quick step hurried along the flags.

Anderson finished his letters, ordered in whisky and soda, and then went to the window and studied the dead wall opposite, and the shadows upon it.

As far as he could remember, Number 14 had been occupied by the lawyer, a staid man who said little at meals, being generally engaged in studying a small bundle of papers beside his plate. Apparently, however, he was in the habit of giving vent to his animal spirits when alone. Why else should he be dancing? The shadow from the next room evidently showed that he was. Again and again his thin form crossed the window, his arms waved, and a gaunt leg was kicked up with surprising agility. He seemed to be barefooted, and the floor must be well laid for no sound betrayed his movements. Sagförer Herr Anders Jensen dancing at ten o'clock at night in a hotel bedroom seemed a fitting subject for a historical painting in the grand style; and Anderson's thoughts, like those of Emily in the *Mysteries of Udolpho,** began to 'arrange themselves in the following lines':

> 'When I return to my hotel,
>   At ten o'clock p.m.,
> The waiters think I am unwell;
>   I do not care for them.
> But when I've locked my chamber door,
>   And put my boots outside,
> I dance all night upon the floor.
> And even if my neighbours swore,
> I'd go on dancing all the more,
> For I'm acquainted with the law,
> And in despite of all their jaw,
> Their protests I deride.'

Had not the landlord at this moment knocked at the door it is probable that quite a long poem might have been laid before the reader.

To judge from his look of surprise when he found himself in the room Herr Kristensen was struck, as Anderson had been, by something unusual in its aspect. But he made no remark. Anderson's photographs interested him mightily and formed the text of many autobiographical discourses. Nor is it quite clear how the conversation could have been diverted into the desired channel of Number 13 had not the lawyer at this moment begun to sing, and to sing in a manner which could leave no doubt in anyone's mind that he was either exceedingly drunk or raving mad. It was a high thin voice that they heard, and it seemed dry as if from long disuse. Of words or tune there was no question. It went sailing up to a surprising height and was carried down with a despairing moan as of a winter wind in a hollow chimney,* or an organ whose wind fails suddenly. It was a really horrible sound, and Anderson felt that if he had been alone he must have fled for refuge and society to some neighbour bagman's room.

The landlord sat open-mouthed.

'I don't understand it,' he said at last, wiping his forehead. 'It is dreadful. I have heard it once before, but I made sure it was a cat.'

'Is he mad?' said Anderson.

'He must be; and what a sad thing! Such a good customer, too, and so successful in his business by what I hear, and a young family to bring up.'

Just then came an impatient knock at the door, and the knocker entered without waiting to be asked. It was the lawyer in deshabille and very rough-haired, and very angry he looked.

'I beg pardon, sir,' he said, 'but I should be much obliged if you would kindly desist——'

Here he stopped, for it was evident that neither of the persons before him was responsible for the disturbance; and after a moment's lull it swelled forth again more wildly than before.

'But what in the name of heaven does it mean?' broke out the lawyer. 'Where is it? Who is it? Am I going out of my mind?'

'Surely, Herr Jensen, it comes from your room next door? Isn't there a cat or something stuck in the chimney?'

This was the best that occurred to Anderson to say, and

he realized its futility as he spoke; but anything was better
than to stand and listen to that horrible voice and look at
the broad white face of the landlord all perspiring and
quivering as he clutched the arms of his chair.

'Impossible,' said the lawyer, 'impossible. There is no
chimney. I came here because I was convinced the noise was
going on here. It was certainly in the next room to mine.'

'Was there no door between yours and mine?' said
Anderson eagerly.

'No, sir,' said Herr Jensen rather sharply. 'At least, not
this morning.'

'Ah,' said Anderson, 'nor tonight?'

'I am not sure,' said the lawyer with some hesitation.

Suddenly the crying or singing voice in the next room
died away, and the singer was heard seemingly to laugh to
himself in a crooning manner. The three men actually
shivered at the sound. Then there was a silence.

'Come,' said the lawyer, 'what have you to say, Herr
Kristensen? What does this mean?'

'Good Heaven!' said Kristensen. 'How should I tell! I know
no more than you, gentlemen.* I pray I may never hear such
a noise again.'

'So do I,' said Herr Jensen, and he added something under
his breath. Anderson thought it sounded like the last words
of the Psalter, '*omnis spiritus laudet Dominum*',* but he
could not be sure.

'But we must do something,' said Anderson, 'the three of
us. Shall we go and investigate in the next room?'

'But that is Herr Jensen's room,' wailed the landlord. 'It
is no use; he has come from there himself.'

'I am not so sure,' said Jensen. 'I think this gentleman is
right: we must go and see.'

The only weapons of defence that could be mustered on
the spot were a stick and umbrella. The expedition went out
into the passage—not without quakings. There was a deadly
quiet outside, but a light shone from under the next door.
Anderson and Jensen approached it. The latter turned the
handle and gave a sudden vigorous push. No use. The door
stood fast.

'Herr Kristensen,' said Jensen, 'will you go and fetch the strongest servant you have in the place? We must see this through.'

The landlord nodded and hurried off, glad to be away from the scene of action. Jensen and Anderson remained outside looking at the door.

'It *is* Number 13, you see,' said the latter.

'Yes, there is your door, and there is mine,' said Jensen.

'My room has three windows in the daytime,' said Anderson, with difficulty suppressing a nervous laugh.

'By George, so has mine!' said the lawyer, turning and looking at Anderson. His back was now to the door. In that moment the door opened and an arm came out and clawed at his shoulder. It was clad in ragged yellowish linen and the bare skin where it could be seen had long grey hair upon it. Anderson was just in time to pull Jensen out of its reach with a cry of disgust and fright when the door shut again, and a low laugh was heard.

Jensen had seen nothing, but when Anderson hurriedly told him what a risk he had run he fell into a great state of agitation and suggested that they should retire from the enterprise and lock themselves up in one or other of their rooms.

However, while he was developing this plan, the landlord and two able-bodied men arrived on the scene, all looking rather serious and alarmed. Jensen met them with a torrent of description and explanation which did not at all tend to encourage them for the fray.

The men dropped the crowbars they had brought and said flatly that they were not going to risk their throats in that devil's den. The landlord was miserably nervous and un-decided—conscious that if the danger were not faced his hotel was ruined, and very loth to face it himself. Luckily Anderson hit upon a way of rallying the demoralized force.

'Is this,' he said, 'the Danish courage I have heard so much of? It isn't a German in there, and if it was, we are five to one.'

The two servants and Jensen were stung into action by this and made a dash at the door.

'Stop!' said Anderson. 'Don't lose your heads. You stay out here with the light, landlord, and one of you two men break in the door, and don't go in when it gives way.'

The men nodded, and the younger stepped forward, raised his crowbar, and dealt a tremendous blow on the upper panel. The result was not in the least what any of them anticipated. There was no cracking or rending of wood—only a dull sound, as if the solid wall had been struck. The man dropped his tool with a shout, and began rubbing his elbow. His cry drew their eyes upon him for a moment. Then Anderson looked at the door again. It was gone. The plaster wall of the passage stared him in the face, with a considerable gash in it where the crowbar had struck it. Number 13 had passed out of existence.

For a brief space they stood perfectly still, gazing at the blank wall. An early cock in the yard beneath was heard to crow; and as Anderson glanced in the direction of the sound he saw through the window at the end of the long passage that the eastern sky was paling to the dawn.

* * * * *

'Perhaps,' said the landlord with hesitation, 'you gentlemen would like another room for tonight—a double-bedded one?'

Neither Jensen nor Anderson was averse to the suggestion. They felt inclined to hunt in couples after their late experience. It was found convenient, when each of them went to his room to collect the articles he wanted for the night, that the other should go with him and hold the candle. They noticed that both Number 12 and Number 14 had *three* windows.

Next morning the same party reassembled in Number 12. The landlord was naturally anxious to avoid engaging outside help and yet it was imperative that the mystery attaching to that part of the house should be cleared up. Accordingly* the two servants had been induced to take upon them the function of carpenters. The furniture was cleared away and, at the cost of a good many irretrievably damaged planks, that portion of the floor was taken up which lay nearest to Number 14.

You will naturally suppose that a skeleton—say that of Mag. Nicolas Francken—was discovered. That was not so. What they did find lying between the beams which supported the flooring was a small copper box. In it was a neatly-folded vellum document with about twenty lines of writing. Both Anderson and Jensen (who proved to be something of a palaeographer) were much excited by this discovery, which promised to afford the key to these extraordinary phenomena.

* * * * *

I possess a copy of an astrological work which I have never read. It has by way of frontispiece a woodcut by Hans Sebald Beham* representing a number of sages seated round a table. This detail may enable connoisseurs to identify the book. I cannot myself recollect its title, and it is not at this moment within reach; but the fly-leaves of it are covered with writing, and during the ten years in which I have owned the volume I have not been able to determine which way up this writing ought to be read, much less in what language it is. Not dissimilar was the position of Anderson and Jensen after the protracted examination to which they submitted the document in the copper box.

After two days' contemplation of it, Jensen, who was the bolder spirit of the two, hazarded the conjecture that the language was either Latin or Old Danish.

Anderson ventured upon no surmises and was very willing to surrender the box and the parchment to the Historical Society of Viborg to be placed in their museum.

I had the whole story from him a few months later as we sat in a wood near Upsala, after a visit to the library there, where we—or rather I—had laughed over the contract by which Daniel Salthenius (in later life Professor of Hebrew at Königsberg) sold himself to Satan.* Anderson was not really amused.

'Young idiot!' he said, meaning Salthenius, who was only an undergraduate when he committed that indiscretion, 'how did he know what company he was courting?'

And when I suggested the usual considerations he only grunted. That same afternoon he told me what you have read; but he refused to draw any inferences from it, and to assent to any that I drew for him.

COUNT MAGNUS

By what means the papers out of which I have made a connected story came into my hands is the last point which the reader will learn from these pages. But it is necessary to prefix to my extracts from them a statement of the form in which I possess them.

They consist, then, partly of a series of collections for a book of travels, such a volume as was a common product of the forties and fifties. Horace Marryat's *Journal of a Residence in Jutland and the Danish Isles** is a fair specimen of the class to which I allude. These books usually treated of some unfamiliar district on the Continent. They were illustrated with woodcuts or steel plates. They gave details of hotel accommodation, and of means of communication, such as we now expect to find in any well-regulated guidebook, and they dealt largely in reported conversations with intelligent foreigners, racy innkeepers and garrulous peasants. In a word, they were chatty.

Begun with the idea of furnishing material for such a book, my papers as they progressed assumed the character of a record of one single personal experience, and this record was continued up to the very eve, almost, of its termination.

The writer was a Mr Wraxall.* For my knowledge of him I have to depend entirely on the evidence his writings afford, and from these I deduce that he was a man past middle age, possessed of some private means, and very much alone in the world. He had, it seems, no settled abode in England, but was a denizen of hotels and boarding-houses. It is probable that he entertained the idea of settling down at some future time which never came; and I think it also likely that the Pantechnicon fire in the early seventies* must have destroyed a great deal that would have thrown light on his antecedents, for he refers once or twice to property of his that was warehoused at that establishment.

It is further apparent that Mr Wraxall had published a book, and that it treated of a holiday he had once taken in

Brittany. More than this I cannot say about his work, because
a diligent search in bibliographical works has convinced me
that it must have appeared either anonymously or under a
pseudonym.

As to his character, it is not difficult to form some superficial opinion. He must have been an intelligent and cultivated man. It seems that he was near being a Fellow of his
college at Oxford—Brasenose, as I judge from the Calendar.
His besetting fault was pretty clearly that of over-
inquisitiveness, possibly a good fault in a traveller, certainly
a fault for which this traveller paid dearly enough in the end.

On what proved to be his last expedition, he was plotting
another book. Scandinavia, a region not widely known to
Englishmen forty years ago, had struck him as an interesting
field. He must have lighted on some old books of Swedish
history or memoirs, and the idea had struck him that there
was room for a book descriptive of travel in Sweden,* inter-
spersed with episodes from the history of some of the great
Swedish families. He procured letters of introduction, therefore, to some persons of quality in Sweden, and set out thither
in the early summer of 1863.

Of his travels in the North there is no need to speak, nor
of his residence of some weeks in Stockholm. I need only
mention that some *savant* resident there put him on the track
of an important collection of family papers belonging to the
proprietors of an ancient manor-house in Vestergothland,
and obtained for him permission to examine them.

The manor-house, or *herrgård*, in question is to be called
Råbäck* (pronounced something like Roebeck), though that is
not its name. It is one of the best buildings of its kind in all
the country, and the picture of it in Dahlenberg's *Suecia
antiqua et moderna*,* engraved in 1694, shows it very much
as the tourist may see it today. It was built soon after 1600,
and is, roughly speaking, very much like an English house
of that period in respect of material—red-brick with stone
facings—and style. The man who built it was a scion of the
great house of De la Gardie,* and his descendants possess it
still. De la Gardie is the name by which I will designate them
when mention of them becomes necessary.

They received Mr Wraxall with great kindness and courtesy, and pressed him to stay in the house as long as his researches lasted. But, preferring to be independent, and mistrusting his powers of conversing in Swedish, he settled himself at the village inn, which turned out quite sufficiently comfortable, at any rate during the summer months. This arrangement would entail a short walk daily to and from the manor-house of something under a mile. The house itself stood in a park, and was protected—we should say grown up—with large old timber. Near it you found the walled garden, and then entered a close wood fringing one of the small lakes with which the whole country is pitted. Then came the wall of the demesne, and you climbed a steep knoll —a knob of rock lightly covered with soil—and on the top of this stood the church, fenced in with tall dark trees. It was a curious building to English eyes. The nave and aisles were low, and filled with pews and galleries. In the western gallery stood the handsome old organ, gaily painted, and with silver pipes. The ceiling was flat, and had been adorned by a seventeenth-century artist with a strange and hideous 'Last Judgment', full of lurid flames, falling cities, burning ships, crying souls, and brown and smiling demons. Handsome brass coronae hung from the roof; the pulpit was like a doll's-house, covered with little painted wooden cherubs and saints; a stand with three hour-glasses was hinged to the preacher's desk. Such sights as these may be seen in many a church in Sweden now, but what distinguished this one was an addition to the original building. At the eastern end of the north aisle the builder of the manor-house had erected a mausoleum* for himself and his family. It was a largish eight-sided building, lighted by a series of oval windows, and it had a domed roof, topped by a kind of pumpkin-shaped object rising into a spire, a form in which Swedish architects greatly delighted. The roof was of copper externally, and was painted black, while the walls, in common with those of the church, were staringly white. To this mausoleum there was no access from the church. It had a portal and steps of its own on the northern side.

Past the churchyard the path to the village goes, and not

more than three or four minutes bring you to the inn door.

On the first day of his stay at Råbäck Mr Wraxall found the church door open, and made those notes of the interior which I have epitomized. Into the mausoleum, however, he could not make his way. He could by looking through the keyhole just descry that there were fine marble effigies and sarcophagi of copper, and a wealth of armorial ornament, which made him very anxious to spend some time in investigation.

The papers he had come to examine at the manor-house proved to be of just the kind he wanted for his book. There were family correspondence, journals, and account-books of the earliest owners of the estate, very carefully kept and clearly written, full of amusing and picturesque detail. The first De la Gardie appeared in them as a strong and capable man. Shortly after the building of the mansion there had been a period of distress in the district, and the peasants had risen and attacked several châteaux and done some damage. The owner of Råbäck took a leading part in suppressing the trouble, and there was reference to executions of ringleaders and severe punishments inflicted with no sparing hand.

The portrait of this Magnus de la Gardie was one of the best in the house, and Mr Wraxall studied it with no little interest after his day's work. He gives no detailed description of it, but I gather that the face impressed him rather by its power than by its beauty or goodness; in fact, he writes that Count Magnus was an almost phenomenally ugly man.

On this day Mr Wraxall took his supper with the family, and walked back in the late but still bright evening.

'I must remember,' he writes, 'to ask the sexton if he can let me into the mausoleum at the church. He evidently has access to it himself, for I saw him tonight standing on the steps, and, as I thought, locking or unlocking the door.'

I find that early on the following day Mr Wraxall had some conversation with his landlord. His setting it down at such length as he does surprised me at first; but I soon realized that the papers I was reading were, at least in their beginning, the materials for the book he was meditating, and that it was to have been one of those quasi-journalistic productions which admit of the introduction of an admixture of conversational matter.

His object, he says, was to find out whether any traditions of Count Magnus de la Gardie lingered on in the scenes of that gentleman's activity, and whether the popular estimate of him were favourable or not. He found that the Count was decidedly not a favourite. If his tenants came late to their work on the days which they owed to him as Lord of the Manor, they were set on the wooden horse, or flogged and branded in the manor-house yard. One or two cases there were of men who had occupied lands which encroached on the lord's domain, and whose houses had been mysteriously burnt on a winter's night, with the whole family inside. But what seemed to dwell on the innkeeper's mind most—for he returned to the subject more than once—was that the Count had been on the Black Pilgrimage,* and had brought something or someone back with him.

You will naturally inquire, as Mr Wraxall did, what the Black Pilgrimage may have been. But your curiosity on the point must remain unsatisfied for the time being, just as his did. The landlord was evidently unwilling to give a full answer, or indeed any answer, on the point, and, being called out for a moment, trotted off with obvious alacrity, only putting his head in at the door a few minutes afterwards to say that he was called away to Skara,* and should not be back till evening.

So Mr Wraxall had to go unsatisfied to his day's work at the manor-house. The papers on which he was just then engaged soon put his thoughts into another channel, for he had to occupy himself with glancing over the correspondence between Sophia Albertina in Stockholm and her married cousin Ulrica Leonora at Råbäck in the years 1705–1710. The letters were of exceptional interest from the light they threw upon the culture of that period in Sweden, as anyone can testify who has read the full edition of them in the publications of the Swedish Historical Manuscripts Commission.

In the afternoon he had done with these, and after returning the boxes in which they were kept to their places on the shelf, he proceeded, very naturally, to take down some of the volumes nearest to them, in order to determine which of them had best be his principal subject of investigation next day. The shelf he had hit upon was occupied mostly by a collection of account-books in the writing of the first Count Magnus. But one among them was not an account-book, but a book of alchemical and other tracts in another sixteenth-century hand. Not being very familiar with alchemical literature, Mr Wraxall spends much space which he might have spared in setting out the names and beginnings of the various treatises: The book of the Phoenix, book of the Thirty Words, book of the Toad, book of Miriam, Turba philo-sophorum,* and so forth; and then he announces with a good deal of circumstance his delight at finding, on a leaf originally left blank near the middle of the book, some writing of Count Magnus himself headed 'Liber nigrae peregrinationis'. It is true that only a few lines were written, but there was quite enough to show that the landlord had that morning been referring to a belief at least as old as the time of Count Magnus, and probably shared by him. This is the English of what was written:

'If any man desires to obtain a long life, if he would obtain a faithful messenger and see the blood of his enemies, it is necessary that he should first go into the city of Chorazin,* and there salute the prince. . . .' Here there was an erasure of one word, not very thoroughly done, so that Mr Wraxall felt pretty sure that he was right in reading it as *aëris* ('of the air'). But there was no more of the text copied, only a line in Latin: 'Quaere reliqua hujus materiei inter secretiora' (See the rest of this matter among the more private things).

It could not be denied that this threw a rather lurid light upon the tastes and beliefs of the Count; but to Mr Wraxall, separated from him by nearly three centuries, the thought that he might have added to his general forcefulness alchemy, and to alchemy something like magic, only made him a more picturesque figure; and when, after a rather prolonged con-templation of his picture in the hall, Mr Wraxall set out on his homeward way, his mind was full of the thought of Count Magnus. He had no eyes for his surroundings, no perception of the evening scents of the woods or the evening light on the lake; and when all of a sudden he pulled up short, he was astonished to find himself already at the gate of the church-yard, and within a few minutes of his dinner. His eyes fell on the mausoleum.

'Ah,' he said, 'Count Magnus, there you are. I should dearly like to see you.'

'Like many solitary men,' he writes, 'I have a habit of talking to myself aloud; and, unlike some of the Greek and Latin particles, I do not expect an answer. Certainly, and perhaps fortunately in this case, there was neither voice nor any that regarded: only the woman who, I suppose, was cleaning up the church, dropped some metallic object on the floor, whose clang startled me. Count Magnus, I think, sleeps sound enough.'

That same evening the landlord of the inn, who had heard Mr Wraxall say that he wished to see the clerk or deacon (as he would be called in Sweden) of the parish, introduced him to that official in the inn parlour. A visit to the De la Gardie tomb-house was soon arranged for the next day, and a little general conversation ensued.

Mr Wraxall, remembering that one function of Scandi-navian deacons is to teach candidates for Confirmation, thought he would refresh his own memory on a Biblical point.

'Can you tell me,' he said, 'anything about Chorazin?'

The deacon seemed startled, but readily reminded him how that village had once been denounced.

'To be sure,' said Mr Wraxall; 'it is, I suppose, quite a ruin now?'

'So I expect,' replied the deacon. 'I have heard some of our old priests say that Antichrist is to be born there; and there are tales——'

'Ah! what tales are those?' Mr Wraxall put in.

'Tales, I was going to say, which I have forgotten,' said the deacon; and soon after that he said good night.

The landlord was now alone, and at Mr Wraxall's mercy; and that inquirer was not inclined to spare him.

'Herr Nielsen,' he said, 'I have found out something about the Black Pilgrimage. You may as well tell me what you know. What did the Count bring back with him?'

Swedes are habitually slow, perhaps, in answering, or perhaps the landlord was an exception. I am not sure; but Mr Wraxall notes that the landlord spent at least one minute in looking at him before he said anything at all. Then he came close up to his guest, and with a good deal of effort he spoke:

'Mr Wraxall, I can tell you this one little tale, and no more—not any more. You must not ask anything when I have done. In my grandfather's time—that is, ninety-two years ago—there were two men who said: "The Count is dead; we do not care for him. We will go tonight and have a free hunt in his wood"—the long wood on the hill that you have seen behind Råbäck. Well, those that heard them say this, they said: "No, do not go; we are sure you will meet with persons walking who should not be walking. They should be resting, not walking." These men laughed. There were no forest-men to keep the wood, because no one wished to hunt there. The family were not here at the house. These men could do what they wished.

'Very well, they go to the wood that night. My grandfather was sitting here in this room. It was the summer, and a light night. With the window open, he could see out to the wood, and hear.

'So he sat there, and two or three men with him, and they listened. At first they hear nothing at all; then they hear someone—you know how far away it is—they hear someone scream, just as if the most inside part of his soul was twisted out of him. All of them in the room caught hold of each other, and they sat so for three-quarters of an hour. Then they hear someone else, only about three hundred ells off. They hear him laugh out loud: it was not one of those two men that laughed, and, indeed, they have all of them said that it was not any man at all. After that they hear a great door shut.

'Then, when it was just light with the sun, they all went to the priest. They said to him:

' "Father, put on your gown and your ruff, and come to bury these men, Anders Bjornsen and Hans Thorbjorn."

'You understand that they were sure these men were dead.

So they went to the wood—my grandfather never forgot this. He said they were all like so many dead men themselves. The priest, too, he was in a white fear. He said when they came to him:

' "I heard one cry in the night, and I heard one laugh afterwards. If I cannot forget that, I shall not be able to sleep again."

'So they went to the wood, and they found these men on the edge of the wood. Hans Thorbjorn was standing with his back against a tree, and all the time he was pushing with his hands—pushing something away from him which was not there. So he was not dead. And they led him away, and took him to the house at Nykjoping, and he died before the winter; but he went on pushing with his hands. Also Anders Bjornsen was there; but he was dead. And I tell you this about Anders Bjornsen, that he was once a beautiful man, but now his face was not there, because the flesh of it was sucked away off the bones. You understand that? My grandfather did not forget that. And they laid him on the bier which they brought, and they put a cloth over his head, and the priest walked before; and they began to sing the psalm for the dead as well as they could. So, as they were singing the end of the first verse, one fell down, who was carrying the head of the bier, and the others looked back, and they saw that the cloth had fallen off, and the eyes of Anders Bjornsen were looking up, because there was nothing to close over them. And this they could not bear. Therefore the priest laid the cloth upon him, and sent for a spade, and they buried him in that place.'

The next day Mr Wraxall records that the deacon called for him soon after his breakfast, and took him to the church and mausoleum. He noticed that the key of the latter was hung on a nail just by the pulpit, and it occurred to him that, as the church door seemed to be left unlocked as a rule, it would not be difficult for him to pay a second and more private visit to the monuments if there proved to be more of interest among them than could be digested at first. The building, when he entered it, he found not unimposing. The monuments, mostly large erections of the seventeenth and

eighteenth centuries, were dignified if luxuriant, and the
epitaphs and heraldry were copious. The central space of the
domed room was occupied by three copper sarcophagi,
covered with finely-engraved ornament. Two of them had,
as is commonly the case in Denmark and Sweden, a large
metal crucifix on the lid. The third, that of Count Magnus,
as it appeared, had, instead of that, a full-length effigy
engraved upon it, and round the edge were several bands
of similar ornament representing various scenes. One was a
battle, with cannon belching out smoke, and walled towns,
and troops of pikemen. Another showed an execution. In a
third, among trees, was a man running at full speed, with
flying hair and outstretched hands. After him followed a
strange form; it would be hard to say whether the artist had
intended it for a man, and was unable to give the requisite
similitude, or whether it was intentionally made as monstrous
as it looked. In view of the skill with which the rest of the
drawing was done, Mr Wraxall felt inclined to adopt the
latter idea. The figure was unduly short, and was for the most
part muffled in a hooded garment which swept the ground.
The only part of the form which projected from that shelter
was not shaped like any hand or arm. Mr Wraxall compares
it to the tentacle of a devil-fish,* and continues: 'On seeing
this, I said to myself, "This, then, which is evidently an
allegorical representation of some kind—a fiend pursuing a
hunted soul—may be the origin of the story of Count
Magnus and his mysterious companion. Let us see how the
huntsman is pictured: doubtless it will be a demon blowing
his horn." ' But, as it turned out, there was no such sensa-
tional figure, only the semblance of a cloaked man on a
hillock, who stood leaning on a stick, and watching the hunt
with an interest which the engraver had tried to express in
his attitude.

Mr Wraxall noted the finely-worked and massive steel
padlocks—three in number—which secured the sarcophagus.
One of them, he saw, was detached, and lay on the pavement.
And then, unwilling to delay the deacon longer or to waste
his own working-time, he made his way onward to the
manor-house.

'It is curious,' he notes, 'how on retracing a familiar path one's thoughts engross one to the absolute exclusion of surrounding objects. Tonight, for the second time, I had entirely failed to notice where I was going (I had planned a private visit to the tomb-house to copy the epitaphs), when I suddenly, as it were, awoke to consciousness, and found myself (as before) turning in at the churchyard gate, and, I believe, singing or chanting some such words as, "Are you awake, Count Magnus? Are you asleep, Count Magnus?" and then something more which I have failed to recollect. It seemed to me that I must have been behaving in this nonsensical way for some time.'

He found the key of the mausoleum where he had expected to find it, and copied the greater part of what he wanted; in fact, he stayed until the light began to fail him.

'I must have been wrong,' he writes, 'in saying that one of the padlocks of my Count's sarcophagus was unfastened; I see tonight that two are loose. I picked both up, and laid them carefully on the window-ledge, after trying unsuccessfully to close them. The remaining one is still firm, and, though I take it to be a spring lock, I cannot guess how it is opened. Had I succeeded in undoing it, I am almost afraid I should have taken the liberty of opening the sarcophagus. It is strange, the interest I feel in the personality of this, I fear, somewhat ferocious and grim old noble.'

The day following was, as it turned out, the last of Mr Wraxall's stay at Råbäck. He received letters connected with certain investments which made it desirable that he should return to England; his work among the papers was practically done, and travelling was slow. He decided, therefore, to make his farewells, put some finishing touches to his notes, and be off.

These finishing touches and farewells, as it turned out, took more time than he had expected. The hospitable family insisted on his staying to dine with them—they dined at three—and it was verging on half-past six before he was outside the iron gates of Råbäck. He dwelt on every step of his walk by the lake, determined to saturate himself, now that he trod it for the last time, in the sentiment of the place and hour. And when he reached the summit of the churchyard knoll, he lingered for many minutes, gazing at the limitless prospect of woods near and distant, all dark beneath a sky of liquid green. When at last he turned to go, the thought struck him that surely he must bid farewell to Count Magnus as well as the rest of the De la Gardies. The church was but twenty yards away, and he knew where the key of the mausoleum hung. It was not long before he was standing over the great copper coffin, and, as usual, talking to himself aloud. 'You may have been a bit of a rascal in your time, Magnus,' he was saying, 'but for all that I should like to see you, or, rather——'

'Just at that instant,' he says, 'I felt a blow on my foot. Hastily enough I drew it back, and something fell on the pavement with a clash. It was the third, the last of the three padlocks which had fastened the sacrophagus. I stooped to pick it up, and—Heaven is my witness that I am writing only the bare truth—before I had raised myself there was a sound of metal hinges creaking, and I distinctly saw the lid shifting upwards. I may have behaved like a coward, but I could not for my life stay for one moment. I was outside that dreadful building in less time than I can write—almost as quickly as I could have said—the words; and what frightens me yet more, I could not turn the key in the lock. As I sit here in my room noting these facts, I ask myself (it was not twenty minutes ago) whether that noise of creaking metal continued, and I cannot tell whether it did or not. I only know that there was something more than I have written that alarmed me, but whether it was sound or sight I am not able to remember. What is this that I have done?'

Poor Mr Wraxall! He set out on his journey to England on the next day, as he had planned, and he reached England in safety; and yet, as I gather from his changed hand and inconsequent jottings, a broken man. One of several small notebooks that have come to me with his papers gives, not a key to, but a kind of inkling of, his experiences. Much of his journey was made by canal-boat, and I find not less than six painful attempts to enumerate and describe his fellow-passengers. The entries are of this kind:

24. Pastor of village in Skåne. Usual black coat and soft black hat.

25. Commercial traveller from Stockholm going to Trollhättan. Black cloak, brown hat.

26. Man in long black cloak, broad-leafed hat, very old-fashioned.

This entry is lined out, and a note added: 'Perhaps identical with No. 13. Have not yet seen his face.' On referring to No. 13, I find that he is a Roman priest in a cassock.

The net result of the recokning is always the same. Twenty-eight people appear in the enumeration, one being always a man in a long black cloak and broad hat, and the other a 'short figure in dark cloak and hood'. On the other hand, it is always noted that only twenty-six passengers appear at meals, and that the man in the cloak is perhaps absent, and the short figure is certainly absent.

On reaching England, it appears that Mr Wraxall landed at Harwich, and that he resolved at once to put himself out of the reach of some person or persons whom he never specifies, but whom he had evidently come to regard as his pursuers. Accordingly he took a vehicle—it was a closed fly—not trusting the railway, and drove across country to the village of Belchamp St Paul.* It was about nine o'clock on a moonlight August night when he neared the place. He was sitting forward, and looking out of the window at the fields and thickets—there was little else to be seen—racing past him. Suddenly he came to a cross-road. At the corner two figures* were standing motionless; both were in dark cloaks; the taller one wore a hat, the shorter a hood. He had no time to see their faces, nor did they make any motion that he could discern. Yet the horse shied violently and broke into a gallop, and Mr Wraxall sank back into his seat in something like desperation. He had seen them before.

Arrived at Belchamp St Paul, he was fortunate enough to find a decent furnished lodging, and for the next twenty-four hours he lived, comparatively speaking, in peace. His last notes were written on this day. They are too disjointed and ejaculatory to be given here in full, but the substance of them is clear enough. He is expecting a visit from his pursuers—how or when he knows not—and his constant cry is 'What has he done?' and 'Is there no hope?' Doctors, he knows, would call him mad, policemen would laugh at him. The parson is away. What can he do but lock his door and cry to God?

People still remembered last year at Belchamp St Paul how a strange gentleman came one evening in August years back; and how the next morning but one he was found dead, and there was an inquest; and the jury that viewed the body fainted, seven of 'em did, and none of 'em wouldn't speak to what they see, and the verdict was visitation of God; and how the people as kep' the 'ouse moved out that same week, and went away from that part. But they do not, I think, know that any glimmer of light has ever been thrown, or could be thrown, on the mystery. It so happened that last year the little house came into my hands as part of a legacy. It had stood empty since 1863, and there seemed no prospect of letting it; so I had it pulled down, and the papers of which I have given you an abstract were found in a forgotten cupboard under the window in the best bedroom.

'OH, WHISTLE, AND I'LL COME TO
YOU, MY LAD'

'I SUPPOSE you will be getting away pretty soon, now Full
term is over, Professor,' said a person not in the story to the
Professor of Ontography, soon after they had sat down next
to each other at a feast in the hospitable hall of St James's
College.*

The Professor was young, neat, and precise in speech.

'Yes,' he said; 'my friends have been making me take up
golf this term, and I mean to go to the East Coast—in point
of fact to Burnstow*—(I dare say you know it) for a week
or ten days, to improve my game. I hope to get off tomorrow.'

'Oh, Parkins,' said his neighbour on the other side, 'if you
are going to Burnstow, I wish you would look at the site
of the Templars' preceptory, and let me know if you think
it would be any good to have a dig there in the summer.'

It was, as you might suppose, a person of antiquarian
pursuits who said this, but, since he merely appears in this
prologue, there is no need to give his entitlements.

'Certainly,' said Parkins, the Professor: 'if you will describe
to me whereabouts the site is, I will do my best to give you
an idea of the lie of the land when I get back; or I could
write to you about it, if you would tell me where you are
likely to be.'

'Don't trouble to do that, thanks. It's only that I'm thinking of taking my family in that direction in the Long,* and
it occurred to me that, as very few of the English preceptories
have ever been properly planned, I might have an opportunity of doing something useful on off-days.'

The Professor rather sniffed at the idea that planning out
a preceptory could be described as useful. His neighbour
continued:

'The site—I doubt if there is anything showing above
ground—must be down quite close to the beach now. The
sea has encroached tremendously, as you know, all along
that bit of coast. I should think, from the map, that it must

be about three-quarters of a mile from the Globe Inn, at the north end of the town. Where are you going to stay?'

'Well, at the Globe Inn, as a matter of fact,' said Parkins; 'I have engaged a room there. I couldn't get in anywhere else; most of the lodging-houses are shut up in winter, it seems; and, as it is, they tell me that the only room of any size I can have is really a double-bedded one, and that they haven't a corner in which to store the other bed, and so on. But I must have a fairly large room, for I am taking some books down, and mean to do a bit of work; and though I don't quite fancy having an empty bed—not to speak of two—in what I may call for the time being my study, I suppose I can manage to rough it for the short time I shall be there.'

'Do you call having an extra bed in your room roughing it, Parkins?' said a bluff person opposite. 'Look here, I shall come down and occupy it for a bit; it'll be company for you.'

The Professor quivered, but managed to laugh in a courteous manner.

'By all means, Rogers; there's nothing I should like better. But I'm afraid you would find it rather dull; you don't play golf, do you?'

'No, thank Heaven!' said rude Mr Rogers.

'Well, you see, when I'm not writing I shall most likely be out on the links, and that, as I say, would be rather dull for you, I'm afraid.'

'Oh, I don't know! There's certain to be somebody I know in the place; but, of course, if you don't want me, speak the word, Parkins; I shan't be offended. Truth, as you always tell us, is never offensive.'

Parkins was, indeed, scrupulously polite and strictly truthful. It is to be feared that Mr Rogers sometimes practised upon his knowledge of these characteristics. In Parkins's breast there was a conflict now raging, which for a moment or two did not allow him to answer. That interval being over, he said:

'Well, if you want the exact truth, Rogers, I was considering whether the room I speak of would really be large enough to accommodate us both comfortably; and also whether (mind, I shouldn't have said this if you hadn't pressed me) you would not constitute something in the nature of a hindrance to my work.'

Rogers laughed loudly.

'Well done, Parkins!' he said. 'It's all right. I promise not to interrupt your work; don't you disturb yourself about that. No, I won't come if you don't want me; but I thought I should do so nicely to keep the ghosts off.' Here he might have been seen to wink and to nudge his next neighbour. Parkins might also have been seen to become pink. 'I beg pardon, Parkins,' Rogers continued; 'I oughtn't to have said that. I forgot you didn't like levity on these topics.'

'Well,' Parkins said, 'as you have mentioned the matter, I freely own that I do *not* like careless talk about what you call ghosts. A man in my position,' he went on, raising his voice a little, 'cannot, I find, be too careful about appearing to sanction the current beliefs on such subjects. As you know, Rogers, or as you ought to know; for I think I have never concealed my views——'

'No, you certainly have not, old man,' put in Rogers *sotto voce*.

'——I hold that any semblance, any appearance of concession to the view that such things might exist is equivalent to a renunciation of all that I hold most sacred. But I'm afraid I have not succeeded in securing your attention.'

'Your *undivided* attention, was what Dr Blimber* actually *said*,'[1] Rogers interrupted, with every appearance of an earnest desire for accuracy. 'But I beg your pardon, Parkins: I'm stopping you.'

'No, not at all,' said Parkins. 'I don't remember Blimber; perhaps he was before my time. But I needn't go on. I'm sure you know what I mean.'

'Yes, yes,' said Rogers, rather hastily—'just so. We'll go into it fully at Burnstow, or somewhere.'

In repeating the above dialogue I have tried to give the impression which it made on me, that Parkins was something of an old woman—rather hen-like, perhaps, in his little ways; totally destitute, alas! of the sense of humour, but at the same time dauntless and sincere in his convictions, and a

[1] Mr Rogers was wrong, *vide Dombey and Son*, Chapter XII.

man deserving of the greatest respect. Whether or not the reader has gathered so much, that was the character which Parkins had.

On the following day Parkins did, as he had hoped, succeed in getting away from his college, and in arriving at Burnstow. He was made welcome at the Globe Inn, was safely installed in the large double-bedded room of which we have heard, and was able before retiring to rest to arrange his materials for work in apple-pie order upon a commodious table which occupied the outer end of the room, and was surrounded on three sides by windows looking out seaward; that is to say, the central window looked straight out to sea, and those on the left and right commanded prospects along the shore to the north and south respectively. On the south you saw the village of Burnstow. On the north no houses were to be seen, but only the beach and the low cliff backing it. Immediately in front was a strip—not considerable—of rough grass, dotted with old anchors, capstans, and so forth; then a broad path; then the beach. Whatever may have been the original distance between the Globe Inn and the sea, not more than sixty yards now separated them.

The rest of the population of the inn was, of course, a golfing one, and included few elements that call for a special description. The most conspicuous figure was, perhaps, that of an *ancien militaire*, secretary of a London club, and possessed of a voice of incredible strength, and of views of a pronouncedly Protestant type. These were apt to find utterance after his attendance upon the ministrations of the Vicar, an estimable man with inclinations towards a picturesque ritual, which he gallantly kept down as far as he could out of deference to East Anglian tradition.*

Professor Parkins, one of whose principal characteristics was pluck, spent the greater part of the day following his arrival at Burnstow in what he had called improving his game, in company with this Colonel Wilson: and during the afternoon—whether the process of improvement were to blame or not, I am not sure—the Colonel's demeanour assumed a colouring so lurid that even Parkins jibbed at the thought of walking home with him from the links. He determined, after a short and furtive look at that bristling moustache and those incarnadined features, that it would be wiser to allow the influences of tea and tobacco to do what they could with the Colonel before the dinner-hour should render a meeting inevitable.

'I might walk home tonight along the beach,' he reflected—'yes, and take a look—there will be light enough for that—at the ruins of which Disney* was talking. I don't exactly know where they are, by the way; but I expect I can hardly help stumbling on them.'

This he accomplished, I may say, in the most literal sense, for in picking his way from the links to the shingle beach his foot caught, partly in a gorse-root and partly in a biggish stone, and over he went. When he got up and surveyed his surroundings, he found himself in a patch of somewhat broken ground covered with small depressions and mounds. These latter, when he came to examine them, proved to be simply masses of flints embedded in mortar and grown over with turf. He must, he quite rightly concluded, be on the site of the preceptory he had promised to look at. It seemed not unlikely to reward the spade of the explorer; enough of the foundations was probably left at no great depth to throw a good deal of light on the general plan. He remembered vaguely that the Templars, to whom this site had belonged, were in the habit of building round churches,* and he thought a particular series of the humps or mounds near him did appear to be arranged in something of a circular form. Few people can resist the temptation to try a little amateur research in a department quite outside their own, if only for the satisfaction of showing how successful they would have been had they only taken it up seriously. Our Professor, however, if he felt something of this mean desire, was also truly anxious to oblige Mr Disney. So he paced with care the circular area he had noticed, and wrote down its rough dimensions in his pocket-book. Then he proceeded to examine an oblong eminence which lay east of the centre of the circle, and seemed to his thinking likely to be the base of a platform or altar. At one end of it, the northern, a patch of the turf was gone—removed by some boy or other creature *ferae naturae*.* It might, he thought, be as well to probe the soil here for evidences of masonry, and he took out his knife and began scraping away the earth. And now followed another little discovery: a portion of soil fell inward as he scraped, and disclosed a small cavity. He lighted one match after another to help him to see of what nature the hole was, but the wind was too strong for them all. By tapping and scratching the sides with his knife, however, he was able to make out that it must be an artificial hole in masonry. It was rectangular, and the sides, top, and bottom, if not actually plastered, were smooth and regular. Of course it was empty. No! As he withdrew the knife he heard a metallic clink, and when he introduced his hand it met with a cylindrical object lying on the floor of the hole. Naturally enough, he picked it up, and when he brought it into the light, now fast fading, he could see that it, too, was of man's making—a metal tube about four inches long, and evidently of some considerable age.

By the time Parkins had made sure that there was nothing else in this odd receptacle, it was too late and too dark for him to think of undertaking any further search. What he had done had proved so unexpectedly interesting that he determined to sacrifice a little more of the daylight on the morrow to archaeology. The object which he now had safe in his pocket was bound to be of some slight value at least, he felt sure.

Bleak and solemn was the view on which he took a last look before starting homeward. A faint yellow light in the west showed the links, on which a few figures moving towards the club-house were still visible, the squat martello tower, the lights of Aldsey village, the pale ribbon of sands intersected at intervals by black wooden groynes, the dim and murmuring sea. The wind was bitter from the north, but was at his back when he set out for the Globe. He quickly rattled and clashed through the shingle and gained the sand, upon which, but for the groynes which had to be got over every few yards, the going was both good and quiet. One last look behind, to measure the distance he had made since leaving the ruined Templars' church, showed him a prospect of company on his walk, in the shape of a rather indistinct personage, who seemed to be making great efforts to catch up with him, but made little, if any, progress. I mean that there was an appearance of running about his movements, but that the distance between him and Parkins did not seem materially to lessen. So, at least, Parkins thought, and decided that he almost certainly did not know him, and that it would be absurd to wait until he came up. For all that, company, he began to think, would really be very welcome on that lonely shore, if only you could choose your companion. In his unenlightened days he had read of meetings in such places which even now would hardly bear thinking of. He went on thinking of them, however, until he reached home, and particularly of one which catches most people's fancy at some time of their childhood. 'Now I saw in my dream that Christian had gone but a very little way when he saw a foul fiend coming over the field to meet him.'* 'What should I do now,' he thought, 'if I looked back and caught sight of a black figure sharply defined against the yellow sky, and saw that it had horns and wings? I wonder whether I should stand or run for it. Luckily, the gentleman behind is not of that kind, and he seems to be about as far off now as when I saw him first. Well, at this rate he won't get his dinner as soon as I shall; and, dear me! it's within a quarter of an hour of the time now. I must run!'

Parkins had, in fact, very little time for dressing. When he met the Colonel at dinner, Peace—or as much of her as that gentleman could manage—reigned once more in the military bosom; nor was she put to flight in the hours of bridge that followed dinner, for Parkins was a more than respectable player. When, therefore, he retired towards twelve o'clock, he felt that he had spent his evening in quite a satisfactory way, and that, even for so long as a fortnight or three weeks, life at the Globe would be supportable under similar conditions—'especially,' thought he, 'if I go on improving my game.'

As he went along the passages he met the boots of the Globe, who stopped and said:

'Beg your pardon, sir, but as I was a-brushing your coat just now there was somethink fell out of the pocket. I put it on your chest of drawers, sir, in your room, sir—a piece of a pipe or somethink of that, sir. Thank you, sir. You'll find it on your chest of drawers, sir—yes, sir. Good night, sir.'

The speech served to remind Parkins of his little discovery of that afternoon. It was with some considerable curiosity that he turned it over by the light of his candles. It was of bronze, he now saw, and was shaped very much after the manner of the modern dog-whistle; in fact it was—yes, certainly it was—actually no more nor less than a whistle. He put it to his lips, but it was quite full of a fine, caked-up sand or earth, which would not yield to knocking, but must be loosened with a knife. Tidy as ever in his habits, Parkins cleared out the earth on to a piece of paper, and took the latter to the window to empty it out. The night was clear and bright, as he saw when he had opened the casement, and he stopped for an instant to look at the sea and note a belated wanderer stationed on the shore in front of the inn. Then he shut the window, a little surprised at the late hours people kept at Burnstow, and took his whistle to the light again. Why, surely there were marks on it, and not merely marks, but letters! A very little rubbing rendered the deeply-cut inscription quite legible, but the Professor had to confess, after some earnest thought, that the meaning of it was as obscure to him as the writing on the wall to Belshazzar.* There were legends both on the front and on the back of the whistle. The one read thus:

$$\begin{array}{c} \text{FLA} \\ \text{FUR} \qquad \text{BIS} \\ \text{FLE} \end{array}$$

The other:

⌘QUIS EST ISTE QUI UENIT⌘

'I ought to be able to make it out,' he thought; 'but I suppose I am a little rusty in my Latin. When I come to think of it, I don't believe I even know the word for a whistle. The long one does seem simple enough. It ought to mean, "Who is this who is coming?" Well, the best way to find out is evidently to whistle for him.'

He blew tentatively and stopped suddenly, startled and yet pleased at the note he had elicited. It had a quality of infinite distance in it, and, soft as it was, he somehow felt it must be audible for miles round. It was a sound, too, that seemed to have the power (which many scents possess) of forming pictures in the brain. He saw quite clearly for a moment a vision of a wide, dark expanse at night, with a fresh wind blowing, and in the midst a lonely figure—how employed, he could not tell. Perhaps he would have seen more had not the picture been broken by the sudden surge of a gust of wind against his casement, so sudden that it made him look up, just in time to see the white glint of a sea-bird's wing somewhere outside the dark panes.

The sound of the whistle had so fascinated him that he could not help trying it once more, this time more boldly. The note was little, if at all, louder than before, and repetition broke the illusion—no picture followed, as he had half hoped it might. 'But what is this? Goodness! what force the wind can get up in a few minutes! What a tremendous gust! There! I knew that window-fastening was no use! Ah! I thought so—both candles out. It's enough to tear the room to pieces.'

The first thing was to get the window shut. While you might count twenty Parkins was struggling with the small casement, and felt almost as if he were pushing back a sturdy burglar, so strong was the pressure. It slackened all at once, and the window banged to and latched itself. Now to relight the candles and see what damage, if any, had been done. No, nothing seemed amiss; no glass even was broken in the casement. But the noise had evidently roused at least one member of the household: the Colonel was to be heard stumping in his stockinged feet on the floor above, and growling.

Quickly as it had risen, the wind did not fall at once. On it went, moaning and rushing past the house, at times rising to a cry so desolate that, as Parkins disinterestedly said, it might have made fanciful people feel quite uncomfortable;

even the unimaginative, he thought after a quarter of an hour, might be happier without it.

Whether it was the wind, or the excitement of golf, or of the researches in the preceptory that kept Parkins awake, he was not sure. Awake he remained, in any case, long enough to fancy (as I am afraid I often do myself under such conditions) that he was the victim of all manner of fatal disorders: he would lie counting the beats of his heart, convinced that it was going to stop work every moment, and would entertain grave suspicions of his lungs, brain, liver, etc.—suspicions which he was sure would be dispelled by the return of daylight, but which until then refused to be put aside. He found a little vicarious comfort in the idea that someone else was in the same boat. A near neighbour (in the darkness it was not easy to tell his direction) was tossing and rustling in his bed, too.

The next stage was that Parkins shut his eyes and determined to give sleep every chance. Here again over-excitement asserted itself in another form—that of making pictures. *Experto crede,** pictures do come to the closed eyes of one trying to sleep, and are often so little to his taste that he must open his eyes and disperse them.

Parkins's experience on this occasion was a very distressing one. He found that the picture which presented itself to him was continuous. When he opened his eyes, of course, it went; but when he shut them once more it framed itself afresh, and acted itself out again, neither quicker nor slower than before. What he saw was this:

A long stretch of shore—shingle edged by sand, and intersected at short intervals with black groynes running down to the water—a scene, in fact, so like that of his afternoon's walk that, in the absence of any landmark, it could not be distinguished therefrom. The light was obscure, conveying an impression of gathering storm, late winter evening, and slight cold rain. On this bleak stage at first no actor was visible. Then, in the distance, a bobbing black object appeared; a moment more, and it was a man running, jumping, clambering over the groynes, and every few seconds looking eagerly back. The nearer he came the more obvious it was that he was not only anxious, but even terribly frightened, though his face was not to be distinguished. He was, moreover, almost at the end of his strength. On he came; each successive obstacle seemed to cause him more difficulty than the last. 'Will he get over this next one?' thought Parkins; 'it seems a little higher than the others.' Yes; half climbing, half throwing himself, he did get over, and fell all in a heap on the other side (the side nearest to the spectator). There, as if really unable to get up again, he remained crouching under the groyne, looking up in an attitude of painful anxiety.*

So far no cause whatever for the fear of the runner had been shown; but now there began to be seen, far up the shore, a little flicker of something light-coloured moving to and fro with great swiftness and irregularity. Rapidly growing larger, it, too, declared itself as a figure in pale, fluttering draperies, ill-defined. There was something about its motion which made Parkins very unwilling to see it at close quarters. It would stop, raise arms, bow itself toward the sand, then run stooping across the beach to the water-edge and back again; and then, rising upright, once more continue its course forward at a speed that was startling and terrifying. The moment came when the pursuer was hovering about from left to right only a few yards beyond the groyne where the runner lay in hiding. After two or three ineffectual castings hither and thither it came to a stop, stood upright, with arms raised high, and then darted straight forward towards the groyne.

It was at this point that Parkins always failed in his resolution to keep his eyes shut. With many misgivings as to incipient failure of eyesight, over-worked brain, excessive smoking, and so on, he finally resigned himself to light his candle, get out a book, and pass the night waking, rather than be tormented by this persistent panorama, which he saw clearly enough could only be a morbid reflection of his walk and his thoughts on that very day.

The scraping of match on box and the glare of light must have startled some creatures of the night—rats or what not—which he heard scurry across the floor from the side of his bed with much rustling. Dear, dear! the match is out! Fool that it is! But the second one burnt better, and a candle and book were duly procured, over which Parkins pored till sleep of a wholesome kind came upon him, and that in no long space. For about the first time in his orderly and prudent life he forgot to blow out the candle, and when he was called next morning at eight there was still a flicker in the socket and a sad mess of guttered grease on top of the little table.

After breakfast he was in his room, putting the finishing touches to his golfing costume—fortune had again allotted the Colonel to him for a partner—when one of the maids came in.

'Oh, if you please,' she said, 'would you like any extra blankets on your bed, sir?'

'Ah! thank you,' said Parkins. 'Yes, I think I should like one. It seems likely to turn rather colder.'

In a very short time the maid was back with the blanket.

'Which bed should I put it on, sir?' she asked.

'What? Why, that one—the one I slept in last night,' he said, pointing to it.

'Oh yes! I beg your pardon, sir, but you seemed to have tried both of 'em; leastways, we had to make 'em both up this morning.'

'Really? How very absurd!' said Parkins. 'I certainly never touched the other, except to lay some things on it. Did it actually seem to have been slept in?'

'Oh yes, sir!' said the maid. 'Why, all the things was crumpled and throwed about all ways, if you'll excuse me, sir—quite as if anyone 'adn't passed but a very poor night, sir.'

'Dear me,' said Parkins. 'Well, I may have disordered it more than I thought when I unpacked my things. I'm very sorry to have given you the extra trouble, I'm sure. I expect a friend of mine soon, by the way—a gentleman from Cambridge—to come and occupy it for a night or two. That will be all right, I suppose, won't it?'

'Oh yes, to be sure, sir. Thank you, sir. It's no trouble, I'm sure,' said the maid, and departed to giggle with her colleagues.

Parkins set forth, with a stern determination to improve his game.

I am glad to be able to report that he succeeded so far in this enterprise that the Colonel, who had been rather repining at the prospect of a second day's play in his company, became quite chatty as the morning advanced; and his voice boomed out over the flats, as certain also of our own minor poets have said, 'like some great bourdon in a minster tower'.*

'Extraordinary wind, that, we had last night,' he said. 'In my old home we should have said someone had been whistling for it.'

'Should you, indeed!' said Parkins. 'Is there a superstition of that kind still current in your part of the country?'

'I don't know about superstition,' said the Colonel. 'They believe in it all over Denmark and Norway, as well as on the Yorkshire coast; and my experience is, mind you, that there's generally something at the bottom of what these country-folk hold to, and have held to for generations. But it's your drive' (or whatever it might have been: the golfing reader will have to imagine appropriate digressions at the proper intervals).

When conversation was resumed, Parkins said, with a slight hesitancy:

'Apropos of what you were saying just now, Colonel, I think I ought to tell you that my own views on such subjects are very strong. I am, in fact, a convinced disbeliever in what is called the "supernatural".'

'What!' said the Colonel, 'do you mean to tell me you don't believe in second-sight, or ghosts, or anything of that kind?'

'In nothing whatever of that kind,' returned Parkins firmly.

'Well,' said the Colonel, 'but it appears to me at that rate, sir, that you must be little better than a Sadducee.'*

Parkins was on the point of answering that, in his opinion, the Sadducees were the most sensible persons he had ever read of in the Old Testament; but, feeling some doubt as to whether much mention of them was to be found in that work, he preferred to laugh the accusation off.

'Perhaps I am,' he said; 'but—— Here, give me my cleek, boy!—Excuse me one moment, Colonel.' A short interval. 'Now, as to whistling for the wind, let me give you my theory about it. The laws which govern winds are really not at all perfectly known—to fisher-folk and such, of course, not known at all. A man or woman of eccentric habits, perhaps, or a stranger, is seen repeatedly on the beach at some unusual hour, and is heard whistling. Soon afterwards a violent wind rises; a man who could read the sky perfectly or who possessed a barometer could have foretold that it would. The simple people of a fishing-village have no barometers, and only a few rough rules for prophesying weather. What more natural than that the eccentric personage I postulated should be regarded as having raised the wind, or that he or she should clutch eagerly at the reputation of being able to do so? Now, take last night's wind: as it happens, I myself was whistling. I blew a whistle twice, and the wind seemed to come absolutely in answer to my call. If anyone had seen me——'

The audience had been a little restive under this harangue, and Parkins had, I fear, fallen somewhat into the tone of a lecturer; but at the last sentence the Colonel stopped.

'Whistling, were you?' he said. 'And what sort of whistle did you use? Play this stroke first.' Interval.

'About that whistle you were asking, Colonel. It's rather a curious one. I have it in my—— No; I see I've left it in my room. As a matter of fact, I found it yesterday.'

And then Parkins narrated the manner of his discovery of the whistle, upon hearing which the Colonel grunted, and opined that, in Parkins's place, he should himself be careful about using a thing that had belonged to a set of Papists, of whom, speaking generally, it might be affirmed that you never knew what they might not have been up to. From this topic he diverged to the enormities of the Vicar, who had given notice on the previous Sunday that Friday would be the Feast of St Thomas the Apostle,* and that there would be service at eleven o'clock in the church. This and other similar proceedings constituted in the Colonel's view a strong presumption that the Vicar was a concealed Papist, if not a

Jesuit; and Parkins, who could not very readily follow the Colonel in this region, did not disagree with him. In fact, they got on so well together in the morning that there was no talk on either side of their separating after lunch.

Both continued to play well during the afternoon, or, at least, well enough to make them forget everything else until the light began to fail them. Not until then did Parkins remember that he had meant to do some more investigating at the preceptory; but it was of no great importance, he reflected. One day was as good as another; he might as well go home with the Colonel.

As they turned the corner of the house, the Colonel was almost knocked down by a boy who rushed into him at the very top of his speed, and then, instead of running away, remained hanging on to him and panting. The first words of the warrior were naturally those of reproof and objurgation, but he very quickly discerned that the boy was almost speechless with fright. Inquiries were useless at first. When the boy got his breath he began to howl, and still clung to the Colonel's legs. He was at last detached, but continued to howl.

'What in the world *is* the matter with you? What have you been up to? What have you seen?' said the two men.

'Ow, I seen it wive at me out of the winder,' wailed the boy, 'and I don't like it.'

'What window?' said the irritated Colonel. 'Come, pull yourself together, my boy.'

'The front winder it was, at the 'otel,' said the boy.

At this point Parkins was in favour of sending the boy home, but the Colonel refused; he wanted to get to the bottom of it, he said; it was most dangerous to give a boy such a fright as this one had had, and if it turned out that people had been playing jokes, they should suffer for it in some way. And by a series of questions he made out this story: The boy had been playing about on the grass in front of the Globe with some others; then they had gone home to their teas, and he was just going, when he happened to look up at the front winder and see it a-wiving at him. It seemed to be a figure of some sort, in white as far as he knew—couldn't see its face;

but it wived at him, and it warn't a right thing—not to say not a right person. Was there a light in the room? No, he didn't think to look if there was a light. Which was the window? Was it the top one or the second one? The seckind one it was—the big winder what got two little uns at the sides.

'Very well, my boy,' said the Colonel, after a few more questions. 'You run away home now. I expect it was some person trying to give you a start. Another time, like a brave English boy, you just throw a stone—well, no, not that exactly, but you go and speak to the waiter, or to Mr Simpson, the landlord, and—yes—and say that I advised you to do so.'

The boy's face expressed some of the doubt he felt as to the likelihood of Mr Simpson's lending a favourable ear to his complaint, but the Colonel did not appear to perceive this, and went on:

'And here's a sixpence—no, I see it's a shilling—and you be off home, and don't think any more about it.'

The youth hurried off with agitated thanks, and the Colonel and Parkins went round to the front of the Globe and reconnoitred. There was only one window answering to the description they had been hearing.

'Well, that's curious,' said Parkins; 'it's evidently my window the lad was talking about. Will you come up for a moment, Colonel Wilson? We ought to be able to see if anyone has been taking liberties in my room.'

They were soon in the passage, and Parkins made as if to open the door. Then he stopped and felt in his pockets.

'This is more serious than I thought,' was his next remark. 'I remember now that before I started this morning I locked the door. It is locked now, and, what is more, here is the key.' And he held it up. 'Now,' he went on, 'if the servants are in the habit of going into one's room during the day when one is away, I can only say that—well, that I don't approve of it at all.' Conscious of a somewhat weak climax, he busied himself in opening the door (which was indeed locked) and in lighting candles. 'No,' he said, 'nothing seems disturbed.'

'Except your bed,' put in the Colonel.

'Excuse me, that isn't my bed,' said Parkins. 'I don't use that one. But it does look as if someone had been playing tricks with it.'

It certainly did: the clothes were bundled up and twisted together in a most tortuous confusion. Parkins pondered.

'That must be it,' he said at last: 'I disordered the clothes last night in unpacking, and they haven't made it since. Perhaps they came in to make it, and that boy saw them through the window; and then they were called away and locked the door after them. Yes, I think that must be it.'

'Well, ring and ask,' said the Colonel, and this appealed to Parkins as practical.

The maid appeared, and, to make a long story short, deposed that she had made the bed in the morning when the gentleman was in the room, and hadn't been there since. No, she hadn't no other key. Mr Simpson he kep' the keys; he'd be able to tell the gentleman if anyone had been up.

This was a puzzle. Investigation showed that nothing of value had been taken, and Parkins remembered the disposition of the small objects on tables and so forth well enough to be pretty sure that no pranks had been played with them. Mr and Mrs Simpson furthermore agreed that neither of them had given the duplicate key of the room to any person whatever during the day. Nor could Parkins, fair-minded man as he was, detect anything in the demeanour of master, mistress, or maid that indicated guilt. He was much more inclined to think that the boy had been imposing on the Colonel.

The latter was unwontedly silent and pensive at dinner and throughout the evening. When he bade good night to Parkins, he murmured in a gruff undertone:

'You know where I am if you want me during the night.'

'Why, yes, thank you, Colonel Wilson, I think I do; but there isn't much prospect of my disturbing you, I hope. By the way,' he added, 'did I show you that old whistle I spoke of? I think not. Well, here it is.'

The Colonel turned it over gingerly in the light of the candle.

'Can you make anything of the inscription?' asked Parkins, as he took it back.

'No, not in this light. What do you mean to do with it?'

'Oh, well, when I get back to Cambridge I shall submit it to some of the archaeologists there, and see what they think of it; and very likely, if they consider it worth having, I may present it to one of the museums.'

"M!' said the Colonel. 'Well, you may be right. All I know is that, if it were mine, I should chuck it straight into the sea. It's no use talking, I'm well aware, but I expect that with you it's a case of live and learn. I hope so, I'm sure, and I wish you a good night.'

He turned away, leaving Parkins in act to speak at the bottom of the stair, and soon each was in his own bed-room.

By some unfortunate accident, there were neither blinds nor curtains to the windows of the Professor's room. The previous night he had thought little of this, but tonight there seemed every prospect of a bright moon rising to shine directly on his bed, and probably wake him later on. When he noticed this he was a good deal annoyed, but, with an ingenuity which I can only envy, he succeeded in rigging up, with the help of a railway-rug, some safety-pins, and a stick and umbrella, a screen which, if it only held together, would completely keep the moonlight off his bed. And shortly afterwards he was comfortably in that bed. When he had read a somewhat solid work long enough to produce a decided wish for sleep, he cast a drowsy glance round the room, blew out the candle, and fell back upon the pillow.

He must have slept soundly for an hour or more, when a sudden clatter shook him up in a most unwelcome manner. In a moment he realized what had happened: his carefully-constructed screen had given way, and a very bright frosty moon was shining directly on his face. This was highly annoying. Could he possibly get up and reconstruct the screen? or could he manage to sleep if he did not?

For some minutes he lay and pondered over the possibili-ties; then he turned over sharply, and with all his eyes open lay breathlessly listening. There had been a movement, he was sure, in the empty bed on the opposite side of the room. Tomorrow he would have it moved, for there must be rats or something playing about in it. It was quiet now. No! the commotion began again. There was a rustling and shaking: surely more than any rat could cause.

I can figure to myself something of the Professor's bewilderment and horror, for I have in a dream thirty years back seen the same thing happen;* but the reader will hardly, perhaps, imagine how dreadful it was to him to see a figure suddenly sit up in what he had known was an empty bed. He was out of his own bed in one bound, and made a dash towards the window, where lay his only weapon, the stick with which he had propped his screen. This was, as it turned out, the worst thing he could have done, because the personage in the empty bed, with a sudden smooth motion, slipped from the bed and took up a position, with outspread arms, between the two beds, and in front of the door. Parkins watched it in a horrid perplexity. Somehow, the idea of getting past it and escaping through the door was intolerable to him; he could not have borne—he didn't known why—to touch it; and as for its touching him, he would sooner dash himself through the window than have that happen. It stood for the moment in a band of dark shadow, and he had not seen what its face was like. Now it began to move, in a stooping posture, and all at once the spectator realized, with some horror and some relief, that it must be blind, for it seemed to feel about it with its muffled arms in a groping and random fashion. Turning half away from him, it became suddenly conscious of the bed he had just left, and darted towards it, and bent over and felt the pillows in a way which made Parkins shudder as he had never in his life thought it possible. In a very few moments it seemed to know that the bed was empty, and then, moving forward into the area of light and facing the window, it showed for the first time what manner of thing it was.

Parkins, who very much dislikes being questioned about it, did once describe something of it in my hearing, and I gathered that what he chiefly remembers about it is a horrible, an intensely horrible, face *of crumpled linen*. What expression he read upon it he could not or would not tell, but that the fear of it went nigh to maddening him is certain.

But he was not at leisure to watch it for long. With formidable quickness it moved into the middle of the room, and, as it groped and waved, one corner of its draperies swept across Parkins's face. He could not—though he knew how perilous a sound was—he could not keep back a cry of disgust, and this gave the searcher an instant clue. It leapt towards him upon the instant,* and the next moment he was half-way through the window backwards, uttering cry upon cry at the utmost pitch of his voice, and the linen face was thrust close into his own. At this, almost the last possible second, deliverance came, as you will have guessed: the Colonel burst the door open, and was just in time to see the dreadful group at the window. When he reached the figures only one was left. Parkins sank forward into the room in a faint, and before him on the floor lay a tumbled heap of bed-clothes.

Colonel Wilson asked no questions, but busied himself in keeping everyone else out of the room and in getting Parkins back to his bed; and himself, wrapped in a rug, occupied the other bed for the rest of the night. Early on the next day Rogers arrived, more welcome than he would have been a day before, and the three of them held a very long consultation in the Professor's room. At the end of it the Colonel left the hotel door carrying a small object between his finger and thumb, which he cast as far into the sea as a very brawny arm could send it. Later on the smoke of a burning ascended from the back premises of the Globe.

Exactly what explanation was patched up for the staff and visitors at the hotel I must confess I do not recollect. The Professor was somehow cleared of the ready suspicion of delirium tremens, and the hotel of the reputation of a troubled house.

There is not much question as to what would have happened to Parkins if the Colonel had not intervened when he did. He would either have fallen out of the window or else lost his wits. But it is not so evident what more the creature that came in answer to the whistle could have done than frighten. There seemed to be absolutely nothing material about it save the bed-clothes of which it had made itself a body. The Colonel, who remembered a not very dissimilar occurrence in India, was of opinion that if Parkins had closed with it it could really have done very little, and that its one power was that of frightening. The whole thing, he said, served to confirm his opinion of the Church of Rome.

There is really nothing more to tell, but, as you may imagine, the Professor's views on certain points are less clear cut than they used to be. His nerves, too, have suffered: he cannot even now see a surplice hanging on a door quite unmoved, and the spectacle of a scarecrow in a field late on a winter afternoon has cost him more than one sleepless night.

THE TREASURE OF ABBOT THOMAS

I

VERUM usque in praesentem diem multa garriunt inter se Canonici de abscondito quodam istius Abbatis Thomae thesauro, quem saepe, quanquam adhuc incassum, quaesiverunt Steinfeldenses. Ipsum enim Thomam adhuc florida in aetate existentem ingentem auri massam circa monasterium defodisse perhibent; de quo multoties interrogatus ubi esset, cum risu respondere solitus erat: 'Job, Johannes, et Zacharias* vel vobis vel posteris indicabunt'; idemque aliquando adiicere se inventuris minime invisurum. Inter alia huius Abbatis opera, hoc memoria praecipue dignum iudico quod fenestram magnam in orientali parte alae australis in ecclesia sua imaginibus optime in vitro depictis impleverit: id quod et ipsius effigies et insignia ibidem posita demonstrant. Domum quoque Abbatialem fere totam restauravit: puteo in atrio ipsius effosso et lapidibus marmoreis pulchre caelatis exornato. Decessit autem, morte aliquantulum subitanea perculsus, aetatis suae anno lxxiido, incarnationis vero Dominicae mdxxixo.

'I suppose I shall have to translate this,' said the antiquary to himself as he finished copying the above lines from that rather rare and exceedingly diffuse book, the *Sertum Steinfeldense Norbertinum*.[1]* 'Well, it may as well be done first as last,' and accordingly the following rendering was very quickly produced:

Up to the present day there is much gossip among the Canons about a certain hidden treasure of this Abbot Thomas, for which those of Steinfeld have often made search, though hitherto in vain. The story is that Thomas, while yet in the vigour of life, concealed a very large quantity of gold somewhere in the monastery. He was often asked where it was and always

---

[1] An account of the Premonstratensian Abbey of Steinfeld in the Eiffel, with lives of the Abbots, published at Cologne in 1712 by Christian Albert Erhard, a resident in the district. The epithet *Norbertinum* is due to the fact that St Norbert was founder of the Premonstratensian Order.

answered with a laugh: Job, John, and Zechariah will tell either you or your successors.' He sometimes added that he should feel no grudge against those who might find it. Among other works carried out by this Abbot I may specially mention his filling the great window at the east end of the south aisle of the church with figures admirably painted on glass, as his effigy and arms in the window attest. He also restored almost the whole of the Abbot's lodging, and dug a well in the court of it, which he adorned with beautiful carvings in marble. He died rather suddenly in the seventy-second year of his age, AD 1529.

The object which the antiquary had before him at the moment was that of tracing the whereabouts of the painted windows of the Abbey Church of Steinfeld. Shortly after the Revolution, a very large quantity of painted glass made its way from the dissolved abbeys of Germany and Belgium to this country and may now be seen adorning various of our parish churches, cathedrals, and private chapels. Steinfeld Abbey was among the most considerable of these involuntary contributors to our artistic possessions (I am quoting the somewhat ponderous preamble of the book which the antiquary wrote) and the greater part of the glass from that institution can be identified without much difficulty by the help either of the numerous inscriptions in which the place is mentioned, or of the subjects of the windows, in which several well-defined cycles or narratives were represented.

The passage with which I began my story had set the antiquary on the track of another identification. In a private chapel*—no matter where—he had seen three large figures each occupying a whole light in a window, and evidently the work of one artist. Their style made it plain that that artist had been a German of the sixteenth century; but hitherto the more exact localizing of them had been a puzzle. They represented (will you be surprised to hear it?) JOB PATRIARCHA,* JOHANNES EVANGELISTA, ZACHARIAS PRO- PHETA, and each of them held a book or scroll inscribed with a sentence from his writings. These as a matter of course the antiquary had noted, and had been struck by the curious way in which they differed from any text of the Vulgate* that he had been able to examine. Thus the scroll in Job's hand was inscribed 'Auro est locus in quo absconditur' (for 'conflatur');[1] on the book of John was 'Habent in vestimentis suis scripturam quam nemo novit'[2] (for 'in vestimento scriptum', the following words being taken from another verse); and Zacharias had: 'Super lapidem unum septem oculi sunt'[3] (which alone of the three presents an unaltered text).*

A sad perplexity it had been to our investigator to think why these three personages should have been placed together in one window. There was no bond of connection between them, either historic, symbolic, or doctrinal, and he could only suppose that they must have formed part of a very large series of prophets and apostles which might have filled, say, all the clearstory* windows of some capacious church. But the passage from the *Sertum* had altered the situation by showing that the names of the actual personages represented in the glass now in Lord D——'s chapel had been constantly on the lips of Abbot Thomas von Eschenhausen of Steinfeld, and that this abbot had put up a painted window probably about the year 1520 in the south aisle of his abbey church. It was no very wild conjecture that the three figures might have formed part of Abbot Thomas's offering; it was one which, moreover, could probably be confirmed or set aside by another careful examination of the glass. And, as Mr Somerton was a man of leisure, he set out on pilgrimage to the private chapel with very little delay. His conjecture was confirmed to the full. Not only did the style and technique of the glass suit perfectly with the date and place required, but, in another window of the chapel, he found some glass, known to have been bought along with the figures, which contained the arms of Abbot Thomas von Eschenhausen.

At intervals during his researches Mr Somerton had been haunted by the recollection of the gossip about the hidden treasure, and as he thought the matter over, it became more and more obvious to him that if the Abbot meant anything

[1] There is a place for gold where it is hidden.
[2] They have on their raiment a writing which no man knoweth.
[3] Upon one stone are seven eyes.

by the enigmatical answer which he gave to his questioners, he must have meant that the secret was to be found somewhere in the window he had placed in the abbey church. It was undeniable, furthermore, that the first of the curiously-selected texts on the scrolls in the window might be taken to have a reference to hidden treasure. Every feature, therefore, or mark which could possibly assist in elucidating the riddle which (he felt sure) the Abbot had set to posterity, he noted with scrupulous care, and returning to his Berkshire manor-house consumed many a pint of the midnight oil over his tracings and sketches. After two or three weeks, a day came when Mr Somerton announced to his man that he must pack his own and his master's things for a short journey abroad, whither for the moment we will not follow him.

II

Mr Gregory, the Rector of Parsbury, had strolled out before breakfast, it being a fine autumn morning, as far as the gate of his carriage-drive with intent to meet the postman and sniff the cool air. Nor was he disappointed of either purpose. Before he had had time to answer more than ten or eleven of the miscellaneous questions propounded to him in the lightness of their hearts by his young offspring, who had accompanied him, the postman was seen approaching; and among the morning's budget was one letter bearing a foreign postmark and stamp (which became at once the objects of an eager competition among the youthful Gregorys) and was addressed in an uneducated but plainly an English hand. When the Rector opened it, and turned to the signature, he realized that it came from the confidential valet of his friend and squire, Mr Somerton. Thus it ran:

Honourd Sir,—

Has I am in a great anxeity about Master I write at is Wish to Beg you Sir if you could be so good as Step over. Master Has add a Nastey Shock and keeps His Bedd. I never Have known Him like this but No wonder and Nothing will serve but you Sir. Master says would I mintion the Short Way Here is Drive to Cobblince* and take a Trap. Hoping I Have maid all Plain, but

am much Confused in Myself what with Anxiatey and Weakful-
ness at Night. If I might be so Bold Sir it will be a Pleasure to see
a Honnest Brish Face among all These Forig ones. I am Sir

Your obed^t Servt

WILLIAM BROWN

P.S.—The Villiage for Town I will not Turm It is name
Steenfeld.

The reader must be left to picture to himself in detail the
surprise, confusion, and hurry of preparation into which the
receipt of such a letter would be likely to plunge a quiet
Berkshire parsonage in the year of grace 1859. It is enough
for me to say that a train to town was caught in the course
of the day, and that Mr Geregory was able to secure a cabin
in the Antwerp boat and a place in the Coblentz train. Nor
was it difficult to manage the transit from that centre to
Steinfeld.

I labour under a grave disadvantage as narrator of this
story in that I have never visited Steinfeld myself, and that
neither of the principal actors in the episode (from whom I
derive my information) was able to give me anything but a
vague and rather dismal idea of its appearance. I gather that
it is a small place with a large church despoiled of its ancient
fittings; a number of rather ruinous great buildings mostly
of the seventeenth century surround this church: for the
abbey, in common with most of those on the Continent, was
rebuilt in a luxurious fashion by its inhabitants at that
period. It has not seemed to me worth while to lavish money
on a visit to the place, for though it is probably far more
attractive than either Mr Somerton or Mr Gregory thought
it, there is evidently little if anything of first-rate interest to
be seen: except, perhaps, one thing, which I should not care
to see.

The inn where the English gentleman and his servant were
lodged is or was the only 'possible' one in the village. Mr
Gregory was taken to it at once by his driver and found
Mr Brown waiting at the door. Mr Brown, a model when in
his Berkshire home of the impassive whiskered race who are
known as confidential valets, was now egregiously out of his

element, in a light tweed suit, anxious, almost irritable, and plainly anything but master of the situation. His relief at the sight of the 'honest British face' of his Rector was unmeasured, but words to describe it were denied him. He could only say:

'Well, I ham pleased I'm sure sir, to see you. And so I'm sure, sir, will master.'

'How is your master, Brown?' Mr Gregory eagerly put in.

'I think he's better, sir, thank you; but he's had a dreadful time of it. I 'ope he's gettin' some sleep now, but——'

'What has been the matter? I couldn't make out from your letter. Was it an accident of any kind?'

'Well, sir, I 'ardly know whether I'd better speak about it. Master was very partickler he should be the one to tell you: but there's no bones broke, that's one thing, I'm sure we ought to be thankful——'

'What does the doctor say?' asked Mr Gregory. They were by this time outside Mr Somerton's bedroom door and speaking in low tones. Mr Gregory, who happened to be in front, was feeling for the handle, and chanced to run his fingers over the panels. Before Brown could answer, there was a terrible cry from within the room.

'In God's name, who is that?' were the first words they heard. 'Brown, is it?'

'Yes, sir—me, sir, and Mr Gregory,' Brown hastened to answer, and there was an audible groan of relief in reply.

They entered the room, which was darkened against the afternoon sun, and Mr Gregory saw, with a shock of pity, how drawn, how damp with drops of fear, was the usually calm face of his friend, who, sitting up in the curtained bed, stretched out a shaking hand to welcome him.

'Better for seeing you, my dear Gregory,' was the reply to the Rector's first question: and it was palpably true.

After five minutes of conversation Mr Somerton was more his own man, Brown afterwards reported, than he had been for days. He was able to eat a more than respectable dinner, and talked confidently of being fit to stand a journey to Coblentz within twenty-four hours.

'But there's one thing,' he said, with a return of agitation which Mr Gregory did not like to see, 'which I must beg you to do for me, my dear Gregory. Don't—' he went on, laying his hand on Gregory's to forestall any interruption, 'don't ask me what it is, or why I want it done. I'm not up to explaining it yet; it would throw me back—undo all the good you have done me by coming. The only word I will say about it is that you run no risk whatever by doing it, and that Brown can and will show you tomorrow what it is. It's merely to put back—to keep something—— no; I can't speak of it yet. Do you mind calling Brown?'

'Well, Somerton,' said Mr Gregory as he crossed the room to the door, 'I won't ask for any explanations till you see fit to give them; and if this bit of business is as easy as you represent it to be, I will very gladly undertake it for you the first thing in the morning.'

'Ah, I was sure you would, my dear Gregory: I was certain I could rely on you. I shall owe you more thanks than I can tell. Now here is Brown. Brown, one word with you.'

'Shall I go?' interjected Mr Gregory.

'Not at all; dear me, no. Brown, the first thing tomorrow morning (you don't mind early hours, I know, Gregory) you must take the Rector to—There, you know' (a nod from Brown, who looked grave and anxious) 'and he and you will put that back. You needn't be in the least alarmed: it's *perfectly* safe in the day-time. You know what I mean: it lies on the step you know, where—where we put it.' (Brown swallowed dryly once or twice and, failing to speak, bowed.) 'And—yes, that's all. Only this one other word, my dear Gregory. If you *can* manage to keep from questioning Brown about this matter I shall be still more bound to you. Tomorrow evening, at latest, if all goes well, I shall be able I believe to tell you the whole story from start to finish. And now I'll wish you good night. Brown will be with me—he sleeps here —and if I were you I should lock my door—yes, be particular to do that. They—they like it, the people here. And it's better. Good night, good night.'

They parted upon this, and if Mr Gregory woke once or twice in the small hours and fancied he heard a fumbling about the lower part of his locked door, it was perhaps no more than what a quiet man, suddenly plunged into a strange bed and the heart of a mystery, might reasonably expect. Certainly he thought, to the end of his days, that he had heard such a sound, twice or three times between midnight and dawn.

He was up with the sun, and out in company with Brown soon after. Perplexing as was the service he had been asked to perform for Mr Somerton, it was not a difficult or an alarming one, and within half an hour from his leaving the inn it was over. What it was I shall not as yet divulge.

Later in the morning Mr Somerton, now almost himself again, was able to make a start from Steinfeld; and that same evening, whether at Coblentz, or at some intermediate stage on the journey I am not certain, he settled down to the promised explanation. Brown was present, but how much of the matter was ever really made plain to his comprehension he would never say, and I am unable to conjecture.

III

This was Mr Somerton's story:

'You know roughly, both of you, that this expedition of mine was undertaken with the object of tracing something in connection with some old painted glass in Lord D——'s private chapel. Well, the starting-point of the whole matter lies in this passage from an old printed book, to which I will ask your attention.'

And at this point Mr Somerton went carefully over some ground with which we are already familiar.

'On my second visit to the chapel,' he went on, 'my purpose was to take every note I could of figures, lettering, diamond-scratchings on the glass, and even apparently accidental markings. The first point which I tackled was that of the inscribed scrolls. I could not doubt that the first of these, that of Job, "There is a place for the gold where it is hidden", with its intentional alteration, must refer to the treasure; so I applied myself with some confidence to the next, that of St John, "They have on their vestures a writing which no man knoweth". The natural question will have occurred to you. Was there an inscription on the robes of the figures? I could see none: each of the three had a broad black border to his mantle, which made a conspicuous and rather ugly feature in the window. I was nonplussed, I will own, and but for a curious bit of luck I think I should have left the search where the Canons of Steinfeld had left it before me. But it so happened that there was a good deal of dust on the surface of the glass, and Lord D—— happening to come in, noticed my blackened hands, and kindly insisted on sending for a Turk's head broom to clean down the window. There must, I suppose, have been a rough piece in the broom; anyhow, as it passed over the border of one of the mantles, I noticed that it left a long scratch and that some yellow stain instantly showed up. I asked the man to stop his work for a moment, and ran up the ladder to examine the place. The yellow stain was there sure enough and what had come away was a thick black pigment, which had evidently been laid on with the brush after the glass had been burnt, and could therefore be easily scraped off without doing any harm. I scraped accordingly, and you will hardly believe—no, I do you an injustice; you will have guessed already—that I found under this black pigment two or three clearly-formed capital letters in yellow stain on a clear ground. Of course I could hardly contain my delight.

'I told Lord D—— that I had detected an inscription which I thought might be very interesting, and begged to be allowed to uncover the whole of it. He made no difficulty about it whatever, told me to do exactly as I pleased, and then, having an engagement, was obliged (rather to my relief, I must say) to leave me. I set to work at once and found the task a fairly easy one. The pigment, disintegrated of course by time, came off almost at a touch, and I don't think that it took me a couple of hours, all told, to clean the whole of the black borders in all three lights. Each of the figures had as the inscription said "a writing on their vestures which nobody knew".

'This discovery of course made it absolutely certain to my mind that I was on the right track. And now, what was the inscription? While I was cleaning the glass I almost took pains not to read the lettering—saving up the treat until I had got the whole thing clear. And when that *was* done—my dear Gregory, I assure you I could almost have cried from sheer disappointment. What I read was only the most hopeless jumble of letters that was ever shaken up in a hat. Here it is:

Job	DREVICIOPEDMOOMSMVIVLISLCAVIBASBA TAOVT
St John	RDIIEAMRLESIPVSPODSEEIRSETTAAESGIAV NNR
Zechariah	FTEEAILNQDPVAIVMTLEEATTOHIOONVM CAAT.H.Q.E.

'Blank as I felt and must have looked for the first few minutes, my disappointment didn't last long. I realized almost at once that I was dealing with a cypher or crypto-gram; and I reflected that it was likely to be of a pretty simple kind, considering its early date. So I copied the letters with the most anxious care. Another little point, I may tell you, turned up in the process which confirmed my belief in the cypher. After copying the letters on Job's robe I counted them, to make sure that I had them right. There were thirty-eight; and just as I finished going through them, my eye fell on a scratching made with a sharp point on the edge of the border. It was simply the number xxxviii in Roman numerals. To cut the matter short, there was a similar note, as I may call it, in each of the other lights; and that made it plain to me that the glass-painter had had very strict orders from Abbot Thomas about the inscription, and had taken pains to get it correct.

'Well, after that discovery, you may imagine how minutely I went over the whole surface of the glass in search of further light. Of course I did not neglect the inscription on the scroll of Zechariah ("Upon one stone are seven eyes"), but I very quickly concluded that this must refer to some mark on a stone which could only be found *in situ*, where the treasure was concealed. To be short, I made all possible notes and sketches and tracings and then came back to Parsbury to work out the cypher at leisure. Oh the agonies I went through! I thought myself very clever at first, for I made sure that the key would be found in some of the old books on secret writing. The *Steganographia* of Joachim Trithemius (who was an earlier contemporary of Abbot Thomas) seemed particularly promising; so I got that, and Selenius's *Cryptographia* and Bacon *de Augmentis Scientiarum*,* and some more: but I could hit upon nothing. Then I tried the principle of the "most frequent letter", taking first Latin and then German as a basis. That didn't help, either: whether it ought to have done so, I am not clear. And then I came back to the window itself and read over my notes hoping, almost against hope, that the Abbot might himself have somewhere supplied the key I wanted. I could make nothing out of the colours or patterns* of the robes: there were no landscape backgrounds with subsidiary objects; there was nothing in the canopies. The only resource possible seemed to be in the attitudes of the figures. "Job," I read, "scroll in left hand, forefinger of right hand extended upwards. John holds inscribed book in left hand; with right hand blesses, with two fingers. Zechariah, scroll in left hand; right hand extended upwards, as Job, but with three fingers pointing up." In other words, I reflected, Job has *one* finger extended, John has *two*, Zechariah has *three*. May not there be a numeral key concealed in that? My dear Gregory,' said Mr Somerton, laying his hand on his friend's knee, 'that *was* the key. I didn't get it to fit at first, but after two or three trials I saw what was meant. After the first letter of the inscription you skip *one* letter, after the next you skip *two* and after that, skip *three*. Now look at the result I got. I've underlined the letters which form words:

DRE<u>VICIOP</u>E<u>DM</u>OOMSMV<u>I</u>VL<u>I</u>SLCAV<u>IBASBATAO</u>V<u>T</u>

R<u>DII</u>EAM<u>RLESIP</u>VSPO<u>DSEEIRSETTAAESGIA</u>V<u>NN</u>R

F<u>TEEAILNQDPVAIVMTLEEEATTOHIOON</u>VMC

<u>AAT</u>.H.Q.E.

'Do you see it? *Decem millia auri reposita sunt in puteo in at . . .* (Ten thousand [pieces] of gold are laid up in a well in . . .), followed by an incomplete word beginning *at*. So far so good. I tried the same plan with the remaining letters; but it wouldn't work, and I fancied that perhaps the placing of dots after the three last letters might indicate some difference of procedure. Then I thought to myself, "Wasn't there some allusion to a well in the account of Abbot Thomas in that book the *Sertum*?" Yes, there was: he built a *puteus in atrio* (a well in the court). There, of course, was my word *atrio*. The next step was to copy out the remaining letters of the inscription, omitting those I had already used. That gave what you will see on this slip:

RVIIOPDOOSMVVISCAVBSBTAOTDIEAMLSIVSPDEERSE TAEGIANRFEEALQDVAIMLEATTHOOVMCA.H.Q.E.

'Now I knew what the three first letters I wanted were, namely RIO, to complete the word *atrio*; and as you will see, these are all to be found in the first five letters. I was a little confused at first by the occurrence of two *i*'s; but very soon I saw that every alternate letter must be taken in the remainder of the inscription. You can work it out for yourself; the result, continuing where the first "round" left off, is this:

—rio domus abbatialis de Steinfeld a me, Thoma, qui posui custodem super ea. Gare à qui la touche.

'So the whole secret was out:

Ten thousand pieces of gold are laid up in the well in the court of the Abbot's house of Steinfeld by me, Thomas, who have set a guardian over them. *Gare à qui la touche.*

'The last words, I ought to say, are a device which Abbot Thomas had adopted. I found it with his arms in another piece of glass at Lord D——'s, and he drafted it bodily into his cypher, though it doesn't quite fit in point of grammar.

'Well, what would any human being have been tempted to do, my dear Gregory, in my place? Could he have helped setting off as I did to Steinfeld and tracing the secret literally to the fountain-head? I don't believe he could: anyhow, I couldn't, and as I needn't tell you, I found myself at Steinfeld as soon as the resources of civilization could put me there, and installed myself in the inn you saw. I must tell you that I was not altogether free from forebodings on one hand of disappointment, on the other of danger. There was always the possibility that Abbot Thomas's well might have been wholly obliterated, or else that someone, ignorant of cryptograms and guided only by luck, might have stumbled on the treasure before me. And then'—there was a very perceptible shaking of the voice here—'I was not entirely easy, I need not mind confessing, as to the meaning of the words about the guardian of the treasure. But if you don't mind, I'll say no more about that until—until it becomes necessary.

'At the first possible opportunity Brown and I began exploring the place. I had naturally represented myself as being interested in the remains of the abbey and we could not avoid paying a visit to the church, impatient as I was to be elsewhere. Still, it did interest me to see the windows where the glass had been, and especially that at the east end of the south aisle. In the tracery lights of that I was startled to see some fragments and coats-of-arms remaining: Abbot Thomas's shield was there, and a small figure with a scroll inscribed *Oculos habent et non videbunt* (They have eyes and shall not see), which, I take it, was a hit of the Abbot's at his Canons.

'But of course the principal object was to find the Abbot's house. There is no prescribed place for this, so far as I know, in the plan of a monastery; you can't predict of it, as you can of the Chapterhouse, that it will be on the eastern side of the cloister, or, as of the dormitory, that it will communicate with a transept of the church. I felt that if I asked many questions I might awaken lingering memories of the treasure, and I thought it best to try first to discover it for myself. It was not a very long or difficult search. That three-sided court south-east of the church, with deserted piles of building round it, and grass-grown pavement, which you saw this morning, was the place. And glad enough I was to see that it was put to no use and was neither very far from our inn nor overlooked by any inhabited building: there were only orchards and paddocks on the slopes east of the church. I can tell you that fine stone glowed wonderfully in the rather watery yellow sunset that we had on the Tuesday afternoon.

'Next, what about the well? There was not much doubt about that, as you can testify. It is really a very remarkable thing. That curb is I think of Italian marble, and the carving I thought must be Italian also. There were reliefs, you will perhaps remember, of Eliezer and Rebekah, and of Jacob opening the well for Rachel* and similar subjects; but by way of disarming suspicion, I suppose, the Abbot had carefully abstained from any of his cynical and allusive inscriptions.

'I examined the whole structure with the keenest interest of course—a square well-head with an opening in one side; an arch over it with a wheel for the rope to pass over, evidently in very good condition still, for it had been used within sixty years, or perhaps even later, though not quite recently. Then there was the question of depth and access to the interior. I suppose the depth was about sixty to seventy feet; and as to the other point, it really seemed as if the Abbot had wished to lead searchers up to the very door of his treasure-house, for, as you tested for yourself, there were big blocks of stone bonded into the masonry and leading down in a regular staircase round and round the inside of the well.

'It seemed almost too good to be true. I wondered if there was a trap—if the stones were so contrived as to tip over when a weight was placed on them; but I tried a good many with my own weight and with my stick and all seemed— and actually were—perfectly firm. Of course I resolved that Brown and I would make an experiment that very night.

'I was well prepared; knowing the sort of place I should have to explore, I had brought a sufficiency of good rope and bands of webbing to surround my body, and crossbars to hold to, as well as lanterns and candles and crowbars: all of which would go into a single carpet-bag and excite no suspicion. I satisfied myself that my rope would be long enough, and that the wheel for the bucket was in good working order, and then we went home to dinner.

'I had a little cautious conversation with the landlord and made out that he would not be overmuch surprised if I went out for a stroll with my man about nine o'clock to make (Heaven forgive me!) a sketch of the abbey by moon-light. I asked no questions about the well, and am not likely to do so now. I fancy I know as much about it as anyone in Steinfeld: at least'—with a strong shudder—'I don't want to know any more.

'Now we come to the crisis, and though I hate to think of it, I feel sure, Gregory, that it will be better for me in all ways to recall it just as it happened. We started, Brown and I, at about nine with our bag, and attracted no attention, for we managed to slip out at the hinder end of the inn yard into an alley which brought us quite to the edge of the village. In five minutes we were at the well, and for some little time we sat on the edge of the well-head to make sure that no one was stirring or spying on us. All we heard was some horses cropping grass out of sight farther down the eastern slope. We were perfectly unobserved and had plenty of light from the gorgeous full moon to allow us to get the rope properly fitted over the wheel. Then I secured the band round my body beneath the arms. We attached the end of the rope very securely to a ring in the stonework. Brown took the lighted lantern and followed me: I had a crowbar. And so we began to descend cautiously, feeling every step before we set foot on it, and scanning the walls in search of any marked stone.

'Half aloud I counted the steps as we went down, and we got as far as the thirty-eighth before I noted anything at all irregular in the surface of the masonry. Even here there was no mark, and I began to feel very blank and to wonder if the Abbot's cryptogram could possibly be an elaborate hoax. At the forty-ninth step the staircase ceased. It was with a very sinking heart that I began retracing my steps, and when I was back on the thirty-eighth—Brown, with the lantern, being a step or two above me—I scrutinized the little bit of irregularity in the stonework with all my might. But there was no vestige of a mark.

'Then it struck me that the texture of the surface looked just a little smoother than the rest, or at least in some way different. It might possibly be cement and not stone. I gave it a good blow with my iron bar. There was a decidedly hollow sound—though that might be the result of our being in a well. But there was more. A great flake of cement dropped on to my feet, and I saw marks on the stone underneath. I had tracked the Abbot down, my dear Gregory: even now I think of it with a certain pride. It took but a very few more taps to clear the whole of the cement away, and I saw a slab of stone about two feet square upon which was engraven a cross. Disappointment again, but only for a moment. It was you, Brown, who reassured me by a casual remark. You said if I remember right: "It's a funny cross; looks like a lot of eyes."

'I snatched the lantern out of your hand, and saw with inexpressible pleasure that the cross *was* composed of seven eyes, four in a vertical line, three horizontal.* The last of the scrolls in the window was explained in the way I had anticipated. Here was my "stone with the seven eyes". So far the Abbot's *data* had been exact, and as I thought of this, the anxiety about the "guardian" returned upon me with increased force. Still, I wasn't going to retreat now.

'Without giving myself time to think I knocked away the cement all round the marked stone, and then gave it a prise on the right side with my crowbar. It moved at once and I saw that it was but a thin light slab, such as I could easily lift out myself, and that it stopped the entrance to a cavity. I did lift it out unbroken, and set it on the step, for it might be very important to us to be able to replace it. Then I waited for several minutes on the step just above. I don't know why, but I think to see if any dreadful thing would rush out. Nothing happened. Next, I lit a candle and very cautiously I placed it inside the cavity, with some idea of seeing whether there were foul air and of getting a glimpse of what was inside. There *was* some foulness of air which nearly extinguished the flame, but in no long time it burned quite steadily. The hole went some little way back, and also on the right and left of the entrance, and I could see some rounded light-coloured objects within which might be bags.

'There was no use in waiting. I faced the cavity and looked in. There was nothing immediately in the front of the hole. I put my arm in and felt to the right, very gingerly—— Just give me a glass of cognac, Brown: I'll go on in a moment, Gregory....

'Well, I felt to the right, and my fingers touched something curved, that felt—yes—more or less like leather; dampish it was, and evidently part of a heavy, full, thing. There was nothing, I must say, to alarm one. I grew bolder and putting both hands in as well as I could I pulled it to me, and it came. It was heavy, but moved more easily than I had expected. As I pulled it towards the entrance, my left elbow knocked over and extinguished the candle. I got the thing fairly in front of the mouth and began drawing it out. Just then Brown gave a sharp ejaculation and ran quickly up the steps with the lantern. He will tell you why, in a moment. Startled as I was, I looked round after him, and saw him stand for a minute at the top and then walk away a few yards. Then I heard him call softly "All right, sir," and went on pulling out the great bag, in complete darkness. It hung for an instant on the edge of the hole, then slipped forward on to my chest and *put its arms round my neck.*

'My dear Gregory, I am telling you the exact truth. I believe I am now acquainted with the extremity of terror and revulsion which a man can endure without losing his mind. I can only just manage to tell you now the bare outline of the experience. I was conscious of a most horrible smell of mould and of a cold kind of face pressed against my own and moving slowly over it; and of several—I don't know how many—legs or arms or tentacles or something clinging to my body. I screamed out, Brown says, like a beast and fell away backward from the step on which I stood, and the creature slipped downwards, I suppose, on to that same step. Providentially the band round me held firm. Brown did not lose his head and was strong enough to pull me up to the top and get me over the edge quite promptly. How he managed it exactly I don't know, and I think he would find it hard to tell you. I believe he contrived to hide our implements in the deserted building near by, and with very great difficulty he got me back to the inn. I was in no state to make explanations and Brown knows no German; but next morning I told the people some tale of having had a bad fall in the abbey ruins, which

I suppose they believed. And now before I go further I should just like you to hear what Brown's experiences during those few minutes were. Tell the Rector, Brown, what you told me.'

'Well, sir,' said Brown, speaking low and nervously, 'it was just this way. Master was busy down in front of the 'ole and I was 'olding the lantern and looking on, when I 'eard somethink drop in the water from the top, as I thought. So I looked up, and I see someone's 'ead lookin' over at us. I s'pose I must ha' said somethink, and I 'eld the light up and run up the steps, and my light shone right on the face. That was a bad un, sir, if ever I see one: a holdish man and the face very much fell in, and larfin, as I thought. And I got up the steps as quick pretty nigh as I'm tellin' you, and when I was out on the ground there warn't a sign of any person. There 'adn't been the time for anyone to get away let alone a hold chap, and I made sure he warn't crouching down by the well nor nothink. Next thing I hear master cry out somethink 'orrible and hall I see was him hanging out by the rope; and as master says, 'ow ever I got him up I couldn't tell you.'

'You hear that, Gregory?' said Mr Somerton. 'Now, does any explanation of that incident strike you?'

'The whole thing is so ghastly and abnormal that I must own it puts me quite off my balance: but the thought did occur to me that possibly the—well, the person who set the trap might have come to see the success of his plan.'

'Just so, Gregory, just so. I can think of nothing else so— *likely*, I should say, if such a word had a place anywhere in my story. I think it must have been the Abbot. . . . Well, I haven't much more to tell you. I spent a miserable night, Brown sitting up with me. Next day I was no better; unable to get up; no doctor to be had, and if one had been available, I doubt if he could have done much for me. I made Brown write off to you, and spent a second terrible night: and, Gregory, of this I am sure, and I think it affected me more than the first shock, for it lasted longer—there was someone or something on the watch outside my door the whole night. I almost fancy there were two. It wasn't only the faint noises I heard from time to time all through the dark hours, but there was the smell—the hideous smell of mould. Every rag

I had had on me on that first evening I had stripped off and made Brown take it away. I believe he stuffed the things into the stove in his room—and yet the smell was there, as intense as it had been in the well; and what is more, it came from outside the door. But with the first glimmer of dawn it faded out and the sounds ceased too: and that convinced me that the thing or things were creatures of darkness and could not stand the daylight, and so I was sure that if anyone could put back the stone, it or they would be powerless until some-one else took it away again. I had to wait until you came to get that done. Of course I couldn't send Brown to do it by himself and still less could I tell anyone who belonged to the place.

'Well, there is my story; and if you don't believe it, I can't help it. But I think you do.'

'Indeed,' said Mr Gregory, 'I can find no alternative. I *must* believe it.* I saw the well and the stone myself, and had a glimpse, I thought, of the bags or something else in the hole. And to be plain with you Somerton, I believe my door was watched last night, too.'

'I dare say it was, Gregory; but thank goodness, that is over. Have you, by the way, anything to tell about your visit to that dreadful place?'

'Very little,' was the answer. 'Brown and I managed easily enough to get the slab into its place, and he fixed it very firmly with the irons and wedges you had desired him to get; and we contrived to smear the surface with mud so that it looks just like the rest of the wall. One thing I did notice in the carving on the well-head, which I think must have escaped you. It was a horrid grotesque shape, perhaps more like a toad than anything else, and there was a label by it inscribed with the two words, "*Depositum custodi*".'[1]

---

[1] Keep that which is committed to thee.

A SCHOOL STORY

Two men in a smoking-room were talking of their private-school days. 'At *our* school,' said A., 'we had a ghost's footmark on the staircase. What was it like? Oh, very unconvincing. Just the shape of a shoe, with a square toe, if I remember right. The staircase was a stone one. I never heard any story about the thing. That seems odd when you come to think of it. Why didn't somebody invent one, I wonder?'

'You can never tell with little boys. They have a mythology of their own. There's a subject for you, by the way, *The Folklore of Private Schools.*'

'Yes: the crop is rather scanty, though. I imagine, if you were to investigate the cycle of ghost stories, for instance, which the boys at private schools tell each other, they would all turn out to be highly-compressed versions of stories out of books.'

'Nowadays the *Strand* and *Pearson's,** and so on, would be extensively drawn upon.'

'No doubt: they weren't born or thought of in my time. Let's see—I wonder if I can remember the staple ones that I was told. First, there was the house with a room in which a series of people insisted on passing a night; and each of them in the morning was found kneeling in a corner and had just time to say "I've seen it", and died.'

'Wasn't that the house in Berkeley Square?'

'I dare say it was. Then there was the man who heard a noise in the passage at night, opened his door, and saw someone crawling towards him on all fours with his eye hanging out on his cheek. There was besides, let me think, yes: the room where a man was found dead in bed with a horseshoe mark on his forehead, and the floor under the bed was covered with marks of horseshoes also; I don't know why. Also there was the lady who on locking her bedroom door in a strange house heard a thin voice among the bed-curtains say, "Now we're shut in for the night." None of those had any explanation or sequel. I wonder if they go on still, those stories.'

'Oh, likely enough—with additions from the magazines, as I said. You never heard, did you, of a real ghost at a private school? I thought not; nobody has that ever I came across.'

'From the way in which you said that, I gather that *you* have.'

'I really don't know; but this is what was in my mind. It happened at my private school thirty odd years ago, and I haven't any explanation of it.

'The school I mean was near London. It was established in a large and fairly old house—a great white building with very fine grounds about it. There were large cedars in the garden, as there are in so many of the older gardens in the Thames valley, and ancient elms in the three or four fields which we used for our games. I think probably it was quite an attractive place, but boys seldom allow that their schools possess any tolerable features.*

'I came to the school in a September soon after the year 1870;* and among the boys who arrived on the same day was one whom I took to: a Highland boy whom I will call McLeod. I needn't spend time in describing him: the main thing is that I got to know him very well. He was not an exceptional boy in any way—not particularly good at books or games—but he suited me.

'The school was a large one: there must have been from 120 to 130 boys there as a rule, and so a considerable staff of masters was required, and there were rather frequent changes among them.

'One term—perhaps it was my third or fourth—a new master made his appearance. His name was Sampson. He was a tallish, stoutish, pale, black-bearded man. I think we liked him: he had travelled a good deal and had stories which amused us on our school walks* so that there was some competition among us to get within earshot of him. I remember too—dear me, I have hardly thought of it since then—that he had a charm on his watch-chain that attracted my attention one day, and he let me examine it. It was, I now suppose, a gold Byzantine coin;* there was an effigy of some

absurd emperor on one side; the other side had been worn
practically smooth and he had had cut on it—rather
barbarously—his own initials, G.W.S., and a date, 24 July
1865. Yes, I can see it now: he told me he had picked it up
in Constantinople: it was about the size of a florin, perhaps
rather smaller.

'Well, the first odd thing that happened was this. Sampson
was doing Latin grammar with us. One of his favourite
methods—perhaps it is rather a good one—was to make us
construct sentences out of our own heads to illustrate the
rules he was trying to make us learn. Of course that is a thing
which gives a silly boy a chance of being impertinent: there
are lots of school stories in which that happens—or anyhow
there might be. But Sampson was too good a disciplinarian for
us to think of trying that on with him. Now, on this occasion
he was telling us how to express *remembering* in Latin: and
he ordered us each to make a sentence bringing in the verb
memini, "I remember". Well, most of us made up some
ordinary sentence such as "I remember my father", or "He
remembers his book", or something equally uninteresting:
and I dare say a good many put down *memino librum meum*
and so forth: but the boy I mentioned—McLeod—was
evidently thinking of something more elaborate than that.
The rest of us wanted to have our sentences passed, and get
on to something else, so some kicked him under the desk, and
I who was next to him poked him and whispered to him to
look sharp. But he didn't seem to attend. I looked at his
paper and saw he had put down nothing at all. So I jogged
him again harder than before and upbraided him sharply for
keeping us all waiting. That did have some effect. He started
and seemed to wake up, and then very quickly he scribbled
about a couple of lines on his paper and showed it up with
the rest. As it was the last, or nearly the last, to come in,
and as Sampson had a good deal to say to the boys who had
written *meminiscimus patri meo* and the rest of it, it turned
out that the clock struck twelve before he had got to McLeod
and McLeod had to wait afterwards to have his sentence
corrected. There was nothing much going on outside when
I got out, so I waited for him to come. He came very slowly

when he did arrive, and I guessed there had been some sort of trouble. "Well," I said, "what did you get?" "Oh, I don't know," said McLeod, "nothing much: but I think Sampson's rather sick with me." "Why, did you show him up some rot?" "No fear," he said. "It was all right as far as I could see: it was like this: *Memento*—that's right enough for remember, and it takes a genitive—*memento putei inter quatuor taxos*." "What silly rot," I said, "what made you shove that down? What does it mean?" "That's the funny part," said McLeod. "I'm not quite sure what it does mean. All I know is, it just came into my head and I corked it down. I know what I *think* it means because just before I wrote it down I had a sort of picture of it in my head: I believe it means 'Remember the well among the four'—what are those dark sort of trees that have red berries on them?" "Mountain ashes, I s'pose you mean." "I never heard of them," said McLeod; "no, I'll tell you—yews." "Well, and what did Sampson say?" "Why, he was jolly odd about it. When he read it he got up and went to the mantelpiece and stopped quite a long time without saying anything, with his back to me. And then he said, without turning round and rather quiet, 'What do you suppose that means?' I told him what I thought, only I couldn't remember the name of the silly tree: and then he wanted to know why I put it down and I had to say something or other. And after that he left off talking about it, and asked me how long I'd been here, and where my people lived, and things like that: and then I came away: but he wasn't looking a bit well."

'I don't remember any more that was said by either of us about this. Next day McLeod took to his bed with a chill or something of the kind, and it was a week or more before he was in school again. And as much as a month went by without anything happening that was noticeable. Whether or not Mr Sampson was really startled, as McLeod had thought, he didn't show it. I am pretty sure, of course, now, that there was something very curious in his past history, but I'm not going to pretend that we boys were sharp enough to guess any such thing.

'There was one other incident of the same kind as the last

which I told you. Several times since that day we had had
to make up examples in school to illustrate different rules,
but there had never been any row except when we did them
wrong. At last there came a day when we were going through
those dismal things which people call Conditional Sentences,
and we were told to make a conditional sentence expressing
a future consequence. We did it, right or wrong, and showed
up our bits of paper, and Sampson began looking through
them. All at once he got up, made some odd sort of noise
in his throat, and rushed out by a door that was just by his
desk. We sat there for a minute or two and then—I suppose
it was incorrect—but we went up—I and one or two others—
to look at the papers on his desk. Of course I thought someone must have put down some nonsense or other and
Sampson had gone off to report him. All the same, I noticed
that he hadn't taken any of the papers with him when he ran
out. Well, the top paper on the desk was written in red
ink—which no one used—and it wasn't in anyone's hand
who was in the class. They all looked at it—McLeod and all
—and took their dying oaths that it wasn't theirs. Then I
thought of counting the bits of paper, and of this I made
quite certain: that there were seventeen bits of paper on the
desk and sixteen boys in the form. Well, I bagged the extra
paper, and kept it, and I believe I have it now. And now you
will want to know what was written on it. It was simple
enough, and harmless enough, I should have said.

Si tu non veneris ad me, ego veniam ad te,

which means, I suppose, "If you don't come to me, I'll come
to you." '

'Could you show me the paper?' interrupted the listener.

'Yes, I could: but there's another odd thing about it. That
same afternoon I took it out of my locker—I know for certain
it was the same bit for I made a finger-mark on it—and no
single trace of writing of any kind was there on it. I kept it,
as I said, and since that time I have tried various experiments
to see whether sympathetic ink had been used, but absolutely
without result.

'So much for that. After about half an hour Sampson

looked in again: said he had felt very unwell and told us
we might go. He came rather gingerly to his desk and gave
just one look at the uppermost paper: and I suppose he
thought he must have been dreaming: anyhow he asked no
questions.

'That day was a half-holiday and next day Sampson was
in school again, much as usual. That night the third and last
incident in my story happened.

'We—McLeod and I—slept in a dormitory at right angles
to the main building. Sampson slept in the main building
on the first floor. There was a very bright full moon. At an
hour which I can't tell exactly, but some time between one
and two, I was woken up by somebody shaking me. It was
McLeod, and a nice state of mind he seemed to be in. "Come,"
he said, "come! there's a burglar getting in through Sampson's window." As soon as I could speak I said, "Well, why
not call out and wake everybody up?" "No, no," he said, "I'm
not sure who it is: don't make a row: come and look."
Naturally I came and looked, and naturally there was no
one there. I was cross enough and should have called McLeod
plenty of names: only—I couldn't tell why—it seemed to me
that there *was* something wrong—something that made me
very glad I wasn't alone to face it. We were still at the
window looking out and as soon as I could, I asked him what
he had heard or seen. "I didn't *hear* anything at all," he said,
"but about five minutes before I woke you I found myself
looking out of this window here, and there was a man sitting
or kneeling on Sampson's window-sill and looking in, and
I thought he was beckoning." "What sort of man?" McLeod
wriggled. "I don't know," he said, "but I can tell you one
thing—he was beastly thin: and he looked as if he was wet
all over: and," he said, looking round and whispering as if
he hardly liked to hear himself, "I'm not at all sure that he
was alive."

'We went on talking in whispers some time longer, and
eventually crept back to bed. No one else in the room woke
or stirred the whole time. I believe we did sleep a bit afterwards, but we were very cheap next day.

'And next day Mr Sampson was gone: not to be found:

and I believe no trace of him has ever come to light since. In thinking it over one of the oddest things about it all has seemed to me to be the fact that neither McLeod nor I ever mentioned what we had seen to any third person whatever. Of course no questions were asked on the subject, and if they had been I am inclined to believe that we could not have made any answer: we seemed unable to speak about it.

'That is my story,' said the narrator. 'The only approach to a ghost story connected with a school that I know, but still, I think, an approach to such a thing.'

* * * * *

The sequel to this may perhaps be reckoned highly conventional; but a sequel there is, and so it must be produced. There had been more than one listener to the story, and in the latter part of that same year, or of the next, one such listener was staying at a country house in Ireland.

One evening his host was turning over a drawer full of odds and ends in the smoking-room. Suddenly he put his hand upon a little box. 'Now,' he said, 'you know about old things; tell me what that is.' My friend opened the little box, and found in it a thin gold chain with an object attached to it. He glanced at the object and then took off his spectacles to examine it more narrowly. 'What's the history of this?' he asked. 'Odd enough,' was the answer. 'You know the yew thicket in the shrubbery: well, a year or two back we were cleaning out the old well that used to be in the clearing here, and what do you suppose we found?'

'Is it possible that you found a body?' said the visitor, with an odd feeling of nervousness.

'We did that: but what's more in every sense of the word, we found two.'

'Good Heavens! Two? Was there anything to show how they got there? Was this thing found with them?'

'It was—amongst the rags of the clothes that were on one of the bodies. A bad business, whatever the story of it may have been. One body had the arms tight round the other. They must have been there thirty years or more—long enough before we came to this place. You may judge we filled the well up fast enough. Do you make anything of what's cut on that gold coin you have there?'

'I think I can,' said my friend, holding it to the light (but he read it without much difficulty): 'it seems to be G.W.S., 24 July 1865.'

THE ROSE GARDEN

MR and Mrs Anstruther were at breakfast in the parlour of Westfield Hall, in the county of Essex.* They were arranging plans for the day.

'George,' said Mrs Anstruther, 'I think you had better take the car to Maldon and see if you can get any of those knitted things I was speaking about which would do for my stall at the bazaar.'

'Oh well, if you wish it, Mary, of course I can do that, but I had half arranged to play a round with Geoffrey Williamson this morning. The bazaar isn't till Thursday of next week, is it?'

'What has that to do with it, George? I should have thought you would have guessed that if I can't get the things I want in Maldon I shall have to write to all manner of shops in town: and they are certain to send something quite unsuitable in price or quality the first time. If you have actually made an appointment with Mr Williamson, you had better keep it, but I must say I think you might have let me know.'

'Oh no, no, it wasn't really an appointment. I quite see what you mean. I'll go. And what shall you do yourself?'

'Why, when the work of the house is arranged for, I must see about laying out my new rose garden. By the way, before you start for Maldon I wish you would just take Collins to look at the place I fixed upon. You know it, of course.'

'Well, I'm not quite sure that I do, Mary. Is it at the upper end, towards the village?'

'Good gracious no, my dear George; I thought I had made that quite clear. No, it's that small clearing just off the shrubbery path that goes towards the church.'

'Oh yes, where we were saying there must have been a summer-house once: the place with the old seat and the posts. But do you think there's enough sun there?'

'My dear George, do allow me *some* common sense, and don't credit me with all your ideas about summer-houses.

Yes, there will be plenty of sun when we have got rid of some
of those box-bushes. I know what you are going to say, and
I have as little wish as you to strip the place bare. All I want
Collins to do is to clear away the old seats and the posts and
things before I come out in an hour's time. And I hope you
will manage to get off fairly soon. After luncheon I think I
shall go on with my sketch of the church; and if you please
you can go over to the links, or——'

'Ah, a good idea—very good! Yes, you finish that sketch,
Mary, and I should be glad of a round.'

'I was going to say, you might call on the Bishop; but I
suppose it is no use my making *any* suggestion. And now do
be getting ready, or half the morning will be gone.'

Mr Anstruther's face, which had shown symptoms of
lengthening, shortened itself again, and he hurried from the
room, and was soon heard giving orders in the passage. Mrs
Anstruther, a stately dame of some fifty summers, proceeded,
after a second consideration of the morning's letters, to her
housekeeping.

Within a few minutes Mr Anstruther had discovered
Collins in the greenhouse, and they were on their way to
the site of the projected rose garden. I do not know much
about the conditions most suitable to these nurseries, but I
am inclined to believe that Mrs Anstruther, though in the
habit of describing herself as 'a great gardener', had not been
well advised in the selection of a spot for the purpose. It was
a small, dank clearing, bounded on one side by a path, and
on the other by thick box-bushes, laurels, and other ever-
greens. The ground was almost bare of grass and dark of
aspect. Remains of rustic seats and an old and corrugated
oak post somewhere near the middle of the clearing had given
rise to Mr Anstruther's conjecture that a summer-house had
once stood there.

Clearly Collins had not been put in possession of his
mistress's intentions with regard to this plot of ground: and
when he learnt them from Mr Anstruther he displayed no
enthusiasm.

'Of course I could clear them seats away soon enough,' he
said. 'They aren't no ornament to the place, Mr Anstruther,

and rotten too. Look 'ere, sir'—and he broke off a large piece—'rotten right through. Yes, clear them away, to be sure we can do that.'

'And the post,' said Mr Anstruther, 'that's got to go too.'

Collins advanced, and shook the post with both hands: then he rubbed his chin.

'That's firm in the ground, that post is,' he said. 'That's been there a number of years, Mr Anstruther. I doubt I shan't get that up not quite so soon as what I can do with them seats.'

'But your mistress specially wishes it to be got out of the way in an hour's time,' said Mr Anstruther.

Collins smiled and shook his head slowly. 'You'll excuse me, sir, but you feel of it for yourself. No, sir, no one can't do what's impossible to 'em, can they, sir? I could git that post up by after tea-time, sir, but that'll want a lot of digging. What you require, you see, sir, if you'll excuse me naming of it, you want the soil loosening round this post 'ere, and me and the boy we shall take a little time doing of that. But now, these 'ere seats,' said Collins, appearing to appropriate this portion of the scheme as due to his own resourcefulness, 'why, I can get the barrer round and 'ave them cleared away in, why less than an hour's time from now, if you'll permit of it. Only——'

'Only what, Collins?'

'Well now, it ain't for me to go against orders no more than what it is for you yourself—or anyone else' (this was added somewhat hurriedly), 'but if you'll pardon me, sir, this ain't the place I should have picked out for no rose garden myself. Why look at them box and laurestinus, 'ow they reg'lar preclude the light from——'

'Ah yes, but we've got to get rid of some of them, of course.'

'Oh, indeed, get rid of them! Yes, to be sure, but—I beg your pardon, Mr Anstruther——'

'I'm sorry, Collins, but I must be getting on now. I hear the car at the door. Your mistress will explain exactly what she wishes. I'll tell her, then, that you can see your way to clearing away the seats at once, and the post this afternoon. Good morning.'

Collins was left rubbing his chin. Mrs Anstruther received the report with some discontent, but did not insist upon any change of plan.

By four o'clock that afternoon she had dismissed her husband to his golf, had dealt faithfully with Collins and with the other duties of the day, and, having sent a campstool and umbrella to the proper spot, had just settled down to her sketch of the church as seen from the shrubbery, when a maid came hurrying down the path to report that Miss Wilkins had called.

Miss Wilkins was one of the few remaining members of the family from whom the Anstruthers had bought the Westfield estate some few years back. She had been staying in the neighbourhood, and this was probably a farewell visit. 'Perhaps you could ask Miss Wilkins to join me here,' said Mrs Anstruther, and soon Miss Wilkins, a person of mature years, approached.

'Yes, I'm leaving the Ashes tomorrow, and I shall be able to tell my brother how tremendously you have improved the place. Of course he can't help regretting the old house just a little—as I do myself—but the garden is really delightful now.'

'I am so glad you can say so. But you mustn't think we've finished our improvements. Let me show you where I mean to put a rose garden. It's close by here.'

The details of the project were laid before Miss Wilkins at some length; but her thoughts were evidently elsewhere.

'Yes, delightful,' she said at last rather absently. 'But do you know, Mrs Anstruther, I'm afraid I was thinking of old times. I'm *very* glad to have seen just this spot again before you altered it. Frank and I had quite a romance about this place.'

'Yes?' said Mrs Anstruther smilingly; 'do tell me what it was. Something quaint and charming, I'm sure.'

'Not so very charming, but it has always seemed to me curious. Neither of us would ever be here alone when we were children, and I'm not sure that I should care about it now in certain moods. It is one of those things that can hardly be put into words—by me at least—and that sound rather foolish if they are not properly expressed. I can tell you after a fashion what it was that gave us—well, almost a horror of the place when we were alone. It was towards the evening of one very hot autumn day, when Frank had disappeared mysteriously about the grounds, and I was looking for him to fetch him to tea, and going down this path I suddenly saw him, not hiding in the bushes, as I rather expected, but sitting on the bench in the old summer-house—there was a wooden summer-house here, you know—up in the corner, asleep, but with such a dreadful look on his face that I really thought he must be ill or even dead. I rushed at him and shook him, and told him to wake up; and wake up he did, with a scream. I assure you the poor boy seemed almost beside himself with fright. He hurried me away to the house, and was in a terrible state all that night, hardly sleeping. Someone had to sit up with him, as far as I remember. He was better very soon, but for days I couldn't get him to say why he had been in such a condition. It came out at last that he had really been asleep and had had a very odd disjointed sort of dream. He never *saw* much of what was around him, but he *felt* the scenes most vividly. First he made out that he was standing in a large room with a number of people in it, and that someone was opposite to him who was "very powerful", and he was being asked questions which he felt to be very important, and, whenever he answered them, someone—either the person opposite to him, or someone else in the room—seemed to be, as he said, making something up against him. All the voices sounded to him very distant, but he remembered bits of the things that were said: "Where were you on the 19th of October?" and "Is this your hand-writing?" and so on. I can see now, of course, that he was dreaming of some trial: but we were never allowed to see the papers, and it was odd that a boy of eight should have such a vivid idea of what went on in a court. All the time he felt, he said, the most intense anxiety and oppression and hope-lessness (though I don't suppose he used such words as that to me). Then, after that, there was an interval in which he remembered being dreadfully restless and miserable, and then there came another sort of picture, when he was aware that he had come out of doors on a dark raw morning with a little snow about. It was in a street, or at any rate among houses, and he felt that there were numbers and numbers of people there too, and that he was taken up some creaking wooden steps and stood on a sort of platform, but the only thing he could actually see was a small fire burning somewhere near him. Someone who had been holding his arm left hold of it and went towards this fire, and then he said the fright he was in was worse than at any other part of his dream, and if I had not wakened him up he didn't know what would have become of him. A curious dream for a child to have, wasn't it? Well, so much for that. It must have been later in the year that Frank and I were here, and I was sitting in the arbour just about sunset. I noticed the sun was going down, and told Frank to run in and see if tea was ready while I finished a chapter in the book I was reading. Frank was away longer than I expected, and the light was going so fast that I had to bend over my book to make it out. All at once I became conscious that someone was whispering to me inside the arbour. The only words I could distinguish, or thought I could, were something like "Pull, pull. I'll push, you pull."

'I started up in something of a fright. The voice—it was little more than a whisper—sounded so hoarse and angry, and yet as if it came from a long, long way off—just as it had done in Frank's dream. But, though I was startled, I had enough courage to look round and try to make out where the sound came from. And—this sounds very foolish, I know, but still it is the fact—I made sure that it was strongest when I put my ear to an old post which was part of the end of the seat. I was so certain of this that I remember making some marks on the post—as deep as I could with the scissors out of my work-basket. I don't know why. I wonder, by the way, whether that isn't the very post itself. . . . Well, yes, it might be: there *are* marks and scratches on it—but one can't be sure. Anyhow, it was just like that post you have there. My father got to know that both of us had had a fright in the arbour, and he went down there himself one evening after dinner, and the arbour was pulled down at very short notice. I recollect hearing my father talking about it to an old man who used to do odd jobs in the place, and the old man saying, "Don't you fear for that, sir: he's fast enough in there without no one don't take and let him out." But when I asked who it was, I could get no satisfactory answer. Possibly my father or mother might have told me more about it when I grew up, but, as you know, they both died when we were still quite children. I must say it has always seemed very odd to me, and I've often asked the older people in the village whether they knew of anything strange: but either they knew nothing or they wouldn't tell me. Dear, dear, how I have been boring you with my childish remembrances! but indeed that arbour did absorb our thoughts quite remarkably for a time. You can fancy, can't you, the kind of stories that we made up for ourselves. Well, dear Mrs Anstruther, I must be leaving you now. We shall meet in town this winter, I hope, shan't we?' etc., etc.

The seats and the post were cleared away and uprooted respectively by that evening. Late summer weather is proverbially treacherous, and during dinner-time Mrs Collins sent up to ask for a little brandy, because her husband had took a nasty chill and she was afraid he would not be able to do much next day.

Mrs Anstruther's morning reflections were not wholly placid. She was sure some roughs had got into the plantation during the night. 'And another thing, George: the moment that Collins is about again, you must tell him to do something about the owls. I never heard anything like them, and I'm positive one came and perched somewhere just outside our window. If it had come in I should have been out of my wits: it must have been a very large bird, from its voice. Didn't you hear it? No, of course not, you were sound asleep as usual. Still, I must say, George, you don't look as if your night had done you much good.'

'My dear, I feel as if another of the same would turn me silly. You have no idea of the dreams I had. I couldn't speak of them when I woke up, and if this room wasn't so bright and sunny I shouldn't care to think of them even now.'

'Well, really, George, that isn't very common with you, I must say. You must have—no, you only had what I had yesterday—unless you had tea at that wretched club house: did you?'

'No, no; nothing but a cup of tea and some bread and butter. I should really like to know how I came to put my dream together—as I suppose one does put one's dreams together from a lot of little things one has been seeing or reading. Look here, Mary, it was like this—if I shan't be boring you——'

'I *wish* to hear what it was, George. I will tell you when I have had enough.'

'All right. I must tell you that it wasn't like other nightmares in one way, because I didn't really *see* anyone who spoke to me or touched me, and yet I was most fearfully impressed with the reality of it all. First I was sitting, no, moving about, in an old-fashioned sort of panelled room. I remember there was a fireplace and a lot of burnt papers in it, and I was in a great state of anxiety about something. There was someone else—a servant, I suppose, because I remember saying to him, "Horses, as quick as you can", and then waiting a bit: and next I heard several people coming upstairs and a noise like spurs on a boarded floor, and then the door opened and whatever it was that I was expecting happened.'

'Yes, but what was that?'

'You see, I couldn't tell: it was the sort of shock that upsets you in a dream. You either wake up or else everything goes black. That was what happened to me. Then I was in a big dark-walled room, panelled, I think, like the other, and a number of people, and I was evidently——'

'Standing your trial, I suppose, George.'

'Goodness! yes, Mary, I was; but did you dream that too? How very odd!'

'No, no; I didn't get enough sleep for that. Go on, George, and I will tell you afterwards.'

'Yes; well, I *was* being tried, for my life, I've no doubt, from the state I was in. I had no one speaking for me, and somewhere there was a most fearful fellow—on the bench, I should have said, only that he seemed to be pitching into me most unfairly, and twisting everything I said, and asking most abominable questions.'

'What about?'

'Why, dates when I was at particular places, and letters I was supposed to have written, and why I had destroyed some papers; and I recollect his laughing at answers I made in a way that quite daunted me. It doesn't sound much, but I can tell you, Mary, it was really appalling at the time. I am quite certain there was such a man once, and a most horrible villain he must have been. The things he said——'

'Thank you, I have no wish to hear them. I can go to the links any day myself. How did it end?'

'Oh, against me; *he* saw to that. I do wish, Mary, I could give you a notion of the strain that came after that, and seemed to me to last for days: waiting and waiting, and sometimes writing things I knew to be enormously important to me, and waiting for answers and none coming, and after that I came out——'

'Ah!'

'What makes you say that? Do you know what sort of thing I saw?'

'Was it a dark cold day, and snow in the streets, and a fire burning somewhere near you?'

'By George, it was! You *have* had the same nightmare! Really not? Well, it is the oddest thing! Yes; I've no doubt it was an execution for high treason. I know I was laid on straw and jolted along most wretchedly, and then had to go up some steps, and someone was holding my arm, and I remember seeing a bit of a ladder and hearing a sound of a lot of people. I really don't think I could bear now to go into a crowd of people and hear the noise they make talking. However, mercifully, I didn't get to the real business. The dream passed off with a sort of thunder inside my head. But, Mary——'

'I know what you are going to ask. I suppose this is an instance of a kind of thought-reading. Miss Wilkins called yesterday and told me of a dream her brother had as a child when they lived here, and something did no doubt make me think of that when I was awake last night listening to those horrible owls and those men talking and laughing in the shrubbery (by the way, I wish you would see if they have done any damage, and speak to the police about it); and so, I suppose, from my brain it must have got into yours while you were asleep. Curious, no doubt, and I am sorry it gave you such a bad night. You had better be as much in the fresh air as you can today.'

'Oh, it's all right now; but I think I *will* go over to the Lodge and see if I can get a game with any of them. And you?'

'I have enough to do for this morning; and this afternoon, if I am not interrupted, there is my drawing.'

'To be sure—I want to see that finished very much.'

No damage was discoverable in the shrubbery. Mr Anstruther surveyed with faint interest the site of the rose garden, where the uprooted post still lay, and the hole it had occupied remained unfilled. Collins, upon inquiry made, proved to be better, but quite unable to come to his work. He expressed, by the mouth of his wife, a hope that he hadn't done nothing wrong clearing away them things. Mrs Collins added that there was a lot of talking people in Westfield, and the hold ones was the worst: seemed to think everything of them having been in the parish longer than what other people had. But as to what they said no more could then be ascertained than that it had quite upset Collins, and was a lot of nonsense.

Recruited* by lunch and a brief period of slumber, Mrs Anstruther settled herself comfortably upon her sketching chair in the path leading through the shrubbery to the side-gate of the churchyard. Trees and buildings were among her favourite subjects, and here she had good studies of both. She worked hard, and the drawing was becoming a really pleasant thing to look upon by the time that the wooded hills to the west had shut off the sun. Still she would have persevered, but the light changed rapidly, and it became obvious that the last touches must be added on the morrow. She rose and turned towards the house, pausing for a time to take delight in the limpid green western sky. Then she passed on between the dark box-bushes, and, at a point just before the path debouched on the lawn, she stopped once again and considered the quiet evening landscape, and made a mental note that that must be the tower of one of the Roothing churches that one caught on the sky-line. Then a bird (perhaps) rustled in the box-bush on her left, and she turned and started at seeing what at first she took to be a Fifth of November mask peeping out among the branches. She looked closer.

It was not a mask. It was a face—large, smooth, and pink. She remembers the minute drops of perspiration which were starting from its forehead: she remembers how the jaws were clean-shaven and the eyes shut. She remembers also, and with an accuracy which makes the thought intolerable to her, how the mouth was open and a single tooth appeared below the upper lip. As she looked the face receded into the darkness of the bush. The shelter of the house was gained and the door shut before she collapsed.

Mr and Mrs Anstruther had been for a week or more recruiting at Brighton before they received a circular from the Essex Archaeological Society, and a query as to whether they possessed certain historical portraits which it was desired to include in the forthcoming work on Essex Portraits, to be published under the Society's auspices. There was an accompanying letter from the Secretary which contained the following passage: 'We are specially anxious to know whether you possess the original of the engraving of which I enclose a photograph. It represents Sir —— ——, Lord Chief Justice under Charles II,* who, as you doubtless know, retired after his disgrace to Westfield, and is supposed to have died there of remorse. It may interest you to hear that a curious entry has recently been found in the registers, not of Westfield but of Priors Roothing, to the effect that the parish was so much troubled after his death that the rector of Westfield summoned the parsons of all the Roothings to come and lay him; which they did. The entry ends by saying: "The stake is in a field adjoining to the churchyard of Westfield, on the west side." Perhaps you can let us know if any tradition to this effect is current in your parish.'

The incidents which the 'enclosed photograph' recalled

were productive of a severe shock to Mrs Anstruther. It was decided that she must spend the winter abroad.

Mr Anstruther, when he went down to Westfield to make the necessary arrangements, not unnaturally told his story to the rector (an old gentleman), who showed little surprise.

'Really I had managed to piece out for myself very much what must have happened, partly from old people's talk and partly from what I saw in your grounds. Of course we have suffered to some extent also. Yes, it was bad at first: like owls, as you say, and men talking sometimes. One night it was in this garden, and at other times about several of the cottages. But lately there has been very little: I think it will die out. There is nothing in our registers except the entry of the burial, and what I for a long time took to be the family motto; but last time I looked at it I noticed that it was added in a later hand and had the initials of one of our rectors quite late in the seventeenth century, A. C.—Augustine Crompton. Here it is, you see—*quieta non movere.** I suppose—— Well, it is rather hard to say exactly what I do suppose.'

THE TRACTATE MIDDOTH

TOWARDS the end of an autumn afternoon an elderly man with a thin face and grey Piccadilly weepers* pushed open the swing-door leading into the vestibule of a certain famous library,* and addressing himself to an attendant, stated that he believed he was entitled to use the library, and inquired if he might take a book out. Yes, if he were on the list of those to whom that privilege was given. He produced his card—Mr John Eldred—and, the register being consulted, a favourable answer was given. 'Now, another point,' said he. 'It is a long time since I was here, and I do not know my way about your building; besides, it is near closing-time, and it is bad for me to hurry up and down stairs. I have here the title of the book I want: is there anyone at liberty who could go and find it for me?' After a moment's thought the doorkeeper beckoned to a young man who was passing. 'Mr Garrett,' he said, 'have you a minute to assist this gentleman?' 'With pleasure,' was Mr Garrett's answer. The slip with the title was handed to him. 'I think I can put my hand on this; it happens to be in the class I inspected last quarter—but I'll just look it up in the catalogue to make sure. I suppose it is that particular edition that you require, sir?' 'Yes, if you please, that and no other,' said Mr Eldred. 'I am exceedingly obliged to you.' 'Don't mention it I beg, sir,' said Mr Garrett, and hurried off.

'I thought so,' he said to himself when his finger, travelling down the pages of the catalogue, stopped at a particular entry. 'Talmud: Tractate Middoth, with the commentary of Nachmanides,* Amsterdam, 1707. 11.3.34. Hebrew class, of course. Not a very difficult job this.'

Mr Eldred, accommodated with a chair in the vestibule, awaited anxiously the return of his messenger—and his disappointment at seeing an empty-handed Mr Garrett running down the staircase was very evident. 'I'm sorry to disappoint you, sir,' said the young man, 'but the book is out.' 'Oh dear!' said Mr Eldred, 'is that so? You are sure there can be no mistake?' 'I don't think there's much chance of it, sir: but it's possible, if you like to wait a minute, that you might meet the very gentleman that's got it. He must be leaving the library soon and I *think* I saw him take that particular book out of the shelf.' 'Indeed! You didn't recognize him, I suppose? Would it be one of the professors or one of the students?' 'I don't think so: certainly not a professor. I should have known him; but the light isn't very good in that part of the library at this time of day, and I didn't see his face. I should have said he was a shortish old gentleman, perhaps a clergyman, in a cloak. If you could wait I can easily find out whether he wants the book very particularly.'

'No, no,' said Mr Eldred, 'I won't—I can't wait now, thank you—no. I must be off. But I'll call again tomorrow if I may, and perhaps you could find out who has it.'

'Certainly, sir, and I'll have the book ready for you if we——' But Mr Eldred was already off and hurrying more than one would have thought wholesome for him.

Garrett had a few moments to spare; and, thought he, 'I'll go back to that case and see if I can find the old man. Most likely he could put off using the book for a few days. I dare say the other one doesn't want to keep it for long.' So off with him to the Hebrew class. But when he got there it was unoccupied and the volume marked 11.3.34 was in its place on the shelf. It was vexatious to Garrett's self-respect to have disappointed an inquirer with so little reason: and he would have liked, had it not been against library rules, to take the book down to the vestibule then and there, so that it might be ready for Mr Eldred when he called. However, next morning he would be on the look out for him and he begged the doorkeeper to send and let him know when the moment came. As a matter of fact he was himself in the vestibule when Mr Eldred arrived, very soon after the library opened, and when hardly anyone besides the staff were in the building.

'I'm very sorry,' he said; 'it's not often that I make such a stupid mistake, but I did feel sure that the old gentleman I saw took out that very book and kept it in his hand without opening it, just as people do, you know, sir, when they mean to take a book out of the library and not merely refer to it. But, however, I'll run up now at once and get it for you this time.'

And here intervened a pause. Mr Eldred paced the entry, read all the notices, consulted his watch, sat and gazed up the staircase, did all that a very impatient man could, until some twenty minutes had run out. At last he addressed himself to the doorkeeper and inquired if it was a very long way to that part of the library to which Mr Garrett had gone.

'Well, I was thinking it was funny, sir: he's a quick man as a rule, but to be sure he might have been sent for by the Librarian, but even so I think he'd have mentioned to him that you was waiting. I'll just speak him up on the toob and see.' And to the tube he addressed himself. As he absorbed the reply to his question his face changed, and he made one or two supplementary inquiries which were shortly answered. Then he came forward to his counter and spoke in a lower tone. 'I'm sorry to hear, sir, that something seems to have 'appened a little awkward. Mr Garrett has been took poorly, it appears, and the Libarian sent him 'ome in a cab by the other way. Something of an attack, by what I can hear.' 'What, really? Do you mean that someone has injured him?' 'No, sir, not violence 'ere, but as I should judge attacted with an attack, what you might term it, of illness. Not a strong constitootion, Mr Garrett. But as to your book, sir, perhaps you might be able to find it for yourself. It's too bad you should be disappointed this way twice over——' 'Er—well, but I'm so sorry that Mr Garrett should have been taken ill in this way while he was obliging me. I think I must leave the book and call and inquire after him. You can give me his address, I suppose.' That was easily done: Mr Garrett, it appeared, lodged in rooms not far from the station. 'And, one other question. Did you happen to notice if an old gentleman, perhaps a clergyman, in a—yes—in a black cloak left the library *after* I did yesterday. I think he may have been a—I think, that is, that he may be staying—or rather that I may have known him.'

'Not in a black cloak, sir, no. There were only two gentlemen left later than what you done, sir, both of them youngish men. There was Mr Carter took out a music-book and one of the prefessors with a couple o' novels. That's the lot, sir; and then I went off to me tea, and glad to get it. Thank you, sir, much obliged.'

Mr Eldred, still a prey to anxiety, betook himself in a cab to Mr Garrett's address, but the young man was not yet in a condition to receive visitors. He was better, but his landlady considered that he must have had a severe shock. She thought most likely from what the doctor said that he would be able to see Mr Eldred tomorrow. Mr Eldred returned to his hotel at dusk and spent, I fear, but a dull evening.

On the next day he was able to see Mr Garrett. When in health Mr Garrett was a cheerful and pleasant-looking young man. Now he was a very white and shaky being, propped up in an armchair by the fire, and inclined to shiver and keep an eye on the door. If, however, there were visitors whom he was not prepared to welcome, Mr Eldred was not among them. 'It really is I who owe you an apology, and I was despairing of being able to pay it, for I didn't know your address. But I am very glad you have called. I do dislike and regret giving all this trouble, but you know I could not have foreseen this—this attack which I had.'

'Of course not; but now—I am something of a doctor— you'll excuse my asking; you have had, I am sure, good advice. Was it a fall you had?'

'No. I did fall on the floor—but not from any height. It was, really, a shock.'

'You mean something startled you. Was it anything you thought you saw?'

'Not much *thinking* in the case, I'm afraid. Yes it was something I saw. You remember when you called the first time at the library?'

'Yes, of course. Well now, let me beg you not to try to describe it—it will not be good for you to recall it, I'm sure.'

'But indeed it would be a relief to me to tell anyone like yourself: you might be able to explain it away. It was just when I was going into the class where your book is——'

'Indeed, Mr Garrett, I insist; besides my watch tells me I have but very little time left in which to get my things together and take the train. No—not another word—it would be more distressing to you than you imagine, perhaps. Now there is just one thing I want to say. I feel that I am really indirectly responsible for this illness of yours, and I think I ought to defray the expense which it has—eh?'

But this offer was quite distinctly declined. Mr Eldred, not pressing it, left almost at once: not, however, before Mr Garrett had insisted upon his taking a note of the classmark of the Tractate Middoth, which, as he said, Mr Eldred could at leisure get for himself. But Mr Eldred did not reappear at the library.

William Garrett had another visitor that day in the person of a contemporary and colleague from the library, one George Earle. Earle had been one of those who found Garrett lying insensible on the floor just inside the 'class' or cubicle (opening upon the central alley of a spacious gallery) in which the Hebrew books were placed, and Earle had naturally been very anxious about his friend's condition. So as soon as library hours were over he appeared at the lodgings. 'Well,' he said (after other conversation), 'I've no notion what it was that put you wrong, but I've got the idea that there's something wrong in the atmosphere of the library. I know this, that just before we found you I was coming along the gallery with Davis and I said to him, "Did ever you know such a musty smell anywhere as there is about here? It can't be wholesome." Well now, if one goes on living a long time with a smell of that kind (I tell you it was worse than I ever knew it) it must get into the system and break out some time, don't you think?'

Garrett shook his head. 'That's all very well about the smell—but it isn't always there, though I've noticed it the last day or two—a sort of unnaturally strong smell of dust. But no—that's not what did for me. It was something I *saw*, and I want to tell you about it. I went into that Hebrew class to get a book for a man that was inquiring for it down below. Now that same book I'd made a mistake about the day before:

I'd been for it, for the same man, and made sure that I saw
an old parson in a cloak taking it out. I told my man it was
out: off he went, to call again next day: I went back to see if
I could get it out of the parson: no parson there, and the book
on the shelf. Well, yesterday, as I say, I went again. This
time, if you please—ten o'clock in the morning, remember,
and as much light as ever you get in those classes, and there
was my parson again, back to me, looking at the books on
the shelf I wanted. His hat was on the table, and he had a
bald head. I waited a second or two looking at him rather
particularly. I tell you, he had a very nasty bald head. It
looked to me dry, and it looked dusty, and the streaks of hair
across it were much less like hair than cobwebs. Well, I made
a bit of a noise on purpose, coughed and moved my feet. He
turned round and let me see his face—which I hadn't seen
before. I tell you again, I'm not mistaken: though for one
reason or another I didn't take in the lower part of his face,
I did see the upper part, and it was perfectly dry and the eyes
were very deep-sunk; and over them from the eyebrows to
the cheek-bone there were *cobwebs*—thick. Now that closed
me up, as they say, and I can't tell you anything more.'

What explanations were furnished by Earle of this pheno-
menon it does not very much concern us to inquire; at all
events they did not convince Garrett that he had not seen
what he had seen.

Before William Garrett returned to work at the library, the
Librarian insisted upon his taking a week's rest and change
of air. Within a few days' time, therefore, he was at the
station with his bag, looking for a desirable smoking compartment in which to travel to Burnstow-on-Sea,* which he had
not previously visited. One compartment and one only
seemed to be suitable. But just as he approached it he saw,
standing in front of the door, a figure so like one bound up
with recent unpleasant associations that with a sickening
qualm and hardly knowing what he did, he tore open the
door of the next compartment and pulled himself into it as
quickly as if death were at his heels. The train moved off,

and he must have turned quite faint for he was next conscious of a smelling-bottle being put to his nose. His physician was a nice-looking old lady, who with her daughter was the only passenger in the carriage.

But for this incident it is not very likely that he would have made any overtures to his fellow-travellers. As it was, thanks and inquiries and general conversation supervened inevitably; and Garrett found himself provided before the journey's end not only with a physician but with a landlady: for Mrs Simpson had apartments to let at Burnstow which seemed in all ways suitable. The place was empty at that season, so that Garrett was thrown a good deal into the society of the mother and daughter. He found them very acceptable company.* On the third evening of his stay he was on such terms with them as to be asked to spend the evening in their private sitting-room.

During their talk it transpired that Garrett's work lay in a library. 'Ah, libraries are fine places,' said Mrs Simpson, putting down her work with a sigh; 'but for all that, books have played me a sad turn, or rather *a* book has.'

'Well, books give me my living, Mrs Simpson, and I should be sorry to say a word against them: I don't like to hear that they have been bad for you.'

'Perhaps Mr Garrett could help us to solve our puzzle mother,' said Miss Simpson.

'I don't want to set Mr Garrett off on a hunt that might waste a lifetime, my dear—nor yet to trouble him with our private affairs.'

'But if you think it in the least likely that I could be of use, I do beg you to tell me what the puzzle is, Mrs Simpson. If it is finding out anything about a book, you see, I am in rather a good position to do it.'

'Yes, I do see that, but the worst of it is that we don't know the name of the book.'

'Nor what it is about?'

'No, nor that either.'

'Except that we don't think it's in English, mother—and that is not much of a clue.'

'Well, Mr Garrett,' said Mrs Simpson, who had not yet

resumed her work and was looking at the fire thoughtfully, 'I *shall* tell you the story. You will please keep it to yourself, if you don't mind? Thank you. Now it is just this. I had an old uncle, a Dr Rant. Perhaps you may have heard of him. Not that he was a distinguished man, but from the odd way he chose to be buried.'

'I rather think I have seen the name in some guidebook.'

'That would be it,' said Miss Simpson. 'He left directions, horrid old man, that he was to be put sitting at a table in his ordinary clothes in a brick room that he'd had made underground in a field near his house. Of course the country people say he's been seen about there in his old black cloak.'

'Well, dear, I don't know much about such things,' Mrs Simpson went on, 'but anyhow he is dead these twenty years and more. He was a clergyman, though I'm sure I can't imagine how he got to be one: but he did no duty for the last part of his life, which I think was a good thing; and he lived on his own property, a very nice estate not a great way from here. He had no wife or family, only one niece, who was myself, and one nephew, and he had no particular liking for either of us—nor for anyone else, as far as that goes. If anything, he liked my cousin better than he did me—for John was much more like him in his temper and, I'm afraid I must say, his very mean sharp ways. It might have been different if I had not married, but I did, and that he very much resented. Very well: here he was with this estate and a good deal of money, as it turned out, of which he had the absolute disposal, and it was understood that we—my cousin and I—would share it equally at his death. In a certain winter, over twenty years back, as I said, he was taken ill, and I was sent for to nurse him. My husband was alive then but the old man would not hear of *his* coming. As I drove up to the house I saw my cousin John driving away from it in an open fly and looking, I noticed, in very good spirits. I went up and did what I could for my uncle, but I was very soon sure that this would be his last illness, and he was convinced of it too. During the day before he died he got me to sit by him all the time, and I could see there was something, and probably something unpleasant, that he was saving up to tell me, and putting it off as long as he felt he could afford the strength—I'm afraid purposely in order to keep me on the stretch. But at last out it came. "Mary," he said, "Mary, I've made my will in John's favour: he has everything, Mary." Well of course that came as a bitter shock to me, for we—my husband and I—were not rich people, and if he could have managed to live a little easier than he was obliged to do, I felt it might be the prolonging of his life. But I said little or nothing to my uncle, except that he had a right to do what he pleased: partly because I couldn't think of anything to say and partly because I was sure there was more to come: and so there was. "But Mary," he said, "I'm not very fond of John, and I've made another will in *your* favour. *You* can have everything. Only you've got to find the will, you see: and I don't mean to tell you where it is." Then he chuckled to himself and I waited, for again I was sure he hadn't finished. "That's a good girl," he said after a time, "—you wait and I'll tell you as much as I told John. But just let me remind you, you can't go into court with what I'm saying to you for *you* won't be able to produce any collateral evidence beyond your own word, and John's a man that can do a little hard swearing if necessary. Very well then, that's understood. Now I had the fancy that I wouldn't write this will quite in the common way, so I wrote it in a book, Mary, a printed book. And there's several thousand books in this house. But there! you needn't trouble yourself with them, for it isn't one of them. It's in safe keeping elsewhere: in a place where John can go and find it any day—if he only knew—and you can't. A good will it is: properly signed and witnessed, but I don't think you'll find the witnesses in a hurry."

'Still I said nothing: if I had moved at all I must have taken hold of the old wretch and shaken him. He lay there laughing to himself, and at last he said:

' "Well, well, you've taken it very quietly, and as I want to start you both on equal terms, and John has a bit of a purchase in being able to go where the book is, I'll tell you just two other things which I didn't tell him. The will's in English, but you won't know that if ever you see it. That's one thing, and another is that when I'm gone you'll find an envelope in my desk directed to you, and inside it something that would help you to find it if only you have the wits to use it."

'In a few hours from that he was gone, and though I made an appeal to John Eldred about it——'

'John Eldred? I beg your pardon, Mrs Simpson—I think I've seen a Mr John Eldred. What is he like to look at?'

'It must be ten years since I saw him: he would be a thin elderly man now, and unless he has shaved them off, he has that sort of whiskers which people used to call Dundreary* or Piccadilly something.'

'——weepers. Yes, that *is* the man.'

'Where did you come across him, Mr Garrett?'

'I don't know if I could tell you,' said Garrett mendaciously. 'In some public place. But you hadn't finished.'

'Really I had nothing much to add, only that John Eldred of course paid no attention whatever to my letters, and has enjoyed the estate ever since, while my daughter and I have had to take to the lodging-house business here—which I must say has not turned out by any means so unpleasant as I feared it might.'

'But about the envelope.'

'To be sure! Why, the puzzle turns on that. Give Mr Garrett the paper out of my desk.'

It was a small slip with nothing whatever on it but five numerals, not divided or punctuated in any way: 11334.

Mr Garrett pondered, but there was a light in his eye. Suddenly he made a face and then asked, 'Do you suppose that Mr Eldred can have any more clue than you have to the title of the book?'

'I have sometimes thought he must,' said Mrs Simpson, 'and in this way: that my uncle must have made the will not very long before he died (that, I think, he said himself), and got rid of the book immediately afterwards. But all his books were very carefully catalogued: and John has the catalogue: and John was most particular that no books whatever should be sold out of the house. And I'm told that he is always journeying about to booksellers and libraries; so I fancy that he must have found out just which books are missing from my uncle's library of those which are entered in the catalogue, and must be hunting for them.'

'Just so, just so,' said Mr Garrett and relapsed into thought.

No later than next day he received a letter which, as he told Mrs Simpson with great regret, made it absolutely necessary for him to cut short his stay at Burnstow.

Sorry as he was to leave them (and they were at least as sorry to part with him), he had begun to feel that a crisis, all-important to Mrs (and shall we add, Miss?) Simpson, was very possibly supervening.

In the train Garrett was uneasy and excited. He racked his brains to think whether the press mark of the book which Mr Eldred had been inquiring after was one in any way corresponding to the numbers of Mrs Simpson's little bit of paper. But he found to his dismay that the shock of the previous week had really so upset him that he could neither remember any vestige of the title or nature of the book, nor even of the locality to which he had gone to seek it. And yet all other parts of library topography and work were clear as ever in his mind.

And another thing—he stamped with annoyance as he thought of it—he had at first hesitated and then had forgotten to ask Mrs Simpson for the name of the place where Eldred lived. That, however, he could write about.

At least he had his clue in the figures on the paper. If they referred to a press mark in his library, they were only susceptible of a limited number of interpretations. They might be divided into 1.13.34, 11.33.4, or 11.3.34. He could try all these in the space of a few minutes, and if any one were missing he had every means of tracing it. He got very quickly to work, though a few minutes had to be spent in explaining his early return to his landlady and his colleagues. 1.13.34. was in place and contained no extraneous writing. As he drew near to Class 11 in the same gallery, its association struck him like a chill. But he *must* go on. After a cursory glance at 11.33.4 (which first confronted him, and was a perfectly new book) he ran his eye along the line of quartos which fills 11.3. The gap he feared was there: 34 was out. A moment was spent in making sure that it had not been misplaced and then he was off to the vestibule.

'Has 11.3.34 gone out? Do you recollect noticing that number?'

'Notice the number? What do you take me for, Mr Garrett? There, take and look over the tickets for yourself if you've got a free day before you.'

'Well then, has a Mr Eldred called again?—the old gentleman who came the day I was taken ill. Come, you'd remember him.'

'What do you suppose? Of course I recollect of him: no, he haven't been in again, not since you went off for your 'oliday. And yet I seem to—there now. Roberts 'll know. Roberts, do you recollect of the name of Heldred?'

'Not arf,' said Roberts. 'You mean the man that sent a bob over the price for the parcel, and I wish they all did.'

'Do you mean to say you've been sending books to Mr Eldred? Come, do speak up: have you?'

'Well now, Mr Garrett, if a gentleman sends the ticket all wrote correct and the secketry says this book may go and the box ready addressed sent with the note, and a sum of money sufficient to deefray the railway charges, what would be *your* action in the matter, Mr Garrett, if I may take the liberty to ask such a question? Would you or would you not have taken the trouble to oblige or would you have chucked the 'ole thing under the counter and——'

'You were perfectly right, of course, Hodgson—perfectly right: only, would you kindly oblige me by showing me the ticket Mr Eldred sent, and letting me know his address?'

'To be sure, Mr Garrett; so long as I'm not 'ectored about and informed that I don't know my duty, I'm willing to oblige in every way feasible to my power. There is the ticket on the file. J. Eldred, 11.3.34. Title of work: T—a—l—m—— well there, you can make what you like of it—not a novel, I should 'azard the guess. And here is Mr Heldred's note applyin' for the book in question, which I see he terms it a track.'*

'Thanks, thanks: but the address? There's none on the note.'

'Ah, indeed; well, now . . . stay now, Mr Garrett, I 'ave it. Why, that note come inside of the parcel, which was directed very thoughtful to save all trouble ready to be sent back with the book inside; and if I *have* made any mistake in this 'ole transaction it lays just in the one point that I neglected to enter the address in my little book here what I keep. Not but what I dare say there was good reasons for me not entering of it: but there, I haven't the time, neither have you I dare say, to go into 'em just now. And—no, Mr Garrett, I do *not* carry it in my 'ed, else what would be the use of me keeping this little book here—just a ordinary common notebook, you see, which I make a practice of entering all such names and addresses in it as I see fit to do?'

'Admirable arrangement, to be sure—but—all right, thank you. When did the parcel go off?'

'Half-past ten this morning.'

'Oh, good; and it's just one now.'

Garrett went upstairs in deep thought. How was he to get the address? A telegram to Mrs Simpson: he might miss a train by waiting for the answer. Yes, there was one other way. She had said that Eldred lived on his uncle's estate. If this were so, he might find that place entered in the donation book. That he could run through quickly now that he knew the title of the book. The register was soon before him, and knowing that the old man had died more than twenty years ago he gave him a good margin and turned back to 1870. There was but one entry possible. '1875, August 14th. *Talmud: Tractatus Middoth cum comm. R. Nachmanidae.* Amstelod. 1707. Given by J. Rant D.D. of Bretfield Manor.'

A gazetteer showed Bretfield to be three miles from a small station on the main line. Now to ask the doorkeeper whether he recollected if the name on the parcel had been anything like Bretfield.

'No, nothing like. It was, now you mention it, Mr Garrett, either Bredfield or Britfield, but nothing like that other name what you coated.'

So far well. Next, a timetable. A train could be got in

twenty minutes—taking two hours over the journey. The only chance—but one not to be missed; and the train was taken.

If he had been fidgety on the journey up he was almost distracted on the journey down. If he found Eldred, what could he say? That it had been discovered that the book was a rarity and must be recalled? An obvious untruth. Or that it was believed to contain important manuscript notes? Eldred would of course show him the book, from which the leaf would already have been removed. He might perhaps find traces of the removal—a torn edge of a fly-leaf probably —and who could disprove, what Eldred was certain to say, that he too had noticed and regretted the mutilation? Altogether the chase seemed very hopeless. The one chance was this. The book had left the library at 10.30: it might not have been put into the first possible train, at 11.20. Granted that, then he might be lucky enough to arrive simultaneously with it and patch up some story which would induce Eldred to give it up.

It was drawing towards evening when he got out upon the platform of his station, and like most country stations this one seemed unnaturally quiet. He waited about till the one or two passengers who got out with him had drifted off, and then inquired of the stationmaster whether Mr Eldred was in the neighbourhood.

'Yes, and pretty near too, I believe. I fancy he means calling here for a parcel he expects. Called for it once today already, didn't he Bob?' (to the porter).

'Yes, sir, he did, and appeared to think it was all along of me that it didn't come by the two o'clock. Anyhow I've got it for him now,' and the porter flourished a square parcel, which a glance assured Garrett contained all that was of any importance to him at that particular moment.

'Bretfield, sir? Yes—three miles just about. Short cut across these three fields brings it down by half a mile. There: there's Mr Eldred's trap.'

A dog-cart drove up with two men in it, of whom Garrett, gazing back as he crossed the little station yard, easily recognized one. The fact that Eldred was driving was slightly in his favour—for most likely he would not open the parcel in the presence of his servant. On the other hand, he would get home quickly and unless Garrett were there within a very few minutes of his arrival, all would be over. He must hurry; and that he did. His short cut took him along one side of a triangle while the cart had two sides to traverse; and it was delayed a little at the station, so that Garrett was in the third of the three fields when he heard the wheels fairly near. He had made the best progress possible but the pace at which the cart was coming made him despair. At this rate it *must* reach home ten minutes before him, and ten minutes would more than suffice for the fulfilment of Mr Eldred's project.

It was just at this time that the luck fairly turned. The evening was still and sounds came clearly. Seldom has any sound given greater relief than that which he now heard: that of the cart pulling up. A few words were exchanged and it drove on. Garrett, halting in the utmost anxiety, was able to see as it drove past the stile (near which he now stood) that it contained only the servant and not Eldred: further, he made out that Eldred was following on foot. From behind the tall hedge by the stile leading into the road he watched the thin wiry figure pass quickly by, with the parcel beneath its arm and feeling in its pockets. Just as he passed the stile something fell out of a pocket upon the grass, but with so little sound that Eldred was not conscious of it. In a moment more it was safe for Garrett to cross the stile into the road and pick up—a box of matches.

Eldred went on and as he went his arms made hasty movements difficult to interpret in the shadow of the trees that overhung the road. But as Garrett followed cautiously, he found at various points the key to them—a piece of string and then the wrapper of the parcel—meant to be thrown *over* the hedge, but sticking in it.

Now Eldred was walking slower and it could just be made out that he had opened the book and was turning over the leaves. He stopped, evidently troubled by the failing light. Garrett slipped into a gate-opening but still watched. Eldred, hastily looking around, sat down on a felled tree-trunk by the roadside and held the open book up close to his eyes.

Suddenly he laid it, still open, on his knee, and felt in all his pockets: clearly in vain, and clearly to his annoyance. 'You would be glad of your matches now,' thought Garrett. Then he took hold of a leaf and was carefully tearing it out when two things happened. First, something black seemed to drop upon the white leaf and run down it, and then as Eldred started and was turning to look behind him a little dark form appeared to rise out of the shadow behind the tree-trunk and from it two arms enclosing a mass of blackness came before Eldred's face and covered his head and neck. His legs and arms were wildly flourished, but no sound came. Then, there was no more movement. Eldred was alone. He had fallen back into the grass behind the tree-trunk. The book was cast into the roadway. Garrett, his anger and suspicion gone for the moment at the sight of this horrid struggle, rushed up with loud cries of 'Help!' and so too, to his enormous relief, did a labourer who had just emerged from a field opposite. Together they bent over and supported Eldred, but to no purpose. The conclusion that he was dead was inevitable. 'Poor gentleman!' said Garrett to the labourer when they had laid him down. 'What happened to him do you think?' 'I wasn't two hundred yards away,' said the man, 'when I see Squire Eldred setting reading in his book, and to my thinking he was took with one of these fits—face seemed to go all over black.' 'Just so,' said Garrett. 'You didn't see anyone near him? It couldn't have been an assault?' 'Not possible—no one couldn't have got away without you or me seeing them.' 'So I thought. Well, we must get some help, and the doctor and the policeman; and perhaps I had better give them this book.'

It was obviously a case for an inquest, and obvious also that Garrett must stay at Bretfield and give his evidence. The medical inspection showed that, though some black dust was found on the face and in the mouth of the deceased, the cause of death was a shock to a weak heart, and not asphyxiation. The fateful book was produced, a respectable quarto printed wholly in Hebrew and not of an aspect likely to excite even the most sensitive.

'You say, Mr Garrett, that the deceased gentleman

appeared at the moment before his attack to be tearing a leaf out of this book?'

'Yes: I think one of the fly-leaves.'

'There is here a fly-leaf partially torn through. It has Hebrew writing on it. Will you kindly inspect it?'

'There are three names in English, sir, also, and a date. But I am sorry to say I cannot read Hebrew writing.'

'Thank you. The names have the appearance of being signatures. They are John Rant, Walter Gibson, and James Frost, and the date is 20 July 1875. Does anyone here know any of these names?'

The Rector, who was present, volunteered a statement that the uncle of the deceased, from whom he inherited, had been named Rant.

The book being handed to him, he shook a puzzled head. 'This is not like any Hebrew I ever learnt.'

'You are sure that it is Hebrew?'

'What? Yes—I suppose. . . . No—my dear sir, you are perfectly right—that is, your suggestion is exactly to the point. Of course—it is not Hebrew at all. It is English, and it is a will.'

It did not take many minutes to show that here was indeed a will of Dr John Rant, bequeathing the whole of the property lately held by John Eldred to Mrs Mary Simpson. Clearly the discovery of such a document would amply justify Mr Eldred's agitation. As to the partial tearing of the leaf, the coroner pointed out that no useful purpose could be attained by speculations whose correctness it would never be possible to establish.

The Tractate Middoth was naturally taken in charge by the coroner for further investigation, and Mr Garrett explained privately to him the history of it, and the position of events so far as he knew or guessed them.

He returned to his work next day and on his walk to the station passed the scene of Mr Eldred's catastrophe. He could hardly leave it without another look, though the recollection of what he had seen there made him shiver, even on that bright morning. He walked round, with some misgivings, behind the felled tree. Something dark that still lay there made him start back for a moment: but it hardly stirred. Looking closer he saw that it was a thick black mass of cobwebs, and as he stirred it gingerly with his stick several large spiders ran out of it into the grass.

There is no great difficulty in imagining the steps by which William Garrett, from being an assistant in a great library, attained to his present position of prospective owner of Bretfield Manor, now in the occupation of his mother-in-law Mrs Mary Simpson.

CASTING THE RUNES

April 15th, 190–

Dear Sir,

I am requested by the Council of the —— Association to return to you the draft of a paper on *The Truth of Alchemy*, which you have been good enough to offer to read at our forthcoming meeting, and to inform you that the Council do not see their way to including it in the programme.

I am,
Yours faithfully,
—— SECRETARY.

April 18th

Dear Sir,

I am sorry to say that my engagements do not permit of my affording you an interview on the subject of your proposed paper. Nor do our laws allow of your discussing the matter with a Committee of our Council, as you suggest. Please allow me to assure you that the fullest consideraion was given to the draft which you submitted, and that it was not declined without having been referred to the judgment of a most competent authority. No personal question (it can hardly be necessary for me to add) can have had the slightest influence on the decision of the Council.

Believe me (*ut supra*).

April 20th

The Secretary of the —— Association begs respectfully to inform Mr Karswell* that it is impossible for him to communicate the name of any person or persons to whom the draft of Mr Karswell's paper may have been submitted; and further desires to intimate that he cannot undertake to reply to any further letters on this subject.

'And who *is* Mr Karswell?' inquired the Secretary's wife. She had called at his office and (perhaps unwarrantably) had picked up the last of these three letters, which the typist had just brought in.

'Why, my dear, just at present Mr Karswell is a very angry man. But I don't know much about him otherwise, except that he is a person of wealth, his address is Lufford Abbey, Warwickshire, and he's an alchemist, apparently, and wants to tell us all about it; and that's about all—except that I don't want to meet him for the next week or two. Now, if you're ready to leave this place, I am.'

'What have you been doing to make him angry?' asked Mrs Secretary.

'The usual thing, my dear, the usual thing: he sent in a draft of a paper he wanted to read at the next meeting, and we referred it to Edward Dunning—almost the only man in England who knows about these things—and he said it was perfectly hopeless, so we declined it. So Karswell has been pelting me with letters ever since. The last thing he wanted was the name of the man we referred his nonsense to: you saw my answer to that. But don't you say anything about it, for goodness' sake.'

'I should think not indeed. Did I ever do such a thing? I do hope, though, he won't get to know that it was poor Mr Dunning.'

'Poor Mr Dunning? I don't know why you call him that; he's a very happy man, is Dunning. Lots of hobbies and a comfortable home, and all his time to himself.'*

'I only meant I should be sorry for him if this man got hold of his name, and came and bothered him.'

'Oh, ah! yes. I dare say he would be poor Mr Dunning then.'

The Secretary and his wife were lunching out, and the friends to whose house they were bound were Warwickshire people. So Mrs Secretary had already settled it in her own mind that she would question them judiciously about Mr Karswell. But she was saved the trouble of leading up to the subject, for the hostess said to the host before many minutes had passed, 'I saw the Abbot of Lufford this morning.' The host whistled. 'Did you? What in the world brings him up to town?' 'Goodness knows; he was coming out of the British Museum gate as I drove past.' It was not unnatural that Mrs Secretary should inquire whether this was a real Abbot who was being spoken of. 'Oh no, my dear: only a neighbour of ours in the country who bought Lufford Abbey a few years ago. His real name is Karswell.' 'Is he a friend of yours?' asked Mr Secretary with a private wink to his wife. The question let loose a torrent of declamation. There was really nothing to be said for Mr Karswell. Nobody knew what he did with himself: his servants were a horrible set of people; he had invented a new religion for himself, and practised no one could tell what appalling rites; he was very easily offended, and never forgave anybody: he had a dreadful face (so the lady insisted, her husband somewhat demurring); he never did a kind action, and whatever influence he did exert was mischievous. 'Do the poor man justice, dear,' the husband interrupted. 'You forget the treat he gave the school children.' 'Forget it, indeed! But I'm glad you mentioned it because it gives an idea of the man. Now, Florence, listen to this. The first winter he was at Lufford this delightful neighbour of ours wrote to the clergyman of his parish (he's not ours, but we know him very well) and offered to show the school children some magic-lantern slides. He said he had some new kinds which he thought would interest them. Well the clergyman was rather surprised because Mr Karswell had shown himself inclined to be unpleasant to the children—complaining of their trespassing or something of the sort; but of course he accepted, and the evening was fixed and our friend went himself to see that everything went right. He said he never had been so thankful for anything as that his own children were all prevented from being there: they were at a children's party at our house as a matter of fact. Because this Mr Karswell had evidently set out with the intention of frightening these poor village children out of their wits, and I do believe if he had been allowed to go on he would actually have done so. He began with some comparatively mild things—Red Riding Hood was one, and even then Mr Farrer said the wolf was so dreadful that several of the smaller children had to be taken out: and he said Mr Karswell began the story by producing a noise like a wolf howling in the distance which was the most gruesome thing he had ever heard. All the slides he showed, Mr Farrer said, were most clever; they were absolutely realistic and where he had got them or how he worked them he could not imagine. Well the show went on, and the stories kept on becoming a little more terrifying each time, and the children were mesmerized into complete silence. At last he produced a series which represented a little boy passing through his own park—Lufford, I mean—in the evening. Every child in the room could recognize the place from the pictures. And this poor boy was followed, and at last pursued and overtaken and either torn in pieces or some-how made away with by a horrible hopping creature in white, which you saw first dodging about among the trees and gradually it appeared more and more plainly. Mr Farrer said it gave him one of the worst nightmares he ever remembered, and what it must have meant to the children doesn't bear thinking of. Of course this was too much, and he spoke very sharply indeed to Mr Karswell and said it couldn't go on. All *he* said was: "Oh, you think it's time to bring our little show to an end and send them home to their beds? Very well!" And then, if you please, he switched on another slide which showed a great mass of snakes, centipedes, and disgusting creatures with wings and somehow or other he made it seem as if they were climbing out of the picture and getting in amongst the audience; and this was accompanied by a sort of dry rustling noise which sent the children nearly mad, and of course they stampeded. A good many of them were rather hurt in getting out of the room, and I don't suppose one of them closed an eye that night. There was the most dreadful trouble in the village afterwards. Of course the mothers threw a good part of the blame on poor Mr Farrer, and if they could have got past the gates I believe the fathers would have broken every window in the Abbey. Well, now, that's Mr Karswell: that's the Abbot of Lufford, my dear, and you can imagine how we covet *his* society.'

'Yes, I think he has *all* the possibilities of a distinguished criminal, has Karswell,' said the host. 'I should be sorry for anyone who got into his bad books.'

'Is he the man—or am I mixing him up with someone else—' asked the Secretary (who for some mintues had been wearing the frown of the man who is trying to recollect something). 'Is he the man who brought out a *History of Witchcraft* some time back—ten years or more?'

'That's the man: do you remember the reviews of it?'

'Certainly I do; and what's equally to the point, I knew the author of the most incisive of the lot. So did you: you must remember John Harrington; he was at John's* in our time.'

'Oh, very well indeed, though I don't think I saw or heard anything of him between the time I went down and the day I read the account of the inquest on him.'

'Inquest?' said one of the ladies. 'What has happened to him?'

'Why, what happened was that he fell out of a tree and broke his neck. But the puzzle was what could have induced him to get up there. It was a mysterious business, I must say. Here was this man, not an athletic fellow—was he?—and with no eccentric twist about him that was ever noticed, walking home along a country road late in the evening: no tramps about—well known and liked in the place—and he suddenly begins to run like mad, loses his hat and stick, and finally shins up a tree—quite a difficult tree—growing in the hedgerow: a dead branch gives way and he comes down with it and breaks his neck, and there he's found next morning with the most dreadful face of fear on him that could be imagined. It was pretty evident, of course, that he had been chased by something, and people talked of savage dogs, and beasts escaped out of menageries; but there was nothing to be made of that. That was in '89, and I believe his brother Henry (whom I remember as well at Cambridge, but *you* probably don't) has been trying to get on the track of an explanation ever since. He, of course, insists there was malice in it, but I don't know. It's difficult to see how it could have come in.'

After a time the talk reverted to the *History of Witchcraft*. 'Did you ever look into it?' asked the host.

'Yes, I did,' said the Secretary. 'I went so far as to read it.'

'Was it as bad as it was made out to be?'

'Oh, in point of style and form, quite hopeless. It deserved all the pulverizing it got. But, besides that, it was an evil book. The man believed every word of what he was saying, and I'm very much mistaken if he hadn't tried the greater part of his receipts.'

'Well, I only remember Harrington's review of it, and I must say if I'd been the author it would have quenched my literary ambition for good. I should never have held up my head again.'

'It hasn't had that effect in the present case. But come, it's half-past three; I must be off.'

On the way home the Secretary's wife said, 'I do hope that horrible man won't find out that Mr Dunning had anything to do with the rejection of his paper.' 'I don't think there's much chance of that,' said the Secretary. 'Dunning won't mention it himself, for these matters are confidential, and none of us will for the same reason. Karswell won't know his name, for Dunning hasn't published anything on the same subject yet. The only danger is that Karswell might find out if he was to ask the British Museum people who was in the habit of consulting alchemical manuscripts: I can't very well tell them not to mention Dunning, can I? It would set them talking at once. Let's hope it won't occur to him.'

However, Mr Karswell was an astute man.

This much is in the way of prologue. On an evening rather later in the same week, Mr Edward Dunning was returning from the British Museum, where he had been engaged in Research, to the comfortable house in a suburb where he lived alone, tended by two excellent women who had been long with him. There is nothing to be added by way of description of him to what we have heard already. Let us follow him as he takes his sober course homewards.

A train took him to within a mile or two of his house, and an electric tram a stage farther. The line ended at a point some three hundred yards from his front door. He had had enough of reading when he got into the car, and indeed the light was not such as to allow him to do more than study the advertisements on the panes of glass that faced him as he sat.

As was not unnatural, the advertisements in this particular line of cars were objects of his frequent contemplation, and, with the possible exception of the brilliant and convincing dialogue between Mr Lamplough and an eminent K.C. on the subject of Pyretic Saline, none of them afforded much scope to his imagination. I am wrong: there was one at the corner of the car farthest from him which did not seem familiar. It was in blue letters on a yellow ground, and all that he could read of it was a name—John Harrington—and something like a date. It could be of no interest to him to know more; but for all that, as the car emptied, he was just curious enough to move along the seat until he could read it well. He felt to a slight extent repaid for his trouble; the advertisement was *not* of the usual type. It ran thus: 'In memory of John Harrington, F.S.A., of The Laurels, Ashbrooke. Died Sept. 18th, 1889. Three months were allowed.'*

The car stopped. Mr Dunning, still contemplating the blue letters on the yellow ground, had to be stimulated to rise by a word from the conductor. 'I beg your pardon,' he said, 'I was looking at that advertisement: it's a very odd one, isn't it?' The conductor read it slowly. 'Well, my word,' he said, 'I never see that one before. Well, that is a cure, ain't it? Someone bin up to their jokes 'ere, I should think.' He got out a duster and applied it, not without saliva, to the pane and then to the outside. 'No,' he said, returning, 'that ain't no transfer: seems to me as if it was reg'lar *in* the glass, what I mean in the substance, as you may say. Don't you think so, sir?' Mr Dunning examined it and rubbed it with his glove, and agreed. 'Who looks after these advertisements and gives leave for them to be put up? I wish you would inquire. I will just take a note of the words.' At this moment there came a call from the driver: 'Look alive, George, time's up.' 'All right, all right; there's somethink else what's up at this end. You come and look at this 'ere glass.' 'What's gorn with the glass?' said the driver, approaching. 'Well, and oo's 'Arrington? What's it all about?' 'I was just asking who was responsible for putting the advertisements up in your cars and saying it would be as well to make some inquiry about this one.' 'Well, sir, that's all done at the Company's orfice that work is: it's our Mr Timms I believe looks into that. When we put up tonight I'll leave word and per'aps I'll be able to tell you tomorrer if you 'appen to be coming this way.'

This was all that passed that evening. Mr Dunning did just go to the trouble of looking up Ashbrooke and found that it was in Warwickshire.

Next day he went to town again. The car (it was the same car) was too full in the morning to allow of his getting a word with the conductor: he could only be sure that the curious advertisement had been made away with. The close of the day brought a further element of mystery into the transaction. He had missed the tram, or else preferred walking home, but at a rather late hour, while he was at work in his study, one of the maids came to say that two men from the tramways was very anxious to speak to him. This was a reminder of the advertisement, which he had—he says—nearly forgotten. He had the men in—they were the conductor and driver of the car—and when the matter of refreshment had been attended to, asked what Mr Timms had had to say about the advertisement. 'Well, sir, that's what we took the liberty to step round about,' said the conductor. 'Mr Timm's 'e give William and me* the rough side of his tongue about that: 'cordin' to 'im there warn't no advertisement of that description sent in nor ordered nor paid for nor put up nor nothink, let alone not bein' there, and we was playing the fool takin' up his time. "Well," I says, "if that's the case, all I ask of you, Mr Timms," I says, "is to take and look at it for yourself," I says. "Of course if it ain't there," I says, "you may take and call me what you like." "Right," he says, "I will": and we went straight off. Now I leave it to you, sir, if that ad., as we term 'em, with 'Arrington on it warn't as plain as ever you see anythink—blue letters on yeller glass, and as I says at the time, and you borne me out, reg'lar *in* the glass, because if you remember you recollect of me swabbing it with my duster.' 'To be sure I do, quite clearly—well?' 'You may say well, I don't think. Mr Timms he gets in that car with a light—no, he told William to 'old the light outside. "Now," he says, "where's your precious ad. what we've 'eard so much about?" " 'Ere it is," I says, "Mr Timms," and I laid my 'and on it.' The conductor paused.

'Well,' said Mr Dunning, 'it was gone, I suppose. Broken?'

'Broke!—not it. There warn't, if you'll believe me, no more trace of them letters—blue letters they was—on that piece o' glass, than—well, it's no good *me* talkin'. I never see such a thing. I leave it to William here if—but there, as I says, where's the benefit in me going on about it?'

'And what did Mr Timms say?'

'Why 'e did what I give 'im leave to—called us pretty much anythink he liked, and I don't know as I blame him so much neither. But what we thought, William and me did, was as we seen you take down a bit of a note about that— well, that letterin'——'

'I certainly did that, and I have it now. Did you wish me to speak to Mr Timms myself, and show it to him? Was that what you came in about?'

'There, didn't I say as much?' said William. 'Deal with a gent if you can get on the track of one, that's my word. Now perhaps, George, you'll allow as I ain't took you very far wrong tonight.'

'Very well, William, very well; no need for you to go on as if you'd 'ad to frog's-march me 'ere. I come quiet, didn't I? All the same for that, we 'adn't ought to take up your time this way, sir; but if it so 'appened you could find time to step round to the Company's orfice in the morning and tell Mr Timms what you seen for yourself, we should lay under a very 'igh obligation to you for the trouble. You see it ain't bein' called—well, one thing and another, as we mind, but if they got it into their 'ead at the orfice as we seen things as warn't there, why, one thing leads to another and where we should be a twelvemunce 'ence—well, you can understand what I mean.'

Amid further elucidations of the proposition, George, conducted by William, left the room.

The incredulity of Mr Timms (who had a nodding acquaintance with Mr Dunning) was greatly modified on the following day by what the latter could tell and show him; and any bad mark that might have been attached to the names of William and George was not suffered to remain on the Company's books; but explanation there was none.

Mr Dunning's interest in the matter was kept alive by an incident of the following afternoon. He was walking from his club to the train, and he noticed some way ahead a man with a handful of leaflets such as are distributed to passers-by by agents of enterprising firms. This agent had not chosen a very crowded street for his operations: in fact Mr Dunning did not see him get rid of a single leaflet before he himself reached the spot. One was thrust into his hand as he passed: the hand that gave it touched his, and he experienced a sort of little shock as it did so. It seemed unnaturally rough and hot. He looked in passing at the giver, but the impression he got was so unclear that however much he tried to reckon it up subsequently nothing would come. He was walking quickly and, as he went on, glanced at the paper. It was a blue one. The name of Harrington in large capitals caught his eye. He stopped, startled, and felt for his glasses. The next instant the leaflet was twitched out of his hand by a man who hurried past, and was irrecoverably gone. He ran back a few paces, but where was the passer-by? and where the distributor?

It was in a somewhat pensive frame of mind that Mr Dunning passed on the following day into the Select Manuscript Room of the British Museum, and filled up tickets for Harley 3586* and some other volumes. After a few minutes they were brought to him and he was settling the one he wanted first upon the desk when he thought he heard his own name whispered behind him. He turned round hastily, and, in doing so, brushed his little portfolio of loose papers on to the floor. He saw no one he recognized except one of the staff in charge of the room, who nodded to him, and he proceeded to pick up his papers. He thought he had them all and was turning to begin work when a stout gentleman at the table behind him, who was just rising to leave and had collected his own belongings, touched him on the shoulder, saying: 'May I give you this? I think it should be yours,' and handed him a missing quire. 'It is mine, thank you,' said Mr Dunning. In another moment the man had left the room.

Upon finishing his work for the afternoon Mr Dunning had some conversation with the assistant in charge and took occasion to ask who the stout gentleman was. 'Oh, he's a man named Karswell,' said the assistant; 'he was asking me a week ago who were the great authorities on alchemy, and of course I told him you were the only one in the country. I'll see if I can't catch him: he'd like to meet you, I'm sure.'

'For heaven's sake don't dream of it!' said Mr Dunning, 'I'm particularly anxious to avoid him.'

'Oh, very well,' said the assistant, 'he doesn't come here often: I dare say you won't meet him.'

More than once on the way home that day Mr Dunning confessed to himself that he did not look forward with his usual cheerfulness to a solitary evening. It seemed to him that something ill-defined and impalpable had stepped in between him and his fellow-men—had taken him in charge, as it were. He wanted to sit close up to his neighbours in the train and in the tram, but as luck would have it both train and car were markedly empty. The conductor George was thoughtful and appeared to be absorbed in calculations as to the number of passengers. On arriving at his house, he found Dr Watson, his medical man, on his doorstep. 'I've had to upset your household arrangements, I'm sorry to say, Dunning. Both your servants *hors de combat*. In fact, I've had to send them to the Nursing Home.'

'Good heavens! what's the matter?'

'It's something like ptomaine poisoning, I should think: you've not suffered yourself, I can see, or you wouldn't be walking about. I think they'll pull through all right.'

'Dear, dear! Have you any idea what brought it on?'

'Well, they tell me they bought some shellfish from a hawker at their dinner-time. It's odd. I've made inquiries, but I can't find that any hawker has been to other houses in the street. I couldn't send word to you—they won't be back for a bit yet. You come and dine with me tonight, anyhow, and we can make arrangements for going on. Eight o'clock. Don't be too anxious.'

The solitary evening was thus obviated; at the expense of some distress and inconvenience, it is true. Mr Dunning spent the time pleasantly enough with the doctor (a rather recent settler) and returned to his lonely home at about 11.30. The night he passed is not one on which he looks back with any satisfaction. He was in bed, and the light was out. He was wondering if the charwoman would come early enough to get him hot water next morning when he heard the unmistakable sound of his study door opening. No step followed it on the passage floor, but the sound must mean mischief, for he knew that he had shut the door that evening after putting his papers away in his desk. It was rather shame than courage that induced him to slip out into the passage and lean over the banister in his nightgown, listening. No light was visible; no further sound came: only a gust of warm or even hot air played for an instant round his shins. He went back and decided to lock himself into his room. There was more unpleasantness, however. Either an economical suburban company had decided that their light would not be required in the small hours, and had stopped working, or else something was wrong with the meter: the effect was in any case that the electric light was off. The obvious course was to find a match and also to consult his watch: he might as well know how many hours of discomfort awaited him. So he put his hand into the well-known nook under the pillow: only, it did not get so far. What he touched was, according to his account, a mouth, with teeth and with hair about it, and, he declares, not the mouth of a human being. I do not think it is any use to guess what he said or did: but he was in a spare room with the door locked and his ear to it before he was clearly conscious again. And there he spent the rest of a most miserable night, looking every moment for some fumbling at the door: but nothing came.

The venturing back to his own room in the morning was attended with many listenings and quiverings. The door stood open, fortunately, and the blinds were up (the servants had been out of the house before the hour of drawing them down). There was, to be short, no trace of an inhabitant. The watch, too, was in its usual place: nothing was disturbed, only the wardrobe door had swung open, in accordance with its confirmed habit. A ring at the back door now announced the charwoman, who had been ordered the night before, and nerved Mr Dunning after letting her in to continue his search in other parts of the house. It was equally fruitless.

The day thus begun went on dismally enough. He dared not go to the Museum: in spite of what the assistant had said, Karswell might turn up there, and Dunning felt he could not cope with a probably hostile stranger. His own house was odious; he hated sponging on the doctor. He spent some little time in a call at the Nursing Home, where he was slightly cheered by a good report of his housekeeper and maid. Towards lunch-time he betook himself to his club, again experiencing a gleam of satisfaction at seeing the Secretary of the Association. At luncheon Dunning told his friend the more material of his woes, but could not bring himself to speak of those that weighed most heavily on his spirits. 'My poor dear man,' said the Secretary, 'what an upset! Look here: we're alone at home, absolutely. You must put up with us. Yes! no excuse: send your things in this afternoon.' Dunning was unable to stand out: he was, in truth, becoming acutely anxious, as the hours went on, as to what that night might have waiting for him. He was almost happy as he hurried home to pack up.

His friends, when they had time to take stock of him, were rather shocked at his lorn appearance, and did their best to keep him up to the mark. Not altogether without success: but when the two men were smoking alone later Dunning became dull again. Suddenly he said, 'Gayton, I believe that alchemist man knows it was I who got his paper rejected.' Gayton whistled. 'What makes you think that?' he said. Dunning told of his conversation with the Museum assistant, and Gayton could only agree that the guess seemed likely to be correct. 'Not that I care much,' Dunning went on, 'only it might be a nuisance if we were to meet. He's a bad-tempered party, I imagine.' Conversation dropped again; Gayton became more and more strongly impressed with the desolateness that came over Dunning's face and bearing, and finally—though with a considerable effort—he asked him point-blank whether something serious was not bothering him. Dunning gave an exclamation of relief. 'I was perishing to get it off my mind,' he said. 'Do you know anything about a man named John Harrington?' Gayton was thoroughly startled and at the moment could only ask why. Then the complete story of Dunning's experiences came out—what had happened in the tramcar, in his own house, and in the street, the troubling of spirit that had crept over him, and still held him; and he ended with the question he had begun with. Gayton was at a loss how to answer him. To tell the story of Harrington's end would perhaps be right; only, Dunning was in a nervous state, the story was a grim one, and he could not help asking himself whether there were not a connecting link between these two cases, in the person of Karswell. It was a difficult concession for a scientific man, but it could be eased by the phrase 'hypnotic suggestion'. In the end he decided that his answer tonight should be guarded: he would talk the situation over with his wife. So he said that he had known Harrington at Cambridge and believed he had died suddenly in 1889, adding a few details about the man and his published work. He did talk over the matter with Mrs Gayton, and as he had anticipated she leapt at once to the conclusion which had been hovering before him. It was she who reminded him of the surviving brother, Henry Harrington, and she also who suggested that he might be got hold of by means of their hosts of the day before. 'He might be a hopeless crank,' objected Gayton. 'That could be ascertained from the Bennetts, who knew him,' Mrs Gayton retorted; and she undertook to see the Bennetts the very next day.

It is not necessary to tell in further detail the steps by which Henry Harrington and Dunning were brought together.

The next scene that does require to be narrated is a conversation that took place between the two. Dunning had told Harrington of the strange ways in which the dead man's name had been brought before him, and had said something, besides, of his own subsequent experiences. Then he had asked if Harrington was disposed, in return, to recall any of the circumstances connected with his brother's death. Harrington's surprise at what he heard can be imagined: but his reply was readily given.

'John,' he said, 'was in a very odd state undeniably from time to time during some weeks before, though not immediately before the catastrophe. There were several things—the principal notion he had was that he thought he was being followed. No doubt he was an impressionable man but he never had had such fancies as this before. I cannot get it out of my mind that there was ill-will at work, and what you tell me about yourself reminds me very much of my brother. Can you think of any possible connecting link?'

'There is just one that has been taking shape vaguely in my mind. I've been told that your brother reviewed a book very severely not long before he died, and just lately I have happened to cross the path of the man who wrote that book in a way he would resent.'

'Don't tell me the man was called Karswell.'

'Why not? that is exactly his name.'

Henry Harrington leant back. 'That is final—to my mind. Now I must explain further. From something he said, I feel sure that my brother John was begining to believe—very much against his will—that Karswell was at the bottom of his trouble. I want to tell you what seems to me to have a bearing on the situation. My brother was a great musician, and used to run up to concerts in town. He came back, three months before he died, from one of these and gave me his programme to look at—an analytical programme: he always kept them. "I nearly missed this one," he said. "I suppose I must have dropped it: anyhow I was looking for it under my seat and in my pockets and so on and my neighbour offered me his: said might he give it me, he had no further use for it, and he went away just afterwards. I don't know who he was—a stout, clean-shaven man. I should have been sorry to miss it: of course I could have bought another, but this cost me nothing." At another time he told me that he had been very uncomfortable both on the way to his hotel and during the night. I piece things together now in thinking it over.

Then not very long after, he was going over these pro-
grammes, putting them in order to have them bound up, and
in this particular one (which by the way I had hardly glanced
at) he found quite near the beginning a strip of paper with
some very odd writing on it in red and black—most carefully
done—it looked to me more like Runic letters than anything
else. "Why," he said, "this must belong to my fat neighbour.
It looks as if it might be worth returning to him; it may be a
copy of something; evidently someone has taken trouble over
it. How can I find his address?" We talked it over for a little
and agreed that it wasn't worth advertising about, and that
my brother had better look out for the man at the next
concert, to which he was going very soon. The paper was
lying on the book and we were both by the fire; it was a cold,
windy summer evening. I suppose the door blew open,
though I didn't notice it: at any rate a gust—a warm gust it
was—came quite suddenly between us, took the paper and
blew it straight into the fire: it was light, thin paper and
flared and went up the chimney in a single ash. "Well," I
said, "you can't give it back now." He said nothing for a
minute: then rather crossly, "No, I can't; but why you should
keep on saying so I don't know." I remarked that I didn't say
it more than once. "Not more than four times, you mean,"
was all he said. I remember all that very clearly, without any
good reason. And now to come to the point. I don't know if
you looked at that book of Karswell's which my unfortunate
brother reviewed. It's not likely that you should: but I did,
both before his death and after it. The first time we made
game of it together. It was written in no style at all—split
infinitives, and every sort of thing that makes an Oxford
gorge rise. Then there was nothing that the man didn't
swallow: mixing up classical myths, and stories out of the
Golden Legend with reports of savage customs of today—all
very proper, no doubt,* if you know how to use them, but
he didn't: he seemed to put the *Golden Legend* and the *Golden
Bough** exactly on a par and to believe both: a pitiable
exhibition, in short. Well, after the misfortune, I looked over
the book again. It was no better than before, but the impression which it left this time on my mind was different. I

suspected—as I told you—that Karswell had borne ill-will to my brother, even that he was in some way responsible for what had happened; and now his book seemed to me to be a very sinister performance indeed. One chapter in particular struck me, in which he spoke of "casting the Runes" on people, either for the purpose of gaining their affection, or of getting them out of the way—perhaps more especially the latter: he spoke of all this in a way that really seemed to me to imply actual knowledge. I've not time to go into details; but the upshot is that I am pretty sure from information received that the civil man at the concert was Karswell. I suspect—more than suspect—that the paper was of importance: and I do believe that if my brother had been able to give it back, he might have been alive now. Therefore, it occurs to me to ask you whether you have anything to put beside what I have told you.'

By way of answer Dunning had the episode in the Manuscript Room at the British Museum to relate. 'Then he did actually hand you some papers; have you examined them? No? because we must, if you'll allow it, look at them at once, and very carefully.'

They went to the still empty house—empty, for the two servants were not yet able to return to work. Dunning's portfolio of papers was gathering dust on the writing-table. In it were the quires of small-sized scribbling páper which he used for his transcripts: and from one of these, as he took it up, there slipped and fluttered out into the room with uncanny quickness a strip of thin light paper. The window was open, but Harrington slammed it to just in time to intercept the paper, which he caught. 'I thought so,' he said; 'it might be the identical thing that was given to my brother. You'll have to look out, Dunning. This may mean something quite serious for you.'

A long consultation took place. The paper was narrowly examined. As Harrington had said, the characters on it were more like Runes than anything else, but not decipherable by either man, and both hesitated to copy them for fear, as they confessed, of perpetuating whatever evil purpose they might conceal. So it has remained impossible (if I may anticipate a little) to ascertain what was conveyed in this curious message or commission: both Dunning and Harrington are firmly convinced that it had the effect of bringing its possessors into very undesirable company. That it must be returned to the source whence it came they were agreed, and further that the only safe and certain way was that of personal service: and here contrivance would be necessary, for Dunning was known by sight to Karswell. He must for one thing alter his appearance by shaving his beard. But then might not the blow fall first? Harrington thought they could time it. He knew the date of the concert at which the 'black spot'* had been put on his brother: it was June 18th. The death had followed on September 18th. Dunning reminded him that three months had been mentioned on the inscription on the car-window. 'Perhaps,' he added with a cheerless laugh, 'mine may be a bill at three months too. I believe I can fix it by my diary. Yes, April 23rd was the day at the Museum—that brings me to July 23rd. Now, you know, it becomes extremely important to me to know anything you will tell me about the progress of your brother's trouble, if it is possible for you to speak of it.' 'Of course. Well, the sense of being watched whenever he was alone was the most distressing thing to him. After a time I took to sleeping in his room, and he was the better for that: still, he talked a great deal in his sleep. What about? Is it wise to dwell on that, at least before things are straightened out? I think not, but I can tell you this: two things came for him by post during those weeks—both with a London postmark and addressed in a commercial hand. One was a woodcut of Bewick's* roughly torn out of the page— one which shows a moonlit road and a man walking along it, followed by an awful demon creature. Under it were written the lines out of the "Ancient Mariner" (which I suppose the cut illustrates) about one who, having once looked round—

> walks on,
> And turns no more his head;
> Because he knows, a frightful fiend
> Doth close behind him tread.*

The other was a calendar such as tradesmen often send. My

brother paid no attention to this but I looked at it after his death, and found that everything after September 18 had been torn out. You may be surprised at his having gone out alone the evening he was killed, but the fact is that during the last ten days or so of his life he had been quite free from the sense of being followed or watched.'

The end of the consultation was this. Harrington, who knew a neighbour of Karswell's, thought he saw a way of keeping a watch on his movements. It would be Dunning's part to be in readiness to try to cross Karswell's path at any moment, to keep the paper safe, and in a place of ready access.

They parted. The next weeks were no doubt a severe strain upon Dunning's nerves: the intangible barrier which had seemed to rise about him on the day when he received the paper gradually developed into a brooding blackness that cut him off from the means of escape to which one might have thought he might resort. No one was at hand who was likely to suggest them to him, and he seemed robbed of all initiative. He waited with inexpressible anxiety as May, June, and early July passed on for a mandate from Harrington. But all this time Karswell remained immovable at Lufford.

At last, in less than a week before the date he had come to look upon as the end of his earthly activities, came a telegram: 'Leaves Victoria by boat train Thursday night. Do not miss. I come to you tonight. Harrington.'

He arrived accordingly, and they concocted plans. The train left Victoria at nine and its last stop before Dover was Croydon West. Harrington would mark down Karswell at Victoria and look out for Dunning at Croydon, calling to him if need were by a name agreed upon. Dunning, disguised as far as might be, was to have no label or initials on any hand luggage, and must at all costs have the paper with him.

Dunning's suspense as he waited on the Croydon platform I need not attempt to describe. His sense of danger during the last days had only been sharpened by the fact that the cloud about him had perceptibly been lighter; but relief was an ominous symptom, and, if Karswell eluded him now, hope was gone: and there were so many chances of that. The rumour of the journey might be itself a device. The twenty minutes in which he paced the platform and persecuted every porter with inquiries as to the boat train were as bitter as any he had spent. Still, the train came, and Harrington was at the window. It was important, of course, that there should be no recognition: so Dunning got in at the farther end of the corridor carriage and only gradually made his way to the compartment where Harrington and Karswell were. He was pleased on the whole to see that the train was far from full.

Karswell was on the alert but gave no sign of recognition. Dunning took the seat not immediately facing him and attempted, vainly at first, then with increasing command of his faculties, to reckon the possibilities of making the desired transfer. Opposite to Karswell and next to Dunning was a heap of Karswell's coats on the seat. It would be of no use to slip the paper into these—he would not be safe, or would not feel so, unless in some way it could be proffered by him and accepted by the other. There was a handbag, open, and with papers in it. Could he manage to conceal this (so that perhaps Karswell might leave the carriage without it), and then find and give it to him? This was the plan that suggested itself. If he could only have counselled with Harrington! but that could not be. The minutes went on. More than once Karswell rose and went out into the corridor. The second time Dunning was on the point of attempting to make the bag fall off the seat, but he caught Harrington's eye, and read in it a warning. Karswell, from the corridor, was watching: probably to see if the two men recognized each other. He returned, but was evidently restless: and when he rose the third time, hope dawned: for something did slip off his seat and fall with hardly a sound to the floor. Karswell went out once more and passed out of range of the corridor window. Dunning picked up what had fallen and saw that the key was in his hands in the form of one of Cook's ticket-cases,* with tickets in it. These cases have a pocket in the cover, and within very few seconds the paper of which we have heard was in the pocket of this one. To make the operation more secure, Harrington stood in the doorway of the compartment and fiddled with the blind. It was done, and done at the right time, for the train was now slowing down towards Dover.

In a moment more Karswell re-entered the compartment. As he did so Dunning, managing, he knew not how, to suppress the tremble in his voice, handed him the ticket-case, saying, 'May I give you this, sir? I believe it is yours.' After a brief glance at the ticket inside, Karswell uttered the hoped-for response, 'Yes, it is; much obliged to you, sir,' and he placed it in his breast pocket.

Even in the few moments that remained—moments of tense anxiety, for they knew not to what a premature finding of the paper might lead—both men noticed that the carriage seemed to darken about them and to grow warmer; that Karswell was fidgety and oppressed; that he drew the heap of loose coats near to him and cast it back as if it repelled him; and that he then sat upright and glanced anxiously at both. They, with sickening anxiety, busied themselves in collecting their belongings: but they both thought that Karswell was on the point of speaking when the train stopped at Dover Town. It was natural that in the short space between town and pier they should both go into the corridor.

At the pier they got out: but so empty was the train that they were forced to linger on the platform until Karswell should have passed ahead of them with his porter on the way to the boat, and only then was it safe for them to exchange a pressure of the hand and a word of concentrated congratulation. The effect upon Dunning was to make him almost faint. Harrington made him lean up against the wall while he himself went forward a few yards within sight of the gangway to the boat, at which Karswell had now arrived. The man at the head of it examined his ticket, and laden with coats he passed down into the boat. Suddenly the official called after him, 'You, sir, beg pardon, did the other gentleman show his ticket?' 'What the devil do you mean by the other gentleman?' Karswell's snarling voice called back from the deck. The man bent over and looked at him. 'The devil? Well, I don't know, I'm sure,' Harrington heard him say to himself, and then aloud, 'My mistake, sir; must have been your rugs! ask your pardon.' And then, to a subordinate near him, ''Ad he got a dog with him, or what? Funny thing: I could 'a' swore 'e wasn't alone. Well, whatever it was, they'll 'ave to see to it aboard. She's off now. Another week and we shall be gettin' the 'oliday customers.' In five minutes more there was nothing but the lessening lights of the boat, the long line of the Dover lamps, the night breeze, and the moon.

Long and long the two sat in their room at the Lord Warden.* In spite of the removal of their greatest anxiety, they were oppressed with a doubt, not of the lightest. Had they been justified in sending a man to his death, as they believed they had? Ought they not to warn him, at least? 'No,' said Harrington; 'if he is the murderer I think him, we have done no more than is just. Still, if you think it better— but how and where can you warn him?' 'He was booked to Abbeville only,' said Dunning. 'I saw that. If I wired to the hotels there in Joanne's guide, "Examine your ticket-case, Dunning", I should feel happier. This is the 21st: he will have a day. But I am afraid he has gone into the dark.' So telegrams were left at the hotel office.

It is not clear whether these reached their destination, or whether, if they did, they were understood. All that is known is that on the afternoon of the 23rd an English traveller examining the front of St Wulfram's Church at Abbeville,* then under extensive repair, was struck on the head and instantly killed by a stone falling from the scaffold erected round the north-western tower, there being, as was clearly proved, no workman on the scaffold at that moment: and the traveller's papers identified him as Mr Karswell.*

Only one detail shall be added. At Karswell's sale a set of Bewick, sold with all faults, was acquired by Harrington. The page with the woodcut of the traveller and the demon was, as he had expected, mutilated. Also, after a judicious interval, Harrington repeated to Dunning something of what he had heard his brother say in his sleep: but it was not long before Dunning stopped him.

THE STALLS OF BARCHESTER
CATHEDRAL

THIS matter began, as far as I am concerned, with the reading of a notice in the obituary section of the *Gentleman's Magazine** for an early year in the nineteenth century:

On February 26th, at his residence in the Cathedral Close of Barchester, the Venerable John Benwell Haynes, D.D., aged 57, Archdeacon of Sowerbridge and Rector of Pickhill and Candley. He was of —— College, Cambridge, and where, by talent and assiduity, he commanded the esteem of his seniors; when, at the usual time, he took his first degree, his name stood high in the list of *wranglers*.* These academical honours procured for him within a short time a Fellowship of his College. In the year 1783 he received Holy Orders, and was shortly afterwards presented to the perpetual Curacy of Ranxton-sub-Ashe by his friend and patron the late truly venerable Bishop of Lichfield. . . . His speedy preferments, first to a Prebend, and subsequently to the dignity of Precentor in the Cathedral of Barchester,* form an eloquent testimony to the respect in which he was held and to his eminent qualifications. He succeeded to the Archdeaconry upon the sudden decease of Archdeacon Pulteney in 1810. His sermons, ever conformable to the principles of the religion and Church which he adorned, displayed in no ordinary degree, without the least trace of enthusiasm, the refinement of the scholar united with the graces of the Christian. Free from sectarian violence, and informed by the spirit of the truest charity, they will long dwell in the memories of his hearers. [Here a further omission.] The productions of his pen include an able defence of Episcopacy, which, though often perused by the author of this tribute to his memory, afford but one additional instance of the want of liberality and enterprise which is a too common characteristic of the publishers of our generation. His published works are, indeed, confined to a spirited and elegant version of the *Argonautica* of Valerius Flaccus,* a volume of *Discourses upon the Several Events in the Life of Joshua*, delivered in his Cathedral, and a number of the charges which he pronounced at various visitations to the clergy of his Archdeaconry. These are distinguished by etc., etc. The urbanity and hospitality of the subject of these lines will not readily be forgotten by those who enjoyed his acquaintance. His interest in the venerable and awful pile under whose hoary vault he was so punctual an attendant, and particularly in the musical portion of its rites, might be termed filial, and formed a strong and delightful contrast to the polite indifference displayed by too many of our Cathedral dignitaries at the present time.

The final paragraph, after informing us that Dr Haynes died a bachelor, says:

It might have been augured that an existence so placid and benevolent would have been terminated in a ripe old age by a dissolution equally gradual and calm. But how unsearchable are the workings of Providence! The peaceful and retired seclusion amid which the honoured evening of Dr Haynes' life was mellowing to its close was destined to be disturbed, nay, shattered, by a tragedy as appalling as it was unexpected. The morning of the 26th of February——

But perhaps I shall do better to keep back the remainder of the narrative until I have told the circumstances which led up to it. These, as far as they are now accessible, I have derived from another source.

I had read the obituary notice which I have been quoting, quite by chance, along with a great many others of the same period. It had excited some little speculation in my mind, but, beyond thinking that, if I ever had an opportunity of examining the local records of the period indicated, I would try to remember Dr Haynes, I made no effort to pursue his case.

Quite lately I was cataloguing the manuscripts in the library of the college to which he belonged. I had reached the end of the numbered volumes on the shelves, and I proceeded to ask the librarian whether there were any more books which he thought I ought to include in my description. 'I don't think there are,' he said, 'but we had better come and look at the manuscript class and make sure. Have you time to do that now?' I had time. We went to the library, checked off the manuscripts, and, at the end of our survey, arrived at a shelf of which I had seen nothing. Its contents consisted for the most part of sermons, bundles of fragmentary papers, college exercises, *Cyrus*, an epic poem in several cantos, the product of a country clergyman's leisure, mathematical tracts by a deceased professor, and other similar material of a kind with which I am only too familiar.* I took brief notes of these. Lastly, there was a tin box, which was pulled out and dusted. Its label, much faded, was thus inscribed: 'Papers of the Ven. Archdeacon Haynes. Bequeathed in 1834 by his sister, Miss Letitia Haynes.'

I knew at once that the name was one which I had somewhere encountered, and could very soon locate it. 'That must be the Archdeacon Haynes who came to a very odd end at Barchester. I've read his obituary in the *Gentleman's Magazine*. May I take the box home? Do you know if there is anything interesting in it?'

The librarian was very willing that I should take the box and examine it at leisure. 'I never looked inside it myself,' he said, 'but I've always been meaning to. I am pretty sure that is the box which our old Master once said ought never to have been accepted by the college. He said that to Martin years ago; and he said also that as long as he had control over the library it should never be opened. Martin told me about it, and said that he wanted terribly to know what was in it; but the Master was librarian, and always kept the box in the lodge, so there was no getting at it in his time, and when he died it was taken away by mistake by his heirs, and only returned a few years ago. I can't think why I haven't opened it; but, as I have to go away from Cambridge this afternoon, you had better have first go at it. I think I can trust you not to publish anything undesirable in our catalogue.'

I took the box home and examined its contents, and thereafter consulted the librarian as to what should be done about publication, and, since I have his leave to make a story out of it, provided I disguise the identity of the people concerned, I will try what can be done.

The materials are, of course, mainly journals and letters. How much I shall quote and how much epitomize must be determined by considerations of space. The proper understanding of the situation has necessitated a little—not very arduous—research, which has been greatly facilitated by the excellent illustrations and text of the Barchester volume in Bell's *Cathedral Series*.

When you enter the choir of Barchester Cathedral now, you pass through a screen of metal and coloured marbles, designed by Sir Gilbert Scott,* and find yourself in what I must call a very bare and odiously furnished place. The stalls are modern, without canopies. The places of the dignitaries and the names of the prebends have fortunately been allowed to survive, and are inscribed on small brass plates affixed to the stalls. The organ is in the triforium, and what is seen of the case is Gothic. The reredos* and its surroundings are like every other.

Careful engravings of a hundred years ago show a very different state of things. The organ is on a massive classical screen. The stalls are also classical and very massive. There is a baldacchino* of wood over the altar, with urns upon its corners. Farther east is a solid altar screen, classical in design, of wood, with a pediment, in which is a triangle surrounded by rays, enclosing certain Hebrew letters in gold. Cherubs contemplate these. There is a pulpit with a great sounding-board at the eastern end of the stalls on the north side, and there is a black and white marble pavement. Two ladies and a gentleman are admiring the general effect. From other sources I gather that the archdeacon's stall then, as now, was next to the bishop's throne at the south-eastern end of the stalls. His house almost faces the west front of the church, and is a fine red-brick building of William the Third's time.

Here Dr Haynes, already a mature man, took up his abode with his sister in the year 1810. The dignity had long been the object of his wishes, but his predecessor refused to depart until he had attained the age of ninety-two. About a week after he had held a modest festival in celebration of that ninety-second birthday, there came a morning, late in the year, when Dr Haynes, hurrying cheerfully into his breakfast-room, rubbing his hands and humming a tune, was greeted, and checked in his genial flow of spirits, by the sight of his sister, seated, indeed, in her usual place behind the tea-urn, but bowed forward and sobbing unrestrainedly into her hand-kerchief. 'What—what is the matter? What bad news?' he began. 'Oh, Johnny, you've not heard? The poor dear arch-deacon!' 'The archdeacon, yes? What is it—ill, is he?' 'No, no; they found him on the staircase this morning; it is so shocking.' 'Is it possible! Dear, dear, poor Pulteney! Had there been any seizure?' 'They don't think so, and that is almost the worst thing about it. It seems to have been all the fault of that stupid maid of theirs, Jane.' Dr Haynes paused. 'I don't quite understand, Letitia. How was the maid at fault?' 'Why, as far as I can make out, there was a stair-rod missing, and she never mentioned it, and the poor arch-deacon set his foot quite on the edge of the step—you know how slippery that oak is—and it seems he must have fallen almost the whole flight and broken his neck. It *is* so sad for poor Miss Pulteney. Of course, they will get rid of the girl at once. I never liked her.' Miss Haynes's grief resumed its sway, but eventually relaxed so far as to permit of her taking some breakfast. Not so her brother, who, after standing in silence before the window for some minutes, left the room, and did not appear again that morning.

I need only add that the careless maid-servant was dis-missed forthwith, but that the missing stair-rod was very shortly afterwards found *under* the stair-carpet—an addi-tional proof, if any were needed, of extreme stupidity and carelessness on her part.

For a good many years Dr Haynes had been marked out by his ability, which seems to have been really considerable, as the likely successor of Archdeacon Pulteney, and no dis-appointment was in store for him. He was duly installed, and entered with zeal upon the discharge of those functions which are appropriate to one in his position. A considerable space in his journals is occupied with exclamations upon the con-fusion in which Archdeacon Pulteney had left the business of his office and the documents appertaining to it. Dues upon Wringham and Barnswood have been uncollected for some-thing like twelve years, and are largely irrecoverable; no visi-tation has been held for seven years; four chancels are almost past mending. The persons deputized by the archdeacon

have been nearly as incapable as himself. It was almost
a matter for thankfulness that this state of things had not
been permitted to continue, and a letter from a friend con-
firms this view. '*ὁ κατέχων*', it says (in rather cruel allusion
to the Second Epistle to the Thessalonians),* 'is removed at
last. My poor friend! Upon what a scene of confusion will
you be entering! I give you my word that, on the last occasion
of my crossing his threshold, there was no single paper that
he could lay hands upon, no syllable of mine that he could
hear, and no fact in connection with my business that he
could remember. But now, thanks to a negligent maid and a
loose stair-carpet, there is some prospect that necessary
business will be transacted without a complete loss alike of
voice and temper.' This letter was tucked into a pocket in the
cover of one of the diaries.

There can be no doubt of the new archdeacon's zeal and
enthusiasm. 'Give me but time to reduce to some semblance
of order the innumerable errors and complications with
which I am confronted, and I shall gladly and sincerely join
with the aged Israelite in the canticle* which too many, I
fear, pronounce but with their lips.' This reflection I find,
not in a diary, but a letter; the doctor's friends seem to have
returned his correspondence to his surviving sister. He does
not confine himself, however, to reflections. His investigation of the rights and duties of his office are very searching
and business-like, and there is a calculation in one place that
a period of three years will just suffice to set the business of
the Archdeaconry upon a proper footing. The estimate
appears to have been an exact one. For just three years he is
occupied in reforms; but I look in vain at the end of that time
for the promised *Nunc dimittis*. He has now found a new
sphere of activity. Hitherto his duties have precluded him
from more than an occasional attendance at the Cathedral
services. Now he begins to take an interest in the fabric
and the music. Upon his struggles with the organist, an old
gentleman who had been in office since 1786, I have no time
to dwell; they were not attended with any marked success.
More to the purpose is his sudden growth of enthusiasm for
the Cathedral itself and its furniture. There is a draft of a

letter to Sylvanus Urban* (which I do not think was ever sent) describing the stalls in the choir. As I have said, these were of fairly late date—of about the year 1700, in fact.

The archdeacon's stall, situated at the south-east end, west of the episcopal throne (now so worthily occupied by the truly excellent prelate who adorns the See of Barchester), is distinguished by some curious ornamentation. In addition to the arms of Dean West, by whose efforts the whole of the internal furniture of the choir was completed, the prayer-desk is terminated at the eastern extremity by three small but remarkable statuettes in the grotesque manner. One is an exquisitely modelled figure of a cat, whose crouching posture suggests with admirable spirit the suppleness, vigilance, and craft of the redoubted adversary of the genus *Mus*.* Opposite to this is a figure seated upon a throne and invested with the attributes of royalty; but it is no earthly monarch whom the carver has sought to portray. His feet are studiously concealed by the long robe in which he is draped: but neither the crown nor the cap which he wears suffice to hide the prick-ears and curving horns which betray his Tartarean origin;* and the hand which rests upon his knee is armed with talons of horrifying length and sharpness. Between these two figures stands a shape muffled in a long mantle. This might at first sight be mistaken for a monk or 'friar of orders gray', for the head is cowled and a knotted cord depends from somewhere about the waist. A slight inspection, however, will lead to a very different conclusion. The knotted cord is quickly seen to be a halter, held by a hand all but concealed within the draperies; while the sunken features and, horrid to relate, the rent flesh upon the cheek-bones, proclaim the King of Terrors. These figures are evidently the production of no unskilled chisel; and should it chance that any of your correspondents are able to throw light upon their origin and significance, my obligations to your valuable miscellany will be largely increased.

There is more description in the paper, and, seeing that the woodwork in question has now disappeared, it has a considerable interest. A paragraph at the end is worth quoting:

Some late researches among the Chapter accounts have shown me that the carving of the stalls was not, as was very usually reported, the work of Dutch artists, but was executed by a native of this city or district named Austin. The timber was procured from an oak copse in the vicinity, the property of the Dean and Chapter, known as Holywood. Upon a recent visit to the parish within whose boundaries it is situated, I learned from the aged and truly respectable incumbent that traditions still lingered amongst the inhabitants of the great size and age of the oaks employed to furnish the materials of the stately structure which has been, however imperfectly, described in the above lines. Of one in particular, which stood near the centre of the grove, it is remembered that it was known as the Hanging Oak. The propriety of that title is confirmed by the fact that a quantity of human bones was found in the soil about its roots, and that at certain times of the year it was the custom for those who wished to secure a successful issue to their affairs, whether of love or the ordinary business of life, to suspend from its boughs small images or puppets rudely fashioned of straw, twigs, or the like rustic materials.

So much for the archdeacon's archaeological investigations. To return to his career as it is to be gathered from his diaries. Those of his first three years of hard and careful work show him throughout in high spirits, and, doubtless, during this time, that reputation for hospitality and urbanity which is mentioned in his obituary notice was well deserved. After that, as time goes on, I see a shadow coming over him— destined to develop into utter blackness—which I cannot but think must have been reflected in his outward demeanour. He commits a good deal of his fears and troubles to his diary; there was no other outlet for them. He was unmarried, and his sister was not always with him. But I am much mistaken if he has told all that he might have told. A series of extracts shall be given:

Aug. 30, 1816. The days begin to draw in more perceptibly than ever. Now that the Archdeaconry papers are reduced to order, I must find some further employment for the evening hours of autumn and winter. It is a great blow that Letitia's health will not allow her to stay through these months. Why not go on with my *Defence of Episcopacy*? It may be useful.

Sept. 15. Letitia has left me for Brighton.

Oct. 11. Candles lit in the choir for the first time at evening prayers. It came as a shock: I find that I absolutely shrink from the dark season.

Nov. 17. Much struck by the character of the carving on my desk: I do not know that I had ever carefully noticed it before. My attention was called to it by an accident. During the *Magnificat* I was, I regret to say, almost overcome with sleep. My hand was resting on the back of the carved figure of a cat which is the nearest to me of the three figures on the end of my stall. I was not aware of this, for I was not looking in that direction, until I was startled by what seemed a softness, a feeling as of rather rough and coarse fur, and a sudden movement, as if the creature were twisting round its head to bite me. I regained complete consciousness in an instant, and I have some idea that I must have uttered a suppressed exclamation, for I noticed that Mr Treasurer turned his head quickly in my direction. The impression of the unpleasant feeling was so strong that I found myself rubbing my hand upon my surplice. This accident led me to examine the figures after prayers more carefully than I had done before, and I realized for the first time with what skill they are executed.

Dec. 6. I do indeed miss Letitia's company. The evenings, after I have worked as long as I can at my *Defence*, are very trying. The house is too large for a lonely man, and visitors of any kind are too rare. I get an uncomfortable impression when going to my room that there *is* company of some kind. The fact is (I may as well formulate it to myself) that I hear voices. This, I am well aware, is a common symptom of incipient decay of the brain—and I believe that I should be less disquieted than I am if I had any suspicion that this was the cause. I have none—none whatever, nor is there anything in my family history to give colour to such an idea. Work, diligent work, and a punctual attention to the duties which fall to me is my best remedy, and I have little doubt that it will prove efficacious.

Jan. 1. My trouble is, I must confess it, increasing upon me. Last night, upon my return after midnight from the Deanery, I lit my candle to go upstairs. I was nearly at the top when something whispered to me, 'Let me wish you a happy New Year.' I could not be mistaken: it spoke distinctly and with a peculiar emphasis. Had I dropped my candle, as I all but did, I tremble to think what the consequences must have been. As it was, I managed to get up the last flight, and was quickly in my room with the door locked, and experienced no other disturbance.

Jan. 15. I had occasion to come downstairs last night to my workroom for my watch, which I had inadvertently left on my table when I went up to bed. I think I was at the top of the last flight when I had a sudden impression of a sharp whisper in my ear '*Take care*'. I clutched the balusters and naturally looked round at once. Of course, there was nothing. After a moment I went on—it was no good turning back—but I had as nearly as possible fallen: a cat—a large one by the feel of it—slipped between my feet, but again, of course, I saw nothing. It *may* have been the kitchen cat, but I do not think it was.

Feb. 27. A curious thing last night, which I should like to forget. Perhaps if I put it down here I may see it in its true proportion. I worked in the library from about 9 to 10. The hall and staircase seemed to be unusually full of what I can only call movement without sound: by this I mean that there seemed to be continuous going and coming, and that whenever I ceased writing to listen, or looked out into the hall, the stillness was absolutely unbroken. Nor, in going to my room at an earlier hour than usual—about half-past ten—was I conscious of anything that I could call a noise. It so happened that I had told John to come to my room for the letter to the bishop which I wished to have delivered early in the morning at the Palace. He was to sit up, therefore, and come for it when he heard me retire. This I had for the moment forgotten, though I had remembered to carry the letter with me to my room. But when, as I was winding up my watch, I heard a light tap at the door, and a low voice saying, 'May I come in?' (which I most undoubtedly did hear), I recollected the fact, and took up the letter from my dressing-table, saying, 'Certainly: come in.' No one, however, answered my summons, and it was now that, as I strongly suspect, I committed an error: for I opened the door and held the letter out. There was certainly no one at that moment in the passage, but, in the instant of my standing there, the door at the end opened and John appeared carrying a candle. I asked him whether he had come to the door earlier; but am satisfied that he had not. I do not like the situation; but although my senses were very much on the alert, and though it was some time before I could sleep, I must allow that I perceived nothing further of an untoward character.

With the return of spring, when his sister came to live with him for some months, Dr Haynes's entries become more cheerful, and, indeed, no symptom of depression is discernible until the early part of September, when he was again left alone. And now, indeed, there is evidence that he was incommoded again, and that more pressingly. To this matter I will return in a moment, but I digress to put in a document which, rightly or wrongly, I believe to have a bearing on the thread of the story.

The account-books of Dr Haynes, preserved along with his other papers, show, from a date but little later than that of his institution as archdeacon, a quarterly payment of £25 to J. L. Nothing could have been made of this, had it stood by itself. But I connect with it a very dirty and ill-written letter, which, like another that I have quoted, was in a pocket in the cover of a diary. Of date or postmark there is no vestige, and the decipherment was not easy. It appears to run:

Dr Sr.

I have bin expctin to her off you theis last wicks, and not Haveing done so must supose you have not got mine witch was saying how me and my man had met in with bad times this season all seems to go cross with us on the farm and which way to look for the rent we have no knowledge of it this been the sad case with us if you would have the great [liberality *probably, but the exact spelling defies reproduction*] to send fourty pounds otherwise steps will have to be took which I should not wish. Has you was the Means of me losing my place with Dr Pulteney I think it is only just what I am asking and you know best what I could say if I was Put to it but I do not wish anything of that unpleasant Nature being one that always wish to have everything Pleasant about me.

Your obedt Servt,

JANE LEE.

About the time at which I suppose this letter to have been written there is, in fact, a payment of £40 to J. L.

We return to the diary:

Oct. 22. At evening prayers, during the Psalms, I had that same experience which I recollect from last year. I was resting my hand on one of the carved figures, as before (I usually avoid that of the cat now), and—I was going to have said—a change came over it, but that seems attributing too much importance to what must, after all, but due to some physical affection in myself: at any rate, the wood seemed to become chilly and soft as if made of wet linen. I can assign the moment at which I became sensible of this. The choir were singing the words [*Set thou an ungodly man to be ruler over him and*] *let Satan stand at his right hand.**

The whispering in my house was more persistent tonight. I seemed not to be rid of it in my room. I have not noticed this before. A nervous man, which I am not, and hope I am not becoming, would have been much annoyed, if not alarmed, by it. The cat was on the stairs tonight. I think it sits there always. There *is* no kitchen cat.

Nov. 15. Here again I must note a matter I do not understand. I am much troubled in sleep. No definite image presented itself, but I was pursued by the very vivid impression that wet lips were whispering into my ear with great rapidity and emphasis for some time together. After this, I suppose, I fell asleep, but was awakened with a start by a feeling as if a hand were laid on my shoulder. To my intense alarm I found myself standing at the top of the lowest flight of the first staircase. The moon was shining brightly enough through the large window to let me see that there was a large cat on the second or third step. I can make no comment. I crept up to bed again, I do not know how. Yes, mine is a heavy burden. [Then follows a line or two which has been scratched out. I fancy I read something like 'acted for the best'.]

Not long after this it is evident to me that the archdeacon's firmness began to give way under the pressure of these phenomena. I omit as unnecessarily painful and distressing the ejaculations and prayers which, in the months of December and January, appear for the first time and become increasingly frequent. Throughout this time, however, he is obstinate in clinging to his post. Why he did not plead ill-health and take refuge at Bath or Brighton I cannot tell; my impression is that it would have done him no good; that he was a man who, if he had confessed himself beaten by the annoyances, would have succumbed at once, and that he was conscious of this. He did seek to palliate them by inviting visitors to his house. The result he has noted in this fashion:

Jan. 7. I have prevailed on my cousin Allen to give me a few days, and he is to occupy the chamber next to mine.

Jan. 8. A still night. Allen slept well, but complained of the wind. My own experiences were as before: still whispering and whispering: what is it that he wants to say?

Jan. 9. Allen thinks this a very noisy house. He thinks, too, that my cat is an unusually large and fine specimen, but very wild.

Jan. 10. Allen and I in the library until 11. He left me twice to see what the maids were doing in the hall: returning the second time he told me he had seen one of them passing through the door at the end of the passage, and said if his wife were here she would soon get them into better order. I asked him what coloured dress the maid wore; he said grey or white. I supposed it would be so.

Jan. 11. Allen left me today. I must be firm.

These words, *I must be firm*, occur again and again on subsequent days; sometimes they are the only entry. In these cases they are in an unusually large hand, and dug into the paper in a way which must have broken the pen that wrote them.

Apparently the archdeacon's friends did not remark any change in his behaviour, and this gives me a high idea of his courage and determination. The diary tells us nothing more than I have indicated of the last days of his life. The end of it all must be told in the polished language of the obituary notice:

The morning of the 26th of February was cold and tempestuous. At an early hour the servants had occasion to go into the front hall of the residence occupied by the lamented subject of these lines. What was their horror upon observing the form of their beloved and respected master lying upon the landing of the principal staircase in an attitude which inspired the gravest fears. Assistance was procured, and an universal consternation was experienced upon the discovery that he had been the object of a brutal and a murderous attack. The vertebral column was fractured in more than one place. This might have been the result of a fall: it appeared that the stair-carpet was loosened at one point. But, in addition to this, there were injuries inflicted upon the eyes, nose and mouth, as if by the agency of some savage animal, which, dreadful to relate, rendered those features unrecognizable. The vital spark was, it is needless to add, completely extinct, and had been so, upon the testimony of respectable medical authorities, for several hours. The author or authors of this mysterious outrage are alike buried in mystery, and the most active conjecture has hitherto failed to suggest a solution of the melancholy problem afforded by this appalling occurrence.

The writer goes on to reflect upon the probability that the writings of Mr Shelley, Lord Byron, and M. Voltaire* may have been instrumental in bringing about the disaster, and concludes by hoping, somewhat vaguely, that this event may 'operate as an example to the rising generation'; but this portion of his remarks need not be quoted in full.

I had already formed the conclusion that Dr Haynes was responsible for the death of Dr Pulteney. But the incident connected with the carved figure of death upon the archdeacon's stall was a very perplexing feature. The conjecture that it had been cut out of the wood of the Hanging Oak was not difficult, but seemed impossible to substantiate. However, I paid a visit to Barchester, partly with the view of finding out whether there were any relics of the woodwork to be heard of. I was introduced by one of the canons to the curator of the local museum, who was, my friend said, more likely to be able to give me information on the point than anyone else. I told this gentleman of the description of certain carved figures and arms formerly on the stalls, and asked whether any had survived. He was able to show me the arms of Dean West and some other fragments. These, he said, had been got from an old resident, who had also once owned a figure— perhaps one of those which I was inquiring for. There was a very odd thing about that figure, he said. 'The old man who had it told me that he picked it up in a wood-yard, whence he had obtained the still extant pieces, and had taken it home for his children. On the way home he was fiddling about with it and it came in two in his hands, and a bit of paper dropped out. This he picked up and, just noticing that there was writing on it, put it into his pocket, and subsequently into a vase on his mantelpiece. I was at his house not very long ago, and happened to pick up the vase and turn it over to see whether there were any marks on it, and the paper fell into my hand. The old man, on my handing it to him, told me the story I have told you, and said I might keep the paper. It was crumpled and rather torn, so I have mounted it on a card, which I have here. If you can tell me what it means I shall be very glad, and also, I may say, a good deal surprised.'

He gave me the card. The paper was quite legibly inscribed in an old hand, and this is what was on it:

> When I grew in the Wood
> I was water'd wth Blood
> Now in the Church I stand
> Who that touches me with his Hand
> If a Bloody hand he bear
> I councell him to be ware
> Lest he be fetcht away
> Whether by night or day,
> But chiefly when the wind blows high
> In a night of February.

This I drempt, 26 Febr. A° 1699. JOHN AUSTIN.

'I suppose it is a charm or a spell: wouldn't you call it something of that kind?' said the curator.

'Yes,' I said, 'I suppose one might. What became of the figure in which it was concealed?'

'Oh, I forgot,' said he. 'The old man told me it was so ugly and frightened his children so much that he burnt it.'

MR HUMPHREYS AND HIS
INHERITANCE

ABOUT fifteen years ago, on a date late in August or early
in September, a train drew up at Wilsthorpe, a country
station in eastern England. Out of it stepped (with other
passengers) a rather tall and reasonably good-looking young
man, carrying a hand bag and some papers tied up in a
packet.

He was expecting to be met, one would say, from the way
in which he looked about him: and he was, as obviously,
expected. The stationmaster ran forward a step or two, and
then, seeming to recollect himself, turned and beckoned to a
stout and consequential person with a short round beard who
was scanning the train with some appearance of bewilderment. 'Mr Cooper,' he called out, 'Mr Cooper, I think this
is your gentleman'; and then, to the passenger who had just
alighted, 'Mr Humphreys, sir? Glad to bid you welcome to
Wilsthorpe.* There's a cart from the Hall for your luggage,
and here's Mr Cooper, what I think you know.' Mr Cooper
had hurried up, and now raised his hat and shook hands.
'Very pleased, I'm sure,' he said, 'to give the echo to Mr
Palmer's kind words. I should have been the first to render
expression to them but for the face not being familiar to me,
Mr Humphreys. May your residence among us be marked
as a red-letter day, sir.' 'Thank you very much, Mr Cooper,'
said Humphreys, 'for your good wishes, and Mr Palmer also.
I do hope very much that this change of—er—tenancy—
which you must all regret, I am sure—will not be to the
detriment of those with whom I shall be brought in contact.'
He stopped, feeling that the words were not fitting themselves
together in the happiest way, and Mr Cooper cut in. 'Oh you
may rest satisfied of that, Mr Humphreys. I'll take it upon
myself to assure you, sir, that a warm welcome awaits you on
all sides. And as to any change of propriety* turning out
detrimental to the neighbourhood, well, your late uncle——'
and here Mr Cooper also stopped, possibly in obedience to an

inner monitor, possibly because Mr Palmer, clearing his throat loudly, asked Humphreys for his ticket. The two men left the little station, and—at Humphreys' suggestion— decided to walk to Mr Cooper's house, where luncheon was awaiting them.

The relation in which these personages stood to each other can be explained in a very few lines. Humphreys had inherited—quite unexpectedly—a property from an uncle: neither the property nor the uncle had he ever seen. He was alone in the world—a man of good ability and kindly nature, whose employment in a government office for the last four or five years had not gone far to fit him for the life of a country gentleman. He was studious and rather diffident, and had few out-of-door pursuits except golf and gardening. Today he had come down for the first time to visit Wilsthorpe and confer with Mr Cooper the bailiff as to the matters which needed immediate attention. It may be asked how this came to be his first visit? Ought he not in decency to have attended his uncle's funeral? The answer is not far to seek: he had been abroad at the time of the death, and his address had not been at once procurable. So he had put off coming to Wilsthorpe till he heard that all things were ready for him. And now we find him arrived at Mr Cooper's comfortable house, facing the parsonage, and having just shaken hands with the smiling Mrs and Miss Cooper.

During the minutes that preceded the announcement of luncheon the party settled themselves on elaborate chairs in the drawing-room, Humphreys, for his part, perspiring quietly in the consciousness that stock was being taken of him.

'I was just saying to Mr Humphreys, my dear,' said Mr Cooper, 'that I hope and trust that his residence among us here in Wilsthorpe will be marked as a red-letter day.'

'Yes indeed, I'm sure,' said Mrs Cooper heartily, 'and many, many of them.'

Miss Cooper murmured words to the same effect, and Humphreys attempted a pleasantry about painting the whole calendar red, which, though greeted with shrill laughter, was evidently not fully understood. At this point they proceeded to luncheon.

'Do you know this part of the country at all, Mr Humphreys?' said Mrs Cooper after a short interval. This was a better opening.

'No, I'm sorry to say I do *not*,' said Humphreys. 'It seems very pleasant, what I could see of it coming down in the train.'

'Oh it *is* a pleasant part. Really, I sometimes say I don't know a nicer district for the country; and the people round, too: such a quantity always going on. But I'm afraid you've come a little late for some of the better garden parties, Mr Humphreys.'

'I suppose I have; dear me, what a pity!' said Humphreys with a gleam of relief; and then, feeling that something more could be got out of this topic, 'But after all, you see, Mrs Cooper, even if I could have been here earlier, I should have been cut off from them, should I not? My poor uncle's recent death, you know——'

'Oh dear, Mr Humphreys, to be sure, what a dreadful thing of me to say!' (And Mr and Miss Cooper seconded the proposition inarticulately.) 'What must you have thought? I *am* so sorry: you must really forgive me.'

'Not at all Mrs Cooper, I assure you. I can't honestly assert that my uncle's death was a great grief to me, for I had never seen him. All I meant was that I supposed I shouldn't be expected to take part for some little time in festivities of that kind.'

'Now really it's very kind of you to take it in that way, Mr Humphreys, isn't it George? And you *do* forgive me? But only fancy! You never saw poor old Mr Wilson!'

'Never in my life; nor did I ever have a letter from him. But, by the way, you have something to forgive *me* for. I've never thanked you except by letter for all the trouble you've taken to find people to look after me at the Hall.'

'Oh I'm sure that was nothing, Mr Humphreys; but I really do think that you'll find them give satisfaction. The man and his wife whom we've got for the butler and housekeeper we've known for a number of years: such a nice respectable couple, and Mr Cooper I'm sure can answer for the men in the stables and gardens.'

'Yes, Mr Humphreys, they're a good lot. The head gardener's the only one who's stopped on from Mr Wilson's time. The major part of the employees, as you no doubt saw by the will, received legacies from the old gentleman and retired from their posts, and as the wife says, your housekeeper and butler are calculated to render you every satisfaction.'

'So everything, Mr Humphreys, is ready for you to step in this very day, according to what I understood you to wish,' said Mrs Cooper. 'Everything, that is, except company, and there I'm afraid you'll find yourself quite at a standstill. Only we did understand it was your intention to move in at once. If not I'm sure you know we should have been only too pleased for you to stay here.'

'I'm quite sure you would, Mrs Cooper, and I'm very grateful to you. But I thought I had really better make the plunge at once. I'm accustomed to living alone, and there will be quite enough to occupy my evenings—looking over papers and books and so on—for some time to come. I thought if Mr Cooper could spare the time this afternoon to go over the house and grounds with me——'

'Certainly, certainly Mr Humphreys. My time is your own, up to any hour you please—'

'Till dinner-time, father, you mean,' said Miss Cooper. 'Don't forget we're going over to the Brasnetts'. And have you got all the garden keys?'

'Are you a great gardener, Miss Cooper?' said Mr Humphreys. 'I wish you would tell me what I'm to expect at the Hall.'

'Oh I don't know about a *great* gardener, Mr Humphreys: I'm very fond of flowers—but the Hall garden might be made quite lovely, I often say. It's very old-fashioned as it is: and a great deal of shrubbery. There's an old temple, besides, and a maze.'

'Really? Have you explored it ever?'

'No-o,' said Miss Cooper drawing in her lips and shaking her head. 'I've often longed to try, but old Mr Wilson always kept it locked. He wouldn't even let Lady Wardrop into it. (She lives near here, at Bentley, you know, and she's a *great* gardener, if you like.) That's why I asked father if he had all the keys.'

'I see: well, I must evidently look into that, and show you over it when I've learnt the way.'

'Oh thank you so much, Mr Humphreys! Now I shall have the laugh of Miss Foster (that's our rector's daughter, you know—they're away on their holiday now—such nice people). We always had a joke between us which should be the first to get into the maze.'

'I think the garden keys must be up at the house,' said Mr Cooper, who had been looking over a large bunch. 'There is a number there in the library. Now, Mr Humphreys, if you're prepared, we might bid goodbye to these ladies and set forward on our little tour of exploration.'

As they came out of Mr Cooper's front gate, Humphreys had to run the gauntlet—not of an organized demonstration, but of a good deal of touching of hats and careful contemplation from the men and women who had gathered in somewhat unusual numbers in the village street. He had further to exchange some remarks with the wife of the lodge-keeper as they passed the park gates, and with the lodge-keeper himself, who was attending to the park road. I cannot, however, spare the time to report the progress fully. As they traversed the half-mile or so between the lodge and the house, Humphreys took occasion to ask his companion some question which brought up the topic of his late uncle, and it did not take long before Mr Cooper was embarked upon a disquisition.

'It is singular to think, as the wife was saying just now, that you should never have seen the old gentleman. And yet—you won't misunderstand me, Mr Humphreys, I feel confident, when I say that in my opinion there would have been but little congeniality betwixt yourself and him. Not that I have a word to say in deprecation—not a single word. I can tell you what he was,' said Mr Cooper, pulling up suddenly and fixing Humphreys with his eye. 'Can tell you what he was in a nutshell, as the saying goes. He was a complete, thorough, valentudinarian.* That describes him to a T. That's what he was, sir, a complete valentudinarian. No participation in what went on around him. I did venture, I think, to send you a few words of cutting from our local paper which I took the occasion to contribute on his decease. If I recollect myself aright such is very much the ghist of them. But don't, Mr Humphreys,' continued Cooper, tapping him impressively on the chest, 'don't you run away with the impression that I wish to say aught but what is most creditable—*most* creditable—of your respected uncle and my late employer. Upright, Mr Humphreys, open as the day; liberal to all in his dealings. He had the heart to feel and the hand to accommodate.* But there it was: there was the stumbling-block—his unfortunate health—or as I might more truly phrase it, his *want* of health.'

'Yes, poor man. Did he suffer from any special disorder before his last illness—which I take it was little more than old age?'

'Just that, Mr Humphreys—just that. The flash flickering slowly away in the pan,' said Cooper with what he considered an appropriate gesture, '—the golden bowl* gradually ceasing to vibrate. But as to your other question I should return a negative answer. General absence of vitality? yes: special complaint? no, unless you reckon a nasty cough he had with him. Why, here we are pretty much at the house. A handsome mansion Mr Humphreys, don't you consider?'

It deserved the epithet on the whole: but it was oddly proportioned—a very tall red-brick house with a plain parapet concealing the roof almost entirely. It gave the impression of a town house set down in the country; there was a basement, and a rather imposing flight of steps leading up to the front door. It seemed also, owing to its height, to desiderate wings, but there were none. The stables and other offices were concealed by trees. Humphreys guessed its probable date at 1770 or thereabouts.

The mature couple who had been engaged to act as butler and cook-housekeeper were waiting inside the front door, and opened it as their new master approached. Their name, Humphreys already knew, was Calton; of their appearance and manner he formed a favourable impression in the few

minutes' talk he had with them. It was agreed that he
should go through the plate and the cellar next day with
Mr Calton, and that Mrs C. should have a talk with him
about linen, bedding, and so on—what there was, and what
there ought to be. Then he and Cooper, dismissing the
Caltons for the present, began their view of the house. Its
topography is not of importance to this story. The large
rooms on the ground floor were satisfactory, especially the
library, which was as large as the dining-room and had three
tall windows facing east. The bedroom prepared for Humphreys was immediately above it. There were many pleasant,
and a few really interesting, old pictures. None of the furniture was new, and hardly any of the books were later than
the seventies. After hearing of and seeing the few changes
his uncle had made in the house, and contemplating a shiny
portrait of him which adorned the drawing-room, Humphreys
was forced to agree with Cooper that in all probability there
would have been little to attract him in his predecessor. It
made him rather sad that he could not be sorry (*dolebat se
dolere non posse**) for the man who, whether with or without
some feeling of kindliness towards his unknown nephew, had
contributed so much to his well-being; for he felt that
Wilsthorpe was a place in which he could be happy, and
especially happy, it might be, in its library.

And now it was time to go over the garden: the empty
stables could wait, and so could the laundry. So to the garden
they addressed themselves, and it was soon evident that Miss
Cooper had been right in thinking that there were possibilities. Also that Mr Cooper had done well in keeping on
the gardener. The deceased Mr Wilson might not have,
indeed plainly had not, been imbued with the latest views
on gardening, but whatever had been done here had been
done under the eye of a knowledgeable man, and the equipment and stock were excellent. Cooper was delighted with
the pleasure Humphreys showed, and with the suggestions
he let fall from time to time. 'I can see,' he said, 'that you've
found your meatear* here, Mr Humphreys: you'll make this
place a regular signosier before very many seasons have
passed over our heads. I wish Clutterham had been here—

that's the head gardener—and here he would have been of course, as I told you, but for his son's being horse doover* with a fever, poor fellow! I should like him to have heard how the place strikes you.'

'Yes, you told me he couldn't be here today, and I was very sorry to hear the reason, but it will be time enough tomorrow. What is that white building on the mound at the end of the grass ride? Is it the temple Miss Cooper mentioned?'

'That it is, Mr Humphreys—the Temple of Friendship. Constructed of marble brought out of Italy for the purpose by your late uncle's grandfather. Would it interest you perhaps to take a turn there? You get a very sweet prospect of the park.'

The general lines of the temple were those of the Sibyl's Temple at Tivoli,* helped out by a dome, only the whole was a good deal smaller. Some ancient sepulchral reliefs were built into the wall and about it all was a pleasant flavour of the grand tour. Cooper produced the key and with some difficulty opened the heavy door. Inside there was a handsome ceiling, but little furniture. Most of the floor was occupied by a pile of thick circular blocks of stone, each of which had a single letter deeply cut on its slightly convex upper surface. 'What is the meaning of these?' Humphreys inquired.

'Meaning? Well, all things we're told have their purpose Mr Humphreys, and I suppose these blocks have had theirs as well as another. But what that purpose is or was [Mr Cooper assumed a didactic attitude here] I for one should be at a loss to point out to you, sir. All I know of them—and it's summed up in a very few words—is just this: that they're stated to have been removed by your late uncle at a period before I entered on the scene, from the maze. That, Mr Humphreys, is——'

'Oh, the maze!' exclaimed Humphreys. 'I'd forgotten that: we must have a look at it. Where is it?'

Cooper drew him to the door of the temple and pointed with his stick. 'Guide your eye,' he said (somewhat in the manner of the second Elder in Handel's *Susanna**—

> Far to the west direct your straining eyes
> Where yon tall holm-tree rises to the skies.)

'Guide your eye by my stick here, and follow out the line directly opposite to the spot where we're standing now, and I'll engage, Mr Humphreys, that you'll catch the archway over the entrance. You'll see it just at the end of the walk answering to the one that leads up to this very building. Did you think of going there at once? because if that be the case, I must go to the house and procure the key. If you would walk on there, I'll rejoin you in a few moments' time.'

Accordingly Humphreys strolled down the ride leading to the temple, past the garden-front of the house, and up the turfy approach to the archway which Cooper had pointed out to him. He was surprised to find that the whole maze was surrounded by a high wall and that the archway was provided with a padlocked iron gate; but then he remembered that Miss Cooper had spoken of his uncle's objection to letting anyone enter this part of the garden. He was now at the gate, and still Cooper came not. For a few minutes he occupied himself in reading the motto cut over the entrance— *Secretum meum mihi et filiis domus meae**—and in trying to recollect the source of it. Then he became impatient, and considered the possibility of scaling the wall. This was clearly not worth while; it might have been done if he had been wearing an older suit: or could the padlock—a very old one— be forced? No, apparently not: and yet, as he gave a final irritated kick at the gate, something gave way, and the lock fell at his feet. He pushed the gate open, inconveniencing a number of nettles as he did so, and stepped into the enclosure.

It was a yew maze* of circular form and the hedges, long untrimmed, had grown out and upwards to a most unorthodox breadth and height. The walks, too, were next door to impassable. Only by entirely disregarding scratches, nettle-stings, and wet could Humphreys force his way along them; but at any rate this condition of things, he reflected, would make it easier for him to find his way out again, for he left a very visible track. So far as he could remember he had never been in a maze before, nor did it seem to him now that he had missed much. The dankness and darkness and smell of crushed goosegrass and nettles were anything but cheerful. Still, it did not seem to be a very intricate specimen of its kind. Here he was (by the way, was that Cooper arrived at last? No) very nearly at the heart of it without having taken much thought as to what path he was following. Ah, there at last was the centre, easily gained. And there was something to reward him.

His first impression was that the central ornament was a sundial, but when he had switched away some portion of the thick growth of brambles and bindweed that had formed over it, he saw that it was a less ordinary decoration. A stone column about four feet high and on the top of it a metal globe—copper, to judge by the green patina—engraved, and finely engraved, too, with figures in outline, and letters. That was what Humphreys saw, and a brief glance at the figures convinced him that it was one of those mysterious things called celestial globes,* from which, one would suppose, no one ever yet derived any information about the heavens. However, it was too dark—at least in the maze—for him to examine this curiosity at all closely, and besides, he now heard Cooper's voice, and sounds as of an elephant in the jungle. Humphreys called to him to follow the track he had beaten out, and soon Cooper emerged panting into the central circle. He was full of apologies for his delay; he had not been able, after all, to find the key. 'But there!' he said, 'you've penetrated into the heart of the mystery unaided and unannealed, as the saying goes. Well! I suppose it's a matter of thirty to forty years since any human foot has trod these precincts. Certain it is that I've never set foot in them before. Well, well, what's the old proverb about angels fearing to tread?* It's proved true once again in this case.' Humphreys' acquaintance with Cooper, though it had been short, was sufficient to assure him that there was no guile in this allusion, and he forbore the obvious remark, merely suggesting that it was fully time to get back to the house for a late cup of tea and to release Cooper for his evening engagement. They left the maze accordingly, experiencing wellnigh the same ease in retracing their path as they had in coming in.

'Have you any idea,' Humphreys asked, as they went

towards the house, 'why my uncle kept that place so carefully locked?'

Cooper pulled up, and Humphreys felt that he must be on the brink of a revelation.

'I should merely be deceiving you, Mr Humphreys, and that to no good purpose, if I laid claim to possess any information whatsoever on that topic. When I first entered upon my duties here some eighteen years back that maze was word for word in the condition you see it now, and the one and only occasion on which the question ever arose within my knowledge was that of which my girl made mention in your hearing. Lady Wardrop—I've not a word to say against her—wrote applying for admission to the maze. Your uncle showed me the note—a most civil note—everything that could be expected from such a quarter. "Cooper," he said, "I wish you'd reply to that note on my behalf." "Certainly Mr Wilson," I said, for I was quite inured to acting as his secretary, "what answer shall I return to it?" "Well," he said, "give Lady Wardrop my compliments and tell her that if ever that portion of the grounds is taken in hand I shall be happy to give her the first opportunity of viewing it, but that it has been shut up now for a number of years and I shall be grateful to her if she kindly won't press the matter." That, Mr Humphreys, was your good uncle's last word on the subject, and I don't think I can add anything to it. Unless,' added Cooper after a pause, 'it might be just this: that, so far as I could form a judgment, he had a dislike (as people often will for one reason or another) to the memory of his grandfather, who, as I mentioned to you, had that maze laid out. A man of peculiar teenets,* Mr Humphreys, and a great traveller. You'll have the opportunity, on the coming Sabbath, of seeing the tablet to him in our little parish church; put up it was some long time after his death.'

'Oh? I should have expected a man who had such a taste for building to have designed a mausoleum for himself.'

'Well, I've never noticed anything of the kind you mention; and in fact, come to think of it, I'm not at all sure that his resting-place is within our boundaries at all: that he lays in the vault I'm pretty confident is not the case. Curious now, that I shouldn't be in a position to inform you on that heading! Still, after all, we can't say, can we Mr Humphreys, that it's a point of crucial importance where the pore mortal coils are bestowed?'

At this point they entered the house, and Cooper's speculations were interrupted.

Tea was laid in the library, where Mr Cooper fell upon subjects appropriate to the scene. 'A fine collection of books! One of the finest, I've understood from connoisseurs, in this part of the country; splendid plates, too, in some of these works. I recollect your uncle showing me one with views of foreign towns—most absorbing it was: got up in first-rate style. And another all done by hand, with the ink as fresh as if it had been laid on yesterday, and yet he told me it was the work of some old monk hundreds of years back. I've always taken a keen interest in literature myself. Hardly anything to my mind can compare with a good hour's reading after a hard day's work; far better than wasting the whole evening at a friend's house—and that reminds me, to be sure. I shall be getting into trouble with the wife if I don't make the best of my way home and get ready to squander away one of these same evenings! I must be off, Mr Humphreys.'

'And that reminds *me*,' said Humphreys, 'if I'm to show Miss Cooper the maze tomorrow, we must have it cleared out a bit. Could you say a word about that to the proper person?'

'Why to be sure. A couple of men with scythes could cut out a track tomorrow morning. I'll leave word as I pass the lodge, and I'll tell them what'll save you the trouble, perhaps, Mr Humphreys, of having to go up and extract them yourself: that they'd better have some sticks or a tape to mark out their way with as they go on.'

'A very good idea—yes, do that; and I'll expect Mrs and Miss Cooper in the afternoon, and yourself about half-past ten in the morning.'

'It'll be a pleasure I'm sure both to them and to myself, Mr Humphreys. Good night!'

Humphreys dined at eight. But for the fact that it was his

first evening, and that Calton was evidently inclined for occasional conversation, he would have finished the novel he had bought for his journey. As it was, he had to listen and reply to some of Calton's impressions of the neighbourhood and the season: the latter, it appeared, was seasonable, and the former had changed considerably—and not altogether for the worse —since Calton's boyhood (which had been spent there). The village shop in particular had greatly improved since the year 1870. It was now possible to procure there pretty much anything you liked in reason: which was a conveniency, because suppose anythink was required of a suddent (and he had known such things before now) he, Calton, could step down there (supposing the shop to be still open) and order it in, without he borrered it of the Rectory, whereas in earlier days it would have been useless to pursue such a course in respect of anything but candles or soap or treacle or perhaps a penny child's picture-book, and nine times out of ten it'd be something more in the nature of a bottle of whisky *you'd* be requiring, leastways—— On the whole Humphreys thought he would be prepared with a book in future.

The library was the obvious place for the after-dinner hours. Candle in hand and pipe in mouth, he moved round the room for some time taking stock of the titles of the books. He had all the predisposition to take interest in an old library, and there was every opportunity for him here to make systematic acquaintance with one, for he had learned from Cooper that there was no catalogue save the very superficial one made for purposes of probate. The drawing up of a *catalogue raisonné** would be a delicious occupation for winter. There were probably treasures to be found, too: even manuscripts if Cooper might be trusted.

As he pursued his round the sense came upon him (as it does upon most of us in similar places) of the extreme unreadableness of a great portion of the collection. 'Editions of classics and Fathers,* and Picart's *Religious Ceremonies*, and the *Harleian Miscellany*, I suppose are all very well, but who is ever going to read Tostatus Abulensis, or Pineda on Job,* or a book like this?' He picked out a small quarto, loose in the binding, and from which the lettered label had fallen off; and observing that coffee was waiting for him, retired to a chair. Eventually he opened the book. It will be observed that his condemnation of it rested wholly on external grounds: for all he knew it might have been a collection of unique plays, but undeniably the outside was blank and forbidding. As a matter of fact, it was a collection of sermons or meditations, and mutilated at that, for the first sheet was gone. It seemed to belong to the latter end of the seventeenth century. He turned over the pages till his eye was caught by a marginal note: 'A *Parable of this Unhappy Condition*', and he thought he would see what aptitudes the author might have for imaginative composition.

'I have heard or read,' so ran the passage, 'whether in the way of *Parable* or true *Relation* I leave my Reader to judge, of a Man who like *Theseus* in the *Attick Tale** should adventure himself, into a *Labyrinth* or *Maze*: and such a one indeed as was not laid out in the Fashion of our *Topiary* artists of this Age, but of a wide compass, in which moreover such unknown Pitfalls and Snares, nay, such ill omened Inhabitants were commonly thought to lurk as could only be encountered at the Hazard of one's very life. Now you may be sure that in such a Case the Disswasions of Friends were not wanting. "Consider of such-an-one" says a Brother "how he went the way you wot of, and was never seen more." "Or of such another" says the Mother "that adventured himself but a little way in, and from that day forth is so troubled in his Wits that he cannot tell what he saw, nor hath passed one good Night." "And have you never heard" cries a Neighbour "of what Faces have been seen to look out over the *Palisadoes* and betwixt the Bars of the Gate?" But all would not do: the Man was set upon his Purpose: for it seems it was the common fireside Talk of that Country that at the Heart and Centre of this *Labyrinth* there was a Jewel of such Price and Rarity that would enrich the Finder thereof for his life: and this should be his by right that could persever to come at it. What then? *Quid multa?* The Adventurer pass'd the Gates and for a whole day's space his Friends without had no news of him, except it might be by some indistinct Cries heard afar off in the Night, such as made them turn in their

restless Beds and sweat for very Fear, not doubting but that
their Son and Brother had put one more to the *Catalogue* of
those unfortunates that had suffer'd shipwreck on that
Voyage. So the next day they went with weeping Tears to
the Clark of the Parish to order the Bell to be toll'd. And their
Way took them hard by the gate of the *Labyrinth*: which
they would have hastened by, from the Horrour they had of
it, but that they caught sight of a sudden of a Man's Body
lying in the Roadway, and going up to it (with what Antici-
pations may be easily figured) found it to be him whom they
reckoned as lost: and not dead, though he were in a Swound
most like death. They then who had gone forth as Mourners
came back rejoycing and set to by all means to revive their
Prodigal. Who being come to himself and hearing of their
Anxieties and their Errand of that Morning, "Ay" says he
"you may as well finish what you were about: for, for all
I have brought back the Jewel (which he shew'd them, and
'twas indeed a rare Piece) I have brought back that with it
that will leave me neither Rest at Night nor Pleasure by
Day." Whereupon they were instant with him to learn his
Meaning, and where his Company should be that went so
sore against his Stomach. "O" says he " 'tis here in my Breast:
I cannot flee from it, do what I may." So it needed no Wizard
to help them to a guess that it was the Recollection of what
he had seen that troubled him so wonderfully. But they
could get no more of him for a long Time but by Fits and
Starts. However at long and at last they made shift to collect
somewhat of this kind: that at first, while the Sun was bright,
he went merrily on, and without any Difficulty reached the
Heart of the *Labyrinth* and got the Jewel, and so set out on
his Way back rejoycing: but as the Night fell, *wherein all
the Beasts of the Forest do move,* he begun to be sensible of
some Creature keeping Pace with him and, as he thought,
peering and looking upon him from the next Alley to that
he was in; and that when he should stop, this Companion
should stop also, which put him in some Disorder of his
Spirits. And indeed as the Darkness increas'd, it seemed to
him that there was more than one, and, it might be, even a
whole Band of such Followers: at least so he judg'd by the

Rustling and Cracking that they kept among the Thickets; besides that there would be at a Time a Sound of Whispering, which seem'd to import a Conference among them. But in regard of who they were or what Form they were of, he would not be persuaded to say what he thought. Upon his Hearers asking him what the Cries were which they heard in the Night (as was observ'd above) he gave them this Account: That about Midnight (so far as he could judge) he heard his Name call'd from a long way off, and he would have been sworn it was his Brother that so call'd him. So he stood still and hilloo'd at the Pitch of his Voice, and he suppos'd that the *Echo*, or the Noyse of his Shouting, disguis'd for the Moment any lesser sound; because, when there fell a Stillness again, he distinguish'd a Trampling (not loud) of running Feet coming very close behind him, wherewith he was so daunted that himself set off to run, and that he continued till the dawn broke. Sometimes when his Breath fail'd him, he would cast himself flat on his Face, and hope that his Pursuers might over-run him in the darkness, but at such a Time they would regularly make a Pause, and he could hear them pant and snuff as it had been a Hound at Fault:* which wrought in him so extream an Horrour of mind, that he would be forc'd to betake himself again to turning and doubling, if by any Means he might throw them off the Scent. And, as if this Exertion was in itself not terrible enough, he had before him the constant Fear of falling into some Pit or Trap, of which he had heard and indeed seen with his own Eyes that there were several, some at the sides and other in the midst, of the Alleys. So that in fine (he said) a more dreadful Night was never spent by Mortal Creature than that he had endur'd in that *Labyrinth*, and not that Jewel which he had in his Wallet nor the richest that was ever brought out of the *Indies* could be a sufficient Recompence to him for the Pains he had suffered.

'I will spare to set down the further Recital of this Man's Troubles, inasmuch as I am confident my Reader's Intelligence will hit the *Parallel* I desire to draw. For is not this Jewel a just Emblem of the Satisfaction which a Man may bring back with him from a Course of this World's Pleasures?

and will not the *Labyrinth* serve for an Image of the World itself wherein such a Treasure (if we may believe the common Voice) is stored up?'

At about this point Humphreys thought that a little Patience* would be an agreeable change, and that the writer's 'improvement' of his Parable might be left to itself. So he put the book back in its former place, wondering as he did so whether his uncle had ever stumbled across that passage; and if so whether it had worked on his fancy so much as to make him dislike the idea of a maze, and determine to shut up the one in the garden. Not long afterwards he went to bed.

The next day brought a morning's hard work with Mr Cooper who, if exuberant in language, had the business of the estate at his fingers' ends. He was very breezy this morning, Mr Cooper was: had not forgotten the order to clear out the maze—the work was going on at that moment: his girl was on the tentacles of expectation about it. He also hoped that Humphreys had slept the sleep of the just and that we should be favoured with a continuance of this congenial weather. At luncheon he enlarged on the pictures in the dining-room and pointed out the portrait of the constructor of the temple and the maze. Humphreys examined this with considerable interest. It was the work of an Italian, and had been painted when old Mr Wilson was visiting Rome as a young man. (There was, indeed, a view of the Colosseum in the background.) A pale thin face and large eyes were the characteristic features. In the hand was a partially unfolded roll of paper on which could be distinguished the plan of a circular building, very probably the temple, and also part of that of a labyrinth. Humphreys got up on a chair to examine it, but it was not painted with sufficient clearness to be worth copying. It suggested to him however that he might as well make a plan of his own maze and hang it in the hall for the use of visitors.

This determination of his was confirmed that same afternoon; for when Mrs and Miss Cooper arrived, eager to be inducted into the maze, he found that he was wholly unable to lead them to the centre. The gardeners had removed the guide-marks they had been using, and even Clutterham, when summoned to assist, was as helpless as the rest. 'The point is, you see, Mr Wilson—I should say 'Umphreys—these mazes is purposely constructed so much alike, with a view to mislead. Still, if you'll foller me, I think I can put you right. I'll just put my 'at down 'ere as a starting-point.' He stumped off and after five minutes brought the party safe to the hat again. 'Now that's a very peculiar thing,' he said, with a sheepish laugh. 'I made sure I'd left that 'at just over against a bramble-bush and you can see for yourself there ain't no bramble-bush not in this walk at all. If you'll allow me, Mr Humphreys—that's the name, ain't it, sir?—I'll just call one of the men in to mark the place like.'

William Crack arrived in answer to repeated shouts. He had some difficulty in making his way to the party. First he was seen or heard in an inside alley, then—almost at the same moment—in an outer one. However, he joined them at last and was first consulted without effect and then stationed by the hat, which Clutterham still considered it necessary to leave on the ground. In spite of this strategy, they spent the best part of three-quarters of an hour in quite fruitless wanderings, and Humphreys was obliged at last, seeing how tired Mrs Cooper was becoming, to suggest a retreat to tea, with profuse apologies to Miss Cooper. 'At any rate you've won your bet with Miss Foster,' he said; 'you have been inside the maze, and I promise you the first thing I do shall be to make a proper plan of it with the lines marked out for you to go by.' 'That's what's wanted, sir,' said Clutterham, 'someone to draw out a plan and keep it by them. It might be very awkward you see anyone getting into that place and a shower of rain come on and them not able to find their way out again; it might be hours before they could be got out, without you'd permit of me makin' a short cut to the middle: what my meanin' is, takin' down a couple of trees in each 'edge in a straight line so as you could git a clear view right through. Of course that'd do away with it as a maze, but I don't know as you'd approve of that.'

'No, I won't have that done yet: I'll make a plan first and

let you have a copy. Later on if we find occasion I'll think of what you say.'

Humphreys was vexed and ashamed at the fiasco of the afternoon and could not be satisfied without making another effort that evening to reach the centre of the maze. His irritation was increased by finding it without a single false step. He had thoughts of beginning his plan at once; but the light was fading, and he felt that by the time he had got the necessary materials together, work would be impossible.

Next morning accordingly, carrying a drawing-board, pencils, compasses, cartridge paper, and so forth (some of which had been borrowed from the Coopers and some found in the library cupboards), he went to the middle of the maze (again without any hesitation) and set out his materials. He was however delayed in making a start. The brambles and weeds that had obscured the column and globe were now all cleared away and it was for the first time possible to see clearly what these were like. The column was featureless, resembling those on which sundials are usually placed. Not so the globe. I have said that it was finely engraved with figures and inscriptions and that on a first glance Humphreys had taken it for a celestial globe: but he soon found that it did not answer to his recollection of such things. One feature seemed familiar: a winged serpent—*Draco*—encircled it about the place which, on a terrestrial globe, is occupied by the equator: but on the other hand, a good part of the upper hemisphere was covered by the outspread wings of a large figure whose head was concealed by a ring at the pole or summit of the whole. Around the place of the head the words *princeps tenebrarum** could be deciphered. In the lower hemisphere there was a space hatched all over with cross-lines and marked as *umbra mortis.** Near it was a range of mountains and among them a valley with flames rising from it. This was lettered (will you be surprised to learn it?) *vallis filiorum Hinnom.** Above and below *Draco* were outlined various figures not unlike the pictures of the ordinary constellations, but not the same. Thus, a nude man with a raised club was described not as *Hercules* but as *Cain*. Another, plunged up to his middle in earth and stretching out despairing arms, was *Chore* not *Ophiuchus*, and a third, hung by his hair to a snaky tree, was *Absolon*. Near the last a man in long robes and high cap standing in a circle and addressing two shaggy demons who hovered outside was described as *Hostanes magus* (a character unfamiliar to Humphreys). The scheme of the whole, indeed, seemed to be an assemblage of the patriarchs of evil, perhaps not uninfluenced by a study of Dante. Humphreys thought it an unusual exhibition of his great-grandfather's taste but reflected that he had probably picked it up in Italy and had never taken the trouble to examine it closely: certainly, had he set much store by it, he would not have exposed it to wind and weather. He tapped the metal; it seemed hollow and not very thick, and, turning from it, addressed himself to his plan. After half an hour's work he found it was impossible to get on without using a clue. So he procured a roll of twine from Clutterham, and laid it out along the alleys from the entrance to the centre, tying the end to the ring at the top of the globe. This expedient helped him to set out a rough plan before luncheon, and in the afternoon he was able to draw it in more neatly. Towards tea-time Mr Cooper joined him and was much interested in his progress. 'Now this——' said Mr Cooper laying his hand on the globe, and then drawing it away hastily. 'Whew! Holds the heat, doesn't it, to a surprising degree Mr Humphreys. I suppose this metal—copper, isn't it?—would be an insulator or conductor, or whatever they call it.'

'The sun has been pretty strong this afternoon,' said Humphreys, evading the scientific point, 'but I didn't notice the globe had got hot. No—it doesn't seem very hot to me,' he added.

'Odd,' said Mr Cooper. 'Now I can't hardly bear my hand on it. Something in the difference of temperament between us, I suppose. I dare say you're a chilly subject, Mr Humphreys: I'm not: and there's where the distinction lies. All this summer I've slept, if you'll believe me, practically *in statu quo*, and had my morning tub as cold as I could get it. Day out and day in—let me assist you with that string.'

'It's all right, thanks; but if you'll collect some of these pencils and things that are lying about I shall be much obliged. Now I think we've got everything, and we might get back to the house.'

They left the maze, Humphreys rolling up the clue as they went. The night was rainy.

Most unfortunately it turned out that, whether by Cooper's fault or not, the plan had been the one thing forgotten the evening before. As was to be expected, it was ruined by the wet. There was nothing for it but to begin again (the job would not be a long one this time). The clue therefore was put in place once more and a fresh start made. But Humphreys had not done much before an interruption came in the shape of Calton with a telegram. His late chief in London wanted to consult him. Only a brief interview was wanted, but the summons was urgent. This was annoying, yet it was not really upsetting. There was a train available in half an hour, and unless things went very cross he could be back, possibly by five o'clock, certainly by eight. He gave the plan to Calton to take to the house, but it was not worth while to remove the clue.

All went as he had hoped. He spent a rather exciting evening in the library, for he lighted tonight upon a cupboard where some of the rarer books were kept. When he went up to bed he was glad to find that the servant had remembered to leave his curtains undrawn and his windows open. He put down his light and went to the window which commanded a view of the garden and the park. It was a brilliant moonlight night. In a few weeks' time the sonorous winds of autumn would break up all this calm, but now the distant woods were in a deep stillness. The slopes of the lawns were shining with dew: the colours of some of the flowers could almost be guessed. The light of the moon just caught the cornice of the temple and the curve of its leaden dome, and Humphreys had to own that so seen these conceits of a past age have a real beauty. In short, the light, the perfume of the woods, and the absolute quiet called up such kind old associations in his mind that he went on ruminating them for a long long time. As he turned from the window he felt he had never seen anything more complete of its sort. The one feature that struck him with a sense of incongruity was a small Irish yew, thin and black, which stood out like an outpost of the shrubbery through which the maze was approached. That, he thought, might as well be away: the wonder was that anyone should have thought it would look well in that position.

However, next morning, in the press of answering letters and going over books with Mr Cooper, the Irish yew was forgotten. One letter, by the way, arrived this day which has to be mentioned. It was from that Lady Wardrop whom Miss Cooper had mentioned and it renewed the application which she had addressed to Mr Wilson. She pleaded in the first place that she was about to publish a Book of Mazes and earnestly desired to include the plan of the Wilsthorpe Maze, and also that it would be a great kindness if Mr Humphreys could let her see it (if at all) at an early date, since she would soon have to go abroad for the winter months. Her house at Bentley was not far distant, so Humphreys was able to send a note by hand to her suggesting the very next day or the day after for her visit; it may be said at once that the messenger brought back a most grateful answer, to the effect that the morrow would suit her admirably.

The only other event of the day was that the plan of the maze was successfully finished.

This night again was fair and brilliant and calm, and Humphreys lingered almost as long at his window. The Irish yew came to his mind again as he was on the point of drawing his curtains: but either he had been misled by a shadow the night before or else the shrub was not really so obtrusive as he had fancied. Anyhow he saw no reason for interfering with it. What he *would* do away with, however, was a clump of dark growth which had usurped a place against the house wall and was threatening to obscure one of the lower range of windows. It did not look as if it could possibly be worth keeping; he fancied it dank and unhealthy, little as he could see of it.

Next day (it was a Friday—he had arrived at Wilsthorpe on a Monday) Lady Wardrop came over in her car soon after luncheon. She was a stout elderly person, very full of talk of all sorts and particularly inclined to make herself agreeable to Humphreys, who had gratified her very much by his ready granting of her request. They made a thorough exploration of the place together and Lady Wardrop's opinion of her host obviously rose sky-high when she found that he really knew something of gardening. She entered enthusiastically into all his plans for improvement, but agreed that it would be a vandalism to interfere with the characteristic laying-out of the ground near the house. With the temple she was particularly delighted and, said she, 'Do you know, Mr Humphreys, I think your bailiff must be right about those lettered blocks of stone. One of my mazes (I'm sorry to say the stupid people have destroyed it now—it was at a place in Hampshire) had the track marked out in that way. They were tiles there but lettered just like yours, and the letters taken in the right order formed an inscription—what it was I forget—something about Theseus and Ariadne. I have a copy of it as well as the plan of the maze where it was. How people can do such things! I shall never forgive you if you injure *your* maze. Do you know, they're becoming very uncommon? Almost every year I hear of one being grubbed up. Now do let's get straight to it: or if you're too busy, I know my way there perfectly, and I'm not afraid of getting lost in it: I know too much about mazes for that. Though I remember missing my lunch—not so very long ago either—through getting entangled in the one at Busbury. Well, of course, if you *can* manage to come with me, that will be all the nicer.'

After this confident prelude justice would seem to require that Lady Wardrop should have been hopelessly muddled by the Wilsthorpe maze. Nothing of that kind happened: yet it is to be doubted whether she got all the enjoyment from her new specimen that she expected. She was interested—keenly interested—to be sure, and pointed out to Humphreys a series of little depressions in the ground which she thought marked the places of the lettered blocks. She told him, too, what other mazes resembled his most closely in arrangement, and explained how it was usually possible to date a maze to within twenty years by means of its plan. This one, she already knew, must be about as old as 1780 and its features were just what might be expected. The globe, furthermore, completely absorbed her. It was unique in her experience, and she pored over it for long. 'I should like a rubbing of that,' she said, 'if it could possibly be made—yes, I am sure you would be most kind about it, Mr Humphreys, but I trust you won't attempt it on my account, I do indeed; I shouldn't like to take any liberties here. I have the feeling that it might be resented. Now, confess,' she went on, turning and facing Humphreys, 'don't you feel—haven't you felt ever since you came in here—that a watch is being kept on us and that if we overstepped the mark in any way there would be a—well, a pounce? No? I do—and I don't care how soon we are outside the gate.

'After all,' she said, when they were once more on their way to the house, 'it may have been only the airlessness and the dull heat of that place that pressed on my brain. Still, I'll take back one thing I said. I'm not sure that I shan't forgive you after all if I find next spring that that maze has been grubbed up.'

'Whether or no that's done, you shall have the plan, Lady Wardrop. I have made one, and no later than tonight I can trace you a copy.'

'Admirable: a pencil tracing will be all I want, with an indication of the scale. I can easily have it brought into line with the rest of my plates. Many, many thanks.'

'Very well, you shall have that tomorrow. I wish you could help me to a solution of my block-puzzle.'

'What, those stones in the summerhouse? That *is* a puzzle; they are in no sort of order? Of course not. But the men who put them down must have had some directions—perhaps you'll find a paper about it among your uncle's things. If not, you'll have to call in somebody who's an expert in cyphers.'

'Advise me about something else, please,' said Humphreys. 'That bush-thing under the library window: you would have that away, wouldn't you?'

'Which? That? Oh I think not,' said Lady Wardrop. 'I can't see it very well from this distance, but it's not unsightly.'

'Perhaps you're right; only looking out of my window just above it last night, I thought it took up too much room. It doesn't seem to, as one sees it from here, certainly. Very well, I'll leave it alone for a bit.'

Tea was the next business, soon after which Lady Wardrop drove off; but half-way down the drive she stopped the car and beckoned to Humphreys, who was still on the front-door steps. He ran to glean her parting words, which were: 'It just occurs to me, it might be worth your while to look at the underside of those stones. They *must* have been numbered, mustn't they? *Good*-bye again. Home, please.'

The main occupation of this evening at any rate was settled. The tracing of the plan for Lady Wardrop and the careful collation of it with the original meant a couple of hours' work at least. Accordingly, soon after nine Humphreys had his materials put out in the library and began. It was a still stuffy evening; windows had to stand open and he had more than one grisly encounter with a bat. These unnerving episodes made him keep the tail of his eye on the window. Once or twice it was a question whether there was—not a bat, but something more considerable—that had a mind to join him. How unpleasant it would be if someone had slipped noiselessly over the sill, and was crouching on the floor!

The tracing of the plan was done: it remained to compare it with the original and to see whether any paths had been wrongly closed or left open. With one finger on each paper he traced out the course that must be followed from the entrance. There were one or two slight mistakes, but here, near the centre, was a bad confusion, probably due to the entry of the second or third bat. Before correcting the copy he followed out carefully the last turnings of the path on the original. These at least were right; they led without a hitch to the middle space. Here was a feature which need not be repeated on the copy—an ugly black spot about the size of a shilling. Ink? No. It resembled a hole, but how should a hole be there? He stared at it with tired eyes: the work of tracing had been very laborious and he was drowsy and oppressed. But surely this was a very odd hole. It seemed to

go not only through the paper but through the table on which it lay. Yes, and through the floor below that, down, and still down, even into infinite depths. He craned over it utterly bewildered. Just as, when you were a child, you may have pored over a square inch of counterpane until it became a landscape with wooded hills, and perhaps even churches and houses, and you lost all thought of the true size of your-self and it, so this hole seemed to Humphreys for the moment the only thing in the world. For some reason it was hateful to him from the first, but he had gazed at it for some moments before any feeling of anxiety came upon him; and then it did come, stronger and stronger—a horror lest some-thing might emerge from it, and a really agonizing conviction that a terror was on its way, from the sight of which he would not be able to escape. Oh yes, far, far down there was a movement, and the movement was upwards—towards the surface. Nearer and nearer it came, and it was of a blackish-grey colour with more than one dark hole. It took shape as a face—a human face—a *burnt* human face: and with the odious writhings of a wasp creeping out of a rotten apple there clambered forth an appearance of a form, waving black arms prepared to clasp the head that was bending over them.*
With a convulsion of despair Humphreys threw himself back, struck his head against a hanging lamp, and fell.

There was concussion of the brain, shock to the system, and a long confinement to bed. The doctor was badly puzzled, not by the symptoms, but by a request which Humphreys made to him as soon as he was able to say anything. 'I wish you would open the ball in the maze.' 'Hardly room enough there, I should have thought,' was the best answer he could summon up; 'but it's more in your way than mine: my dancing days are over.' At which Humphreys muttered and turned over to sleep, and the doctor intimated to the nurses that the patient was not out of the wood yet. When he was better able to express his views, Humphreys made his meaning clear, and received a promise that the thing should be done at once. He was so anxious to learn the result that the doctor, who seemed a little pensive next morning, saw that more harm than good would be done by saving up his report.

'Well,' he said, 'I am afraid the ball is done for; the metal must have worn thin I suppose. Anyhow it went all to bits with the first blow of the chisel.' 'Well? go on, do!' said Humphreys impatiently. 'Oh, you want to know what we found in it, of course. Well, it was half full of stuff like ashes.' 'Ashes? What did you make of them?' 'I haven't thoroughly examined them yet; there's hardly been time: but Cooper's made up his mind—I dare say from something I ˙said—that it's a case of cremation. Now don't excite yourself, my good sir: yes, I must allow I think he's probably right.'

The maze is gone, and Lady Wardrop has forgiven Humphreys; in fact I believe he married her niece. She was right, too, in her conjecture that the stones in the temple were numbered. There had been a numeral painted on the bottom of each. Some few of these had rubbed off, but enough remained to enable Humphreys to reconstruct the inscription. It ran thus:

PENETRANS AD INTERIORA MORTIS.*

Grateful as Humphreys was to the memory of his uncle, he could not quite forgive him for having burnt the journals and letters of the James Wilson who had gifted Wilsthorpe with the maze and the temple. As to the circumstances of that ancestor's death and burial no tradition survived; but his will, which was almost the only record of him accessible, assigned an unusually generous legacy to a servant who bore an Italian name.

Mr Cooper's view is that, humanly speaking, all these many solemn events have a meaning for us, if our limited intelligence permitted of our disintegrating it, while Mr Calton has been reminded of an aunt now gone from us, who about the year 1866 had been lost for upwards of an hour and a half in the maze at Covent Gardens, or it might be Hampton Court.

One of the oddest things in the whole series of transactions is that the book which contained the Parable has entirely disappeared. Humphreys has never been able to find it since he copied out the passage to send to Lady Wardrop.

THE DIARY OF MR POYNTER

THE sale-room of an old and famous firm of book auctioneers in London is, of course, a great meeting-place for collectors, librarians, and dealers: not only when an auction is in progress, but perhaps even more notably when books that are coming on for sale are upon view. It was in such a sale-room that the remarkable series of events began which were detailed to me not many months ago by the person whom they principally affected—namely, Mr James Denton, M.A., F.S.A.,* etc., etc., sometime of Trinity Hall, now, or lately, of Rendcomb Manor in the county of Warwick.

He, on a certain spring day in a recent year, was in London for a few days upon business connected principally with the furnishing of the house which he had just finished building at Rendcomb. It may be a disappointment to you to learn that Rendcomb Manor was new; that I cannot help. There had, no doubt, been an old house; but it was not remarkable for beauty or interest. Even had it been, neither beauty nor interest would have enabled it to resist the disastrous fire which about a couple of years before the date of my story had razed it to the ground. I am glad to say that all that was most valuable in it had been saved, and that it was fully insured. So that it was with a comparatively light heart that Mr Denton was able to face the task of building a new and considerably more convenient dwelling for himself and his aunt who constituted his whole *ménage*.

Being in London, with time on his hands, and not far from the sale-room at which I have obscurely hinted, Mr Denton thought that he would spend an hour there upon the chance of finding, among that portion of the famous Thomas collection of MSS, which he knew to be then on view, something bearing upon the history or topography of his part of Warwickshire.

He turned in accordingly, purchased a catalogue and ascended to the sale-room, where, as usual, the books were disposed in cases and some laid out upon the long tables. At the shelves, or sitting about at the tables, were figures, many of whom were familiar to him. He exchanged nods and greetings with several, and then settled down to examine his catalogue and note likely items. He had made good progress through about two hundred of the five hundred lots —every now and then rising to take a volume from the shelf and give it a cursory glance—when a hand was laid on his shoulder, and he looked up. His interrupter was one of those intelligent men with a pointed beard and a flannel shirt, of whom the last quarter of the nineteenth century was, it seems to me, very prolific.

It is no part of my plan to repeat the whole conversation which ensued between the two. I must content myself with stating that it largely referred to common acquaintances, e.g., to the nephew of Mr Denton's friend who had recently married and settled in Chelsea, to the sister-in-law of Mr Denton's friend who had been seriously indisposed, but was now better, and to a piece of china which Mr Denton's friend had purchased some months before at a price much below its true value. From which you will rightly infer that the conversation was rather in the nature of a monologue. In due time, however, the friend bethought himself that Mr Denton was there for a purpose, and said he, 'What are you looking out for in particular? I don't think there's much in this lot.' 'Why, I thought there might be some Warwickshire collections, but I don't see anything under Warwick in the catalogue.' 'No, apparently not,' said the friend. 'All the same, I believe I noticed something like a Warwickshire diary. What was the name again? Drayton? Potter? Painter—either a P or a D, I feel sure.' He turned over the leaves quickly. 'Yes, here it is. Poynter. Lot 486. That might interest you. There are the books, I think: out on the table. Someone has been looking at them. Well, I must be getting on. Good-bye— you'll look us up, won't you? Couldn't you come this afternoon? we've got a little music about four. Well, then, when you're next in town.' He went off. Mr Denton looked at his watch and found to his confusion that he could spare no more than a moment before retrieving his luggage and going for the train. The moment was just enough to show him that there were four largish volumes of the diary—that it concerned the years about 1710, and that there seemed to be a good many insertions in it of various kinds. It seemed quite worth while to leave a commission of five and twenty pounds for it, and this he was able to do, for his usual agent entered the room as he was on the point of leaving it.

That evening he rejoined his aunt at their temporary abode, which was a small dower-house not many hundred yards from the Manor. On the following morning the two resumed a discussion that had now lasted for some weeks as to the equipment of the new house. Mr Denton laid before his relative a statement of the results of his visit to town—particulars of carpets, of chairs, of wardrobes, and of bedroom china. 'Yes, dear,' said his aunt, 'but I don't see any chintzes here. Did you go to ——?' Mr Denton stamped on the floor (where else, indeed, could he have stamped?). 'Oh dear, oh dear,' he said, 'the one thing I missed. I *am* sorry. The fact is I was on my way there and I happened to be passing Robins's.' His aunt threw up her hands. 'Robins's! Then the next thing will be another parcel of horrible old books at some outrageous price. I do think, James, when I am taking all this trouble for you, you might contrive to remember the one or two things which I specially begged you to see after. It's not as if I was asking it for myself. I don't know whether you think I get any pleasure out of it, but if so I can assure you it's very much the reverse. The thought and worry and trouble I have over it you have no idea of, and *you* have simply to go to the shops and order the things.' Mr Denton interposed a moan of penitence. Oh, aunt——' 'Yes, that's all very well, dear, and I don't want to speak sharply, but you *must* know how very annoying it is: particularly as it delays the whole of our business for I can't tell how long: here is Wednesday—the Simpsons come tomorrow, and you can't leave them. Then on Saturday we have friends, as you know, coming for tennis. Yes, indeed, you spoke of asking them yourself, but, of course, I had to write the notes, and it is ridiculous, James, to look like that. We must occasionally be civil to our neighbours: you wouldn't like to have it said we were perfect bears. What was I saying? Well, anyhow it comes to this, that it must be Thursday in next week at least, before you can go to town again, and until we have decided upon the chintzes it is impossible to settle upon one single other thing.'

Mr Denton ventured to suggest that as the paint and wallpapers had been dealt with, this was too severe a view: but this his aunt was not prepared to admit at the moment. Nor, indeed, was there any proposition he could have advanced which she would have found herself able to accept. However, as the day went on, she receded a little from this position: examined with lessening disfavour the samples and price lists submitted by her nephew, and even in some cases gave a qualified approval to his choice.

As for him, he was naturally somewhat dashed by the consciousness of duty unfulfilled, but more so by the prospect of a lawn-tennis party, which, though an inevitable evil in August, he had thought there was no occasion to fear in May. But he was to some extent cheered by the arrival on the Friday morning of an intimation that he had secured at the price of £12 10s. the four volumes of Poynter's manuscript diary, and still more by the arrival on the next morning of the diary itself.

The necessity of taking Mr and Mrs Simpson for a drive in the car on Saturday morning and of attending to his neighbours and guests that afternoon prevented him from doing more than open the parcel until the party had retired to bed on the Saturday night. It was then that he made certain of the fact, which he had before only suspected, that he had indeed acquired the diary of Mr William Poynter, Squire of Acrington (about four miles from his own parish)— that same Poynter who was for a time a member of the circle of Oxford antiquaries, the centre of which was Thomas Hearne,* and with whom Hearne seems ultimately to have quarrelled—a not uncommon episode in the career of that excellent man. As is the case with Hearne's own collections, the diary of Poynter contained a good many notes from printed books, descriptions of coins and other antiquities that had been brought to his notice, and drafts of letters on these subjects, besides the chronicle of everyday events. The description in the sale catalogue had given Mr Denton no idea of the amount of interest which seemed to lie in the book, and he sat up reading in the first of the four volumes until a reprehensibly late hour.

On the Sunday morning, after church, his aunt came into the study and was diverted from what she had been going to say to him by the sight of the four brown leather quartos on the table. 'What are these?' she said suspiciously. 'New, aren't they? Oh! are these the things that made you forget my chintzes? I thought so. Disgusting. What did you give for them, I should like to know? Over Ten Pounds? James, it is really sinful. Well, if you have money to throw away on this kind of thing, there *can* be no reason why you should not subscribe—and subscribe handsomely—to my anti-Vivisection League. There is not, indeed, James, and I shall be very seriously annoyed it——. Who did you say wrote them? Old Mr Poynter, of Acrington? Well, of course, there is some interest in getting together old papers about this neighbourhood. But Ten Pounds!' She picked up one of the volumes—not that which her nephew had been reading —and opened it at random, dashing it to the floor the next instant with a cry of disgust as an earwig fell from between the pages. Mr Denton picked it up with a smothered expletive and said, 'Poor book! I think you're rather hard on Mr Poynter.' 'Was I, my dear? I beg his pardon, but you know I cannot abide those horrid creatures. Let me see if I've done any mischief.' 'No, I think all's well: but look here what you've opened him on.' 'Dear me, yes, to be sure! how very interesting. Do unpin it, James, and let me look at it.'

It was a piece of patterned stuff about the size of the quarto page, to which it was fastened by an old-fashioned pin. James detached it and handed it to his aunt, carefully replacing the pin in the paper.

Now, I do not know exactly what the fabric was; but it had a design printed upon it, which completely fascinated Miss Denton. She went into raptures over it, held it against the wall, made James do the same, that she might retire to contemplate it from a distance: then pored over it at close quarters, and ended her examination by expressing in the warmest terms her appreciation of the taste of the ancient Mr Poynter who had had the happy idea of preserving this sample in his diary. 'It is a most charming pattern,' she said, 'and remarkable too. Look, James, how delightfully the lines ripple. It reminds one of hair, very much, doesn't it? And then these knots of ribbon at intervals. They give just the relief of colour that is wanted. I wonder——' 'I was going to say,' said James with deference, 'I wonder if it would cost much to have it copied for our curtains.' 'Copied? how could you have it copied, James?' 'Well, I don't know the details, but I suppose that is a printed pattern, and that you could have a block cut from it in wood or metal.' 'Now, really, that is a capital idea, James. I am almost inclined to be glad that you were so—that you forgot the chintzes on Wednesday. At any rate, I'll promise to forgive and forget if you get this *lovely* old thing copied. No one will have anything in the least like it, and mind, James, we won't allow it to be sold. Now I *must* go, and I've totally forgotten what it was I came in to say: never mind, it'll keep.'

After his aunt had gone James Denton devoted a few minutes to examining the pattern more closely than he had yet had a chance of doing. He was puzzled to think why it should have struck Miss Denton so forcibly. It seemed to him not specially remarkable or pretty. No doubt it was suitable enough for a curtain pattern: it ran in vertical bands, and there was some indication that these were intended to converge at the top. She was right, too, in thinking that these main bands resembled rippling—almost curling—tresses of hair. Well, the main thing was to find out by means of trade directories, or otherwise, what firm would undertake the reproduction of an old pattern of this kind. Not to delay the reader over this portion of the story, a list of likely names was made out, and Mr Denton fixed a day for calling on them, or some of them, with his sample.

The first two visits which he paid were unsuccessful: but there is luck in odd numbers. The firm in Bermondsey which was third on his list was accustomed to handling this line. The evidence they were able to produce justified their being entrusted with the job. 'Our Mr Cattell' took a fervent personal interest in it. 'It's 'eartrending, isn't it, sir,' he said, 'to picture the quantity of reelly lovely medeevial stuff of this kind that lays wellnigh unnoticed in many of our residential country 'ouses: much of it in peril, I take it, of being cast aside as so much rubbish. What is it Shakespeare says—unconsidered trifles.* Ah, I often say he 'as a word for us all, sir. I say Shakespeare, but I'm well aware all don't 'old with me there—I 'ad something of an upset the other day when a gentleman came in—a titled man, too, he was, and I think he told me he'd wrote on the topic, and I 'appened to cite out something about 'Ercules and the painted cloth.* Dear me, you never see such a pother. But as to this, what you've kindly confided to us, it's a piece of work we shall take a reel enthusiasm in achieving it out to the very best of our ability. What man 'as done, as I was observing only a few weeks back to another esteemed client, man can do, and in three to four weeks' time, all being well, we shall 'ope to lay before you evidence to that effect, sir. Take the address, Mr 'Iggins, if you please.'

Such was the general drift of Mr Cattell's observations on the occasion of his first interview with Mr Denton. About a month later, being advised that some samples were ready for his inspection, Mr Denton met him again, and had, it seems, reason to be satisfied with the faithfulness of the reproduction of the design. It had been finished off at the top in accordance with the indication I mentioned, so that the vertical bands joined. But something still needed to be done in the way of matching the colour of the original. Mr Cattell had suggestions of a technical kind to offer, with which I need not trouble you. He had also views as to the general desirability of the pattern which were vaguely adverse. 'You say you don't wish this to be supplied excepting to personal friends equipped with a authorization from yourself, sir. It shall be done. I quite understand your wish to keep it exclusive: lends a catchit,* does it not, to the suite? What's every man's, it's been said, is no man's.'

'Do you think it would be popular if it were generally obtainable?' asked Mr Denton.

'I 'ardly think it, sir,' said Cattell, pensively clasping his beard. 'I 'ardly think it. Not popular: it wasn't popular with the man that cut the block, was it, Mr 'Iggins?'

'Did he find it a difficult job?'

'He'd no call to do so, sir; but the fact is that the artistic temperament—and our men are artists, sir, every one of them—true artists as much as many that the world styles by that term—it's apt to take some strange 'ardly accountable likes or dislikes, and here was an example. The twice or thrice that I went to inspect his progress: language I could understand, for that's 'abitual to him, but reel distaste for what I should call a dainty enough thing, I did not, nor am I now able to fathom. It seemed,' said Mr Cattell, looking narrowly upon Mr Denton, 'as if the man scented something almost Hevil in the design.'

'Indeed? did he tell you so? I can't say I see anything sinister in it myself.'

'Neether can I, sir. In fact I said as much. "Come, Gatwick," I said, "what's to do here? What's the reason of your prejudice—for I can call it no more than that?" But, no! no explanation was forthcoming. And I was merely reduced, as I am now, to a shrug of the shoulders, and a *cui bono*. However, here it is,' and with that the technical side of the question came to the front again.

The matching of the colours for the background, the hem, and the knots of ribbon was by far the longest part of the business, and necessitated many sendings to and fro of the original pattern and of new samples. During part of August and September, too, the Dentons were away from the Manor. So that it was not until October was well in that a sufficient quantity of the stuff had been manufactured to furnish curtains for the three or four bedrooms which were to be fitted up with it.

On the feast of Simon and Jude* the aunt and nephew returned from a short visit to find all completed, and their satisfaction at the general effect was great. The new curtains, in particular, agreed to admiration with their surroundings. When Mr Denton was dressing for dinner, and took stock of his room, in which there was a large amount of the chintz displayed, he congratulated himself over and over again on the luck which had first made him forget his aunt's commission and had then put into his hands this extremely effective means of remedying his mistake. The pattern was, as he said at dinner, so restful and yet so far from being dull. And Miss Denton—who, by the way, had none of the stuff in her own room—was much disposed to agree with him.

At breakfast next morning he was induced to qualify his satisfaction to some extent—but very slightly. 'There is one thing I rather regret,' he said, 'that we allowed them to join up the vertical bands of the pattern at the top. I think it would have been better to leave that alone.'

'Oh?' said his aunt interrogatively.

'Yes: as I was reading in bed last night they kept catching my eye rather. That is, I found myself looking across at them every now and then. There was an effect as if someone kept peeping out between the curtains in one place or another, where there was no edge, and I think that was due to the joining up of the bands at the top. The only other thing that troubled me was the wind.'

'Why, I thought it was a perfectly still night.'

'Perhaps it was only on my side of the house, but there was enough to sway my curtains and rustle them more than I wanted.'

That night a bachelor friend of James Denton's came to stay, and was lodged in a room on the same floor as his host, but at the end of a long passage, half-way down which was a red baize door, put there to cut off the draught and intercept noise.

The party of three had separated. Miss Denton a good first, the two men at about eleven. James Denton, not yet inclined for bed, sat him down in an arm-chair and read for a time. Then he dozed, and then he woke, and bethought himself that his brown spaniel, which ordinarily slept in his room, had not come upstairs with him. Then he thought he was mistaken: for happening to move his hand which hung down over the arm of the chair within a few inches of the floor, he felt on the back of it just the slightest touch of a surface of hair, and stretching it out in that direction he stroked and patted a rounded something. But the feel of it, and still more the fact that instead of a responsive movement, absolute stillness greeted his touch, made him look over the arm. What he had been touching rose to meet him. It was in the attitude of one that had crept along the floor on its belly, and it was, so far as could be recollected, a human figure. But of the face which was now rising to within a few inches of his own no feature was discernible, only hair. Shapeless as it was, there was about it so horrible an air of menace that as he bounded from his chair and rushed from the room he heard himself moaning with fear: and doubtless he did right to fly. As he dashed into the baize door that cut the passage in two, and—forgetting that it opened towards him—beat against it with all the force in him, he felt a soft ineffectual tearing at his back which, all the same, seemed to be growing in power, as if the hand, or whatever worse than a hand was there, were becoming more material as the pursuer's rage was more concentrated. Then he remembered the trick of the door—he got it open—he shut it behind him —he gained his friend's room, and that is all we need know.

It seems curious that, during all the time that had elapsed since the purchase of Poynter's diary, James Denton should not have sought an explanation of the presence of the pattern that had been pinned into it. Well, he had read the diary through without finding it mentioned, and had concluded that there was nothing to be said. But, on leaving Rendcomb Manor (he did not know whether for good), as he naturally insisted upon doing on the day after experiencing the horror I have tried to put into words, he took the diary with him. And at his seaside lodgings he examined more narrowly the portion whence the pattern had been taken. What he remembered having suspected about it turned out to be correct. Two or three leaves were pasted together, but written upon, as was patent when they were held up to the light. They yielded easily to steaming, for the paste had lost much of its strength and they contained something relevant to the pattern.

The entry was made in 1707.

Old Mr Casbury, of Acrington, told me this day much of young Sir Everard Charlett, whom he remember'd Commoner of University College, and thought was of the same family as Dr Arthur

Charlett, now master of yᵉ Coll. This Charlett was a personable young gent., but a loose atheistical companion, and a great Lifter, as they then call'd the hard drinkers, and for what I know do so now. He was noted, and subject to severall censures at different times for his extravagancies: and if the full history of his debaucheries had bin known, no doubt would have been expell'd yᵉ Coll., supposing that no interest had been imploy'd on his behalf, of which Mr Casbury had some suspicion. He was a very beautiful person, and constantly wore his own Hair, which was very abundant, from which, and his loose way of living, the cant name for him was Absalom,* and he was accustom'd to say that indeed he believ'd he had shortened old David's days, meaning his father, Sir Job Charlett, an old worthy cavalier.

Note that Mr Casbury said that he remembers not the year of Sir Everard Charlett's death, but it was 1692 or 3. He died suddenly in October. [Several lines describing his unpleasant habits and reputed delinquencies are omitted.] Having seen him in such topping spirits the night before, Mr Casbury was amaz'd when he learn'd the death. He was found in the town ditch, the hair as was said pluck'd clean off his head. Most bells in Oxford rung out for him, being a nobleman, and he was buried next night in St Peter's in the East. But two years after, being to be moved to his country estate by his successor, it was said the coffin, breaking by mischance, proved quite full of Hair: which sounds fabulous, but yet I believe precedents are upon record, as in Dr Plot's *History of Staffordshire.**

His chambers being afterwards stripp'd, Mr Casbury came by part of the hangings of it, which 'twas said this Charlett had design'd expressly for a memoriall of his Hair, giving the Fellow that drew it a lock to work by, and the piece which I have fasten'd in here was parcel of the same, which Mr Casbury gave to me. He said he believ'd there was a subtlety in the drawing, but had never discover'd it himself, nor much liked to pore upon it.

The money spent upon the curtains might as well have been thrown into the fire, as they were. Mr Cattell's comment upon what he heard of the story took the form of a quotation from Shakespeare. You may guess it without difficulty. It began with the words 'There are more things.'*

AN EPISODE OF CATHEDRAL
HISTORY

THERE was once a learned gentleman who was deputed to examine and report upon the archives of the cathedral of Southminster.* The examination of these records demanded a very considerable expenditure of time: hence it became advisable for him to engage lodgings in the city: for though the cathedral body were profuse in their offers of hospitality, Mr Lake felt that he would prefer to be master of his day. This was recognized as reasonable. The dean eventually wrote advising Mr Lake, if he were not already suited, to communicate with Mr Worby* the principal Verger, who occupied a house convenient to the church and was prepared to take in a quiet lodger for three or four weeks. Such an arrangement was precisely what Mr Lake desired. Terms were easily agreed upon, and early in December, like another Mr Datchery* (as he remarked to himself), the investigator found himself in the occupation of a very comfortable room in an ancient and cathedraly house.

One so familiar with the customs of cathedral churches, and treated with such obvious consideration by the dean and Chapter of this cathedral in particular, could not fail to command the respect of the Head Verger. Mr Worby even acquiesced in certain modifications of statements he had been accustomed to offer for years to parties of visitors. Mr Lake, on his part, found the Verger a very cheery companion and took advantage of any occasion that presented itself for enjoying his conversation when the day's work was over.

One evening about nine o'clock Mr Worby knocked at his lodger's door. 'I've occasion,' he said, 'to go across to the cathedral, Mr Lake, and I think I made you a promise when I did so next I would give you the opportunity to see what it looks like at night time. It's quite fine and dry outside if you care to come.'

'To be sure I will: very much obliged to you, Mr Worby, for thinking of it. Just let me get my coat.'

'Here it is, sir, and I've another lantern here that you'll find advisable for the steps, as there's no moon.'

'Anyone might think we were Jasper and Durdles,* over again, mightn't they?' said Lake as they crossed the close—for he had ascertained that the Verger had read *Edwin Drood*.

'Well, so they might,' said Mr Worby with a short laugh, 'though I don't know whether we ought to take it as a compliment. Odd ways, I often thinks, they had at that cathedral, don't it seem so to you, sir? Full choral matins at seven o'clock in the morning all the year round. Wouldn't suit our boys' voices nowadays, and I think there's one or two of the men would be applying for a rise if the Chapter was to bring it in—particular the alltoes.'

They were now at the south-west door. As Mr Worby was unlocking it Lake said, 'Did you ever find anybody locked in here by accident?'

'Twice I did. One was a drunk sailor; how ever he got in I don't know. I s'pose he went to sleep in the service, but by the time I got to him he was praying fit to bring the roof in. Lor what a noise that man did make! said it was the first time he'd been inside a church for ten year and blest if ever he'd try it again. The other was an old sheep: them boys it was, up to their games. That was the last time they tried it on, though. There, sir, now you see what we look like; our late dean used now and again to bring parties in, but he preferred a moonlight night and there was a piece of verse he'd coat to 'em, relating to a Scotch cathedral* I understand; but I don't know: I almost think the effect's better when it's all dark-like. Seems to add to the size and heighth. Now if you won't mind stopping down here in the nave while I go up into the choir where my business lays, you'll see what I mean.'

Accordingly Lake waited leaning against a pillar and watched the light wavering along the length of the church, and up the steps into the choir until it was intercepted by some screen or other furniture, which only allowed the reflection to be seen on the piers and roof. Not many minutes had passed before Worby reappeared at the door of the choir and by waving his lantern signalled to Lake to rejoin him.

'I suppose it *is* Worby, and not a substitute,' thought Lake to himself, as he walked up the nave. There was, in fact, nothing untoward. Worby showed him the papers which he had come to fetch out of the dean's stall, and asked him what he thought of the spectacle: Lake agreed that it was well worth seeing. 'I suppose,' he said, as they walked towards the altar-steps together, 'that you're too much used to going about here at night to feel nervous—but you must get a start every now and then, don't you? when a book falls down or a door swings to?'

'No, Mr Lake, I can't say I think much about noises, not now-a-days: I'm much more afraid of finding an escape of gas or a burst in the 'otwater pipes than anything else. Still there *have* been times, years ago. Did you notice that plain altar tomb there—fifteenth century we say it is, I don't know if you agree to that? Well if you didn't look at it, just come back and give it a glance if you'd be so good.' It was on the north side of the choir and rather awkwardly placed: only about three feet from the enclosing stone screen. Quite plain, as the Verger had said, but for some ordinary stone panelling. A metal cross of some size on the northern side (that next to the screen) was the solitary feature of any interest.

Lake agreed that it was not earlier than the Perpendicular period: 'but,' he said, 'unless it's the tomb of some remarkable person, you'll forgive me for saying that I don't think it's particularly noteworthy.'

'Well I can't say as it is the tomb of anybody noted in 'istry,' said Worby, who had a dry smile on his face, 'for we don't own any record whatsoever of who it was put up to. For all that, if you've half an hour to spare, sir, when we get back to the house, Mr Lake, I could tell you a tale about that tomb. I won't begin on it now; it strikes cold here, and we don't want to be dawdling about all night.'

'Of course I should like to hear it immensely.'

'Very well, sir, you shall. Now if I might put a question to you,' he went on, as they passed down the choir aisle. 'In our little local guide—and not only there but in the little book on our cathedral in the series—you'll find it stated that this portion of the building was erected previous to the twelfth century. Now of course I should be glad enough to take that view; but—mind the step, sir—but I put it to you—does the lay of the stone 'ere in this portion of the wall (which he tapped with his key), does it to your eye carry the flavour of what you might call Saxon masonry? No, I thought not; no more it does to me: now, if you'll believe me, I've said as much to those men—one's the librarian of our Free Libry here, and the other came down from London on purpose—fifty times, if I have once, but I might just as well have talked to that bit of stonework. But there it is; I suppose every one's got their opinions.'

The discussion of this peculiar trait of human nature occupied Mr Worby almost up to the moment when he and Lake re-entered the former's house. The condition of the fire in Lake's sitting room led to a suggestion from Mr Worby that they should finish the evening in his own parlour. We find them accordingly settled there some short time afterwards.

Mr Worby made his story a long one, and I will not undertake to tell it wholly in his own words, or in his own order. Lake committed the substance of it to paper immediately after hearing it, together with some few passages of the narrative which had fixed themselves verbatim in his mind; I shall probably find it expedient to condense Lake's record to some extent.

Mr Worby was born, it appeared, about the year 1828. His father before him had been connected with the cathedral, and likewise his grandfather. One or both had been choristers and in later life both had done work as mason and carpenter respectively about the fabric. Worby himself, though possessed as he frankly acknowledged of an indifferent voice, had been drafted into the choir at about ten years of age.

It was in 1840 that the wave of the Gothic revival smote the cathedral of Southminster.* 'There was a lot of lovely stuff went then, sir,' said Worby with a sigh. 'My father couldn't hardly believe it when he got his orders to clear out

the choir. There was a new dean just come in—Dean Burscough it was—and my father had been 'prenticed to a good
firm of joiners in the city and knew what good work was
when he saw it. Crool it was he used to say: all that beautiful
wainscot oak, as good as the day it was put up, and garlands-
like of foliage and fruit, and lovely old gilding work on the
coats of arms and the organ-pipes. All went to the timber
yard—every bit except some little pieces worked up in the
Lady Chapel and 'ere in this overmantel. Well—I may be
mistook, but I say our choir's never looked as well since.
Still there was a lot found out about the history of the
church and no doubt but what it did stand in need of repair.
There was very few winters passed by but what we'd lose a
pinnicle.' Mr Lake expressed his concurrence with Worby's
views of restoration, but owns to a fear about this point lest
the story proper should never be reached. Possibly this was
perceptible in his manner. Worby hastened to reassure him.
'Not but what I could carry on about that topic for hours at a
time, and do do when I see my opportunity. But Dean
Burscough he was very set on the Gothic period and nothing
would serve him but everything must be made agreeable to
that. And one morning after service he appointed for my
father to meet him in the choir, and he come back after he'd
taken off his robes in the vestry, and he'd got a roll of paper
with him, and the verger that was then brought in a table
and they begun spreading it out on the table with prayer
books to keep it down, and my father helped 'em and he saw
it was a picture of the inside of a choir in a cathedral: and
the dean—he was a quick-spoken gentleman—he says, "Well,
Worby—what do you think of that?" "Why," says my
father, "I don't think I 'ave the pleasure of knowing that
view. Would that be Hereford Cathedral, Mr Dean?" "No
Worby," says the dean, "that's Southminster Cathedral as
we hope to see it before many years." "Indeed, sir," says my
father, and that was all he did say—leastways to the dean—
but he used to tell me he felt reelly faint in himself when
he looked round our choir as I can remember it, all comfortable and furnished-like, and then see this nasty little dry
picter as he called it drawn out by some London architect.

Well, there I am again. But you'll see what I mean if you look at this old view.'

Worby reached down a framed print from the wall. 'Well, the long and the short of it was that the dean he handed over to my father a copy of an order of the Chapter that he was to clear out every bit of the choir—make a clean sweep—ready for the new work that was being designed up in town, and he was to put it in hand as soon as ever he could get the breakers together. Now then, sir, if you look at that view, you'll see where the pulpit used to stand: that's what I want you to notice, if you please.' It was, indeed, easily seen; an unusually large structure of timber with a domed sounding board, standing at the east end of the stalls on the north side of the choir, facing the Bishop's throne. Worby proceeded to explain that during the alterations, services were held in the nave—the members of the choir being thereby disappointed of an anticipated holiday, and the organist in particular incurring the suspicion of having wilfully damaged the mechanism of the temporary organ that was hired at considerable expense from London.

The work of demolition began with the choir screen and organ loft and proceeded gradually eastwards, disclosing as Worby said many interesting features of older work. While this was going on, the members of the Chapter were, naturally, in and about the choir a great deal, and it soon became apparent to the elder Worby—who could not help overhearing some of their talk—that on the part of the senior Canons especially there must have been a good deal of disagreement before the policy now being carried out had been adopted. Some were of opinion that they should catch their deaths of cold in the return stalls, unprotected by a screen from the draughts in the nave: others objected to being exposed to the view of persons in the choir aisles, especially, they said, during the sermons, when they found it helpful to listen in a posture which was liable to misconstruction. The strongest opposition however came from the oldest of the body, who up to the last moment objected to the removal of the pulpit. 'You ought not to touch it, Mr Dean,' he said with great emphasis one morning, when the two were standing

before it: 'you don't know what mischief you may do.'
'Mischief? it's not a work of any particular merit, Canon.'
'Don't call me Canon,' said the old man with great asperity,
'—that is, for thirty years I've been known as Dr Ayloff and
I shall be obliged, Mr Dean, if you would kindly humour me
in that matter. And as to the pulpit (which I've preached
from for these thirty years, though I don't insist on that),
all I'll say is I *know* you're doing wrong in moving it.' 'But
what sense could there be, my dear Doctor, in leaving it
where it is when we're fitting up the rest of the choir in a
totally different *style*? What reason could be given—apart
from the look of the thing?' 'Reason! reason!' said old Dr
Ayloff, 'if you young men—if I may say so without any
disrespect Mr Dean—if you'd only listen to reason a little,
and not be always asking for it we should get on better.
But there, I've said my say.' The old gentleman hobbled off,
and as it proved, never entered the cathedral again. The
season—it was a hot summer—turned sickly on a sudden.
Dr Ayloff was one of the first to go with some affection of the
muscles of the thorax, which took him painfully at night.
And at many services the number of choirmen and boys was
very thin.

Meanwhile the pulpit had been done away with. In fact,
the sounding board (part of which still exists as a table in a
summerhouse in the Palace garden) was taken down within
an hour or two of Dr Ayloff's protest. The removal of the
base—not effected without considerable trouble—disclosed to
view greatly to the exultation of the restoring party, an altar
tomb—the tomb, of course, to which Worby had attracted
Lake's attention that same evening. Much fruitless research
was expended in attempts to identify the occupant: from
that day to this he has never had a name put to him. The
structure had been most carefully boxed in under the pulpit
floor, so that such slight ornament as it possessed was not
defaced. Only on the north side of it there was what
looked like an injury: a gap between two of the slabs com-
posing the side. It might be two or three inches across. Palmer
the mason was directed to fill it up in a week's time, when he
came to do some other small jobs near that part of the choir.

The season was undoubtedly a very trying one. Whether the church was built on a site that had once been a marsh, as was suggested, or for whatever reason, the residents in its immediate neighbourhood had, many of them, but little enjoyment of the exquisite sunny days and the calm nights of August and September. To several of the older people—Dr Ayloff among others, as we have seen—the summer proved downright fatal; but even among the younger, few escaped either a sojourn in bed for a matter of weeks, or at the least, a brooding sense of oppression, accompanied by hateful nightmares. Gradually there formulated itself a suspicion, which grew into a conviction, that the alterations in the cathedral had something to say in the matter. The widow of a former old verger, a pensioner of the Chapter of Southminster, was visited by dreams, which she retailed to her friends, of a shape that slipped out of the little door of the south transept as the dark fell,* and flitted—taking a fresh direction every night—about the close, disappearing for a while in house after house and finally emerging again when the night sky was paling. She could see nothing of it, she said, but that it was a moving form: only she had an impression that when it returned to the church, as it seemed to do in the end of the dream, it turned its head: and then, she could not tell why, but she thought it had red eyes. Worby remembered hearing the old lady tell this dream at a tea party in the house of the chapter clerk. Its recurrence might perhaps, he said, be taken as a symptom of approaching illness; at any rate before the end of September the old lady was in her grave.

The interest excited by the restoration of this great church was not confined to its own county. One day that summer an F.S.A.* of some celebrity visited the place. His business was to write an account of the discoveries that had been made, for the Society of Antiquaries, and his wife, who accompanied him, was to make a series of illustrative drawings for his report. In the morning she employed herself in making a general sketch of the choir: in the afternon she devoted herself to details. She first drew the newly exposed altar tomb, and when that was finished, she called her husband's attention to a beautiful piece of diaper-ornament* on the screen just behind it, which had, like the tomb itself, been completely concealed by the pulpit. Of course, he said, an illustration of that must be made: so she seated herself on the tomb and began a careful drawing which occupied her till dusk.

Her husband had by this time finished his work of measuring and description, and they agreed that it was time to be getting back to their hotel. 'You may as well brush my skirt, Frank,' said the lady, 'it must have got covered with dust I'm sure.' He obeyed dutifully; but after a moment, he said, 'I don't know whether you value this dress particularly, my dear, but I'm inclined to think it's seen its best days. There's a great bit of it gone.' 'Gone? Where?' said she. 'I don't know *where* it's gone, but it's off at the bottom edge behind here.' She pulled it hastily into sight, and was horrified to find a jagged tear extending some way into the substance of the stuff: very much, she said, as if a dog had rent it away. The dress was, in any case, hopelessly spoilt, to her great vexation, and though they looked everywhere, the missing piece could not be found. There were many ways, they concluded, in which the injury might have come about, for the choir was full of old bits of woodwork with nails sticking out of them. Finally they could only suppose that one of these had caused the mischief, and that the workmen, who had been about all day, had carried off the particular piece with the fragment of dress still attached to it.

It was about this time, Worby thought, that his little dog began to wear an anxious expression when the hour for it to be put into the shed in the back yard approached. (For his mother had ordained that it must not sleep in the house.) One evening, he said, when he was just going to pick it up and carry it out, it looked at him 'like a Christian and waved its 'and I was going to say—well, you know 'ow they do carry on sometimes, and the end of it was I put it under my coat, and 'uddled it upstairs—and I'm afraid I as good as deceived my poor mother on the subject. After that the dog acted very artful with 'iding itself under the bed for half an hour or more before bed-time came, and we worked it so as my mother never found out what we'd done.' Of course Worby was glad of its company anyhow, but more particularly when the nuisance that is still remembered in Southminster as 'the crying' set in. 'Night after night,' said Worby, 'that dog seemed to know it was coming; he'd creep out he would and snuggle into the bed and cuddle right up to me shivering, and when the crying come he'd be like a wild thing, shoving his head under my arm, and I was fully near as bad. Six or seven times we'd hear it, not more, and when he'd dror out his 'ed again I'd know it was over for that night. What was it like, sir? Well I never heard but one thing that seemed to hit it off. I happened to be playing about in the close and there was two of the Canons met and said good morning one to another. "Sleep well last night?" says one—it was Mr Henslow that one, and Mr Lyall* was the other. "Can't say I did," says Mr Lyall, "rather too much of Isaiah 34: 14 for me."* "34: 14, says Mr Henslow, "what's that?" "You call yourself a Bible reader!" says Mr Lyall. (Mr Henslow, you must know, he was one of what used to be termed Simeon's lot—pretty much what we should call the Evangelical party.*) "You go and look it up." I wanted to know what he was getting at myself and so off I ran home and got out my own Bible and there it was: "the satyr shall cry to his fellow." Well, I thought, is that what we've been listening to these past nights? and I tell you it made me look over my shoulder a time or two. Of course I'd asked my father and mother about what it could be before that, but they both said it was most likely cats: but they spoke very short and I could see they was troubled. My word! that was a noise—'ungry like, as if it was calling after some one that wouldn't come. If ever you felt you wanted company, it would be when you was waiting for it to begin again. I believe two or three nights there was men put on to watch in different parts of the close; but they all used to get together in one corner the nearest they could to the High Street, and nothing came of it.

'Well then the next thing was this. Me and another of the boys—he's in business in the city now as a grocer, like his father before him—we'd gone up in the choir after morning service was over and we heard old Palmer the mason talking to one of his men. So we went up nearer because we knew he was a rusty old chap and there might be some fun going. It appears Palmer 'd told this man to stop up the chink in that old tomb. Well there was this man keeping on saying he'd done it the best he could and there was Palmer carrying on like all possessed about it. "Call that making a job of it?" he says. "If you had your rights you'd get the sack for this. What do you suppose I pay you your wages for? What do you suppose I'm going to say to the Dean and Chapter when they come round, as come they may do anytime and see where you've been bungling about covering the 'ole place with mess and plaster and Lord knows what?" "Well, master, I done the best I could," says the man. "I don't know no more than what you do 'ow it come to fall out this way. I tamped it right in the 'ole," he says, "and now it's fell out," he says, "I never see."

' "Fell out?" says old Palmer, "why it's nowhere near the place. Blowed out you mean"; and he picked up a bit of plaster, and so did I, that was laying up against the screen three or four feet off and not dry yet: and old Palmer he looked at it curious-like and then he turned round on me and he says, "Now then you boys, have you been up to some of your games here?" "No," I says, "I haven't, Mr Palmer; there's none of us been about here till just this minute": and while I was talking the other boy, Evans, he got looking in through the chink and I heard him draw in his breath, and he came away sharp and up to us and says he, "I believe there's something in there. I saw something shiny." "Oh ah! I dare say," says old Palmer: "well, I ain't got time to stop about here. You William, you go off and get some more stuff and make a job of it this time: if not, there'll be trouble in my yard," he says.

'So the man he went off, and Palmer too, and us boys stopped behind and I says to Evans, "Did you really see anything in there?" "Yes," he says, "I did indeed." So then I says, "Let's shove something in and stir it up." And we tried several of the bits of wood that was laying about, but they were all too big. Then Evans he had a sheet of music he'd brought with him, an anthem or a service, I forget which it was now—and he rolled it up small and shoved it in the chink: two or three times he did it and nothing happened. "Give it me, boy," I said, and I had a try. No, nothing happened. Then, I don't know why I thought of it, I'm sure, but I stooped down just opposite the chink and put my two fingers in my mouth and whistled—you know the way—and at that I seemed to think I heard something stirring, and I says to Evans, "Come away," I says, "I don't like this." "Oh rot," he says, "give me that roll", and he took it and shoved it in. And I don't think ever I see any one go so pale as he did. "I say Worby," he says, "it's caught or else someone's got hold of it." "Pull it out or leave it," I says. "Come and let's get off." So he gave a good pull, and it came away; leastways most of it did, but the end was gone, torn off it was, and Evans looked at it for a second and then he gave a sort of a croak and let it drop and we both made off out of there as quick as ever we could. When we got outside Evans says to me, "Did you see the end of that paper?" "No," I says, "only it was torn." "Yes it was," he says, "but it was wet too, and black!" Well, partly because of the fright we had, and partly because that music was wanted in a day or two, and we knew there'd be a set-out about it with the organist, we didn't say nothing to anyone else, and I suppose the workmen they swept up the bit that was left along with the rest of the rubbish. But Evans—if you were to ask him this very day about it—he'd stick to it he saw that paper wet and black at the end where it was torn.'

After that the boys gave the choir a wide berth, so that Worby was not sure what was the result of the mason's renewed mending of the tomb. Only he made out from fragments of conversation dropped by the workmen passing through the choir that some difficulty had been met with and that the governor—Mr Palmer to wit—had tried his own hand at the job. A little later, he happened to see Mr Palmer himself knocking at the door of the deanery and being admitted by the butler. A day or so after that, he gathered from a remark his father let fall at breakfast that something a little out of the common was to be done in the cathedral after morning service on the morrow. 'And I'd just as soon it was today,' his father added. 'I don't see the use of running risks.' ' "Father," I says, "what are you going to do in the cathedral tomorrow?" And he turned on me as savage as I ever see him—he was a wonderful good tempered man as a general thing, my poor father was. "My lad," he says, "I'll trouble you not to go picking up your elders' and betters' talk: it's not manners and it's not straight. What I'm going to do or not going to do in the cathedral tomorrow is none of your business: and if I catch sight of you hanging about the place tomorrow after your work's done I'll send you home with a flea in your ear. Now you mind that." Of course I said I was very sorry and that, and equally of course I went off and laid my plans with Evans. We knew there was a stair up in the corner of the transept which you can get up to the triforium, and in them days the door to it was pretty well always open, and even if it wasn't we knew the key usually laid under a bit of matting hard by. So we made up our minds we'd be putting away music and that next morning while the rest of the boys was clearing off, and then slip up the stairs and watch from the triforium if there was any signs of work going on.

'Well that same night I dropped off asleep as sound as a boy does, and all of a sudden the dog woke me up coming into the bed, and thought I, now we're going to get it sharp, for he seemed more frightened than usual. After about five minutes sure enough came this cry. I can't give you no idea what it was like: and so near too—nearer than I'd heard it yet —and a funny thing, Mr Lake; you know what a place this close is for an echo, and particular if you stand this side of it. Well, this crying never made no sign of an echo at all. But as I said, it was dreadful near this night, and on the top of the start I got with hearing it, I got another fright, for I heard something rustling outside in the passage. Now to be sure I thought I was done; but I noticed the dog seemed to perk up a bit, and next there was some one whispered outside the door, and I very near laughed out loud for I knew it was my father and mother that had got out of bed with the noise. "Whatever is it?" says my mother. "Hush! I don't know," says my father, excited-like, "don't disturb the boy. I hope he didn't hear nothing."

'So me knowing they were just outside, it made me bolder, and I slipped out of bed across to my little window giving on the close—but the dog he bored right down to the bottom of the bed—and I looked out. First go off I couldn't see anything. Then right down in the shadow under a buttress I made out what I shall always say was two spots of red—a dull red it was, nothing like a lamp nor a fire but just so as you could pick 'em out of the black shadow. I hadn't but just sighted 'em when it seemed we wasn't the only people that had been disturbed, because I see a window in a house on the left-hand side become lighted up and the light moving. I just turned my head to make sure of it and then looked back into the shadow for those two red things, and they were gone, and for all I peered about and stared, there was not a sign more of them. Then come my last fright that night—something come against my bare leg—but that was all right: that was my little dog had come out of bed and prancing about making a great to-do only holding his tongue, and me seeing he was quite in spirits again, I took him back to bed and we slept the night out.

'Next morning I made out to tell my mother I'd had the dog in my room, and I was surprised, after all she'd said about it before, how quiet she took it. "Did you?" she says. "Well, by good rights you ought to go without your breakfast for doing such a thing behind my back: but I don't know as there's any great harm done, only another time you ask my permission, do you hear?" A bit after that I said something to my father about having heard the cats again. "*Cats?*" he says, and he looked over at my poor mother, and she coughed and he says, "Oh, ah, yes, cats. I believe I heard 'em myself."

'That was a funny morning altogether: nothing seemed to go right. The organist he stopped in bed, and the minor canon he forgot it was the 19th day and waited for the *Venite* and after a bit the deputy he set off playing the chant for even-song, which was a minor; and then the Decani boys* were laughing so much they couldn't sing, and when it came to the anthem the solo boy he got took with the giggles and made out his nose was bleeding and shoved the book at me what hadn't practised the verse and wasn't much of a singer if I had known it. Well, things was rougher you see fifty years ago, and I got a nip from the counter-tenor behind me that I remembered.

'So we got through somehow and neither the men nor the boys weren't by way of waiting to see whether the canon in residence—Mr Henslow it was—would come to the vestries and fine 'em, but I don't believe he did: for one thing I fancy he'd read the wrong lesson for the first time in his life and knew it. Anyhow Evans and me didn't find no difficulty in slipping up the stairs as I told you, and when we got up we laid ourselves down flat on our stomachs where we could just stretch our heads out over the old tomb, and we hadn't but just done so when we heard the verger that was then shutting the iron porch-gates and locking the southwest door, and then the transept door, so we knew there was something up and they meant to keep the public out for a bit.

'Next thing was, the dean and the canon come in by their door on the north, and then I see my father, and old Palmer and a couple of their best men, and Palmer stood a talking for a bit with the dean in the middle of the choir. He had a coil of rope and the men had crows. All of 'em looked a bit nervous. So there they stood talking, and at last I heard the dean say, "Well, I've no time to waste, Palmer. If you think this'll satisfy Southminster people, I'll permit it to be done; but I must say this, that never in the whole course of my life have I heard such arrant nonsense from a practical man as I have from you. Don't you agree with me, Henslow?" As far as I could hear Mr Henslow said something like "Oh well, we're told aren't we Mr Dean not to judge others" and the dean he gave a kind of sniff and walked straight up to the tomb and took his stand behind it with his back to the screen, and the others they come edging up rather gingerly. Henslow he stopped on the south side and scratched on his chin, he did. Then the dean spoke up: "Palmer," he says, "which can you do easiest, get the slab off the top or shift one of the side slabs?"

'Old Palmer and his men they pottered about a bit looking round the edge of the top slab and sounding the sides on the south and east and west and everywhere but the north. Henslow said something about it being better to have a try at the south side because there was more light and more room to move about in. Then my father, who'd been watching of them, went round to the north side, and knelt down and felt of the slab by the chink, and he got up and dusted his knees and says to the dean: "Beg pardon, Mr Dean, but I think if Mr Palmer'll try this here slab he'll find it'll come out easy enough. Seems to me one of the men could prise it out with his crow by means of this chink." "Ah, thank you Worby," says the dean, "that's a good suggestion. Palmer, let one of your men do that, will you?"

'So the man come round and put his bar in and bore on it, and just that minute when they were all bending over, and us boys got our heads well stuck out over the edge of the triforium, there come a most fearful crash down at the west end of the choir, as if a whole stack of big timber had fallen down a flight of stairs. Well you can't expect me to tell you everything that happened all in a minute. Of course there was a terrible commotion. I heard the slab fall out, and the crowbar on the floor, and I heard the dean say "Good God".

'When I looked down again I saw the dean tumbled over on the floor, the men was making off down the choir, Henslow was just going to help the dean up, Palmer was going to stop the men, as he said afterwards, and my father was sitting on the altar step with his face in his hands. The dean he was very cross. "I wish to goodness you'd look where you're coming to, Henslow," he says. "Why you should all take to your heels when a stick of wood tumbles down I cannot imagine"; and all Henslow could do, explaining he was right away on the other side of the tomb, would not satisfy him.

'Then Palmer came back and reported there was nothing to account for this noise and nothing seemingly fallen down, and when the dean finished feeling of himself they gathered round—except my father, he sat where he was—and some one lighted up a bit of candle and they looked into the tomb. "Nothing there," says the dean—"what did I tell you? Stay, here's something. What's this? a bit of music-paper, and a piece of torn stuff—part of a dress it looks like. Both quite modern—no interest whatever. Another time perhaps you'll take the advice of an educated man"—or something like that, and off he went, limping a bit, and out through the north door, only as he went he called back angry to Palmer for leaving the door standing open. Palmer called out "Very sorry sir," but he shrugged his shoulders, and Henslow says, "I fancy Mr Dean's mistaken. I closed the door behind me, but he's a little upset." Then Palmer says, "Why, where's Worby?" and they saw him sitting on the step and went up to him. He was recovering himself it seemed and wiping his forehead, and Palmer helped him up on to his legs, as I was glad to see.

'They were too far off for me to hear what they said but my father pointed to the north door in the aisle, and Palmer and Henslow both of them looked very surprised and scared. After a bit my father and Henslow went out of the church, and the others made what haste they could to put the slab back and plaster it in. And about as the clock struck twelve the Cathedral was opened again and us boys made the best of our way home.

'I was in a great taking to know what it was had given my poor father such a turn, and when I got in and found him sitting in his chair taking a glass of spirits and my mother standing looking anxious at him I couldn't keep from bursting out and making confession where I'd been. But he didn't seem to take on, not in the way of losing his temper. "You was there, was you? Well did you see it?" "I see everything father," I says, "except when the noise came." "Did you see what it was knocked the dean over?" he says, "that what come out of the monument? You didn't? Well that's a mercy." "Why what was it father?" I said. "Come, you must have seen it," he says. "*Didn't* you see? A thing like a man, all over hair, and two great eyes to it?"

'Well, that was all I could get out of him that time, and later on he seemed as if he was ashamed of being so frightened, and he used to put me off when I asked him about it. But years after, when I was got to be a grown man, we had some talk now and again on the matter, and he always said the same thing. "Black it was," he'd say, "and a mass of hair and two legs, and the light caught on its eyes."

'Well that's the tale of that tomb Mr Lake: it's one we don't tell to our visitors, and I should be obliged to you not to make any use of it till I'm out of the way. I doubt Mr Evans'll feel the same as I do if you ask him.'

This proved to be the case. But over twenty years have passed by, and the grass is growing over both Worby and Evans: so Mr Lake felt no difficulty about communicating his notes—taken in 1890—to me. He accompanied them with a sketch of the tomb and a copy of the short inscription on the metal cross which was affixed at the expense of Dr Lyall to the centre of the northern side. It was from the Vulgate of Isaiah xxxiv, and consisted merely of the three words—

IBI CUBAVIT LAMIA.*

THE UNCOMMON PRAYER-BOOK

MR DAVIDSON was spending the first week in January alone in a country town. A combination of circumstances had driven him to that drastic course: his nearest relations were enjoying winter sports abroad, and the friends who had been kindly anxious to replace them had an infectious complaint in the house. Doubtless he might have found someone else to take pity on him; 'but,' he reflected, 'most of them have made up their parties, and after all it is only for three or four days at most that I have to fend for myself, and it will be just as well if I can get a move on with my introduction to the Leventhorp Papers. I might use the time by going down as near as I can to Gaulsford and making acquaintance with the neighbourhood. I ought to see the remains of the Leventhorp house,* and the tombs in the church.'

The first day after his arrival at the Swan Hotel at Longbridge was so stormy that he got no farther than the tobacconist's. The next, comparatively bright, he used for his visit to Gaulsford, which interested him more than a little, but had no ulterior consequences. The third, which was really a pearl of a day for early January, was too fine to be spent indoors. He gathered from the landlord that a favourite practice of visitors in the summer was to take a morning train to a couple of stations westward and walk back down the valley of the Tent,* through Stanford St Thomas and Stanford Magdalene, both of which were accounted highly picturesque villages. He closed with this plan, and we now find him seated in a third-class carriage at 9.45 a.m., on his way to Kingsbourne Junction, and studying the map of the district.

One old man was his only fellow-traveller, a piping old man, who seemed inclined for conversation. So Mr Davidson, after going through the necessary versicles and responses* about the weather, inquired whether he was going far.

'No, sir, not far, not this morning, sir,' said the old man. 'I ain't only goin' so far as what they call Kingsbourne

Junction. There isn't but two stations betwixt here and there. Yes, they calls it Kingsbourne Junction.'

'I'm going there, too,' said Mr Davidson.

'Oh indeed, sir! do you know that part?'

'No, I'm only going for the sake of taking a walk back to Longbridge, and seeing a bit of the country.'

'Oh indeed, sir! Well, 'tis a beautiful day for a gentleman as enjoys a bit of a walk.'

'Yes, to be sure. Have you got far to go when you get to Kingsbourne?'

'No, sir, I ain't got far to go, once I get to Kingsbourne Junction. I'm agoin' to see my daughter, sir. She live at Brockstone. That's about two mile across the fields from what they call Kingsbourne Junction, that is. You've got that marked down on your map, I expect, sir.'

'I expect I have. Let me see, Brockstone, did you say? Here's Kingsbourne, yes; and which way is Brockstone— toward the Stanfords? Ah, I see it: Brockstone Court, in a park. I don't see the village, though.'

'No, sir, you wouldn't see no village of Brockstone. There ain't only the Court and the chapel at Brockstone.'

'Chapel? Oh yes, that's marked here too. The chapel; close by the Court, it seems to be. Does it belong to the Court?'

'Yes, sir, that's close up to the Court, only a step. Yes, that belong to the Court. My daughter, you see, sir, she's the keeper's wife now, and she live at the Court and look after things now the family's away.'

'No one living there now, then?'

'No, sir, not for a number of years. The old gentleman he lived there when I was a lad, and the lady she lived on after him to very near upon ninety years of age. And then she died, and them that have it now, they've got this other place, in Warwickshire I believe it is, and they don't do nothin' about lettin' the Court out; but Colonel Wildman he have the shooting, and young Mr Clark, he's the agent, he come over once in so many weeks to see to things, and my daughter's husband he's the keeper.'

'And who uses the chapel? just the people round about, I suppose.'

'Oh no, no one don't use the chapel. Why, there ain't no one to go. All the people about, they go to Stanford St Thomas Church; but my son-in-law he go to Kingsbourne Church now, because the gentleman at Stanford he have this Gregory singin',* and my son-in-law he don't like that; he say he can hear the old donkey brayin' any day of the week, and he like something a little cheerful on the Sunday.' The old man drew his hand across his mouth and laughed. 'That's what my son-in-law say: he say he can hear the old donkey [etc., *da capo**].'

Mr Davidson also laughed as honestly as he could, thinking meanwhile that Brockstone Court and chapel would probably be worth including in his walk, for the map showed that from Brockstone he could strike the Tent Valley quite as easily as by following the main Kingsbourne–Longbridge road. So, when the mirth excited by the remembrance of the son-in-law's *bon mot* had died down, he returned to the charge, and ascertained that both the Court and the chapel were of the class known as 'old-fashioned places', and that the old man would be very willing to take him thither, and his daughter would be happy to show him whatever she could.

'But that ain't a lot, sir, not as if the family was livin' there; all the lookin'-glasses is covered up, and the paintin's, and the curtains and carpets folded away: not but what I dare say she could show you a pair just to look at, because she go over them to see as the morth shouldn't get into 'em.'

'I shan't mind about that, thank you: if she can show me the inside of the chapel, that's what I'd like best to see.'

'Oh, she can show you that right enough, sir. She have the key of the door, you see, and most weeks she go in and dust about. That's a nice chapel, that is. My son-in-law he say he'll be bound they didn't have none of this Gregory singin' there. Dear! I can't help but smile when I think of him sayin' that about th' old donkey. "I can hear him bray," he say, "any day of the week"; and so he can, sir, that's true, anyway.'

The walk across the fields from Kingsbourne to Brockstone was very pleasant. It lay for the most part on the top of the country, and commanded wide views over a succession of ridges, plough and pasture, or covered with dark-blue woods

—all ending, more or less abruptly, on the right, in headlands that overlooked the wide valley of a great western river. The last field they crossed was bounded by a close copse, and no sooner were they in it than the path turned downwards very sharply, and it became evident that Brockstone was neatly fitted into a sudden and very narrow valley. It was not long before they had glimpses of groups of smokeless stone chimneys, and stone-tiled roofs, close beneath their feet; and not many minutes after that, they were wiping their shoes at the back door of Brockstone Court, while the keeper's dogs barked very loudly in unseen places, and Mrs Porter in quick succession screamed at them to be quiet, greeted her father, and begged both her visitors to step in.

It was not to be expected that Mr Davidson should escape being taken through the principal rooms of the Court, in spite of the fact that the house was entirely out of commission. Pictures, carpets, curtains, furniture, were all covered up or put away, as old Mr Avery had said, and the admiration which our friend was very ready to bestow had to be lavished on the proportions of the rooms, and on the one painted ceiling, upon which an artist who had fled from London in the Plague-year* had depicted the Triumph of Loyalty and Defeat of Sedition.* In this Mr Davidson could show an unfeigned interest. The portraits of Cromwell, Ireton, Bradshaw, Peters, and the rest,* writhing in carefully-devised torments, were evidently the part of the design to which most pains had been devoted.

'That were the old Lady Sadleir* had that paintin' done, same as the one what put up the chapel. They say she were the first that went up to London to dance on Oliver Cromwell's grave.'* So said Mr Avery, and continued musingly: 'Well, I suppose she got some satisfaction to 'er mind, but I don't know as I should want to pay the fare to London and back just for that, and my son-in-law he say the same: he say he don't know as he should have cared to pay all that money only for that. I was tellin' the gentleman as we come along in the train, Mary, what your 'Arry says about this Gregory singin' down at Stanford here. We 'ad a bit of a laugh over that, sir, didn't us?'

'Yes, to be sure we did; ha! ha!' Once again Mr Davidson strove to do justice to the pleasantry of the keeper. 'But,' he said, 'if Mrs Porter can show me the chapel, I think it should be now, for the days aren't long, and I want to get back to Longbridge before it falls quite dark.'

Even if Brockstone Court has not been illustrated in *Rural Life* (and I think it has not) I do not propose to point out its excellences here; but of the chapel a word must be said. It stands about a hundred yards from the house, and has its own little graveyard and trees about it. It is a stone building about seventy feet long, and in the gothic style, as that style was understood in the middle of the seventeenth century. On the whole it resembles some of the Oxford college chapels as much as anything, save that it has a distinct chancel, like a parish church, and a fanciful domed bell-turret at the south-west angle.

When the west door was thrown open, Mr Davidson could not repress an exclamation of pleased surprise at the completeness and richness of the interior. Screen-work, pulpit, seating, and glass—all were of the same period; and as he advanced into the nave and sighted the organ-case with its gold embossed pipes in the western gallery, his cup of satisfaction was filled. The glass in the nave windows was chiefly armorial; in the chancel were figure-subjects, of the kind that may be seen at Abbey Dore, of Lord Scudamore's work.* But this is not an archaeological Review.

While Mr Davidson was still busy examining the remains of the organ (attributed to one of the Dallams,* I believe) old Mr Avery had stumped up into the chancel and was lifting the dust-cloths from the blue velvet cushions of the stall-desks—evidently it was here that the family sat. Mr Davidson heard him say in a rather hushed tone of surprise, 'Why, Mary, here's all the books open agin!'

The reply was in a voice that sounded peevish rather than surprised. 'Tt-tt-tt, well, there, I never!'

Mrs Porter went over to where her father was standing, and they continued talking in a lower key. Mr Davidson saw plainly that something not quite in the common run was under discussion: so he came down the gallery stairs and joined them. There was no sign of disorder in the chancel any more than in the rest of the chapel, which was beautifully clean, but the eight folio Prayer-Books on the cushions of the stall-desks were indubitably open.

Mrs Porter was inclined to be fretful over it. 'Whoever can it be as does it?' she said, 'for there's no key but mine, nor yet door but the one we come in by, and the winders is barred, every one of 'em: I don't like it, father, that I don't.'

'What is it, Mrs Porter? Anything wrong?' said Mr Davidson.

'No, sir, nothing reely wrong, only these books. Every time pretty near that I come in to do up the place, I shuts 'em and spreads the cloths over 'em to keep off the dust, ever since Mr Clark spoke about it when I first come; and yet there they are again, and always the same page—and as I says, whoever it can be as does it with the door and winders shut; and as I says, it makes anyone feel queer comin' in here alone as I 'ave to do, not as I'm given that way myself, not to be frightened easy, I mean to say; and there's not a rat in the place—not as no rat wouldn't trouble to do a thing like that, do you think, sir?'

'Hardly, I should say; but it sounds very queer. Are they always open at the same place, did you say?'

'Always the same place, sir, one of the psalms it is, and I didn't particular notice it the first time or two, till I see a little red line of printing, and it's always caught my eye since.'

Mr Davidson walked along the stalls and looked at the open books. Sure enough, they all stood at the same page: Psalm cix, and at the head of it, just between the number and the *Deus laudem*,* was a rubric, 'For the 25th day of April'. Without pretending to minute knowledge of the history of the Book of Common Prayer, he knew enough to be sure that this was a very odd and wholly unauthorized addition to its text; and though he remembered that April 25 is St Mark's Day, he could not imagine what appropriateness this very savage psalm could have to that festival. With slight misgivings, he ventured to turn over the leaves to examine the title-page, and knowing the need for particular accuracy in these matters, he devoted some ten minutes to making a line-for-line transcript of it. The date was 1653; the printer called himself Anthony Cadman. He turned to the list of Proper Psalms for certain days: yes, added to it was that same inexplicable entry: *For the 25th day of April: the* 109th *Psalm.* An expert would no doubt have thought of many other points to inquire into, but this antiquary, as I have said, was no expert. He took stock, however, of the binding, a handsome one of tooled blue leather, bearing the arms that figured in several of the nave windows in various combinations.

'How often,' he said at last to Mrs Porter, 'have you found these books lying open like this?'

'Reely I couldn't say, sir, but it's a great many times now. Do you recollect, father, me telling you about it the first time I noticed it?'

'That I do, my dear: you was in a rare taking, and I don't so much wonder at it; that was five year ago I was paying you a visit at Michaelmas time, and you come in at tea-time, and says you, "Father, there's the books layin' open under the cloths agin"; and I didn't know what my daughter was speakin' about, you see, sir, and I says, "Books?" just like that, I says; and then it all came out. But as Harry says,— that's my son-in-law, sir,—"whoever it can be," he says, "as does it, because there ain't only the one door, and we keeps the key locked up," he says, "and the winders is barred, every one on 'em. Well," he says, "I lay once I could catch 'em at it they wouldn't do it a second time," he says. And no more they wouldn't, I don't believe, sir. Well that was five year ago, and it's been happenin' constant ever since by your account, my dear. Young Mr Clark he don't seem to think much to it, but then he don't live here, you see, and 'tisn't his business to come and clean up here of a dark afternoon, is it?'

'I suppose you never notice anything else odd when you are at work here, Mrs Porter?' said Mr Davidson.

'No, sir, I do not,' said Mrs Porter, 'and it's a funny thing to me I don't, with the feeling I have as there's someone

settin' here—no, it's the other side, just within the screen—
and lookin' at me all the time I'm dustin' in the gallery and
pews. But I never yet see nothin' worse than myself, as the
sayin' goes, and I kindly hope I never may.'

In the conversation that followed (there was not much of it)
nothing was added to the statement of the case. Having
parted on good terms with Mr Avery and his daughter, Mr
Davidson addressed himself to his eight-mile walk. The little
valley of Brockstone soon led him down into the broader one
of the Tent, and on to Stanford St Thomas, where he found
refreshment.

We need not accompany him all the way to Longbridge.
But as he was changing his socks before dinner, he suddenly
paused and said half-aloud, 'By Jove, that *is* a rum thing!' It
had not occurred to him before how strange it was that any
edition of the Prayer-Book should have been issued in 1653,
seven years before the Restoration, five years before Cromwell's death, and when the use of the book, let alone the
printing of it, was penal. He must have been a bold man who
put his name and a date on that title-page. Only, Mr Davidson reflected, it probably was not his name at all, for the ways
of printers in difficult times were devious.

As he was in the front hall of the Swan that evening,
making some investigations about trains, a small motor
stopped in front of the door, and out of it came a small man
in a fur coat, who stood on the steps and gave directions in a
rather yapping foreign accent to his chauffeur. When he
came into the hotel, he was seen to be black-haired and pale-
faced, with a little pointed beard, and gold pince-nez;
altogether, very neatly turned out.

He went to his room, and Mr Davidson saw no more of him
till dinner-time. As they were the only two dining that night,
it was not difficult for the newcomer to find an excuse for falling into talk; he was evidently wishing to make out what
brought Mr Davidson into that neighbourhood at that season.

'Can you tell me how far it is from here to Arlingworth?'
was one of his early questions, and it was one which threw
some light on his own plans, for Mr Davidson recollected

having seen at the station an advertisement of a sale at Arlingworth Hall, comprising old furniture, pictures, and books. This, then, was a London dealer.

'No,' he said, 'I've never been there. I believe it lies out by Kingsbourne—it can't be less than twelve miles. I see there's a sale there shortly.'

The other looked at him inquisitively, and he laughed. 'No,' he said, as if answering a question, 'you needn't be afraid of my competing; I'm leaving this place tomorrow.'

This cleared the air, and the dealer, whose name was Homberger,* admitted that he was interested in books, and thought there might be in these old country-house libraries something to repay a journey. 'For,' said he, 'we English have always this marvellous talent for accumulating rarities in the most unexpected places, ain't it?'

And in the course of the evening he was most interesting on the subject of finds made by himself and others. 'I shall take the occasion after this sale to look round the district a bit: perhaps you could inform me of some likely spots, Mr Davidson?' But Davidson, though he had seen some very tempting locked-up bookcases at Brockstone Court, kept his counsel. He did not really like Mr Homberger.

Next day, as he sat in the train, a little ray of light came to illuminate one of yesterday's puzzles. He happened to take out an almanac-diary that he had bought for the new year, and it occurred to him to look at the remarkable events for April 25. There it was: 'St Mark. Oliver Cromwell born, 1599.'

That, coupled with the painted ceiling, seemed to explain a good deal. The figure of old Lady Sadleir became more substantial to his imagination, as of one in whom love for Church and King had gradually given place to intense hate of the power that had silenced the one and slaughtered the other. What curious evil service was that which she and a few like her had been wont to celebrate year by year in that remote valley? and how in the world had she managed to elude authority? And again, did not this persistent opening of the books agree oddly with the other traits of her portrait known to him?

It would be interesting for anyone who chanced to be near Brockstone on the twenty-fifth of April to look in at the chapel and see if anything exceptional happened. When he came to think of it, there seemed to be no reason why he should not be that person himself: he, and if possible, some congenial friend. He resolved that so it should be.

Knowing that he knew really nothing about the printing of Prayer-Books, he realized that he must make it his business to get the best light on the matter without divulging his reasons. I may say at once that his search was entirely fruitless. One writer of the early part of the nineteenth century, a writer of rather windy and rhapsodical chat about books, professed to have heard of a special anti-Cromwellian issue of the Prayer-Book in the very midst of the Commonwealth period. But he did not claim to have seen a copy, and no one had believed him. Looking into this matter, Mr Davidson found that the statement was based on letters from a correspondent who had lived near Longbridge: so he was inclined to think that the Brockstone Prayer-Books were at the bottom of it, and had excited a momentary interest.

Months went on, and St Mark's Day came near. Nothing interfered with Mr Davidson's plans of visiting Brockstone, or with those of the friend whom he had persuaded to go with him, and to whom alone he had confided the puzzle. The same 9.45 train which had taken him in January took them now to Kingsbourne; the same field-path led them to Brockstone. But today they stopped more than once to pick a cowslip; the distant woods and ploughed uplands were of another colour, and in the copse there was, as Mrs Porter said, 'a regular charm of birds; why you couldn't hardly collect your mind sometimes with it.'

She recognized Mr Davidson at once and was very ready to do the honours of the chapel. The new visitor, Mr Witham, was as much struck by the completeness of it as Mr Davidson had been. 'There can't be such another in England,' he said.

'Books open again, Mrs Porter?' said Davidson, as they walked up to the chancel.

'Dear, yes, I expect so, sir,' said Mrs Porter, as she drew off the cloths. 'Well, there!' she exclaimed the next moment, 'if they ain't shut! That's the first time ever I've found 'em so. But it's not for want of care on my part, I do assure you, gentlemen, if they wasn't, for I felt the cloths the last thing before I shut up last week, when the gentleman had done photografting the heast winder, and every one was shut, and where there was ribbons left I tied 'em. Now I think of it, I don't remember ever to 'ave done that before, and per'aps, whoever it is it just made the difference to 'em. Well, it only shows, don't it? If at first you don't succeed, try, try, try again.'

Meanwhile the two men had been examining the books, and now Davidson spoke.

'I'm sorry to say I'm afraid there's something wrong here, Mrs Porter. These are not the same books.'

It would make too long a business to detail all Mrs Porter's outcries, and the questionings that followed. The upshot was this. Early in January the gentleman had come to see over the chapel and thought a great deal of it and said he must come back in the spring weather and take some photografts. And only a week ago he had drove up in his motoring car, and a very 'eavy box with the slides in it, and she had locked him in because he said something about a long explosion, and she was afraid of some damage happening; and he says, no, not explosion, but it appeared the lantern what they take the slides with worked very slow, and so he was in there the best part of an hour and she come and let him out, and he drove off with his box and all and gave her his visiting-card, and oh, dear, dear, to think of such a thing! he must have changed the books and took the old ones away with him in his box.

'What sort of man was he?'

'Oh, dear, he was a small-made gentleman, if you can call him so after the way he've behaved, with black hair, that is if it was hair, and gold eye-glasses, if they was gold: reely, one don't know what to believe. Sometimes I doubt he weren't a reel Englishman at all, and yet he seemed to know the language, and had the name on his visiting-card like anybody else might.'

'Just so; might we see the card? Yes: T. W. Henderson, and

an address somewhere near Bristol. Well, Mrs Porter, it's quite plain this Mr Henderson, as he calls himself, has walked off with your eight Prayer-Books and put eight others about the same size in place of them. Now listen to me. I suppose you must tell your husband about this, but neither you nor he must say one word about it to anyone else. If you'll give me the address of the agent—Mr Clark, isn't it?—I will write to him and tell him exactly what has happened, and that it really is no fault of yours. But, you understand, we must keep it very quiet: and why? Because this man who has stolen the books will of course try to sell them one at a time—for I may tell you they are worth a good deal of money—and the only way we can bring it home to him is by keeping a sharp look out and saying nothing.'

By dint of repeating the same advice in various forms they succeeded in impressing Mrs Porter with the real need for silence, and were forced to make a concession only in the case of Mr Avery, who was expected on a visit shortly: 'But you may be safe with father, sir,' said Mrs Porter. 'Father ain't a talkin' man.'

It was not quite Mr Davidson's experience of him; still, there were no neighbours at Brockstone, and even Mr Avery must be aware that gossip with anybody on such a subject would be likely to end in the Porters having to look out for another situation.

A last question was whether Mr Henderson, so-called, had anyone with him.

'No, sir, not when he come he hadn't: he was working his own motoring car himself, and what luggage he had, let me see: there was his lantern and this box of slides inside the carriage, which I helped him into the chapel and out of it myself with it, if only I'd knowed! And as he drove away under the big yew tree by the monument I see the long white bundle laying on the top of the coach, what I didn't notice when he drove up. But he set in front, sir, and only the boxes inside behind him. And do you reely think, sir, as his name weren't Henderson at all? Oh dear me, what a dreadful thing! Why fancy what trouble it might bring to a innocent person that might never have set foot in the place but for that!'

They left Mrs Porter in tears. On the way home there was much discussion as to the best means of keeping watch upon possible sales. What Henderson-Homberger (for there could be no real doubt of the identity) had done was, obviously, to bring down the requisite number of folio Prayer-Books—disused copies from college chapels and the like, bought ostensibly for the sake of the bindings, which were superficially like enough to the old ones—and to substitute them at his leisure for the genuine articles. A week had now passed without any public notice being taken of the theft. He would take a little time himself to find out about the rarity of the books, and would ultimately, no doubt, 'place' them cautiously. Between them, Davidson and Witham were in a position to know a good deal of what was passing in the book-world, and they could map out the ground pretty completely. A weak point with them at the moment was that neither of them knew under what other name or names Henderson-Homberger carried on business. But there are ways of solving these problems.

And yet all this planning proved unnecessary.

* * * * *

We are transported to a London office on this same 25th of April. We find there, within closed doors, late in the day, two police inspectors, a commissionaire, and a youthful clerk. The two latter, both rather pale and agitated in appearance, are sitting on chairs and being questioned.

'How long do you say you've been in this Mr Poschwitz's employment? Six months? And what was his business? Attended sales in various parts and brought home parcels of books. Did he keep a shop anywhere? No? Disposed of 'em here and there, and sometimes to private collectors. Right. Now then, when did he go out last? Rather better than a week ago. Tell you where he was going? No? Said he was going to start next day from his private residence, and shouldn't be at the office—that's here, eh?—before two days: you was to attend as usual. Where is his private residence? Oh, that's the address, Norwood way; I see. Any family? Not in this country? Now, then, what account do you give of what's happened since he came back? Came back on the Tuesday, did he? and this is the Saturday. Bring any books? One package: where is it? In the safe: you got the key? No, to be sure, it's open, of course. How did he seem when he got back—cheerful? Well, but how do you mean curious? Thought he might be in for an illness: he said that, did he? Odd smell got in his nose, couldn't get rid of it: told you to let him know who wanted to see him before you let 'em in? That wasn't usual with him? Much the same all Wednesday, Thursday, Friday. Out a good deal; said he was going to the British Museum. Often went there to make inquiries in the way of his business. Walked up and down a lot in the office when he was in? Anyone call in on those days? Mostly when he was out. Anyone find him in? Oh, Mr Collinson? Who's Mr Collinson? An old customer: know his address? All right, give it us afterwards. Well, now, what about this morning? You left Mr Poschwitz's here at twelve and went home. Anybody see you? Commissionaire, you did? Remained at home till summoned here. Very well.

'Now commissionaire; we have your name—Watkins, eh? Very well, make your statement: don't go too quick, so as we can get it down.'

'I was on duty 'ere later than usual, Mr Potwitch 'aving asked me to remain on, and ordered his lunching to be sent in, which come as ordered. I was in the lobby from eleven-thirty on, and see Mr Bligh [the clerk] leave at about twelve. After that no one come in at all except Mr Potwitch's lunching come at one o'clock and the man left in five minutes' time. Towards the afternoon I became tired of waitin' and I come upstairs to this first floor. The outer door what lead to the orfice stood open, and I come up to the plate-glass door here. Mr Potwitch he was standing behind the table smoking a cigar, and he laid it down on the mantelpiece and felt in his trouser pockets and took out a key and went across to the safe. And I knocked on the glass, thinkin' to see if he wanted me to come and take away his tray, but he didn't take no notice, bein' engaged with the safe door. Then he got it open and stooped down and seemed to be lifting up a package off of the floor of the safe. And then, sir, I see what looked to be like a great roll of old shabby white flannel about four to five feet high fall for'ards out of the inside of the safe right against Mr Potwitch's shoulder as he was stooping over: and Mr Potwitch he raised himself up as it were, resting his hands on the package, and give a exclamation. And I can't hardly expect you should take what I says, but as true as I stand here I see this roll had a kind of a face in the upper end of it, sir. You can't be more surprised than what I was, I can assure you, and I've seen a lot in me time . . . Yes, I can describe it if you wish it, sir: it was very much the same as this wall here in colour [the wall had an earth-coloured distemper] and it had a bit of a band tied round underneath, and the eyes, well they was dry-like, and much as if there was two big spiders' bodies in the holes. . . Hair? no, I don't know as there was much hair to be seen: the flannel-stuff was over the top of the 'ead. . . I'm very sure it warn't what it should have been. . . No, I only see it in a flash, but I took it in like a photograft —wish I hadn't. . . Yest, sir, it fell right over on to Mr Potwitch's shoulder, and this face hid in his neck—yes, sir, about where the injury was—more like a ferret goin' for a rabbit than anythink else, and he rolled over, and of course I tried to get in at the door, but as you know, sir, it were locked on the inside, and all I could do, I rung up everyone, and the surgeon come, and the police and you gentlemen, and you know as much as what I do. If you won't be requirin' me any more today I'd be glad to be gettin' off home: it's shook me up more than I thought for.'

'Well,' said one of the inspectors, when they were left alone, and 'Well?' said the other inspector: and, after a pause, 'What's the surgeon's report again? You've got it there. Yes. Effect on the blood like the worst kind of snake-bite: death almost instantaneous. I'm glad of that for his sake; he was a nasty sight. No case for detaining this man Watkins, anyway; we know all about him. And what about this safe, now? We'd better go over it again, and, by the way, we haven't opened that package he was busy with when he died.'

'Well, handle it careful,' said the other. 'There might be this snake in it, for what you know. Get a light into the corners of the place, too. Well: there's room for a shortish person to stand up in; but what about ventilation?'

'Perhaps,' said the other slowly, as he explored the safe with an electric torch, 'perhaps they didn't require much of that. My word! it strikes warm coming out of that place! like a vault, it is. But here, what's this bank-like of dust all spread out into the room? That must have come there since the door was opened; it would sweep it all away if you moved it—see? Now what do you make of that?'

'Make of it? About as much as I make of anything else in this case. One of London's mysteries this is going to be, by what I can see, and I don't believe a photographer's box full of large-size old fashioned Prayer-Books is going to take us much further. For that's just what your package is.'

It was a natural but hasty utterance. The preceding narrative shows that there was in fact plenty of material for constructing a case; and when once Messrs. Davidson and Witham had brought their end to Scotland Yard, the join-up was soon made, and the circle completed.

To the relief of Mrs Porter, the owners of Brockstone decided not to replace the books in the chapel: they repose, I believe, in a safe-deposit in town. The police have their own methods of keeping certain matters out of the newspapers: otherwise it can hardly be supposed that Watkins's evidence about Mr Poschwitz's death could have failed to furnish a good many headlines of a startling character to the press.

A NEIGHBOUR'S LANDMARK

THOSE who spend the greater part of their time in reading or writing books are, of course, apt to take rather particular notice of accumulations of books when they come across them. They will not pass a stall, a shop, or even a bedroom-shelf without reading some title, and if they find themselves in an unfamiliar library, no host need trouble himself further about their entertainment. The putting of dispersed sets of volumes together, or the turning right way up of those which the dusting housemaid has left in an apoplectic condition, appeals to them as one of the lesser Works of Mercy. Happy in these employments, and in occasionally opening an eighteenth-century octavo, to see 'what it is all about', and to conclude after five minutes that it deserves the seclusion it now enjoys, I had reached the middle of a wet August afternoon at Betton Court——

'You begin in a deeply Victorian manner,' I said; 'is this to continue?'

'Remember, if you please,' said my friend, looking at me over his spectacles, 'that I am a Victorian by birth and education, and that the Victorian tree may not unreasonably be expected to bear Victorian fruit. Further, remember that an immense quantity of clever and thoughtful Rubbish is now being written about the Victorian age. Now,' he went on, laying his papers on his knee, 'that article, "The Stricken Years", in *The Times* Literary Supplement* the other day,—able? of course it is able; but, oh! my soul and body, do just hand it over here, will you? it's on the table by you.'

'I thought you were to read me something you had written,' I said, without moving, 'but, of course——'

'Yes, I know,' he said. 'Very well, then, I'll do that first. But I *should* like to show you afterwards what I mean. How-ever——' And he lifted the sheets of paper and adjusted his spectacles.

——at Betton Court, where, generations back, two country-house libraries had been fused together, and no descendant of either stock had ever faced the task of picking them over or getting rid of duplicates. Now I am not setting out to tell of rarities I may have discovered, of Shakespeare quartos bound up in volumes of political tracts, or anything of that kind, but of an experience which befell me in the course of my search—an experience which I cannot either explain away or fit into the scheme of my ordinary life.

It was, I said, a wet August afternoon, rather windy, rather warm. Outside the window great trees were stirring and weeping. Between them were stretches of green and yellow country (for the Court stands high on a hill-side), and blue hills far off, veiled with rain. Up above was a very restless and hopeless movement of low clouds travelling northwest. I had suspended my work—if you call it work—for some minutes to stand at the window and look at these things, and at the greenhouse roof on the right with the water sliding off it, and the Church tower that rose behind that. It was all in favour of my going steadily on; no likelihood of a clearing up for hours to come. I, therefore, returned to the shelves, lifted out a set of eight or nine volumes, lettered *Tracts*, and conveyed them to the table for closer examination.

They were for the most part of the reign of Anne. There was a good deal of *The Late Peace, The Late War, The Conduct of the Allies*: there were also *Letters to a Convocation Man; Sermons preached at St Michael's, Queenhithe; Enquiries into a late Charge of the Rt. Rev. the Lord Bishop of Winchester* (or more probably Winton) *to his Clergy*: things all very lively once, and indeed still keeping so much of their old sting that I was tempted to betake myself into an arm-chair in the window, and give them more time than I had intended. Besides, I was somewhat tired by the day. The Church clock struck four, and it really was four, for in 1889 there was no saving of daylight.

So I settled myself. And first I glanced over some of the War pamphlets, and pleased myself by trying to pick out Swift by his style from among the undistinguished. But the War pamphlets needed more knowledge of the geography of the Low Countries than I had. I turned to the Church, and read several pages of what the Dean of Canterbury said to the Society for Promoting Christian Knowledge on the occasion of their anniversary meeting in 1711. When I turned over to a Letter from a Beneficed Clergyman in the Country to the Bishop of C . . . . r, I was becoming languid, and I gazed for some moments at the following sentence without surprise:

'This Abuse (for I think myself justified in calling it by that name) is one which I am persuaded Your Lordship would (if 'twere known to you) exert your utmost efforts to do away. But I am also persuaded that you know no more of its existence than (in the words of the Country Song)

That which walks in Betton Wood
Knows why it walks or why it cries.'*

Then indeed I did sit up in my chair, and run my finger along the lines to make sure that I had read them right. There was no mistake. Nothing more was to be gathered from the rest of the pamphlet. The next paragraph definitely changed the subject: 'But I have said enough upon this Topick' were its opening words. So discreet, too, was the namelessness of the Beneficed Clergyman that he refrained even from initials, and had his letter printed in London.

The riddle was of a kind that might faintly interest anyone: to me, who have dabbled a good deal in works of folk-lore, it was really exciting. I was set upon solving it—on finding out, I mean, what story lay behind it; and, at least, I felt myself lucky in one point, that, whereas I might have come on the paragraph in some College Library far away, here I was at Betton, on the very scene of action.

The Church clock struck five, and a single stroke on a gong followed. This, I knew, meant tea. I heaved myself out of the deep chair, and obeyed the summons.

My host and I were alone at the Court. He came in soon, wet from a round of landlord's errands, and with pieces of local news which had to be passed on before I could make an opportunity of asking whether there was a particular place in the parish that was still known as Betton Wood.

'Betton Wood,' he said, 'was a short mile away, just on the crest of Betton Hill, and my father stubbed up the last bit of

it when it paid better to grow corn than scrub oaks. Why do
you want to know about Betton Wood?'

'Because,' I said, 'in an old pamphlet I was reading just
now, there are two lines of a country song which mention it,
and they sound as if there was a story belonging to them.
Someone says that someone else knows no more of whatever
it may be—

> Than that which walks in Betton Wood
> Knows why it walks or why it cries.'

'Goodness,' said Philipson, 'I wonder whether that was
why . . . I must ask old Mitchell.' He muttered something else
to himself, and took some more tea, thoughtfully.

'Whether that was why——?' I said.

'Yes, I was going to say, whether that was why my father
had the Wood stubbed up. I said just now it was to get more
plough-land, but I don't really know if it was. I don't believe
he ever broke it up: it's rough pasture at this moment. But
there's one old chap at least who'd remember something of
it—old Mitchell.' He looked at his watch. 'Blest if I don't go
down there and ask him. I don't think I'll take you,' he went
on; 'he's not so likely to tell anything he thinks is odd if
there's a stranger by.'

'Well, mind you remember every single thing he does
tell. As for me, if it clears up, I shall go out, and if it doesn't,
I shall go on with the books.'

It did clear up, sufficiently at least to make me think
it worth while to walk up the nearest hill and look over the
country. I did not know the lie of the land; it was the first
visit I had paid to Philipson, and this was the first day of it.
So I went down the garden and through the wet shrubberies
with a very open mind, and offered no resistance to the
indistinct impulse—was it, however, so very indistinct?—
which kept urging me to bear to the left whenever there was
a forking of the path. The result was that after ten minutes
or more of dark going between dripping rows of box and laurel
and privet, I was confronted by a stone arch in the Gothic
style set in the stone wall which encircled the whole demesne.
The door was fastened by a spring-lock, and I took the precaution of leaving this on the jar as I passed out into the

road. That road I crossed, and entered a narrow lane between hedges which led upward; and that lane I pursued at a leisurely pace for as much as half a mile, and went on to the field to which it led. I was now on a good point of vantage for taking in the situation of the Court, the village, and the environment; and I leant upon a gate and gazed westward and downward.

I think we must all know the landscapes—are they by Birket Foster,* or somewhat earlier?—which, in the form of wood-cuts, decorate the volumes of poetry that lay on the drawing-room tables of our fathers and grandfathers—volumes in 'Art Cloth, embossed bindings'; that strikes me as being the right phrase. I confess myself an admirer of them, and especially of those which show the peasant leaning over a gate in a hedge and surveying, at the bottom of a downward slope, the village church spire—embosomed amid venerable trees, and a fertile plain intersected by hedgerows, and bounded by distant hills, behind which the orb of day is sinking (or it may be rising) amid level clouds illumined by his dying (or nascent) ray. The expressions employed here are those which seem appropriate to the pictures I have in mind; and were there opportunity, I would try to work in the Vale, the Grove, the Cot, and the Flood. Anyhow, they are beautiful to me, these landscapes, and it was just such a one that I was now surveying. It might have come straight out of *Gems of Sacred Song, selected by a Lady* and given as a birthday present to Eleanor Philipson in 1852 by her attached friend Millicent Graves. All at once I turned as if I had been stung. There thrilled into my right ear and pierced my head a note of incredible sharpness, like the shriek of a bat, only ten times intensified—the kind of thing that makes one wonder if something has not given way in one's brain. I held my breath, and covered my ear, and shivered. Something in the circulation: another minute or two, I thought, and I return home. But I must fix the view a little more firmly in my mind. Only, when I turned to it again, the taste was gone out of it. The sun was down behind the hill, and the light was off the fields, and when the clock bell in the Church tower struck seven, I thought no longer of kind mellow evening hours of rest, and scents of flowers and woods on evening air; and of how someone on a farm a mile or two off would be saying 'How clear Betton bell sounds tonight after the rain!'; but instead images came to me of dusty beams and creeping spiders and savage owls up in the tower, and forgotten graves and their ugly contents below, and of flying Time and all it had taken out of my life. And just then into my left ear—close as if lips had been put within an inch of my head, the frightful scream came thrilling again.

There was no mistake possible now. It *was* from outside. 'With no language but a cry'* was the thought that flashed into my mind. Hideous it was beyond anything I had heard or have heard since, but I could read no emotion in it, and doubted if I could read any intelligence. All its effect was to take away every vestige, every possibility, of enjoyment, and make this no place to stay in one moment more. Of course there was nothing to be seen: but I was convinced that, if I waited, the thing would pass me again on its aimless, end-less beat, and I could not bear the notion of a third repetition. I hurried back to the lane and down the hill. But when I came to the arch in the wall I stopped. Could I be sure of my way among those dank alleys, which would be danker and darker now! No, I confessed to myself that I was afraid: so jarred were all my nerves with the cry on the hill that I really felt I could not afford to be startled even by a little bird in a bush, or a rabbit. I followed the road which followed the wall, and I was not sorry when I came to the gate and the lodge, and descried Philipson coming up towards it from the direc-tion of the village.

'And where have you been?' said he.

'I took that lane that goes up the hill opposite the stone arch in the wall.'

'Oh! did you? Then you've been very near where Betton Wood used to be: at least, if you followed it up to the top, and out into the field.'

And if the reader will believe it, that was the first time that I put two and two together. Did I at once tell Philipson what had happened to me? I did not. I have not had other experiences of the kind which are called super-natural, or

-normal, or -physical, but, though I knew very well I must speak of this one before long, I was not at all anxious to do so; and I think I have read that this is a common case.

So all I said was: 'Did you see the old man you meant to?'

'Old Mitchell? Yes, I did; and got something of a story out of him. I'll keep it till after dinner. It really is rather odd.'

So when we were settled after dinner he began to report, faithfully, as he said, the dialogue that had taken place. Mitchell, not far off eighty years old, was in his elbow-chair. The married daughter with whom he lived was in and out preparing for tea.

After the usual salutations: 'Mitchell, I want you to tell me something about the Wood.'

'What Wood's that, Master Reginald?'

'Betton Wood. Do you remember it?'

Mitchell slowly raised his hand and pointed an accusing forefinger. 'It were your father done away with Betton Wood, Master Reginald, I can tell you that much.'

'Well, I know it was, Mitchell. You needn't look at me as if it were my fault.'

'Your fault? No, I says it were your father done it, before your time.'

'Yes, and I dare say if the truth was known, it was your father that advised him to do it, and I want to know why.'

Mitchell seemed a little amused. 'Well,' he said, 'my father were woodman to your father and your grandfather before him, and if he didn't know what belonged to his business, he'd oughter done. And if he did give advice that way, I suppose he might have had his reasons, mightn't he now?'

'Of course he might, and I want you to tell me what they were.'

'Well now, Master Reginald, whatever makes you think as I know what his reasons might 'a been I don't know how many year ago?'

'Well, to be sure, it is a long time, and you might easily have forgotten, if ever you knew. I suppose the only thing is for me to go and ask old Ellis what he can recollect about it.'

That had the effect I hoped for.

'Old Ellis!' he growled. 'First time ever I hear anyone say old Ellis were any use for any purpose. I should 'a thought you know'd better than that yourself, Master Reginald. What do you suppose old Ellis can tell you better'n what I can about Betton Wood, and what call have he got to be put afore me, I should like to know. His father warn't woodman on the place: he were ploughman—that's what he was, and so anyone could tell you what knows; anyone could tell you that, I says.'

'Just so, Mitchell, but if you know all about Betton Wood and won't tell me, why, I must do the next best I can, and try and get it out of somebody else; and old Ellis has been on the place very nearly as long as you have.'

'That he ain't, not by eighteen months! Who says I wouldn't tell you nothing about the Wood? I ain't no objection; only it's a funny kind of a tale, and 'taint right to my thinkin' it should be all about the parish. You, Lizzie, do you keep in your kitchen a bit. Me and Master Reginald wants to have a word or two private. But one thing I'd like to know, Master Reginald, what come to put you upon asking about it today?'

'Oh! well, I happened to hear of an old saying about something that walks in Betton Wood. And I wondered if that had anything to do with its being cleared away: that's all.'

'Well, you was in the right, Master Reginald, however you come to hear of it, and I believe I can tell you the rights of it better than anyone in this parish, let alone old Ellis. You see it came about this way: that the shortest road to Allen's Farm laid through the Wood, and when we was little my poor mother she used to go so many times in the week to the farm to fetch a quart of milk, because Mr Allen what had the farm then under your father, he was a good man, and anyone that had a young family to bring up, he was willing to allow 'em so much in the week. But never you mind about that now. And my poor mother she never liked to go through the Wood, because there was a lot of talk in the place, and sayings like what you spoke about just now. But every now and again, when she happened to be late with her work, she'd

have to take the short road through the Wood, and as sure
as ever she did, she'd come home in a rare state. I remember
her and my father talking about it, and he'd say, "Well, but
it can't do you no harm, Emma," and she'd say, "Oh! but
you haven't an idear of it, George. Why, it went right
through my head," she says, "and I came over all bewildered-
like, and as if I didn't know where I was. You see, George,"
she says, "it ain't as if you was about there in the dusk. You
always goes there in the daytime, now don't you?" and he
says: "Why, to be sure I do; do you take me for a fool?" And
so they'd go on. And time passed by, and I think it wore her
out, because, you understand, it warn't no use to go for the
milk not till the afternoon, and she wouldn't never send none
of us children instead, for fear we should get a fright. Nor
she wouldn't tell us about it herself. "No," she says, "it's bad
enough for me. I don't want no one else to go through it, nor
yet hear talk about it." But one time I recollect she says,
"Well, first it's a rustling-like all along in the bushes, coming
very quick, either towards me or after me according to the
time, and then there comes this scream as appears to pierce
right through from the one ear to the other, and the later
I am coming through, the more like I am to hear it twice
over; but thanks be, I never yet heard it the three times."
And then I asked her, and I says: "Why, that seems like
someone walking to and fro all the time, don't it?" and she
says, "Yes, it do, and whatever it is she wants, I can't
think": and I says, "Is it a woman, mother?" and she says,
"Yes, I've heard it is a woman."

'Anyway, the end of it was my father he spoke to your
father, and told him the Wood was a bad wood. "There's
never a bit of game in it, and there's never a bird's nest there,"
he says, "and it ain't no manner of use to you." And after
a lot of talk, your father he come and see my mother about
it, and he see she warn't one of these silly women as gets
nervish about nothink at all, and he made up his mind there
was somethink in it, and after that he asked about in the
neighbourhood, and I believe he made out somethink, and
wrote it down in a paper what very like you've got up at the
Court, Master Reginald. And then he gave the order, and

the Wood was stubbed up. They done all the work in the daytime, I recollect, and was never there after three o'clock.'

'Didn't they find anything to explain it, Mitchell? No bones or anything of that kind?'

'Nothink at all, Master Reginald, only the mark of a hedge and ditch along the middle, much about where the quickset hedge run now; and with all the work they done, if there had been anyone put away there, they was bound to find 'em. But I don't know whether it done much good, after all. People here don't seem to like the place no better than they did afore.'

'That's about what I got out of Mitchell,' said Philipson, 'and as far as any explanation goes, it leaves us very much where we were. I must see if I can't find that paper.'

'Why didn't your father ever tell you about the business?' I said.

'He died before I went to school, you know, and I imagine he didn't want to frighten us children by any such story. I can remember being shaken and slapped by my nurse for running up that lane towards the Wood when we were coming back rather late one winter afternoon: but in the daytime no one interfered with our going into the Wood if we wanted to—only we never did want.'

'Hm!' I said, and then, 'Do you you think you'll be able to find that paper that your father wrote?'

'Yes,' he said, 'I do. I expect it's no farther away than that cupboard behind you. There's a bundle or two of things specially put aside, most of which I've looked through at various times, and I know there's one envelope labelled Betton Wood: but as there was no Betton Wood any more, I never thought it would be worth while to open it, and I never have. We'll do it now, though.'

'Before you do,' I said (I was still reluctant, but I thought this was perhaps the moment for my disclosure), 'I'd better tell you I think Mitchell was right when he doubted if clearing away the Wood had put things straight.' And I gave the account you have heard already: I need not say Philipson was interested. 'Still there?' he said. 'It's amazing. Look here, will you come out there with me now, and see what happens?'

'I will do no such thing,' I said, 'and if you knew the feeling, you'd be glad to walk ten miles in the opposite direction. Don't talk of it. Open your envelope, and let's hear what your father made out.'

He did so, and read me the three or four pages of jottings which it contained. At the top was written a motto from Scott's *Glenfinlas*,* which seemed to me well-chosen:

Where walks, they say, the shrieking ghost.

Then there were notes of his talk with Mitchell's mother, from which I extract only this much. 'I asked her if she never thought she saw anything to account for the sounds she heard. She told me, no more than once, on the darkest evening she ever came through the Wood; and then she seemed forced to look behind her as the rustling came in the bushes, and she thought she saw something all in tatters with the two arms held out in front of it coming on very fast, and at that she ran for the stile, and tore her gown all to flinders getting over it.'

Then he had gone to two other people whom he found very shy of talking. They seemed to think, among other things, that it reflected discredit on the parish. However, one, Mrs Emma Frost, was prevailed upon to repeat what her mother had told her. 'They say it was a lady of title that married twice over, and her first husband went by the name of Brown, or it might have been Bryan ['Yes, there were Bryans at the Court before it came into our family,' Philipson put in], and she removed her neighbour's landmark: leastways she took in a fair piece of the best pasture in Betton parish what belonged by rights to two children as hadn't no one to speak for them, and they say years after she went from bad to worse, and made out false papers to gain thousands of pounds up in London, and at last they was proved in law to be false, and she would have been tried and put to death very like, only she escaped away for the time. But no one can't avoid the curse that's laid on them that removes the landmark, and so we take it she can't leave Betton before someone take and put it right again.'

At the end of the paper there was a note to this effect. 'I

regret that I cannot find any clue to previous owners of the fields adjoining the Wood. I do not hesitate to say that if I could discover their representatives, I should do my best to indemnify them for the wrong done to them in years now long past: for it is undeniable that the Wood is very curiously disturbed in the manner described by the people of the place. In my present ignorance alike of the extent of the land wrongly appropriated, and of the rightful owners, I am reduced to keeping a separate note of the profits derived from this part of the estate, and my custom has been to apply the sum that would represent the annual yield of about five acres to the common benefit of the parish and to charitable uses: and I hope that those who succeed me may see fit to continue this practice.'

So much for the elder Mr Philipson's paper. To those who, like myself, are readers of the State Trials* it will have gone far to illuminate the situation. They will remember how between the years 1678 and 1684 the Lady Ivy, formerly Theodosia Bryan,* was alternately Plaintiff and Defendant in a series of trials in which she was trying to establish a claim against the Dean and Chapter of St Paul's for a considerable and very valuable tract of land in Shadwell: how in the last of those trials, presided over by L. C. J. Jeffreys, it was proved up to the hilt that the deeds upon which she based her claim were forgeries executed under her orders: and how, after an information for perjury and forgery was issued against her, she disappeared completely—so completely, indeed, that no expert has ever been able to tell me what became of her.

Does not the story I have told suggest that she may still be heard of on the scene of one of her earlier and more successful exploits?

*   *   *   *   *

'That,' said my friend, as he folded up his papers, 'is a very faithful record of my one extraordinary experience. And now——'

But I had so many questions to ask him, as for instance, whether his friend had found the proper owner of the land, whether he had done anything about the hedge, whether the sounds were ever heard now, what was the exact title and date of his pamphlet, etc., etc., that bed-time came and passed, without his having an opportunity to revert to the Literary Supplement of The Times.

[Thanks to the researches of Sir John Fox, in his book on The Lady Ivie's Trial (Oxford, 1929), we now know that my heroine died in her bed in 1695, having—heaven knows how —been acquitted of the forgery, for which she had undoubtedly been responsible.*]

A WARNING TO THE CURIOUS

THE place on the east coast which the reader is asked to consider is Seaburgh.* It is not very different now from what I remember it to have been when I was a child. Marshes intersected by dykes to the south, recalling the early chapters of *Great Expectations*; flat fields to the north, merging into heath; heath, fir woods, and, above all, gorse, inland. A long sea-front and a street: behind that a spacious church of flint, with a broad, solid western tower and a peal of six bells. How well I remember their sound on a hot Sunday in August, as our party went slowly up the white, dusty slope of road towards them, for the church stands at the top of a short, steep incline. They rang with a flat clacking sort of sound on those hot days, but when the air was softer they were mellower too. The railway ran down to its little terminus farther along the same road. There was a gay white windmill just before you came to the station, and another down near the shingle at the south end of the town, and yet others on higher ground to the north. There were cottages of bright red brick with slate roofs . . . but why do I encumber you with these commonplace details? The fact is that they come crowding to the point of the pencil when it begins to write of Seaburgh. I should like to be sure that I had allowed the right ones to get on to the paper. But I forgot. I have not quite done with the word-painting business yet.

Walk away from the sea and the town, pass the station, and turn up the road on the right. It is a sandy road, parallel with the railway, and if you follow it, it climbs to somewhat higher ground. On your left (you are now going northward) is heath, on your right (the side towards the sea) is a belt of old firs, wind-beaten, thick at the top, with the slope that old seaside trees have; seen on the skyline from the train they would tell you in an instant, if you did not know it, that you were approaching a windy coast. Well, at the top of my little hill, a line of these firs strikes out and runs towards the sea, for there is a ridge that goes that way; and the ridge ends in a rather well-defined mound commanding the level fields of rough grass, and a little knot of fir trees crowns it. And here you may sit on a hot spring day, very well content to look at blue sea, white windmills, red cottages, bright green grass, church tower, and distant martello tower on the south.

As I have said, I began to know Seaburgh as a child; but a gap of a good many years separates my early knowledge from that which is more recent. Still it keeps its place in my affections, and any tales of it that I pick up have an interest for me. One such tale is this: it came to me in a place very remote from Seaburgh, and quite accidentally, from a man whom I had been able to oblige—enough in his opinion to justify his making me his confidant to this extent.

I know all that country more or less (he said). I used to go to Seaburgh pretty regularly for golf in the spring. I generally put up at the 'Bear', with a friend—Henry Long it was, you knew him perhaps—('Slightly,' I said) and we used to take a sitting-room and be very happy there. Since he died I haven't cared to go there. And I don't know that I should anyhow after the particular thing that happened on our last visit.

It was in April 19— we were there, and by some chance we were almost the only people in the hotel. So the ordinary public rooms were practically empty, and we were the more surprised when, after dinner, our sitting-room door opened, and a young man put his head in. We were aware of this young man. He was rather a rabbity anaemic subject—light hair and light eyes—but not unpleasing. So when he said: 'I beg your pardon, is this a private room?' we did not growl and say: 'Yes, it is,' but Long said, or I did—no matter which: 'Please come in.' 'Oh, may I?' he said, and seemed relieved. Of course it was obvious that he wanted company; and as he was a reasonable kind of person—not the sort to bestow his whole family history on you—we urged him to make himself at home. 'I dare say you find the other rooms rather bleak,' I said. Yes, he did: but it was really too good of us, and so on. That being got over, he made some pretence of reading a book. Long was playing Patience, I was writing. It became plain to me after a few minutes that this visitor of ours was in rather a state of fidgets or nerves, which communicated itself to me, and so I put away my writing and turned to at engaging him in talk.

After some remarks, which I forget, he became rather confidential. 'You'll think it very odd of me' (this was the sort of way he began), 'but the fact is I've had something of a shock.' Well, I recommended a drink of some cheering kind, and we had it. The waiter coming in made an interruption (and I thought our young man seemed very jumpy when the door opened), but after a while he got back to his woes again. There was nobody he knew in the place, and he did happen to know who we both were (it turned out there was some common acquaintance in town), and really he did want a word of advice, if we didn't mind. Of course we both said: 'By all means,' or 'Not at all,' and Long put away his cards. And we settled down to hear what his difficulty was.

'It began,' he said, 'more than a week ago, when I bicycled over to Froston,* only about five or six miles, to see the church; I'm very much interested in architecture, and it's got one of those pretty porches with niches and shields. I took a photograph of it, and then an old man who was tidying up in the churchyard came and asked if I'd care to look into the church. I said yes, and he produced a key and let me in. There wasn't much inside, but I told him it was a nice little church, and he kept it very clean, "but," I said, "the porch is the best part of it." We were just outside the porch then, and he said, "Ah, yes, that is a nice porch; and do you know, sir, what's the meanin' of that coat of arms there?"

'It was the one with the three crowns, and though I'm not much of a herald, I was able to say yes, I thought it was the old arms of the kingdom of East Anglia.

' "That's right, sir," he said, "and do you know the meanin' of them three crowns that's on it?"

'I said I'd no doubt it was known, but I couldn't recollect to have heard it myself.

' "Well, then," he said, "for all you're a scholard, I can tell you something you don't know. Them's the three 'oly crowns what was buried in the ground near by the coast to keep the Germans from landing—ah, I can see you don't believe that. But I tell you, if it hadn't have been for one of them 'oly crowns bein' there still, them Germans would a landed here time and again, they would. Landed with their ships, and killed man, woman and child in their beds. Now then, that's the truth what I'm telling you, that is; and if you don't believe me, you ast the rector. There he comes: you ast him, I says."

'I looked round, and there was the rector, a nice-looking old man, coming up the path; and before I could begin assuring my old man, who was getting quite excited, that I didn't disbelieve him, the rector struck in, and said: "What's all this about, John? Good day to you, sir. Have you been looking at our little church?"

'So then there was a little talk which allowed the old man to calm down, and then the rector asked him again what was the matter.

' "Oh," he said, "it warn't nothink, only I was telling this gentleman he'd ought to ast you about them 'oly crowns."

' "Ah, yes, to be sure," said the rector, "that's a very curious matter, isn't it? But I don't know whether the gentleman is interested in our old stories, eh?"

' "Oh, he'll be interested fast enough," says the old man, "he'll put his confidence in what you tells him, sir; why, you known William Ager yourself, father and son too."

'Then I put in a word to say how much I should like to hear all about it, and before many minutes I was walking up the village street with the rector, who had one or two words to say to parishioners, and then to the rectory, where he took me into his study. He had made out, on the way, that I really was capable of taking an intelligent interest in a piece of folk-lore, and not quite the ordinary tripper. So he was very willing to talk, and it is rather surprising to me that the particular legend he told me has not made its way into print before. His account of it was this: "There has always been a belief in these parts in the three holy crowns. The old people say they were buried in different places near the coast to keep off the Danes or the French or the Germans. And they say that one of the three was dug up a long time ago, an danother has disappeared by the encroaching of the sea, and one's still left doing its work, keeping off invaders. Well, now, if you have read the ordinary guides and histories of this county, you will remember perhaps that in 1687 a crown, which was said to be the crown of Redwald, King of the East Angles, was dug up at Rendlesham,* and alas! alas! melted down before it was even properly described or drawn. Well, Rendlesham isn't on the coast, but it isn't so very far inland, and it's on a very important line of access. And I believe that is the crown which the people mean when they say that one has been dug up. Then on the south you don't want me to tell you where there was a Saxon royal palace which is now under the sea, eh? Well, there was the second crown, I take it. And up beyond these two, they say, lies the third."

' "Do they say where it is?" of course I asked.

'He said, "Yes, indeed, they do, but they don't tell," and his manner did not encourage me to put the obvious question. Instead of that I waited a moment, and said: "What did the old man mean when he said you knew William Ager, as if that had something to do with the crowns?"

' "To be sure," he said, "now that's another curious story. These Agers—it's a very old name in these parts, but I can't find that they were ever people of quality or big owners— these Agers say, or said, that their branch of the family were the guardians of the last crown. A certain old Nathaniel Ager was the first one I knew—I was born and brought up quite near here—and he, I believe, camped out at the place during the whole of the war of 1870. William, his son, did the same, I know, during the South African War.* And young William, *his* son, who has only died fairly recently, took lodgings at the cottage nearest the spot, and I've no doubt hastened his end, for he was a consumptive, by exposure and night watching. And he was the last of that branch. It was a dreadful grief to him to think that he was the last, but he could do nothing, the only relations at all near to him were in the colonies. I wrote letters for him to them imploring them to come over on business very important to the family, but there has been no answer. So the last of the holy crowns, if it's there, has no guardian now."

'That was what the rector told me, and you can fancy how interesting I found it. The only thing I could think of when I left him was how to hit upon the spot where the crown was supposed to be. I wish I'd left it alone.

'But there was a sort of fate in it, for as I bicycled back past the churchyard wall my eye caught a fairly new gravestone, and on it was the name of William Ager. Of course I got off and read it. It said "of this parish, died at Seaburgh 19—, aged 28." There it was, you see. A little judicious questioning in the right place, and I should at least find the cottage nearest the spot. Only I didn't quite know what was the right place to begin my questioning at. Again there was fate: it took me to the curiosity-shop down that way—you know—and I turned over some old books, and, if you please, one was a prayer-book of 1740 odd, in a rather handsome binding—I'll just go and get it, it's in my room.'

He left us in a state of some surprise, but we had hardly time to exchange any remarks when he was back, panting, and handed us the book opened at the fly-leaf, on which was, in a straggly hand:

> Nathaniel Ager is my name and England is my nation,
> Seaburgh is my dwelling-place and Christ is my Salvation,
> When I am dead and in my Grave, and all my bones are
>   rotton,
> I hope the Lord will think on me when I am quite forgotton.

This poem was dated 1754, and there were many more entries of Agers, Nathaniel, Frederick, William, and so on, ending with William, 19—.

'You see,' he said, 'anybody would call it the greatest bit of luck. I did, but I don't now. Of course I asked the shopman about William Ager, and of course he happened to remember that he lodged in a cottage in the North Field and died there. This was just chalking the road for me. I knew which the cottage must be: there is only one sizable one about there. The next thing was to scrape some sort of acquaintance with the people, and I took a walk that way at once. A dog did the business for me: he made at me so fiercely that they had to run out and beat him off, and then naturally begged my pardon, and we got into talk. I had only to bring up Ager's name, and pretend I knew, or thought I knew something of him, and then the woman said how sad it was him dying so young, and she was sure it came of him spending the night out of doors in the cold weather. Then I had to say: "Did he go out on the sea at night?" and she said: "Oh, no, it was on the hillock yonder with the trees on it." And there I was.

'I know something about digging in these barrows: I've opened many of them in the down country. But that was with owner's leave, and in broad daylight and with men to help. I had to prospect very carefully here before I put a spade in: I couldn't trench across the mound, and with those old firs growing there I knew there would be awkward tree roots. Still the soil was very light and sandy and easy, and there was a rabbit hole or so that might be developed into a sort of tunnel. The going out and coming back at odd hours to the hotel was going to be the awkward part. When I made up my mind about the way to excavate I told the people that I was called away for a night, and I spent it out there. I made my tunnel: I won't bore you with the details of how I supported it and filled it in when I'd done, but the main thing is that I got the crown.'

Naturally we both broke out into exclamations of surprise and interest. I for one had long known about the finding of the crown at Rendlesham and had often lamented its fate. No one has ever seen an Anglo-Saxon crown—at least no one had. But our man gazed at us with a rueful eye. 'Yes,' he said, 'and the worst of it is I don't know how to put it back.'

'Put it back?' we cried out. 'Why, my dear sir, you've made one of the most exciting finds ever heard of in this country. Of course it ought to go to the Jewel House at the Tower. What's your difficulty? If you're thinking about the owner of the land, and treasure-trove, and all that, we can certainly help you through. Nobody's going to make a fuss about technicalities in a case of this kind.'

Probably more was said, but all he did was to put his face in his hands, and mutter: 'I don't know how to put it back.'

At last Long said: 'You'll forgive me, I hope, if I seem impertinent, but are you *quite* sure you've got it?' I was

wanting to ask much the same question myself, for of course
the story did seem a lunatic's dream when one thought over
it. But I hadn't quite dared to say what might hurt the poor
young man's feelings. However, he took it quite calmly—
really, with the calm of despair, you might say. He sat up
and said: 'Oh yes, there's no doubt of that: I have it here,
in my room, locked up in my bag. You can come and look
at it if you like: I won't offer to bring it here.'

We were not likely to let the chance slip. We went with
him; his room was only a few doors off. The boots was just
collecting shoes in the passage: or so we thought: afterwards
we were not sure. Our visitor—his name was Paxton—was
in a worse state of shivers than before, and went hurriedly
into the room, and beckoned us after him, turned on the
light, and shut the door carefully. Then he unlocked his kit-
bag, and produced a bundle of clean pocket-handkerchiefs in
which something was wrapped, laid it on the bed, and undid
it. I can now say I *have* seen an actual Anglo-Saxon crown.
It was of silver—as the Rendlesham one is always said to have
been—it was set with some gems, mostly antique intaglios
and cameos, and was of rather plain, almost rough work-
manship. In fact, it was like those you see on the coins and
in the manuscripts. I found no reason to think it was later
than the ninth century. I was intensely interested, of course,
and I wanted to turn it over in my hands, but Paxton
prevented me. 'Don't *you* touch it,' he said, 'I'll do that.'
And with a sigh that was, I declare to you, dreadful to hear,
he took it up and turned it about so that we could see every
part of it. 'Seen enough?' he said at last, and we nodded. He
wrapped it up and locked it in his bag, and stood looking at
us dumbly. 'Come back to our room,' Long said, 'and tell us
what the trouble is.' He thanked us, and said: 'Will you
go first and see if—if the coast is clear?' That wasn't very
intelligible, for our proceedings hadn't been, after all, very
suspicious, and the hotel, as I said, was practically empty.
However, we were beginning to have inklings of—we didn't
know what, and anyhow nerves are infectious. So we did
go, first peering out as we opened the door, and fancying
(I found we both had the fancy) that a shadow, or more than

a shadow—but it made no sound—passed from before us to one side as we came out into the passage. 'It's all right,' we whispered to Paxton—whispering seemed the proper tone—and we went, with him between us, back to our sitting-room. I was preparing, when we got there, to be ecstatic about the unique interest of what we had seen, but when I looked at Paxton I saw that would be terribly out of place, and I left it to him to begin.

'What *is* to be done?' was his opening. Long thought it right (as he explained to me afterwards) to be obtuse, and said: 'Why not find out who the owner of the land is, and inform——' 'Oh, no, no!' Paxton broke in impatiently, 'I beg your pardon: you've been very kind, but don't you see it's got to go back, and I daren't be there at night, and daytime's impossible. Perhaps, though, you don't see: well, then, the truth is that I've never been alone since I touched it.' I was beginning some fairly stupid comment, but Long caught my eye, and I stopped. Long said: 'I think I do see, perhaps: but wouldn't it be—a relief—to tell us a little more clearly what the situation is?'

Then it all came out: Paxton looked over his shoulder and beckoned to us to come nearer to him, and began speaking in a low voice: we listened most intently, of course, and compared notes afterwards, and I wrote down our version, so I am confident I have what he told us almost word for word. He said: 'It began when I was first prospecting, and put me off again and again. There was always somebody—a man—standing by one of the firs. This was in daylight, you know. He was never in front of me. I always saw him with the tail of my eye on the left or the right, and he was never there when I looked straight for him. I would lie down for quite a long time and take careful observations, and make sure there was no one, and then when I got up and began prospecting again, there he was. And he began to give me hints, besides; for wherever I put that prayer-book—short of locking it up, which I did at last—when I came back to my room it was always out on my table open at the fly-leaf where the names are, and one of my razors across it to keep it open. I'm sure he just can't open my bag, or something more would have happened. You see, he's light and weak, but all the same I daren't face him. Well, then, when I was making the tunnel, of course it was worse, and if I hadn't been so keen I should have dropped the whole thing and run. It was like someone scraping at my back all the time: I thought for a long time it was only soil dropping on me, but as I got nearer the —the crown, it was unmistakable. And when I actually laid it bare and got my fingers into the ring of it and pulled it out, there came a sort of cry behind me—oh, I can't tell you how desolate it was! And horribly threatening too. It spoilt all my pleasure in my find—cut it off that moment. And if I hadn't been the wretched fool I am, I should have put the thing back and left it. But I didn't. The rest of the time was just awful. I had hours to get through before I could decently come back to the hotel. First I spent time filling up my tunnel and covering my tracks, and all the while he was there trying to thwart me. Sometimes, you know, you see him, and sometimes you don't, just as he pleases, I think: he's there, but he has some power over your eyes. Well, I wasn't off the spot very long before sunrise, and then I had to get to the junction for Seaburgh, and take a train back. And though it was daylight fairly soon, I don't know if that made it much better. There were always hedges, or gorse-bushes, or park fences along the road—some sort of cover, I mean—and I was never easy for a second. And then when I began to meet people going to work, they always looked behind me very strangely: it might have been that they were surprised at seeing anyone so early; but I didn't think it was only that, and I don't now: they didn't look exactly at *me*. And the porter at the train was like that too. And the guard held open the door after I'd got into the carriage—just as he would if there was somebody else coming, you know. Oh, you may be very sure it isn't my fancy,' he said with a dull sort of laugh. Then he went on: 'And even if I do get it put back, he won't forgive me: I can tell that. And I was so happy a fortnight ago.' He dropped into a chair, and I believe he began to cry.

We didn't know what to say, but we felt we must come to the rescue somehow, and so—it really seemed the only thing—we said if he was so set on putting the crown back in its place, we would help him. And I must say that after what we had heard it did seem the right thing. If these horrid consequences had come on this poor man, might there not really be something in the original idea of the crown having some curious power bound up with it, to guard the coast? At least, that was my feeling, and I think it was Long's too. Our offer was very welcome to Paxton, anyhow. When could we do it? It was nearing half-past ten. Could we contrive to make a late walk plausible to the hotel people that very night? We looked out of the window: there was a brilliant full moon—the Paschal moon.* Long undertook to tackle the boots and propitiate him. He was to say that we should not be much over the hour, and if we did find it so pleasant that we stopped out a bit longer we would see that he didn't lose by sitting up. Well, we were pretty regular customers of the hotel, and did not give much trouble, and were considered by the servants to be not under the mark in the way of tips; and so the boots *was* propitiated, and let us out on to the sea-front, and remained, as we heard later, looking after us. Paxton had a large coat over his arm, under which was the wrapped-up crown.

So we were off on this strange errand before we had time to think how very much out of the way it was. I have told this part quite shortly on purpose, for it really does represent the haste with which we settled our plan and took action. 'The shortest way is up the hill and through the churchyard,' Paxton said, as we stood a moment before the hotel looking up and down the front. There was nobody about—nobody at all. Seaburgh out of the season is an early, quiet place. 'We can't go along the dyke by the cottage, because of the dog,' Paxton also said, when I pointed to what I thought a shorter way along the front and across two fields. The reason he gave was good enough. We went up the road to the church, and turned in at the churchyard gate. I confess to having thought that there might be some lying there who might be conscious of our business: but if it was so, they were also conscious that one who was on their side, so to say, had us under surveillance, and we saw no sign of them. But under observation we felt we were, as I have never felt it at another time.

Specially was it so when we passed out of the churchyard into a narrow path with close high hedges, through which we hurried as Christian did through that Valley;* and so got out into open fields. Then along hedges, though I would sooner have been in the open, where I could see if anyone was visible behind me; over a gate or two, and then a swerve to the left, taking us up on to the ridge which ended in that mound.

As we neared it, Henry Long felt, and I felt too, that there were what I can only call dim presences waiting for us, as well as a far more actual one attending us. Of Paxton's agitation all this time I can give you no adequate picture: he breathed like a hunted beast, and we could not either of us look at his face. How he would manage when we got to the very place we had not troubled to think: he had seemed so sure that that would not be difficult. Nor was it. I never saw anything like the dash with which he flung himself at a particular spot in the side of the mound, and tore at it, so that in a very few minutes the greater part of his body was out of sight. We stood holding the coat and that bundle of handkerchiefs, and looking, very fearfully, I must admit, about us. There was nothing to be seen: a line of dark firs behind us made one skyline, more trees and the church tower half a mile off on the right, cottages and a windmill on the horizon on the left, calm sea dead in front, faint barking of a dog at a cottage on a gleaming dyke between us and it: full moon making that path we know across the sea: the eternal whisper of the Scotch firs just above us, and of the sea in front. Yet, in all this quiet, an acute, an acrid consciousness of a restrained hostility very near us, like a dog on a leash that might be let go at any moment.

Paxton pulled himself out of the hole, and stretched a hand back to us. 'Give it to me,' he whispered, 'unwrapped.' We pulled off the handkerchiefs, and he took the crown. The moonlight just fell on it as he snatched it. We had not ourselves touched that bit of metal, and I have thought since that it was just as well. In another moment Paxton was out of the hole again and busy shovelling back the soil with hands that were already bleeding. He would have none of our help, though. It was much the longest part of the job to get the place to look undisturbed: yet—I don't know how—he made a wonderful success of it. At last he was satisfied, and we turned back.

We were a couple of hundred yards from the hill when Long suddenly said to him: 'I say, you've left your coat there. That won't do. See?' And I certainly did see it—the long dark overcoat lying where the tunnel had been. Paxton had not stopped, however: he only shook his head, and held up the coat on his arm. And when we joined him, he said, without any excitement, but as if nothing mattered any more: 'That wasn't my coat.' And, indeed, when we looked back again, that dark thing was not to be seen.

Well, we got out on to the road, and came rapidly back that way. It was well before twelve when we got in, trying to put a good face on it, and saying—Long and I—what a lovely night it was for a walk. The boots was on the look-out for us, and we made remarks like that for his edification as we entered the hotel. He gave another look up and down the sea-front before he locked the front door, and said: 'You didn't meet many people about, I s'pose, sir?' 'No, indeed, not a soul,' I said; at which I remember Paxton looked oddly at me. 'Only I thought I see someone turn up the station road after you gentlemen,' said the boots. 'Still, you was three together, and I don't suppose he meant mischief.' I didn't know what to say; Long merely said 'Good night,' and we went off upstairs, promising to turn out all lights, and to go to bed in a few minutes.

Back in our room, we did our very best to make Paxton take a cheerful view. 'There's the crown safe back,' we said; 'very likely you'd have done better not to touch it' (and he heavily assented to that), 'but no real harm has been done, and we shall never give this away to anyone who would be so mad as to go near it. Besides, don't you feel better yourself? I don't mind confessing,' I said, 'that on the way there I was very much inclined to take your view about—well, about being followed; but going back, it wasn't at all the same thing, was it?' No, it wouldn't do: 'You've nothing to trouble yourselves about,' he said, 'but I'm not forgiven. I've got to pay for that miserable sacrilege still. I know what you are going to say. The Church might help. Yes, but it's the body that has to suffer. It's true I'm not feeling that he's waiting outside for me just now. But——' Then he stopped. Then he turned to thanking us, and we put him off as soon as we could. And naturally we pressed him to use our sitting-room next day, and said we should be glad to go out with him. Or did he play golf, perhaps? Yes, he did, but he didn't think he should care about that tomorrow. Well, we recommended him to get up late and sit in our room in the morning while we were playing, and we would have a walk later in the day. He was very submissive and *piano* about it all: ready to do just what we thought best, but clearly quite certain in his own mind that what was coming could not be averted or palliated. You'll wonder why we didn't insist on accompanying him to his home and seeing him safe into the care of brothers or someone. The fact was he had nobody. He had had a flat in town, but lately he had made up his mind to settle for a time in Sweden, and he had dismantled his flat and shipped off his belongings, and was whiling away a fortnight or three weeks before he made a start. Anyhow, we didn't see what we could do better than sleep on it—or not sleep very much, as was my case—and see what we felt like tomorrow morning.

We felt very different, Long and I, on as beautiful an April morning as you could desire; and Paxton also looked very different when we saw him at breakfast. 'The first approach to a decent night I seem ever to have had,' was what he said. But he was going to do as we had settled: stay in probably all the morning, and come out with us later. We went to the links; we met some other men and played with them in the morning, and had lunch there rather early, so as not to be late back. All the same, the snares of death overtook him.

Whether it could have been prevented, I don't know. I think he would have been got at somehow, do what we might. Anyhow, this is what happened.

We went straight up to our room. Paxton was there, reading quite peaceably. 'Ready to come out shortly?' said Long, 'say in half an hour's time?' 'Certainly,' he said: and

I said we would change first, and perhaps have baths, and call for him in half an hour. I had my bath first, and went and lay down on my bed, and slept for about ten minutes. We came out of our rooms at the same time, and went together to the sitting-room. Paxton wasn't there—only his book. Nor was he in his room, nor in the downstair rooms. We shouted for him. A servant came out and said: 'Why, I thought you gentlemen was gone out already, and so did the other gentleman. He heard you a-calling from the path there, and run out in a hurry, and I looked out of the coffee-room window, but I didn't see you. 'Owever, he run off down the beach that way.'

Without a word we ran that way too—it was the opposite direction to that of last night's expedition. It wasn't quite four o'clock, and the day was fair, though not so fair as it had been, so there was really no reason, you'd say, for anxiety: with people about, surely a man couldn't come to much harm.

But something in our look as we ran out must have struck the servant, for she came out on the steps, and pointed, and said, 'Yes, that's the way he went.' We ran on as far as the top of the shingle bank, and there pulled up. There was a choice of ways: past the houses on the sea-front, or along the sand at the bottom of the beach, which, the tide being now out, was fairly broad. Or of course we might keep along the shingle between these two tracks and have some view of both of them; only that was heavy going. We chose the sand, for that was the loneliest, and someone *might* come to harm there without being seen from the public path.

Long said he saw Paxton some distance ahead, running and waving his stick, as if he wanted to signal to people who were on ahead of him. I couldn't be sure: one of these sea-mists was coming up very quickly from the south. There was someone, that's all I could say. And there were tracks on the sand as of someone running who wore shoes; and there were other tracks made before those—for the shoes sometimes trod in them and interfered with them—of some-one not in shoes. Oh, of course, it's only my word you've got to take for all this: Long's dead, we'd no time or means to make sketches or take casts, and the next tide washed everything away. All we could do was to notice these marks as we hurried on. But there they were over and over again, and we had no doubt whatever that what we saw was the track of a bare foot, and one that showed more bones than flesh.

The notion of Paxton running after—after anything like this, and supposing it to be the friends he was looking for, was very dreadful to us. You can guess what we fancied: how the thing he was following might stop suddenly and turn round on him, and what sort of face it would show, half-seen at first in the mist—which all the while was getting thicker and thicker. And as I ran on wondering how the poor wretch could have been lured into mistaking that other thing for us, I remembered his saying, 'He has some power over your eyes.' And then I wondered what the end would be, for I had no hope now that the end could be averted, and—well, there is no need to tell all the dismal and horrid thoughts that flitted through my head as we ran on into the mist. It was uncanny, too, that the sun should still be bright in the sky and we could see nothing. We could only tell that we were now past the houses and had reached that gap there is between them and the old martello tower. When you are past the tower, you know, there is nothing but shingle for a long way—not a house, not a human creature, just that spit of land, or rather shingle, with the river on your right and the sea on your left.

But just before that, just by the martello tower, you remember there is the old battery, close to the sea. I believe there are only a few blocks of concrete left now the rest has all been washed away, but at this time there was a lot more, though the place was a ruin. Well, when we got there, we clambered to the top as quick as we could to take breath and look over the shingle in front if by chance the mist would let us see anything. But a moment's rest we must have. We had run a mile at least. Nothing whatever was visible ahead of us, and we were just turning by common consent to get down and run hopelessly on, when we heard what I can only call a laugh: and if you can understand what I mean by a breathless, a lungless laugh, you have it: but I don't suppose you can. It came from below, and swerved away into the mist. That was enough. We bent over the wall. Paxton was there at the bottom.

You don't need to be told that he was dead. His tracks showed that he had run along the side of the battery, had turned sharp round the corner of it, and, small doubt of it, must have dashed straight into the open arms of someone who was waiting there. His mouth was full of sand and stones, and his teeth and jaws were broken to bits. I only glanced once at his face.

At the same moment, just as we were scrambling down from the battery to get to the body, we heard a shout, and saw a man running down the bank of the martello tower. He was the caretaker stationed there, and his keen old eyes had managed to descry through the mist that something was wrong. He had seen Paxton fall, and had seen us a moment after, running up—fortunate this, for otherwise we could hardly have escaped suspicion of being concerned in the dreadful business. Had he, we asked, caught sight of anybody attacking our friend? He could not be sure.

We sent him off for help, and stayed by the dead man till they came with the stretcher. It was then that we traced out how he had come, on the narrow fringe of sand under the battery wall. The rest was shingle, and it was hopelessly impossible to tell whither the other had gone.

What were we to say at the inquest? It was a duty, we felt, not to give up, there and then, the secret of the crown, to be published in every paper. I don't know how much you would have told; but what we did agree upon was this: to say that we had only made acquaintance with Paxton the day before, and that he had told us he was under some apprehension of danger at the hands of a man called William Ager. Also that we had seen some other tracks besides Paxton's when we followed him along the beach. But of course by that time everything was gone from the sands.

No one had any knowledge, fortunately, of any William Ager living in the district. The evidence of the man at the martello tower freed us from all suspicion. All that could be done was to return a verdict of wilful murder by some person or persons unknown.

Paxton was so totally without connections that all the inquiries that were subsequently made ended in a No Thoroughfare. And I have never been at Seaburgh, or even near it, since.

RATS

'And if you was to walk through the bedrooms now, you'd see the ragged, mouldy bedclothes a-heaving and a-heaving like seas.' 'And a-heaving and a-heaving with what?' he says. Why, with the rats under 'em.'*

BUT was it with the rats? I ask, because in another case it was not. I cannot put a date to the story, but I was young when I heard it, and the teller was old. It is an ill-proportioned tale, but that is my fault, not his.

It happened in Suffolk, near the coast. In a place where the road makes a sudden dip and then a sudden rise; as you go northward, at the top of that rise, stands a house on the left of the road. It is a tall red-brick house, narrow for its height; perhaps it was built about 1770. The top of the front has a low triangular pediment with a round window in the centre. Behind it are stables and offices, and such garden as it has is behind them. Scraggy Scotch firs are near it: an expanse of gorse-covered land stretches away from it. It commands a view of the distant sea from the upper windows of the front. A sign on a post stands before the door; or did so stand, for though it was an inn of repute once, I believe it is so no longer.

To this inn came my acquaintance, Mr Thomson, when he was a young man, on a fine spring day, coming from the University of Cambridge, and desirous of solitude in tolerable quarters and time for reading. These he found, for the land-lord and his wife had been in service and could make a visitor comfortable, and there was no one else staying in the inn. He had a large room on the first floor commanding the road and the view, and if it faced east, why, that could not be helped; the house was well built and warm.

He spent very tranquil and uneventful days: work all the morning, an afternoon perambulation of the country round, a little conversation with country company or the people of the inn in the evening over the then fashionable drink of brandy and water, a little more reading and writing, and bed; and he would have been content that this should continue for the full month he had at disposal, so well was his work progressing, and so fine was the April of that year—which I have reason to believe was that which Orlando Whistlecraft chronicles in his weather record as the 'Charming Year'.*

One of his walks took him along the northern road, which stands high and traverses a wide common, called a heath. On the bright afternoon when he first chose this direction his eye caught a white object some hundreds of yards to the left of the road, and he felt it necessary to make sure what this might be. It was not long before he was standing by it, and found himself looking at a square block of white stone fashioned somewhat like the base of a pillar, with a square hole in the upper surface. Just such another you may see at this day on Thetford Heath.* After taking stock of it he contemplated for a few minutes the view, which offered a church tower or two, some red roofs of cottages and windows winking in the sun, and the expanse of sea—also with an occasional wink and gleam upon it— and so pursued his way.

In the desultory evening talk in the bar, he asked why the white stone was there on the common.

'A old-fashioned thing, that is,' said the landlord (Mr Betts), 'we was none of us alive when that was put there.' 'That's right,' said another. 'It stands pretty high,' said Mr Thomson, 'I dare say a sea-mark was on it some time back.' 'Ah! yes,' Mr Betts agreed, 'I 'ave 'eard they could see it from the boats; but whatever there was, it's fell to bits this long time.' 'Good job too,' said a third, ''twarn't a lucky mark, by what the old men used to say; not lucky for the fishin', I mean to say.' 'Why ever not?' said Thomson. 'Well, I never see it myself,' was the answer, 'but they 'ad some funny ideas, what I mean, peculiar, them old chaps, and I shouldn't wonder but what they made away with it theirselves.'

It was impossible to get anything clearer than this: the company, never very voluble, fell silent, and when next someone spoke it was of village affairs and crops. Mr Betts was the speaker.

Not every day did Thomson consult his health by taking a country walk. One very fine afternoon found him busily writing at three o'clock. Then he stretched himself and rose, and walked out of his room into the passage. Facing him was another room, then the stair-head, then two more rooms, one looking out to the back, the other to the south. At the south end of the passage was a window, to which he went, considering with himself that it was rather a shame to waste such a fine afternoon. However, work was paramount just at the moment; he thought he would just take five minutes off and go back to it, and those five minutes he would employ— the Bettses could not possibly object—to looking at the other rooms in the passage, which he had never seen. Nobody at all, it seemed, was indoors; probably, as it was market day, they were all gone to the town, except perhaps a maid in the bar. Very still the house was, and the sun shone really hot; early flies buzzed in the window-panes. So he explored. The room facing his own was undistinguished except for an old print of Bury St Edmunds; the two next him on his side of the passage were gay and clean, with one window apiece, whereas his had two. Remained the south-west room, opposite to the last which he had entered. This was locked; but Thomson was in a mood of quite indefensible curiosity, and feeling confident that there could be no damaging secrets in a place so easily got at, he proceeded to fetch the key of his own room, and when that did not answer, to collect the keys of the other three. One of them fitted, and he opened the door. The room had two windows looking south and west, so it was as bright and the sun as hot upon it as could be. Here there was no carpet, but bare boards; no pictures, no washing-stand, only a bed, in the farther corner: an iron bed, with mattress and bolster, covered with a bluish check counterpane. As featureless a room as you can well imagine, and yet there was something that made Thomson close the door very quickly and yet quietly behind him and lean against the window-sill in the passage, actually quivering all over. It was this, that under the counterpane someone lay, and not only lay, but stirred. That it was some *one* and not some *thing* was certain, because the shape of a head was unmistakable on the bolster; and yet it was all covered, and no one lies with covered head but a dead person; and this was not dead, not truly dead, for it heaved and shivered. If he had seen these things in dusk or by the light of a flickering candle, Thomson could have comforted himself and talked of fancy. On this bright day that was impossible. What was to be done? First, lock the door at all costs. Very gingerly he approached it and bending down listened, holding his breath; perhaps there might be a sound of heavy breathing, and a prosaic explanation. There was absolute silence. But as, with a rather tremulous hand, he put the key into its hole and turned it, it rattled, and on the instant a stumbling padding tread was heard coming towards the door. Thomson fled like a rabbit to his room and locked himself in: futile enough, he knew it was; would doors and locks be any obstacle to what he suspected? but it was all he could think of at the moment, and in fact nothing happened; only there was a time of acute suspense—followed by a misery of doubt as to what to do. The impulse, of course, was to slip away as soon as possible from a house which contained such an inmate. But only the day before he had said he should be staying for at least a week more, and how if he changed plans could he avoid the suspicion of having pried into places where he certainly had no business? Moreover, either the Bettses knew all about the inmate, and yet did not leave the house, or knew nothing, which equally meant that there was nothing to be afraid of, or knew just enough to make them shut up the room, but not enough to weigh on their spirits: in any of these cases it seemed that not much was to be feared, and certainly so far as he had had no sort of ugly experience. On the whole the line of least resistance was to stay.

Well, he stayed out his week. Nothing took him past that door, and, often as he would pause in a quiet hour of day or night in the passage and listen, and listen, no sound whatever issued from that direction. You might have thought that Thomson would have made some attempt at ferreting out stories connected with the inn—hardly perhaps from Betts, but from the parson of the parish, or old people in the village; but no, the reticence which commonly falls on people who have had strange experiences, and believe in them, was upon him. Nevertheless, as the end of his stay drew near, his yearning after some kind of explanation grew more and more acute. On his solitary walks he persisted in planning out some way, the least obtrusive, of getting another daylight glimpse into that room, and eventually arrived at this scheme. He would leave by an afternoon train—about four o'clock. When his fly was waiting, and his luggage on it, he would make one last expedition up-stairs to look round his own room and see if anything was left unpacked, and then, with that key, which he had contrived to oil (as if that made any difference!), the door should once more be opened, for a moment, and shut.

So it worked out. The bill was paid, the consequent small talk gone through while the fly was loaded: 'pleasant part of the country—been very comfortable, thanks to you and Mrs Betts—hope to come back some time', on one side: on the other, 'very glad you've found satisfaction, sir, done our best—always glad to 'ave your good word—very much favoured we've been with the weather, to be sure.' Then, 'I'll just take a look upstairs in case I've left a book or some-thing out—no, don't trouble, I'll be back in a minute.' And as noiselessly as possible he stole to the door and opened it. The shattering of the illusion! He almost laughed aloud. Propped, or you might say sitting, on the edge of the bed was—nothing in the round world but a scarecrow! A scare-crow out of the garden, of course, dumped into the deserted room. . . . Yes; but here amusement ceased. Have scarecrows bare bony feet? Do their heads loll on to their shoulders? Have they iron collars and links of chain about their necks? Can they get up and move, if never so stiffly, across a floor, with wagging head and arms close at their sides? and shiver?

The slam of the door, the dash to the stair-head, the leap downstairs, were followed by a faint. Awakening, Thomson saw Betts standing over him with the brandy bottle and a very reproachful face. 'You shouldn't a done so, sir, really you shouldn't. It ain't a kind way to act by persons as done

the best they could for you.' Thomson heard words of this
kind, but what he said in reply he did not know. Mr Betts,
and perhaps even more Mrs Betts, found it hard to accept
his apologies and his assurances that he would say no word
that could damage the good name of the house. However,
they *were* accepted. Since the train could not now be caught,
it was arranged that Thomson should be driven to the town
to sleep there. Before he went the Bettses told him what little
they knew. 'They says he was landlord 'ere a long time back,
and was in with the 'ighwaymen that 'ad their beat about
the 'eath. That's how he come by his end: 'ung in chains,
they say, up where you see that stone what the gallus stood
in. Yes, the fishermen made away with that, I believe,
because they see it out at sea and it kep' the fish off, according to their idea. Yes, we 'ad the account from the people
that 'ad the 'ouse before we come. "You keep that room shut
up," they says, "but don't move the bed out, and you'll find
there won't be no trouble." And no more there 'as been; not
once he haven't come out into the 'ouse, though what he
may do now there ain't no sayin'. Anyway, you're the first
I know on that's seen him since we've been 'ere: I never set
eyes on him myself, nor don't want. And ever since we've
made the servants' rooms in the stablin', we ain't 'ad no
difficulty that way. Only I do 'ope, sir, as you'll keep a close
tongue, considerin' 'ow an 'ouse do get talked about': with
more to this effect.

The promise of silence was kept for many years. The occasion of my hearing the story at last was this: that when Mr
Thomson came to stay with my father it fell to me to show
him to his room, and instead of letting me open the door for
him, he stepped forward and threw it open himself, and then
for some moments stood in the doorway holding up his candle
and looking narrowly into the interior. Then he seemed to
recollect himself and said: 'I beg your pardon. Very absurd,
but I can't help doing that, for a particular reason.' What
that reason was I heard some days afterwards, and you have
heard now.

THE EXPERIMENT

A NEW YEAR'S EVE GHOST STORY
(Full Directions will be found at the End)

THE Reverend Dr Hall was in his study making up the entries for the year in the parish register: it being his custom to note baptisms, weddings and burials in a paper book as they occurred, and in the last days of December to write them out fairly in the vellum book that was kept in the parish chest.

To him entered his housekeeper, in evident agitation. 'Oh, sir,' said she, 'whatever do you think? The poor Squire's gone!'

'The Squire? Squire Bowles? What are you talking about, woman? Why, only yesterday——.'

'Yes, I know, sir, but it's the truth. Wickem, the clerk, just left word on his way down to toll the bell—you'll hear it yourself in a minute. There now, just listen.'

Sure enough the sound broke on the still night—not loud, for the Rectory did not immediately adjoin the churchyard. Dr Hall rose hastily.

'Terrible, terrible,' he said. 'I must see them at the Hall at once. He seemed so greatly better yesterday.' He paused. 'Did you hear any word of the sickness having come this way at all? There was nothing said in Norwich. It seems so sudden.'

'No, indeed, sir, no such thing. Just caught away with a choking in his throat, Wickem says. It do make one feel—well, I'm sure I had to set down as much as a minute or more, I come over that queer when I heard the words—and by what I could understand they'll be asking for the burial very quick. There's some can't bear the thought of the cold corpse laying in the house, and——.'

'Yes: well, I must find out from Madam Bowles herself or Mr Joseph. Get me my cloak, will you? Ah, and could

you let Wickem know that I desire to see him when the
tolling is over?' He hurried off.

'In an hour's time he was back and found Wickem waiting
for him. 'There is work for you, Wickem,' he said, as he
threw off his cloak, 'and not overmuch time to do it in.'

'Yes, sir,' said Wickem, 'the vault to be opened to be
sure——.'

'No, no, that's not the message I have. The poor Squire,
they tell me, charged them before now not to lay him in the
chancel. It was to be an earth grave in the yard, on the
north side.' He stopped at an inarticulate exclamation from
the clerk. 'Well?' he said.

'I ask pardon, sir,' said Wickem in a shocked voice, 'but
did I understand you right? No vault, you say, and on the
north side? Tt-tt-! Why the poor gentleman must a been
wandering.'

'Yes, it does seem strange to me, too,' said Dr Hall, 'but
no, Mr Joseph tells me it was his father's—I should say
stepfather's—clear wish, expressed more than once, and
when he was in good health. Clean earth and open air. You
know, of course, the poor Squire had his fancies, though he
never spoke of this one to me. And there's another thing,
Wickem. No coffin.'

'Oh dear, dear, sir,' said Wickem, yet more shocked. 'Oh,
but that'll make sad talk, that will, and what a disappointment for Wright, too! I know he'd looked out some beautiful wood for the Squire, and had it by him years past.'

'Well, well, perhaps the family will make it up to Wright
in some way,' said the Rector, rather impatiently, 'but what
you have to do is to get the grave dug and all things in a
readiness—torches from Wright you must not forget—by
ten o'clock tomorrow night. I don't doubt but there will be
somewhat coming to you for your pains and hurry.'

'Very well, sir, if those be the orders, I must do my best
to carry them out. And should I call in on my way down
and send the women up to the Hall to lay out the body,
sir?'

'No: that, I think—I am sure—was not spoken of. Mr Joseph will send, no doubt, if they are needed. No, you have enough without that. Good-night, Wickem. I was making up the registers when this doleful news came. Little had I thought to add such an entry to them as I must now.'

All things had been done in decent order. The torchlighted cortège had passed from the Hall through the park, up the lime avenue to the top of the knoll on which the church stood. All the village had been there, and such neighbours as could be warned in the few hours available. There was no great surprise at the hurry.

Formalities of law there were none then, and no one blamed the stricken widow for hastening to lay her dead to rest. Nor did anyone look to see her following in the funeral train. Her son Joseph—only issue of her first marriage with a Calvert of Yorkshire—was the chief mourner.

There were, indeed, no kinsfolk on Squire Bowles's side who could have been bidden. The will, executed at the time of the Squire's second marriage, left everything to the widow.

And what was 'everything'? Land, house, furniture, pictures, plate were all obvious. But there should have been accumulations in coin, and beyond a few hundreds in the hands of agents—honest men and no embezzlers—cash there was none. Yet Francis Bowles had for years received good rents and paid little out. Nor was he a reputed miser; he kept a good table, and money was always forthcoming for the moderate spendings of his wife and stepson. Joseph Calvert had been maintained ungrudgingly at school and college.

What, then, had he done with it all? No ransacking of the house brought any secret hoard to light; no servant, old or young, had any tale to tell of meeting the Squire in unexpected places at strange hours. No, Madam Bowles and her son were fairly non-plussed. As they sat one evening in the parlour discussing the problem for the twentieth time:

'You have been at his books and papers, Joseph, again today, haven't you?'

'Yes, mother, and no forwarder.'

'What was it he would be writing at, and why was he always sending letters to Mr Fowler at Gloucester?'

'Why, you know he had a maggot about the Middle State of the Soul. 'Twas over that he and that other were always busy. The last thing he wrote would be a letter that he never finished. I'll fetch it. . . . Yes, the same song over again.

' "Honoured friend,—I make some slow advance in our studies, but I know not well how far to trust our authors. Here is one lately come my way who will have it that for a time after death the soul is under control of certain spirits, as Raphael, and another whom I doubtfully read as Nares; but still so near to this state of life that on prayer to them he may be free to come and disclose matters to the living. Come, indeed, he must, if he be rightly called, the manner of which is set forth in an experiment. But having come, and once opened his mouth, it may chance that his summoner shall see and hear more than of the hid treasure which it is likely he bargained for; since the experiment puts this in the forefront of things to be enquired. But the eftest way is to send you the whole, which herewith I do; copied from a book of recipes which I had of good Bishop Moore." '*

Here Joseph stopped, and made no comment, gazing on the paper. For more than a minute nothing was said, then Madam Bowles, drawing her needle through her work and looking at it, coughed and said, 'There was no more written?'

'No, nothing, mother.'

'No? Well, it is strange stuff. Did ever you meet this Mr Fowler?'

'Yes, it might be once or twice, in Oxford, a civil gentleman enough.'

'Now I think of it,' said she, 'it would be but right to acquaint him with—with what has happened: they were close friends. Yes, Joseph, you should do that: you will know what should be said. And the letter is his, after all.'

'You are in the right, mother, and I'll not delay it.' And forthwith he sat down to write.

From Norfolk to Gloucester was no quick transit. But a letter went, and a larger packet came in answer; and there were more evening talks in the panelled parlour at the Hall. At the close of one, these words were said: 'Tonight, then, if you are certain of yourself, go round by the field path. Ay, and here is a cloth will serve.'

'What cloth is that, mother? A napkin?'

'Yes, of a kind: what matter?' So he went out by the way of the garden, and she stood in the door, musing, with her hand on her mouth. Then the hand dropped and she said half aloud: 'If only I had not been so hurried! But it *was* the face cloth, sure enough.'

It was a very dark night, and the spring wind blew loud over the black fields: loud enough to drown all sounds of shouting or calling. If calling there was, there was no voice, nor any that answered, nor any that regarded—yet.

Next morning, Joseph's mother was early in his chamber. 'Give me the cloth,' she said, 'the maids must not find it. And tell me, tell me, quick!'

Joseph, seated on the side of the bed with his head in his hands, looked up at her with bloodshot eyes. 'We have opened his mouth,' he said. 'Why in God's name did you leave his face bare?'

'How could I help it? You know how I was hurried that day? But do you mean you saw it?'

Joseph only groaned and sunk his head in his hands again. Then, in a low voice, 'He said you should see it, too.'

With a dreadful gasp she clutched at the bedpost and clung to it. 'Oh, but he's angry,' Joseph went on. 'He was only biding his time, I'm sure. The words were scarce out of my mouth when I heard like the snarl of a dog in under there.' He got up and paced the room. 'And what can we do? He's free! And I daren't meet him! I daren't take the drink and go where he is! I daren't lie here another night. Oh, why did you do it? We could have waited.'

'Hush,' said his mother: her lips were dry. ''Twas you, you know it, as much as I. Besides, what use in talking?

Listen to me: 'tis but six o'clock. There's money to cross the water: such as they can't follow. Yarmouth's not so far, and most night boats sail for Holland, I've heard. See you to the horses. I can be ready.'

Joseph stared at her. 'What will they say here?'

'What? Why, cannot you tell the parson we have wind of property lying in Amsterdam which we must claim or lose? Go, go; or if you are not man enough for that, lie here again tonight.' He shivered and went.

That evening after dark a boatman lumbered into an inn on Yarmouth Quay, where a man and a woman sat, with saddle-bags on the floor by them.

'Ready, are you, mistress and gentleman?' he said. 'She sails before the hour, and my other passenger he's waitin' on the quay. Be there all your baggage?' and he picked up the bags.

'Yes, we travel light,' said Joseph. 'And you have more company bound for Holland?'

'Just the one,' said the boatman, 'and he seem to travel lighter yet.'

'Do you know him?' said Madam Bowles: she laid her hand on Joseph's arm, and they both paused in the doorway.

'Why no, but for all he's hooded I'd know him again fast enough, he have such a cur'ous way of speakin', and I doubt you'll find he know you, by what he said. "Goo you and fetch 'em out," he say, "and I'll wait on 'em here," he say, and sure enough he's a-comin' this way now.'

Poisoning of a husband was petty treason then, and women guilty of it were strangled at the stake and burnt. The Assize records of Norwich tell of a woman so dealt with and of her son hanged thereafter, convict on their own confession, made before the Rector of their parish, the name of which I withhold, for there is still hid treasure to be found there.

Bishop Moore's book of recipes is now in the University Library at Cambridge, marked Dd 11, 45, and on the leaf numbered 144 this is written:

An experiment most ofte proved true, to find out tresure hidden in the ground, theft, manslaughter, or anie other thynge. Go to the grave of a ded man, and three tymes call hym by his nam at the hed of the grave, and say. Thou, N., N., N., I coniure the, I require the, and I charge the, by thi Christendome that thou takest leave of the Lord Raffael and Nares and then askest leave this night to come and tell me trewlie of the tresure that lyith hid in such a place. Then take of the earth of the grave at the dead bodyes hed and knitt it in a lynnen clothe and put itt under thi right eare and sleape theruppon: and wheresoever thou lyest or slepest, that night he will com and tell thee trewlie in waking or sleping.

THE MALICE OF INANIMATE
OBJECTS

THE Malice of Inanimate Objects is a subject upon which
an old friend of mine was fond of dilating, and not without
justification. In the lives of all of us, short or long, there
have been days, dreadful days, on which we have had to
acknowledge with gloomy resignation that our world has
turned against us. I do not mean the human world of our
relations and friends: to enlarge on that is the province of
nearly every modern novelist. In their books it is called 'Life'
and an odd enough hash it is as they portray it. No, it is the
world of things that do not speak or work or hold congresses
and conferences. It includes such beings as the collar stud,
the inkstand, the fire, the razor, and, as age increases, the
extra step on the staircase which leads you either to expect
or not to expect it. By these and such as these (for I have
named but the merest fraction of them) the word is passed
round, and the day of misery arranged. Is the tale still
remembered of how the Cock and Hen went to pay a visit
to Squire Korbes? How on the journey they met with and
picked up a number of associates, encouraging each with the
announcement:

> To Squire Korbes we are going
> For a visit is owing.

Thus they secured the company of the Needle, the Egg, the
Duck, the Cat, possibly—for memory is a little treacherous
here—and finally the Millstone: and when it was discovered
that Squire Korbes was for the moment out, they took up
positions in his mansion and awaited his return. He did
return, wearied no doubt by a day's work among his extensive properties. His nerves were first jarred by the raucous
cry of the Cock. He threw himself into his armchair and was
lacerated by the Needle. He went to the sink for a refreshing
wash and was splashed all over by the Duck. Attempting to
dry himself with the towel he broke the Egg upon his face.

He suffered other indignities from the Hen and her accomplices, which I cannot now recollect, and finally, maddened with pain and fear, rushed out by the back door and had his brains dashed out by the Millstone that had perched itself in the appropriate place. 'Truly,' in the concluding words of the story, 'this Squire Korbes must have been either a very wicked or a very unfortunate man.' It is the latter alternative which I incline to accept. There is nothing in the preliminaries to show that any slur rested on his name, or that his visitors had any injury to avenge. And will not this narrative serve as a striking example of that Malice of which I have taken upon me to treat? It is, I know, the fact that Squire Korbes's visitors were not all of them, strictly speaking, inanimate. But are we sure that the perpetrators of this Malice are really inanimate either? There are tales which seem to justify a doubt.

Two men of mature years were seated in a pleasant garden after breakfast. One was reading the day's paper, the other sat with folded arms, plunged in thought, and on his face were a piece of sticking plaster and lines of care. His companion lowered his paper. 'What,' said he, 'is the matter with you? The morning is bright, the birds are singing, I can hear no aeroplanes or motor bikes.'

'No,' replied Mr Burton, 'it is nice enough, I agree, but I have a bad day before me. I cut myself shaving and spilt my tooth powder.'

'Ah,' said Mr Manners, 'some people have all the luck,' and with this expression of sympathy he reverted to his paper. 'Hullo,' he exclaimed, after a moment, 'here's George Wilkins dead! You won't have any more bother with him, anyhow.'

'George Wilkins?' said Mr Burton, more than a little excitedly, 'Why, I didn't even know he was ill.'

'No more he was, poor chap. Seems to have thrown up the sponge and put an end to himself. Yes,' he went on, 'it's some days back: this is the inquest. Seemed very much worried and depressed, they say. What about, I wonder?

Could it have been that will you and he were having a row about?'

'Row?' said Mr Burton angrily, 'there was no row: he hadn't a leg to stand on: he couldn't bring a scrap of evidence. No, it may have been half-a-dozen things: but Lord! I never imagined he'd take anything so hard as that.'

'I don't know,' said Mr Manners, 'he was a man, I thought, who did take things hard: they rankled. Well, I'm sorry, though I never saw much of him. He must have gone through a lot to make him cut his throat. Not the way I should choose, by a long sight. Ugh! Lucky he hadn't a family, anyhow. Look here, what about a walk round before lunch? I've an errand in the village.'

Mr Burton assented rather heavily. He was perhaps reluctant to give the inanimate objects of the district a chance of getting at him. If so, he was right. He just escaped a nasty purl over the scraper at the top of the steps: a thorny branch swept off his hat and scratched his fingers, and as they climbed a grassy slope he fairly leapt into the air with a cry and came down flat on his face. 'What in the world?' said his friend coming up. 'A great string, of all things! What business—Oh, I see—belongs to that kite' (which lay on the grass a little farther up). 'Now if I can find out what little beast has left that kicking about, I'll let him have it— or rather I won't, for he shan't see his kite again. It's rather a good one, too.' As they approached, a puff of wind raised the kite and it seemed to sit up on its end and look at them with two large round eyes painted red, and, below them, three large printed red letters, I.C.U. Mr Manners was amused and scanned the device with care. 'Ingenious,' he said, 'it's a bit off a poster, of course: I see! Full Particulars, the word was.' Mr Burton on the other hand was not amused, but thrust his stick through the kite. Mr Manners was inclined to regret this. 'I dare say it serves him right,' he said, 'but he'd taken a lot of trouble to make it.'

'Who had?' said Mr Burton sharply. 'Oh, I see, you mean the boy.'

'Yes, to be sure, who else? But come on down now: I want to leave a message before lunch. As they turned a corner into the main street, a rather muffled and choky voice was heard to say 'Look out! I'm coming. They both stopped as if they had been shot.

'Who *was* that?' said Manners. 'Blest if I didn't think I knew'—then, with almost a yell of laughter he pointed with his stick. A cage with a grey parrot in it was hanging in an open window across the way. 'I *was* startled, by George: it gave you a bit of a turn, too, didn't it?' Burton was inaudible. 'Well, I shan't be a minute: you can go and make friends with the bird.' But when he rejoined Burton, that unfortunate was not, it seemed, in trim for talking with either birds or men; he was some way ahead and going rather quickly. Manners paused for an instant at the parrot window and then hurried on laughing more than ever. 'Have a good talk with Polly?' said he, as he came up.

'No, of course not,' said Burton, testily. 'I didn't bother about the beastly thing.'

'Well, you wouldn't have got much out of her if you'd tried,' said Manners. 'I remembered after a bit; they've had her in the window for years: she's stuffed.' Burton seemed about to make a remark, but suppressed it.

Decidedly this was not Burton's day out. He choked at lunch, he broke a pipe, he tripped in the carpet, he dropped his book in the pond in the garden. Later on he had or professed to have a telephone call summoning him back to town next day and cutting short what should have been a week's visit. And so glum was he all the evening that Manners' disappointment in losing an ordinarily cheerful companion was not very sharp.

At breakfast Mr Burton said little about his night: but he did intimate that he thought of looking in on his doctor. 'My hand's so shaky,' he said, 'I really daren't shave this morning.'

'Oh, I'm sorry,' said Mr Manners, 'my man could have managed that for you: but they'll put you right in no time.'

Farewells were said. By some means and for some reason Mr Burton contrived to reserve a compartment to himself. (The train was not of the corridor type.) But these precautions avail little against the angry dead.

I will not put dots or stars, for I dislike them, but I will say that apparently someone tried to shave Mr Burton in the train, and did not succeed overly well. He was however satisfied with what he had done, if we may judge from the fact that on a once white napkin spread on Mr Burton's chest was an inscription in red letters: GEO. W. FECI.

Do not these facts—if facts they are—bear out my suggestion that there is something not inanimate behind the Malice of Inanimate Objects? Do they not further suggest that when this malice begins to show itself we should be very particular to examine and if possible rectify any obliquities in our recent conduct? And do they not, finally, almost force upon us the conclusion that, like Squire Korbes, Mr Burton must have been either a very wicked or a singularly unfortunate man?

A VIGNETTE

YOU are asked to think of the spacious garden of a country rectory,* adjacent to a park of many acres, and separated therefrom by a belt of trees of some age which we knew as the Plantation. It is but about thirty or forty yards broad. A close gate of split oak leads to it from the path encircling the garden, and when you enter it from that side you put your hand through a square hole cut in it and lift the hook to pass along to the iron gate which admits to the park from the Plantation. It has further to be added that from some windows of the rectory, which stands on a somewhat lower level than the Plantation, parts of the path leading thereto, and the oak gate itself can be seen. Some of the trees, Scotch firs and others, which form a backing and a surrounding, are of considerable size, but there is nothing that diffuses a mysterious gloom or imparts a sinister flavour—nothing of melancholy or funereal associations. The place is well clad, and there are secret nooks and retreats among the bushes, but there is neither offensive bleakness nor oppressive darkness. It is, indeed, a matter for some surprise when one thinks it over, that any cause for misgivings of a nervous sort have attached itself to so normal and cheerful a spot, the more so, since neither our childish mind when we lived there nor the more inquisitive years that came later ever nosed out any legend or reminiscence of old or recent unhappy things.

Yet to me they came, even to me, leading an exceptionally happy wholesome existence, and guarded—not strictly but as carefully as was any way necessary—from uncanny fancies and fear. Not that such guarding avails to close up all gates. I should be puzzled to fix the date at which any sort of misgiving about the Plantation gate first visited me. Possibly it was in the years just before I went to school, possibly on one later summer afternoon of which I have a faint memory, when I was coming back after solitary roaming in the park, or, as I bethink me, from tea at the Hall:*

anyhow, alone, and fell in with one of the villagers also homeward bound just as I was about to turn off the road on to the track leading to the Plantation. We broke off our talk with 'good nights', and when I looked back at him after a minute or so I was just a little surprised to see him standing still and looking after me. But no remark passed, and on I went. By the time I was within the iron gate and outside the park, dusk had undoubtedly come on; but there was no lack yet of light, and I could not account to myself for the questionings which certainly did rise as to the presence of anyone else among the trees, questionings to which I could not very certainly say 'No', nor, I was glad to feel, 'Yes', because if there were anyone they could not well have any business there. To be sure, it is difficult, in anything like a grove, to be quite certain that nobody is making a screen out of a tree trunk and keeping it between you and him as he moves round it and you walk on. All I can say is that if such an one was there he was no neighbour or acquaintance of mine, and there was some indication about him of being cloaked or hooded. But I think I may have moved at a rather quicker pace than before, and have been particular about shutting the gate. I think, too, that after that evening something of what Hamlet calls a 'gain-giving'* may have been present in my mind when I thought of the Plantation. I do seem to remember looking out of a window which gave in that direction, and questioning whether there was or was not any appearance of a moving form among the trees. If I did, and perhaps I did, hint a suspicion to the nurse the only answer to it will have been 'the hidea of such a thing!'* and an injunction to make haste and get into my bed.

Whether it was on that night or a later one that I seem to see myself again in the small hours gazing out of the window across moonlit grass and hoping I was mistaken in fancying any movement in that half-hidden corner of the garden, I cannot now be sure. But it was certainly within a short while that I began to be visited by dreams which I would much rather not have had—which, in fact, I came to dread acutely; and the point round which they centred was the Plantation gate.

As years go on it but seldom happens that a dream is disturbing. Awkward it may be, as when, while I am drying myself after a bath, I open the bedroom door and step out on to a populous railway platform and have to invent rapid and flimsy excuses for the deplorable *déshabille*. But such a vision is not alarming, though it may make one despair of ever holding up one's head again. But in the times of which I am thinking, it did happen, not often, but oftener than I liked, that the moment a dream set in I knew that it was going to turn out ill, and that there was nothing I could do to keep it on cheerful lines.

Ellis the gardener might be wholesomely employed with rake and spade as I watched at the window; other familiar figures might pass and repass on harmless errands; but I was not deceived. I could see that the time was coming when the gardener and the rest would be gathering up their properties and setting off on paths that led homeward or into some safe outer world, and the garden would be left—to itself, shall we say, or to denizens who did not desire quite ordinary company and were only waiting for the word 'all clear' to slip into their posts of vantage.

Now, too, was the moment near when the surroundings began to take on a threatening look; that the sunlight lost power and a quality of light replaced it which, though I did not know it at the time. my memory years after told me was the lifeless pallor of an eclipse. The effect of all this was to intensify the foreboding that had begun to possess me, and to make me look anxiously about, dreading that in some quarter my fear would take a visible shape. I had not much doubt which way to look. Surely behind those bushes, among those trees, there was motion, yes, and surely—and more quickly than seemed possible—there was motion, not now among the trees, but on the very path towards the house. I was still at the window, and before I could adjust myself to the new fear there came the impression of a tread on the stairs and a hand on the door. That was as far as the dream got, at first; and for me it was far enough. I had no notion what would have been the next development, more than that it was bound to be horrifying,

That is enough in all conscience about the beginning of my dreams. A beginning it was only, for something like it came again and again; how often I can't tell, but often enough to give me an acute distaste for being left alone in that region of the garden. I came to fancy that I could see in the behaviour of the village people whose work took them that way an anxiety to be past a certain point, and moreover a welcoming of company as they approached that corner of the park. But on this it will not do to lay over-much stress, for, as I have said, I could never glean any kind of story bound up with the place.

However, the strong probability that there had been one once I cannot deny.

I must not by the way give the impression that the whole of the Plantation was haunted ground. There were trees there most admirably devised for climbing and reading in; there was a wall, along the top of which you could walk for many hundred yards and reach a frequented road, passing farmyard and familiar houses; and once in the park, which had its own delights of wood and water, you were well out of range of anything suspicious—or, if that is too much to say, of anything that suggested the Plantation gate.

But I am reminded, as I look on these pages, that so far we have had only preamble, and that there is very little in the way of actual incident to come, and that the criticism attributed to the devil when he sheared the sow is like to be justified. What, after all, was the outcome of the dreams to which without saying a word about them I was liable during a good space of time? Well, it presents itself to me thus. One afternoon—the day being neither overcast nor threatening—I was at my window in the upper floor of the house. All the family were out. From some obscure shelf in a disused room I had worried out a book, not very recondite: it was, in fact, a bound volume of a magazine in which were contained parts of a novel.* I know now what novel it was, but I did not then, and a sentence struck and arrested me. Someone was walking at dusk up a solitary lane by an old mansion in Ireland, and being a man of imagination he was suddenly forcibly impressed by what he calls 'the aerial image of the old house, with its peculiar malign, scared, and skulking aspect' peering out of the shade of its neglected old trees. The words were quite enough to set my own fancy on a bleak track. Inevitably I looked and looked with apprehension, to the Plantation gate. As was but right it was shut, and nobody was upon the path that led to it or from it. But as I said a while ago, there was in it a square hole giving access to the fastening; and through that hole, I could see—and it struck like a blow on the diaphragm—something white or partly white. Now this I could not bear, and with an access of something like courage—only it was more like desperation, like determining that I must know the worst—I did steal down and, quite uselessly, of course, taking cover behind bushes as I went, I made progress until I was within range of the gate and the hole. Things were, alas! worse than I had feared; through that hole a face was looking my way. It was not monstrous, not pale, fleshless, spectral. Malevolent I thought and think it was; at any rate the eyes were large and open and fixed. It was pink and, I thought, hot, and just above the eyes the border of a white linen drapery hung down from the brows.

There is something horrifying in the sight of a face looking at one out of a frame as this did; more particularly if its gaze is unmistakably fixed upon you. Nor does it make the matter any better if the expression gives no clue to what is to come next. I said just now that I took this face to be malevolent, and so I did, but not in regard of any positive dislike or fierceness which it expressed. It was, indeed, quite without emotion: I was only conscious that I could see the whites of the eyes all round the pupil, and that, we know, has a glamour of madness about it. The immovable face was enough for me. I fled, but at what I thought must be a safe distance inside my own precincts I could not but halt and look back. There was no white thing framed in the hole of the gate, but there was a draped form shambling away among the trees.

Do not press me with questions as to how I bore myself when it became necessary to face my family again. That

I was upset by something I had seen must have been pretty clear, but I am very sure that I fought off all attempts to describe it. Why I make a lame effort to do it now I cannot very well explain: it undoubtedly has had some formidable power of clinging through many years to my imagination. I feel that even now I should be circumspect in passing that Plantation gate; and every now and again the query haunts me: Are there here and there sequestered places which some curious creatures still frequent, whom once on a time anybody could see and speak to as they went about on their daily occasions, whereas now only at rare intervals in a series of years does one cross their paths and become aware of them; and perhaps that is just as well for the peace of mind of simple people.

EXPLANATORY NOTES

ABBREVIATIONS

CGS	*Collected Ghost Stories* (1931)
E&K	*Eton and King's* (1926)
GSA	*Ghost Stories of an Antiquary* (1904)
Memoir	Lubbock, *Montague Rhodes James: A Memoir* (1939)
MGSA	*More Ghost Stories of an Antiquary* (1911)
SOED	*Shorter Oxford Dictionary*
TG	*A Thin Ghost* (1919)
WTC	*A Warning to the Curious* (1925)

CANON ALBERIC'S SCRAP-BOOK

1 *Title*: originally called blandly 'A Curious Book', this story, probably MRJ's first, was published initially in the *National Review* for March 1895, retitled for publication 'The Scrap-book of Canon Alberic'. It was republished in 1904 as the opening story of GSA, with a final slight modification of the title. In the Preface to CGS MRJ states incorrectly that the story was written in 1894. In fact it must have been written between mid-April 1892, after MRJ visited S. Bertrand de Comminges (see below), and 28 October 1893, when it was read to the Chitchat Society at Cambridge together with 'Lost Hearts' (see Introduction, p. xviii). *MS*: King's College, Cambridge. *Text*: MS, collated with printed versions.

S. Bertrand de Comminges: an ancient Pyrenean town that MRJ had long wished to visit, from at least 1887. It was not until the Easter vacation of 1892 that he was able to go there, with a party that included two friends from Christ's College, Cambridge: J. Armitage Robinson and Arthur (later Sir Arthur) Shipley. The 'wonderful church' of the story was described by MRJ in a letter to his parents, and he provided them with a sketch plan on which he marked many details that are mentioned in the story—including the stuffed crocodile. MRJ revisited Comminges at Easter 1899, and also in 1902. He made trips to France, the country that was 'his first and greatest love' (*Memoir*,

p. 32), nearly every year of his adult life—often, from 1895, on a bicycle.

notebook: Dennistoun's notetaking reflects MRJ's own practice when travelling. Many of his notebooks survive (at the Fitzwilliam Museum, Cambridge) and show the extraordinary attention to architectural and iconographic detail that made MRJ, somewhat like Dennistoun, a most untypical tourist.

Chapeau Rouge: this seems to be an invented establishment. MRJ himself never stayed in Comminges.

weazened: MS. Printed versions have 'wizened'.

2 *let us call him Dennistoun*: in the MS and *National Review* he is called Anderson. The name was changed for GSA (and subsequently CGS), presumably to distinguish this protagonist from Mr Anderson in 'Number 13'. Dennistoun reappears briefly in the preamble to 'The Mezzotint' (GSA).

the Englishman . . . sacristan: this was the caption to McBryde's first illustration for the story, which formed the frontispiece to GSA.

3 *Angelus*: from the Latin 'Angelus domini nuntiavit Mariae'; 'a devotional exercise commemorating the Incarnation, in which the Angelic Salutation is thrice repeated, said by Roman Catholics, at morning, noon, and sunset, at the sound of a bell' (SOED).

4 *At once all Dennistoun's cherished dreams . . . flashed up*: it is entirely fitting that MRJ's first published ghost story should draw on his scholarly interest in Western manuscripts, for the period in which it was written coincides with the growth of his reputation as an outstanding palaeographer and cataloguer. He became Director of the Fitzwilliam Museum, Cambridge, in 1893, the year 'Canon Alberic' was probably written, having been Assistant Director since 1886. In this position he was responsible for the Museum's acquisitions policy and under him the Fitzwilliam attracted a number of important manuscripts. His descriptive catalogue of the manuscripts in the Fitzwilliam, as well as catalogues for Jesus College, Sidney Sussex, and Eton, were all published in 1895. He went on to produce catalogues for all the other Cambridge colleges, ending with St Catharine's in 1925.

Dennistoun's thrill at discovering the scrap-book strikes another personal note: cf. *The Wanderings and Homes of Manuscripts* (1919), p. 93:

To find, as the late Mr Greenwell of Durham found, a leaf of a sixth-century Latin Bible . . . in a curiosity shop, is a chance that comes to few. But I have always lamented that I did not pass through the streets of Orleans at the time . . . when an illustrated Greek MS of the Gospels on purple vellum and in gold and silver uncials was exposed for sale in a shop window . . .

The pleasure of discovering treasures in unlikely places, however, was tasted by MRJ in 1890, when he came across a cache of MSS—including the unique Life of St William of Norwich—in a small dank building in the churchyard at Brent Eleigh, Suffolk.

Plantin's printing: Christophe Plantin (1514–89), French printer, born at St Avertin near Tours and known principally for his Bibles in Latin, Hebrew, and Dutch. MRJ had visited the Plantin Museum in Antwerp in April 1891 and recorded examining 'an early illuminated Sedulius 10th century'.

5   *missal . . . antiphoner*: *missal*—book containing the words and directions for celebrating Mass; *antiphoner*—'originally the liturgical book in the Western Church containing the parts of the Office and Mass which were sung by the choir antiphonally, i.e. alternating by sections' (*Concise Oxford Dictionary of the Christian Church*).

6   *uncial writing*: the large, rounded, unjoined form of writing used in early Greek and Latin manuscripts. MRJ whose normal hand could be unreadable, often inscribed presentation copies of books to friends in beautiful uncial letters (see for example the dedication page of *The Story of a Troll-hunt*).

Papias On the Words of Our Lord: not an invented reference, but a work known to have existed in the early Church. Papias (*c*.60–130) was Bishop of Hierapolis in Asia Minor. His writings survive only in quotations in Irenaeus and Eusebius. The work is mentioned by MRJ in his *Wanderings and Homes of Manuscripts* (1919), where it is described as 'supremely desirable' (p. 76).

scrap-book: in *The Wanderings and Homes of Manuscripts*

MRJ called the practice of cutting out illuminations from manuscripts and making scrapbooks of them 'reprehensible' (pp. 91–2), though as an Eton schoolboy he had indulged in an innocent form of this practice, obtaining manuscript fragments from London booksellers and pasting them into a scrapbook. It may be that Canon Alberic's fictitious compilation was suggested by the scrapbook acquired by Samuel Sandars in 1890, which contained two leaves of an exceptionally beautiful and early Book of Hours (now known as the Grey–FitzPayn Hours). These were given to the Fitzwilliam in 1892, when MRJ was Assistant Director. Eventually, through William Morris, the manuscript from which the leaves had been taken was also acquired by the Museum.

7 *Responsa . . . Ita*: the Latin in the MS, and in the *National Review* text, differs slightly from later versions. The form of the questions is: '*Si inveniam? . . . Si fiam dives? . . . Si vivam invidendus? . . . Si moriar in lecto meo?*'. CGS is followed here.

Mr Minor Canon Quatremain . . . Old St Paul's: a character in W. H. Ainsworth's *Old St Paul's* (1841)—'a grave, sallow-complexioned man, with a morose and repulsive physiognomy' (ch. 8). By means of astrological calculations and dowsing rods he believes he has located treasure in the cathedral: ' "Mercury is posited in the north angle of the fourth house; the dragon's tail is likewise within it; and as Sol is the significator, it must be gold." ' This seems to be the passage Dennistoun has in mind.

The picture in question . . . trust in their master: the general composition and attitudes of the figures in the picture may perhaps be based on Raphael's cartoon 'The Death of Ananias', which was in the South Kensington Museum (now the Victoria and Albert Museum).

8 *a Lecturer in Morphology*: perhaps a reference to MRJ's friend Arthur Shipley, who became Tutor in Natural Sciences at Christ's College, Cambridge, in 1892; from 1894–1908 he was University Lecturer on Advanced Morphology of the Invertebrata.

9 *a glass of wine . . . drunk*: this is the MS reading. The *National Review* and GSA have simply 'a glass of wine

drunk'. This wholly typical aside, which doubtless raised smiles when the story was first read to the Chitchat, is here reinstated.

perhaps, like Gehazi . . . spared: 2 Kings 5, the story of Elisha's servant Gehazi, who runs after the Syrian general Naaman after the prophet has cured him of leprosy. Gehazi tries to defraud Naaman of the payment for his cure that Elisha has refused to take. When the fraud is discovered Elisha pronounces that Gehazi and his descendants will suffer from Naaman's leprosy forever.

10   *a large spider?*: MRJ had a deep, almost pathological, dislike of spiders. In E&K he spoke admiringly of McBryde's courage in seizing 'by its sinewy leg the largest spider I have ever seen in a derelict bath at Verdun' (p. 219). Cf. the 'awful bird-catching spiders of South America' on p. 8, and see 'The Ash-tree'.

a hand like the hand in that picture!: the caption to McBryde's second illustration to the story. The intended resemblance of Dennistoun to MRJ is clear in this drawing.

12   *Contradictio Salomonis . . . Dec. 29, 1701*: no English translation was provided in the MS, nor, consequently, in the *National Review* version. One infers that the Latin was left untranslated for the classically proficient audience at the story's first reading.

Psalm: Whoso dwelleth (xci): the celebrated hymn of protection enjoyed by the elect containing the lines 'Thou shalt not be afraid for the terror by night; nor for the arrow that flieth by day; / Nor for the pestilence that walketh in darkness; nor for the destruction that wasteth at noonday.'

the 'Gallia Christiana' . . . Sammarthani: the *Gallia Christiana*, first published by Claude Robert in 1626, contains a documentary account of the bishoprics, bishops, abbeys, and abbots of France. A later edition appeared in 1656. A thorough revision was undertaken early in the eighteenth century by Denys de Sainte-Marthe (1650–1725), a Maurist—i.e. a Benedictine monk of the Congregation of St-Maur, founded in 1621. From 1672 the Maurists devoted themselves to historical and literary scholarship, of which the *Gallia* is a notable example.

Ecclesiasticus: in the Old Testament Apocrypha, 39–28.

Isaiah: Isaiah 34, pronouncing God's vengeance on Edom.

soutane: the cassock of a Roman Catholic priest.

'*I hope it isn't wrong . . . Alberic de Mauléon's rest*': MS and *National Review*. GSA and CGS amend the sentence slightly to remove the obscure word 'trental', which means a set of thirty requiem masses.

13 *Wentworth Collection*: a fictitious institution but intended probably for the Fitzwilliam Museum at Cambridge.

THE MEZZOTINT

14 *Title*: first published in GSA (1904). MS: School Library, Eton. *Text*: MS, collated with printed versions.

Dennistoun: the main character in 'Canon Alberic's Scrapbook'. The MS has 'Anderson': see note to 'Canon Alberic' p. 300.

another University: i.e. Oxford. The MS has 'at a sister University'.

Shelburnian Library: i.e. the Bodleian Library, at which MRJ was working in June 1899.

his museum: the Ashmolean Museum, called the Ashleian at the end of the story.

Mr J. W. Britnell: 'Mr E. V. Daniells' in the MS.

15 *mezzotint*: 'a method of engraving on copper or steel, in which the surface of the plate is first roughened uniformly, the lights and half-lights being then produced by scraping away the "nap" thus formed, and the untouched parts giving the deepest shadows . . . a print produced by this process' (SOED).

16 *manor-house of the last century*: i.e. the eighteenth century. The story was written in the second half of the 1890s.

sculpsit: 'he carved it'.

17 *Professor Binks*: a parenthetical comment in the MS—'(it seems a good enough name for a man in his position)'—was never printed.

18 *whist was played and tobacco smoked*: cards and tobacco were prominent features of MRJ's entertaining at King's.

19 *sported*: in University slang, 'to sport one's oak' meant to keep one's outer door shut, i.e. as a signal that the occupant is out or does not wish to be disturbed.

His host was not quite dressed . . . even at this late hour: another self-reference. MRJ had a lifelong aversion to early rising.

Canterbury College: fictional. Both Christ Church and St John's, Oxford, have Canterbury Quadrangles.

The morning pipe: another self-reference. MRJ was very much a pipe man; cf. *Memoir*, p. 20, describing MRJ's rooms in Wilkins' Buildings at King's: 'Even the card table has upon it a good assortment of MSS and notebooks with tins of "Sun Dew" tobacco and a dozen or so of pipes.'

21 *Bursar*: the college treasurer.

22 *Phasmatological Society*: a hit probably at the Society for Psychical Research, founded in 1882, a precursor of which was the Ghost Club at Cambridge. The SPR's first President was Henry Sidgwick of Trinity. MRJ never showed any interest in psychical research.

23 *a Doré Bible*: i.e. a Bible illustrated by Gustave Doré (1832–83), who combined a taste for the romantic and the bizarre.

Murray's Guide to Essex: i.e. [John Murray, the publisher's] *Handbook for Essex, Suffolk, Norfolk, and Cambridgeshire* [by Richard J. King] (London, 1870; 2nd edn., 1875; 3rd edn., 1892).

24 *like the man in Tess of the D'Urbervilles?*: in Thomas Hardy's *Tess of the d'Urbervilles* (1891), Jack Durbeyfield, a Blackmoor Vale villager, is besotted by the knowledge that he is a descendant of the ancient family of d'Urbervilles.

Gawdy: the name was probably borrowed from a Norfolk family whose papers were the subject of a Historical Manuscripts Commission Report in 1885 which MRJ would almost certainly have known.

25 *north side of the church*: it was an old belief that only

evil-doers should be buried on the north side of the church. Cf. Coverdale's 'Praying for the Dead': 'As men die, so shall they arise; if in faith in the Lord, towards the south . . . if in unbelief . . . towards the north.' What is possibly MRJ's earliest piece of supernatural fiction (written as an Eton schoolboy) describes an incident on the north side of a church; cf. also the burial of Mrs Mothersole in 'The Ash-tree' and see 'The Experiment'.

spes ultima gentis: 'The last [or final] hope of the race'.

the Sadducean Professor of Ophiology: cf. the 'Professor of Ontography' in ' "Oh, Whistle, and I'll Come to You, My Lad" '. The Sadducees believed neither in angels nor the Resurrection (see note to ' "Oh, Whistle" ', p. 314). In the MS the professor's chair is the more prosaic one of Biology. The narrator's comment that the Professor's remark 'met with the reception it deserved' may perhaps indicate MRJ's own attitude towards rationalistic debunking of supernatural events.

Bridgeford: 'Oxford' in the MS.

NUMBER 13

26 *Title*: first published as the fifth story in GSA (1904). The idea of the story, according to Lubbock (*Memoir*, p. 32), was suggested by Will Stone (see below). For the dating of the story see next note. The MS is at King's, but lacks the conclusion. There is a cancelled opening:

Too few Englishmen travel in Jutland. Too few that is if we are taking the unselfish view that the pleasantest parts of the world ought to be visited by the largest possible number of people: not one too few, on the other hand [,] if we are expressing what are most likely our genuine feelings that there ought to be certain parts of this earth kept sacred from the mass of tourists. Still I am not really apprehensive that Jutland will ever become a crowded tourist resort. Its beauties are of a tranquil, a tame, a melancholy kind. Its literature is luckily not popularized by translations, and its sights in the way of [   ], galleries and museums are few. I am therefore the less afraid that I shall do it the disservice of bringing the curse of trippers and hotel coupons upon it by singing its praises. Perhaps the story that I am to tell may even have the opposite effect.

Text: MS, collated with printed versions.

Viborg: in the summer of 1899, MRJ, James McBryde, and another young Cambridge friend, Will Stone, visited Denmark on a cycling holiday. According to MRJ's statement in the Preface to *CGS*, the story was written that year. Perhaps Stone thought of the idea in 1899, but it seems more likely that the story itself was written the following year, 1900, when they revisited Denmark. For one thing, they did not (apparently) stay in or visit Viborg in 1899, but they did stay there the following summer: for another, on 10 September 1900 Stone wrote to MRJ: 'No 13 must be finished before you come to Marlborough [where Stone had been an assistant master since 1899].' Stone died of pneumonia in February 1901—a great blow for MRJ. The first Danish trip also inspired *The Story of a Troll-hunt*, a comic tale written and illustrated by McBryde from an idea of MRJ's. It was published by subscription, at MRJ's instigation, after McBryde's death in 1904.

Of Denmark, MRJ wrote: 'Perhaps . . . the expeditions I made in [McBryde's] company to Denmark and Sweden . . . were the most blissful of all that I ever had' (*E&K*, p. 219). He was particularly fond of Denmark and its people (whom he described as 'very un-foreign on the whole')—as indicated at several points in the story. He became proficient in Danish and later translated forty stories by Hans Andersen, published in 1930.

Preisler's . . . Golden Lion: MRJ stayed at Preisler's in August 1900. The Golden Lion is fictitious: no such building survived the fire of 1726.

the last days of Roman Catholicism: Denmark adopted Lutheranism in 1536. Viborg was particularly associated with the Reformation in Denmark, since it was there that Hans Tansen (or Tarsen), the leading Danish reformer, first preached.

27 '*1 Bog Mose, Cap. 22*,'; i.e. Genesis 22.

bagmen: commercial travellers.

29 *Bishop Jorgen Friis*: presumably Johan Friis (1494–1570).

Troldmand: magician, sorcerer.

30 *terrier*: a book recording site, boundaries, etc., of land of private persons or corporations.

his game of patience: MRJ was an enthusiastic card player, especially of jacoby, piquet, and patience. The two latter games were listed as his recreations in *Who's Who*.

31 *drawers and wardrobe*: MS. Printed texts omit 'drawers and'.

stuepige: chambermaid, servant.

32 *no Number 13 at all*: in the MS there follows the cancelled sentences ' "Well, I can only say that I must have been drunk. There is no other possible explanation, drunk or dreaming: and I never do either." '

33 *casus belli*: an act or situation that percipitates war.

36 *Emily in the Mysteries of Udolpho*: *The Mysteries of Udolpho* by Ann Radcliffe, published in 1794, was one of the most celebrated and influential of all Gothic romances. Its heroine is Emily de St Aubert, who is prone to expressing her thoughts in verse. MRJ specifically has in mind here the opening paragraph of ch. 7: 'and while she leaned on her window . . . her ideas arranged themselves in the following lines [there follows the poem 'The First Hour of Morning']'.

37 *a winter wind . . . chimney*: MS reads 'a bitter wind on a lonely hearth'.

38 *I know no more . . . gentlemen*: MS continues ' "It sounds like a lost soul" ' (deleted).

omnis spiritus laudet Dominum: the closing verse of Psalm 150: 'Let everything that hath breath praise the Lord.' This passage (from 'and he added something' to 'he could not be sure') is not in the MS, which reads ' "So do I," said Herr Jensen, "either here or hereafter." '

40 *Accordingly . . .* : the MS ends here and the final folios have not been traced. From this point to the end the punctuation of *CGS* has been emended at the present editor's discretion.

41 *Hans Sebald Beham*: 1500–50; one of two brothers from Nuremberg, painters and engravers, and followers of

Dürer. I have not identified the book alluded to here—
assuming it exists.

Upsala . . . Salthenius . . . Satan: MRJ visited Sweden in
August 1901 and wrote to his parents from Uppsala: 'I also
saw two contracts with the devil written (and signed in
blood) in 1718 by Daniel Salthenius who was condemned
to death for writing them. He escaped that & died professor
of divinity [Hebrew in the story] at Konigsberg.' MRJ
may have known of Salthenius's contracts before going to
Uppsala, but it is possible that this passage was added in
1901, when the story had been substantially completed.

COUNT MAGNUS

43 *Title*: first published in GSA (1904), the sixth story. The
MS, sold at Sotheby's on 9 November 1936 to Bumpus,
remains untraced, though there is one sheet of what seems
to be an early draft at King's (see note to p. oo, below).
The story was probably written in 1901 or 1902 (see
below). When A. E. Housman sent Thomas Hardy a copy
of GSA in November 1913 he particularly recommended
this story (see Inroduction, p. xx). *Text*: CGS.

Horace Marryat's Journal . . . Danish Isles: published in
2 vols., 1860. The full title is *Journal of a Residence in
Jutland, the Danish Isles, and Copenhagen*. Marryat was
also the author of *One Year in Sweden* (2 vols., 1862).

Mr Wraxall: the unusual name of the story's main
character interestingly recalls (Sir) Nathaniel Wraxall,
one-time agent of ex-Queen Caroline Matilda of Denmark
and MP for Hindon, whose *Historical Memoirs* (1815) contained a highly fanciful account of Sir Francis Dashwood's
convivial gatherings (known generally, but erroneously, as
the Hell-Fire Club) on the Thames at Medmenham in
Buckinghamshire, not far upstream from Eton.

the Pantechnicon fire in the early seventies: the Pantechnicon occupied about two acres of ground in Motcomb
Street, Belgrave Square, and was a repository for ware-
housing furniture, pictures, plate, etc. The fire of 12
February 1872 completely destroyed the building and much
of its contents. The name pantechnicon came to be used to
describe a furniture-removing van.

44   *Sweden*: having crossed briefly to Sweden from Denmark
     in 1899, MRJ spent the summer vacation of 1901 there
     with McBryde, touring the southern part of the country.

     Råbäck: part of the 1901 itinerary (see previous note).
     MRJ wrote to his parents from Råbäck on 10 August 1901.

     Dahlenberg's Suecia antiqua et moderna: i.e. Erik Jonsson,
     Count Dahlbergh, *Suecia antiqua et hodierna*, a collection
     of engravings from original paintings and drawings prin-
     cipally by Count Dahlbergh (3 vols., 1723).

     De la Gardie: the De la Gardie family played a prominent
     part in Swedish history. There was a Magnus De la
     Gardie, a contemporary of Queen Christina and a patron
     of the arts, but he had nothing in common with MRJ's
     creation.

45   *a mausoleum*: the actual De la Gardie mausoleum is at the
     Cistercian abbey of Varnhem, which MRJ visited in August
     1901. Count Magnus's mausoleum formed the subject of
     an unfinished drawing by McBryde. On 6 May 1904 he
     wrote to MRJ: 'It is difficult to do an octagonal mausoleum
     with oval windows and to put the right thickness of wall
     through each . . . I have drawn the tombs . . . I mean the
     sarcophagi or stone shrines or whatever you call them . . .
     the only thing against it is that you say once on looking
     down onto the sarcophagus. They can easily be put on the
     floor if you like or on stone small slabs . . . Still I suppose
     that doesn't matter as it makes a better picture the height
     of a man stooping to pick up a padlock. The rest is scienti-
     fically correct as to position of doors, windows and light
     and correctly orientated.' (James papers, Cambridge Uni-
     versity Library).

47   *the Black Pilgrimage*: in the *Monthly Repository of
     Theology and General Literature*, vol. X, no. CX (Feb.
     1815), p. 121, appeared a curious item of foreign intel-
     ligence that seems to bear on Count Magnus's Black
     Pilgrimage:

     The late King of Sweden has published a very curious address.
     He says, he has received the Grand Seignior's permission to
     make a pilgrimage to the Holy Land: in consequence, he
     invites ten persons to accompany him, one from each of the
     nations of Europe: they are to wear black robes, to let their
     beards grow, take the style and title of Black Brethren, and

are each to be attended by a servant in black and grey livery . . . the Black Brethren are to assemble at Trieste, on the 24th of June.

Skara: visited by MRJ in August 1901.

48 *The book of the Phoenix . . . Turba philosophorum*: Book of the Toad—perhaps Trinity MS 1399, *Bufo Gradiens*, etc. The first three volumes of MRJ's catalogue of Trinity MSS were published between 1900 and 1902. An alchemical work ascribed to Miriam (Moses' sister) is quoted by Zosimos (*c.* AD 300). The *Turba philosophorum* is an early Latin alchemical text of the twelfth century published in *Artis Auriferae* (1593) and J. J. Mangentus's *Bibliotheca Chemica Curiosa* (1702); a translation by A. E. Waite was issued by George Redway in 1896. MRJ would have known of the MSS of the work at St John's (MS 182) and Trinity (MS 1122), and also perhaps the sixteenth-century MS in the Bodleian at Oxford (Codex Latinus 7171).

Chorazin: mentioned in the woe pronounced by Jesus in Matthew 11:21 and Luke 10:13:

Woe unto thee, Chorazin! woe unto thee, Bethsaida! for if the mighty works, which were done in you, had been done in Tyre and Sidon, they would have repented long ago in sackcloth and ashes.

But I say unto you, it shall be more tolerable for Tyre and Sidon at the day of judgment, than for you.

H. Russell Wakefield uses the name Chorazin for a Soho club in his story 'He Cometh and He Passeth By' (*They Return at Evening*, 1928).

52 *devil-fish*: a name for the angler fish, which attracts prey by moving wormlike filaments on its head and mouth. The term is also used to describe the octopus, cuttle-fish, and other cephalopods, which is perhaps the meaning here.

55 *Belchamp St Paul*: a village in Essex, not far from Sudbury.

he came to a cross-road . . . two figures: the subject of the second of McBryde's unfinished illustrations for this story. 'I think the best picture', he told MRJ in May 1904, 'will be Mr Wraxall seeing the two figures standing in the moonlight by the crossroads while arriving in his closed fly. The fly is going directly along on the left, the horses are shying and the fly tipped up away from the figures. Mr Wraxall's sinewy hand . . . is seen clutching the

window sash on the moonlit side. Signpost at corner. Much
trouble about inclined plane of trap and shadows. I mean
to get them quite correct.' (James papers, Cambridge University Library).

'OH, WHISTLE, AND I'LL COME TO
YOU, MY LAD'

57 *Title*: first published in *GSA* (1904), the seventh story. The
MS was sold at Sotheby's in November 1936, to Bain. It is
untraced. The source of the quotation used as the title is
from Burns:

> O whistle, an' I'll come to you, my lad;
> O whistle, an' I'll come to you, my lad:
> Tho' father and mither should baith gae mad,
> O whistle, an' I'll come to you, my lad.

'Oh, Whistle . . .' is also the 'lively Scottish air' that
Wandering Willie plays to the captive Darsie Latimer in
Scott's *Redgauntlet* (1824, ch. 9), which contained the
classic supernatural tale, 'Wandering Willie's Tale'. Two
references suggest that the story was first read to the
Christmas 1903 gathering at King's: H. E. Luxmoore,
MRJ's former Eton tutor, recorded hearing what he called
'Fur flebis' (i.e. ' "Oh, Whistle" ') read that Christmas,
together with 'Number 13'; and an entry in Arthur
Benson's diary for December 1903 noted that 'MRJ read us
one of his medieval ghost stories—this is a pleasant habit
of his—the local colour is excellent, and the stories grim—
but there is a certain want of depth about them. The
people are all like elderly dons' (Magdalene College).
Benson read his own story, 'Basil Netherby', written for
the occasion, that same Christmas. ' "Oh, Whistle" ' was
admired by A. E. Housman and Thomas Hardy, to whom
Housman recommended the tale in 1913 (see Introduction,
p. xx). There is a reference to the ' "Oh, Whistle" ' ghost
in H. Russell Wakefield's 'The Triumph of Death', in
which the helpless companion of Miss Prunella Pendleham
is made to read 'a tale about some bedclothes forming into
a figure and frightening an old man in the other bed'. See
also Richard Holmes, *Shelley: The Pursuit* (1974), where
' "Oh, Whistle" ' is interpreted as 'a tale with sexual

undertones . . . especially [James's] comments on the *expressions* of linen'. *Text*: CGS.

Ontography . . . St James's College: both the professor's subject and his college are of course fictitious.

Burnstow: i.e. Felixstowe, Suffolk, where his friend Felix Cobbold lived. MRJ was there in 1893 and 1897–8; the latter visit may perhaps have a bearing on the dating of the story. Burnstow also appears in The Tractate Middoth'.

the Long: i.e. the Cambridge Long Vacation in the summer.

59 *Dr Blimber*: Dr Blimber was the principal of the boys' school at Brighton to which Paul Dombey is sent in Dickens's *Dombey and Son*. The nearest quotation in ch. 12 of the novel to that alluded to by Mr Rogers and in MRJ's note appears to be: ' "It is, Mr Feeder—if you are doing me the honour to attend—remarkable: VERY remarkable, Sir—" '.

60 *inclinations towards a picturesque ritual . . . East Anglian tradition*: MRJ's father (see Introduction) had an East Anglian living and was a loyal member of the Anglican Church's Evangelical wing. MRJ, though he had a sympathetic interest in Catholicism and ritualism from an antiquarian point of view, had himself an 'East Anglian' attitude towards it theologically. It was recorded by Arthur Benson in his diary that as Provost of King's MRJ refused to let Elgar's *Dream of Gerontius* be performed in the Chapel because it was 'too papistical'. On the other hand, he certainly did not share the Colonel's ultra-Protestant paranoia.

61 *Disney*: a Cambridge allusion. The Professor of Archaeology in the University is the Disney Professor. MRJ thought of standing for this chair in 1891.

round churches: such as Holy Sepulchre Church in Cambridge, at the junction of Bridge Street, Sidney Street, and St John's Street.

62 *ferae naturae*: in a wild state, undomesticated.

63 *'Now I saw in my dream . . . meet him'*: John Bunyan, *The Pilgrim's Progress*, Christian meeting Apollyon in the Valley of Humiliation. MRJ's quotation is inaccurate.

64 *Belshazzar*: see Daniel 5. Belshazzar was the son of

Nebuchadnezzar. During a great feast given by the king writing appeared on the palace wall which no one could interpret except the prophet. The message, MENE, MENE, TEKEL, UPHARSIN, foretold Belshazzar's doom and the destruction of his kingdom.

66 *Experto crede*: i.e. believe one who knows, or who has experienced it.

67 *looking up in an attitude of painful anxiety*: the caption to McBryde's first illustration to this story.

69 *'like some great bourdon in a minster tower'*: I have not traced this quotation. A bourdon is the bass stop of an organ, usually of 16-foot tone.

little better than a Sadducee: the Sadducees, according to the New Testament, denied the resurrection of the dead and the existence of angels. Professor Parkins's doubts were correct: there is no mention of them in the Old Testament. Cf. the 'Sadducean Professor of Ophiology' in 'The Mezzotint'.

70 *the Feast of St Thomas the Apostle*: i.e. 21 December.

75 *I can figure to myself . . . the same thing happen*: this is the exception to MRJ's denial, in the Preface to *CGS* (1931), that his stories were based on his own experience. 'Thirty years back' would place the dream around 1873, when MRJ was about eleven years old—another link, perhaps, with the childhood images of 'A Vignette' (p. 293), in which the ghost bears a resemblance to the entity in the present story (see Inroduction, p. xxix).

76 *It leapt towards him upon the instant*: the caption to McBryde's second illustration for the story.

THE TREASURE OF ABBOT THOMAS

78 *Title*: first published as the final story of *GSA* (1904). *MS*: Eton College. The MS was sold at Sotheby's in November 1936 to MRJ's friend Owen Hugh Smith. The story was written, in the summer of 1904, to fill up the volume (see below). *Text*: MS collated with printed versions.

Job, Johannes, et Zacharias: in the MS, 'Job' was changed from 'Salomon' and 'Zacharias' from 'Paulus'.

Sertum Steinfeldense Norbertinum: although works on the (actual: see next note) Premonstratensian abbey at Steinfeld exist, both this work and its author, Christian Albert Erhard, appear to be fictitious.

79 *a private chapel*: this is based on the chapel at Ashridge, near Berkhamsted in Hertfordshire, the home of Lord Brownlow (a relative of MRJ's Eton friend and contemporary Harry Cust). MRJ had camped at Ashridge with the Eton Rifle Corps in the summer of 1882, and doubtless noted the chapel. In July 1904 he was there examining the glass and in 1906 published a privately printed pamphlet, *Notes of Glass in Ashridge Chapel*. Of relevance to the background of the story is the following paragraph:

All the glass seems to me to be cent. XVI . . . I imagine that all of it probably came from one Church, the Abbatial Church of Steinfeld in the Eifel district. This was founded as a Benedictine Abbey in 920 . . . after 177 years (*i.e.* in 1099) the Benedictines, grown lax, were turned out . . . in favour of the Premonstratensians. Some fine glass from the same district is in the east window of St Stephen's Church at Norwich, and there is, I believe, a good deal in situ in the village churches. There is an account of Steinfeld in the Gallia Christiana, vol. III (Diocese of Cologne). I have not yet hit on a modern guide which will tell me whether there are any remains of it at the present day.

It is clear from this that MRJ never visited Steinfeld.

JOB PATRIARCHA: changed in the MS from 'REX SALOMON'.

Vulgate: the most widely used Latin version of the Bible in the West, mainly the work of St Jerome.

80 *Super lapidem . . . unaltered text*: the MS reads 'and Zacharias had: Super lapidem septem oculi sunt,[3] (where the word *unum* is omitted).' The note (3) in MS reads: 'Upon a (or the) stone are seven eyes.' The text in question (Zechariah 3: 9) is: 'For behold the stone that I have laid before Joshua; upon one stone shall be seven eyes: behold, I will engrave the graving thereof, saith the Lord of hosts, and I will remove the iniquity of that land in one day' (Authorized Version).

clearstory: this is the MS spelling; the more common variant 'clerestory' appears in all printed versions of the story.

81 *Cobblince*: i.e. Coblenz. The MS originally had 'Collong', i.e. Cologne.

88 *Steganographia . . . Cryptographia . . . de Augmentis Scientiarum*: Johann Trithemius (1462–1516), German monk and scholar, devised a system of shorthand, described in his *Steganographia*, first printed at Frankfurt in 1606, though it circulated earlier in manuscript. It was, Dr John Dee told Lord Cecil in 1563, a work 'for which many a learned man hath long sought and dayley yet doth seek' (Charlotte Fell Smith, *John Dee* (1909), p. 21). Selenius is Gustavus Selenus (i.e. Augustus II, Duke of Brunswick-Luneburg), *Gustavi Seleni Cryptomenytices et Cryptographiae . . .* (Luneburg, 1624). The *de Augmentis Scientiarum* (1623) is the expanded Latin version of Francis Bacon's *The Advancement of Learning* (1605).

   colours or patterns: the plurals are clear in the MS, but both GSA and CGS have 'colour or pattern'. There seems no reason why the MS reading should not stand, for the text nowhere states that the figures in the windows are dressed identically.

91 *Eliezer and Rebekah . . . Jacob . . . Rachel*: Genesis 24: the point of the reference is that Eliezer, Abraham's steward, sent to find a wife for Isaac, finds Rebekah by a well outside the city of Nahor in Mesopotamia; Genesis 29, Jacob meeting Rachel at the well of Haran.

93 *four in a vertical line, three horizontal*: in the copy of the 1919 edition of GSA in the Cambridge University Library (Adv.d.110.1), MRJ deleted the word 'four' and wrote 'five' in the margin, but then apparently crossed out the correction. The configuration of the 'eyes' strictly needs five in a vertical line, flanked by two others, making seven altogether.

96 *I must believe it*: this is followed in the MS by the deleted exclamation 'But what vistas it opens up!'

A SCHOOL STORY

97 *Title*: first published in *MGSA* (1911). MS: King's College, Cambridge. Arthur Benson, in his diary for 28 December 1906, records that 'After dinner L[uxmoore] told the story

(by MRJ) of the ashes, memento putei—a good story' (Magdalene College, Cambridge). The story was composed to entertain the King's College Choir School, in which MRJ took a keen interest. As Dean of King's he had direct responsibility for the school; as Provost he sent the boys a copy of GSA and in 1906 played in the annual cricket match between the Choir School and the Fellows. In the mid-1890s he wrote two comic plays for the choristers, *The Dismal Tragedy of Henry Blew Beard Esq* (in which he took the title role) and the *Historia de Alexandro Barberio et XL Latronibus*. Lyrics for both productions were by E. G. Swain, the College Chaplain and author of *The Stoneground Ghost Tales* (1912). See E&K, pp. 235-7. *Text*: MS collated with printed versions.

the Strand and Pearson's: the MS reads 'Nowadays the *Strand* would be a large contributor'. *Pearson's Magazine* ran in 88 volumes from 1896–1939; the *Strand*, the monthly best remembered for its serialization of the Sherlock Holmes stories, ran from 1891–1950. *Pearson's* published illustrated abridgements of some of MRJ's stories in the 1930s. He told Gwendolen McBryde in February 1932 that he had been 'startled to see a story of mine ['Number 13'] reprinted in Pearson's Mag. and promise of more to come—the publisher "thought I wouldn't mind" and no more I do, particularly as they pay. But I also noticed that they left out a number of sentences, and this I protest against. The publisher palliates his crime by saying he has sold about 3000 copies of the number—which is doubtless a good result' (*Letters to a Friend*, ed. Gwendolen McBryde, p. 179).

98 *The school I mean was near London . . . features*: this is Temple Grove, East Sheen, MRJ's own preparatory school, a once grand mansion standing in its own grounds between Mortlake and Richmond Park that had earlier been the home of Sir William Temple. It is described in some detail, but not named, in the first chapter of *Changing Eton* (1937) by L. S. R. Byrne and E. L. Churchill, who drew on MRJ's own memories of the school. See also Meston Batchelor, *Cradle of Empire* (1981) and MRJ's recollections of Temple Grove in E&K, pp. 5-14. The phrase 'quite an attractive place' is toned down from MS 'very attractive place'.

I came to the school . . . 1870: MRJ entered Temple Grove in September 1873. As he later recalled, the day—a rainy one—of his arrival there was 'one of the most lachrymose in my remembrance'.

stories which amused us on our school walks: perhaps a reference to the 'incredible romances about himself' invented by the writing master at Temple Grove, Mr Prior, 'and retailed to us when we were out for school walks of a winter afternoon' (E&K, p. 12).

a gold Byzantine coin: could this object be based on the 'silver coin of Vonones II, King of Parthia' which MRJ lost on the road to Richmond when a Temple Grove boy? See E&K, p. 6.

THE ROSE GARDEN

105 *Title*: first published in *MGSA* (1911). MS sold at Sotheby's, 9 November 1936, to Elkin Matthews; untraced. *Text*: *CGS* (1931). In *The Gothic Quest* (1938), p. 409, Montague Summers records 'how the late Dr M. R. James told me that one of his Ghost Stories—I am not sure which, but I rather fancy it might be *The Rose Garden*— was suggested to him by his recollection of a peculiarly vivid dream.' Cf. explanatory note to ' "Oh, Whistle, and I'll Come to You, My Lad" ', p. 312.

Westfield Hall . . . Essex: Westfield seems to be an invented location with no precise original, though Roothing, mentioned later in the story, is presumably derived from the Roothings, or Rodings, a few miles to the west of Chelmsford in Essex. 'Priors Roothing' suggests Abbess Roding (formerly Abbots Roothing).

114 *Recruited*: in the sense of refreshed, replenished, reinvigorated; the word is used in the same sense two paragraphs later.

115 *Sir —— —— . . . Charles II*: this would seem to refer to Sir William Scroggs (?1623–83), Chief Justice of the King's Bench from 1678 and Judge Jeffreys's predecessor. He displayed brutal zeal during the Popish Plot trials—for instance in the case of Oliver Plunkett, Archbishop of Armagh, who was tried for treason in 1681 and convicted

by Scroggs, on dubious evidence, to be hung, drawn, and quartered. MRJ would have come across Scroggs in the State Trials, which he greatly enjoyed reading: 'those of the period of the Popish Plot,' he wrote, 'the reign of James II, and the years immediately following the Revolution are undoubtedly the richest.' (Preface to *The Lady Ivie's Trial*, ed. Sir John Fox, 1929; see note to 'A Neighbour's Landmark', p. 333.)

116 *quieta non movere*: 'let sleeping dogs lie'.

THE TRACTATE MIDDOTH

117 *Title*: first published in *MGSA* (1911). MS: King's College, Cambridge. *Text*: MS collated with printed versions.

Piccadilly weepers: drooping whiskers of the kind fashionable in the 1860s (see note to p. 126, below).

the vestibule of a certain famous library: the Old Cambridge University Library (now the Squire Law Library and Seeley Historical Library) is situated north of the Old Schools and west of the Senate House in the centre of Cambridge. It was built 1837–42 as an extension of the library which by then occupied most of the Old Schools quadrangle.

Talmud . . . Nachmanides: The Talmud is the corpus of Jewish civil and ceremonial law, consisting of the Mishnah, or oral teachings, and the Gemara, or commentaries on the Mishnah. Tractate, from the Latin *tractatus*, is a treatise; the *Tractate Middoth* seems to be an invented work. Nachmanides, or Nahmanides (Moses ben Nahman Gerondi), the Spanish Talmudist of Gerona, was born in 1194 and died in Palestine *c.*1270. Of some slight relevance to MRJ's use of him here is a note on Nahmanides by the occult historiographer A. E. Waite: 'As regards the practical part of the Kabbalah, he treated it with grave consideration, including its art of necromancy, the evocation of evil spirits and the methods of their control' (Waite, *The Holy Kabbalah*, 1929, p. 111).

122 *Burnstow-on-Sea*: i.e. Felixstowe. Burnstow was the setting for ' "Oh, Whistle, and I'll Come to You, My Lad" '.

123 *The place was empty . . . acceptable company*: MS wording differs slightly: 'The place was empty at that season and Garrett found both mother and daughter very acceptable company. They were people of education and intelligence [this phrase is not in printed versions] and on the third evening . . . [continues]'.

126 *Dundreary*: Lord Dundreary was a character in Tom Taylor's *Our American Cousin* (1858). His long drooping whiskers became proverbial.

128 *a track*: Hodgson of course is reading the abbreviation for 'tractate'—i.e. 'trac.'.

CASTING THE RUNES

135 *Title*: first published in *MGSA* (1911). MS: British Library (Egerton 3141), acquired from the Sotheby's sale on 9 November 1936. A missing folio from the MS was later found among MRJ's papers at King's and presented to the Museum through A. N. L. Munby in 1948. A note by Eric Millar, a friend of MRJ's, in the *British Museum Quarterly* later stated that the purchase of the MS had been felt to be especially appropriate 'as the scene of the actual "casting" of the runes is laid in the Students' Room, in which the author was for so many years a familiar and honoured figure'. *Text*: MS collated with printed versions. The MS contains several lengthy cancelled passages.

Karswell: it is sometimes assumed that Karswell is based on the self-styled 'Great Beast', the occultist Aleister Crowley (1875–1947), though on what authority is not clear. I cannot find that MRJ ever mentioned Crowley or his nefarious activities either publicly or in private, although Crowley went up to Trinity College, Cambridge, in 1895 and might conceivably have come to the attention of MRJ, who was then Dean of King's and had many friends in Trinity. The first number of Crowley's 'magickal' periodical *The Equinox* appeared in 1909, and the previous year Somerset Maugham had cast him as Oliver Haddo in his novel *The Magician*. On the other hand, Crowley did not come to wide public prominence as 'the wickedest man in the world' until the 1920s, and there is no direct evidence to support the claim that Karswell is based on

Crowley. In a cancelled MS passage Karswell is described as 'formerly a Roman [Catholic] . . . thirsting I believe for recognition by the literary and scientific world'.

136 *he's a very happy man . . . all his time to himself*: it is hard not to feel that this summation of Dunning's bachelor life in some way articulates James's desire to escape from the administrative burdens of University life and live quietly as a self-sufficient gentleman scholar. A cancelled MS passage describes Mr Dunning more fully as being 'of middle age and size, of regular habits, with a turn for investigations genealogical, topographical, and antiquarian; a familiar figure in the Reading Room and Select Manuscripts of the [British] Museum, and at the Record Office, by no means uninteresting or uninterested in life, but one who had never experienced any deep convulsion of his being.'

139 *John's*: i.e. St John's College, Cambridge.

141 *Three months were allowed*: in the MS, Harrington was given six months.

142 *William and me*: MS. MGSA (and CGS) has 'William 'ere', which seems to be a misreading.

144 *Select Manuscript Room of the British Museum . . . Harley 3586*: MRJ became a Trustee of the British Museum in 1925, and of course used the Museum frequently over the years. See note to title, above. Harley 3586 actually consists of two monastic registers (in Latin) from the fourteenth century with which are bound two English letters of the seventeenth century (from Thomas Blount and Thomas Goad). It is difficult to see what the joke is—if there is one—in this reference.

150 *all very proper, no doubt*: MS reads 'quite scientific'. See next note.

the Golden Legend . . . Golden Bough: the *Golden Legend* is a medieval compilation of ecclesiastical lore, lives of saints, homilies, etc. A version of it was one of Caxton's most popular productions. Sir J. G. Frazer (1854–1941), a Fellow of Trinity College, Cambridge, published *The Golden Bough*, an immense comparative study of religion, magic, and folklore in 12 volumes, 1890–1915. It may be inferred that MRJ did not have a very high opinion of

Frazer's work or of comparative mythology in general. Confirmation is found in his polemical review of an article in the *Classical Review* (Dec. 1916) by the Cambridge archaeologist Jane Harrison on 'The Head of John the Baptist', in which she interpreted the dance of Salome as 'the dance of the daimon of the New Year with the head of the Old Year': 'Crude and inconsequent speculations of this kind . . .', wrote MRJ, 'go far to justify those who deny to Comparative Mythology the name and dignity of a science.'

152   the *'black spot'*: see R. L. Stevenson's *Treasure Island* (1883), ch. 3.

    a woodcut of Bewick's: Thomas Bewick (1753–1828), the celebrated wood-engraver whose work included Gay's *Fables* (1779) and the *Fables of Aesop* (1818).

    'Walks on . . . behind him tread': from S. T. Coleridge's 'The Rime of the Ancient Mariner' (first published in *Lyrical Ballads*, 1798).

154   *Cook's ticket-cases*: i.e. Thomas Cook (1808–92), pioneer of the modern tourist industry.

156   *the Lord Warden*: an actual Dover hotel at which MRJ occasionally stayed on his way to or from France.

    St Wulfram's Church at Abbeville: a church MRJ knew well.

    identified him as Mr Karswell: in the MS there follows a cancelled passage describing how, on the evening of Karswell's death, 'between Abbeville and St Riquier', a large bird 'of the vulture type' was sighted heading northward by a local naturalist: 'The failing light prevented the man from making an accurate observation; but he states his conviction that the creature was not in fact a vulture.'

THE STALLS OF BARCHESTER CATHEDRAL

157   *Title*: first published in the *Contemporary Review*, XCVII, 35 (1910), 449–60, subtitled 'Materials for a Ghost Story'; reprinted in MGSA (1911). MS: sold at Sotheby's, November 1936, to Bain; untraced. *Text*: CGS (1931).

    Gentleman's Magazine: founded by Edward Cave (1691–1754) in 1731. See note on Sylvanus Urban below.

wranglers: a Cambridge term meaning someone placed in the first class of the Mathematical Tripos.

Barchester: the name of the imaginary cathedral town in the county of Barsetshire created by Anthony Trollope in his sequence of novels beginning with *The Warden* (1855) and ending with *The Last Chronicle of Barset* (1867). Barsetshire and Barchester were also used as a setting by the novelist Angela Thirkell. MRJ's Barchester, like his Southminster in 'An Episode of Cathedral History', was a blend of Canterbury, Salisbury, and Hereford.

Argonautica of Valerius Flaccus: Valerius Flaccus's epic poem on the Argonauts was begun *c*.AD 70 but was left unfinished.

159 *material of a kind with which I am only too familiar*: the voice here is that of M. R. James the cataloguer.

160 *Sir Gilbert Scott*: Sir George Gilbert Scott (1811–78), one of the leading architects of the Gothic Revival. Here and in 'An Episode of Cathedral History' MRJ expresses something of his disapproval of the destruction carried out in the name of restoration during the Revival.

prebends . . . triforium . . . reredos: a prebend is an endowment to a cathedral or collegiate church *in praebendam* (i.e. to maintain a secular priest or regular canon); hence a prebendary. A triforium is a gallery or arcade above the arches of the nave, choir, or occasionally transept. A reredos is an ornamental screen of stone or wood at the rear of the altar.

baldacchino: a canopy placed above the altar, and often supported by pillars, that was popular during the Jacobean period.

162 *Second Epistle to the Thessalonians*: 2 Thessalonians 7, 'For the mystery of iniquity doth already work: only he who now letteth will let, until he be taken out of the way.'

the aged Israelite in the canticle: Simeon, in Luke 2: 29. The 'Song of Simeon' ('Lord, now lettest thou thy servant depart in peace, according to thy word') is the canticle *Nunc dimittis*, ordered for Evensong in the Book of Common Prayer.

163 *Sylvanus Urban*: the pseudonym of Edward Cave, founder of the *Gentleman's Magazine*.

the genus Mus: a pedantic phrase for a mouse.

Tartarean origin: pertaining to hell. Tartarus was the infernal region in Greek and Roman mythology.

168 *Set thou an ungodly man . . . right hand*: Psalm 109: 6.

170 *the writings of Mr Shelley, Lord Byron, and M. Voltaire*: i.e. subversive and, from the writer's conventional point of view, atheistical modern writers.

MR HUMPHREYS AND HIS INHERITANCE

172 *Title*: first published as the final story of MGSA (1911). *MS*: sold at Sotheby's, November 1936, to Owen Hugh Smith; now at Eton. *Text*: MS collated with printed versions. One reader, MRJ's friend Arthur Hort, was puzzled by the story and MRJ obliged with the following résumé:

As far as I can give it the explanation is this. That old Mr Wilson who made the maze had remained in the globe with his ashes, quiescent as long as the gate was not opened. When they opened it and laid out the clue, and left the gate open, he woke up and came out. It was he who was mistaken on two successive nights for an Irish yew and a growth against the house wall, and on the last evening he made himself visible to his descendant creeping up as it were out of unknown depths and emerging at the appropriate spot—the centre of the plan of the maze.

(3 January 1912; letter in private hands)

At King's there is an undated draft of a story involving a young man called John Humphreys which has elements in common with the published story (for example, the episode of the small Irish yew). The plots, however, have nothing in common and there is no maze in the MS story, 'which should be described rather as an earlier story about John Humphreys than as an early draft of the published story' (Michael Halls, 'A Handlist of the Papers of Montague Rhodes James, D. Litt., in the Modern Archives, King's College, Cambridge', 1981, p. 4).

welcome to Wilsthorpe: in the MS, MRJ's first choice of a name is illegible; his second was 'Haydon', deleted in favour of Wilsthorpe.

change of propriety: Cooper means 'change of proprietorship'.

176 *valentudinarian*: i.e. valetudinarian—someone of infirm health or who is unduly anxious about his health.

177 *the heart to feel and the hand to accommodate*: cf. Charles Churchill, 'The Prophecy of Famine': 'And Nature gave thee, open to distress,/A heart to pity, and a hand to bless.'

flash . . . pan . . . golden bowl: Ecclesiastes 12: 1, 'Or ever the silver cord be loosed, or the golden bowl be broken. . .'.

178 *dolebat se dolore non posse*: lit. 'grieved that he could not grieve'.

meatear: i.e. *métier*, one's trade, profession, or calling.

179 *horse doover*: either meant for 'hors de combat', or perhaps literally 'out of work' (from 'hors d'œuvre'). The MS has 'hors', not 'horse': the latter more accurately gives us Cooper's pronunciation.

Sibyl's Temple at Tivoli: Tivoli is the ancient Tibur, some twenty miles north of Rome. A replica of the Sibyl's Temple is erected by Sir Richard Fell at Castringham in 'The Ash-tree' (GSA).

Handel's 'Susanna': Handel was one of MRJ's favourite composers. *Susanna* would have had a double appeal for him, being also an apocryphal book of the Old Testament.

180 *Secretum meum mihi et filiis domus meae*: lit. 'my secret is for me and for the sons of my house'.

a yew maze: the topiary labyrinth became fashionable in the late sixteenth century. In England a well-known example was the hedge maze made about 1560 for Lord Burghley at Theobalds in Hertfordshire. The most famous English hedge maze is at Hampton Court, constructed in 1690 but probably replacing an earlier one, immortalized by Jerome K. Jerome in *Three Men in a Boat* (1889). The fruitless wanderings of the Wilsthorpe party later in the story may indeed deliberately recall the Hampton Court Maze episode in Jerome's book. In Suffolk there was a maze which MRJ may have known of at Somerleyton Hall.

181   *celestial globe*: a globe showing the arrangement of the stars.

      the old proverb . . . tread: Alexander Pope, *An Essay on Criticism* (1711), l.625: 'For fools rush in where angels fear to tread.'

182   *teenets*: i.e. tenets.

184   *catalogue raisonné*: a descriptive catalogue.

      Fathers: i.e. the Fathers of the early Christian Church.

      Picart's Religious Ceremonies . . . Harleian Miscellany . . . Tostatus Abulensis . . . Pineda on Job: (i) Bernard Picart, *Cérémonies et coutumes religieuses de tous les peuples du monde . . .* 8 vols. (Amsterdam, 1723–43), translated into English in 1733 and again in 1828. (ii) The Harleian Miscellany was a reprint of selected tracts from the library of Edward Harley (1689–1741), 2nd Earl of Oxford; published in 1744–6, it was edited by William Oldys (whose surname was borrowed by MRJ for a character in 'The Residence at Whitminster', TG, 1919) and Samuel Johnson. (iii) Tostatus Abulensis, i.e. Alfonso Tostado de Madrigal, Bishop of Avila; see J. de Almonazid, *El Abulense ilustrado* (1672). (iv) Pineda, i.e. Joannes de Pineda, of Seville, *Commentariorum in Iob* (1598).

185   *Theseus in the Attick Tale*: the legend of Theseus and Ariadne in the labyrinth of the Minotaur.

187   *a Hound at Fault*: in hunting parlance, 'fault' denotes loss of scent by the hounds, and thus a check in the pursuit so caused. This is the kind of linguistic detail that lends authenticity and immediacy to MRJ's literary and historical pastiches.

188   *Patience*: Mr Humphreys, like Mr Anderson in 'Number 13', enjoys one of MRJ's own favourite card games.

190   *princeps tenebrarum*: Prince of Darkness.

      umbra mortis: the shadow of death.

      vallis filiorum Hinnom: the valley (of the sons) of Hinnom, close to the walls of Jerusalem, acquired an evil reputation because of idolatrous practices carried out there. See 2 Kings 23: 10, and Milton, *Paradise Lost*, i. 403–5:

> and made his [Moloch's] grave
> The pleasant valley of Hinnom, Tophet thence
> And black Gehenna called, the type of Hell.

197 *Nearer and nearer . . . over them*: in the MS this passage—
the climax of the story—is conveyed in the present tense
and the pivotal phrase 'there clambered forth an appearance of a form' is less effectively rendered 'there came an
appearance'.

198 PENETRANS AD INTERIORA MORTIS: lit. 'penetrating to the
inner places of death'.

THE DIARY OF MR POYNTER

199 *Title*: first published in *TG* (1919). *MS*: untraced. *Text*:
CGS (1931).
F.S.A.: Fellow of the Society of Antiquaries. See note to
'An Episode of Cathedral History', p. 329.

202 *the circle of Oxford antiquaries . . . Thomas Hearne*:
Thomas Hearne (1678–1735), bibliophile and antiquary,
second Keeper of the Bodleian Library (1712), whose
Collectanea, 6 vols. (1715), compiled from the notes of
John Leland, Henry VIII's librarian, was a bibliographical
event of great importance and formed part of the historical
substructure of MRJ's own work. Hearne was an MA of
St Edmund Hall, Oxford.

205 *unconsidered trifles*: Shakespeare, *The Winter's Tale*,
IV.ii.26, 'a snapper-up of unconsidered trifles'.
I say Shakespeare . . . 'Ercules and the painted cloth: a
curious passage which seems to refer to the Bacon–
Shakespeare controversy. Mr Cattell appears to be mis-
quoting *Henry IV, Part I*, iv.ii: 'slaves as ragged as
Lazarus in the painted cloth'.
lends a catchit: i.e. lends a cachet, a mark of distinction,
authenticity, or prestige.

206 *the feast of Simon and Jude*: 28 October.

209 *Absalom*: third son of David by Maacah. See 2 Samuel 18:
25–6:

But in all Israel there was none to be so much praised as
Absalom for his beauty: from the sole of his foot even to
the crown of his head there was no blemish in him.
And when he polled his head, (for it was at every year's
end that he polled it: because the hair was heavy on him,
therefore he polled it:) he weighed the hair of his head at
two hundred shekels after the king's weight.

Dr Plot's History of Staffordshire: the *Natural History of Staffordshire* (1686) by Dr Robert Plot (1640–96), antiquary, first 'custos' of the Ashmolean Museum at Oxford, Professor of Chemistry at Oxford 1683, Historiographer Royal 1688.

There are more things: *Hamlet*, I.v.166, 'There are more things in heaven and earth, Horatio,/Than are dreamt of in your philosophy.'

AN EPISODE OF CATHEDRAL HISTORY

210 *Title*: first published in the *Cambridge Review*, 10 June 1914, pp. 533–8. Reprinted as the third story in TG (1919). MS: King's College, Cambridge. The MS was sold at Sotheby's in November 1936, together with 'The Story of a Disappearance and an Appearance', to J. M. Keynes, who later bequeathed both MSS to King's. The story had been written by May 1913, for it was referred to by Arthur Benson in his diary on the 18th of that month: 'Monty read us a very good ghost story, with an admirable verger very humorously portrayed—the ghost part weak' (Diary of A. C. Benson, Magdalene College, Cambridge). *Text*: MS collated with printed versions.

Southminster: according to James (Preface to CGS, 1931), this and Barchester (in 'The Stalls of Barchester Cathedral') were 'blends of Canterbury, Salisbury, and Hereford'.

Mr Worby: A Worby is buried in Livermere churchyard.

like another Mr Datchery: Dick Datchery is the name assumed by a character, whose true identity remains unrevealed, in Dickens's unfinished last novel, *The Mystery of Edwin Drood* (1870). MRJ had read Dickens with great delight from his early years at Eton and he remained one of his favourite authors. *Edwin Drood* had a particular fascination for MRJ, who was constitutionally drawn to puzzles and mysteries of all kinds—from the provenance of manuscripts to crosswords and detective fiction. His interest in the book resulted in an article for the *Cambridge Review* ('The Edwin Drood Syndicate'), which appeared in two parts in November–December 1905, soon after he became Provost of King's. In 1909 he joined five other Drood enthusiasts—including Henry Jackson of

Trinity, author of *About Edwin Drood* (1911)—on an investigatory excursion to Rochester (see E&K, pp. 215–16). MRJ's view was that Dick Datchery was Edwin Drood himself in disguise.

211 *Jasper and Durdles*: two more characters from *Edwin Drood* (see note above); John Jasper, Edwin Drood's sinister uncle and precentor of the cathedral at Cloisterham (Rochester), and Durdles the stonemason.

 . . . *a piece of verse . . . Scotch cathedral* . . . : Mr Worby seems to have in mind the following lines from Sir Walter Scott's *The Lord of the Isles* (1813):

> If thou would'st view fair Melrose aright,
> Go visit it by the pale moonlight;
> For the gay beams of lightsome day
> Gild, but to flout, the ruins of grey.

213 *It was in 1840 . . . Southminster*: MRJ strongly disapproved of needless architectural 'restoration'. An indication of his attitude on this matter is given by an exchange of views in 1900 concerning the glass in the Priory Church at Malvern, where his brother Sydney was then Headmaster. A Mrs McClure wished to 'restore' the mutilated pictures in the windows. MRJ dismissed the argument that this could be done on the grounds of 'reverence': 'I must confess that the question of reverence or irreverence seems to me not to arise here at all. Did we mutilate these windows? do we keep them thus mutilated in order to make the personages and scenes represented ridiculous? . . . We would gladly have had the whole, but that was denied us. We treasure what we have, neither adding to it, nor taking from it.' These views should be borne in mind whenever the theme of architectural restoration occurs in the ghost stories.

217 *as the dark fell*: MS and *Cambridge Review*; TG and CGS have 'as the dark fell in', which seems wrong. MRJ had originally written 'as the dark closed in' but did not delete 'closed in' when he wrote 'fell' over the top.

F.S.A.: Fellow of the Society of Antiquaries. MRJ had been FSA since the mid-1890s. In the MS he deleted the words 'draughtsman', 'artist', and 'antiquarian' before deciding on 'F.S.A.'.

diaper-ornament: a diamond-shaped design.

219 *Henslow . . . Lyall*: it is perhaps no accident that MRJ
names his canons after two eminent Victorians: John
Stevens Henslow (1796–1861), botanist and naturalist on
the *Beagle*, who presided over the celebrated debate on
Darwin's *Origin of Species* at the British Association in
1861; and Alfred Lyall (1795–1865), philosopher and
traveller, educated at Eton and Trinity College, Cambridge.

Isaiah 34:14: 'The wild beasts of the desert shall also meet
with the wild beasts of the island, and the satyr shall cry
to his fellow; the screech owl [night monster] also shall
rest there, and find for herself a place of rest.' See last
note.

Simeon's lot . . . Evangelical party: there is a personal
aspect to the reference. MRJ's father, the Revd Herbert
James, whilst a Cambridge undergraduate in the 1840s,
had come under the posthumous influence of Charles
Simeon (1759–1836), one of the leading Evangelicals of his
day, a Fellow of King's, and a founder of the Church
Missionary Society. He remained closely associated with
the Evangelical wing of the Church of England and in
him, as his obituary in *The Times* said, 'the Simeon spirit
worked strongly'.

223 *the 19th day . . . Venite . . . Decani boys*: the *Venite* is a
canticle consisting of Psalm 95, the opening words of
which are 'O come, let us sing unto the Lord' (Venite,
exultemus). It is ordered for Morning Prayer on Day 19
in the Book of Common Prayer. *Decani boys* are those on
the dean's (south) side of the choir, opposite the cantorial,
or precentor's, side.

227 *Isaiah xxxiv . . .* IBI CUBAVIT LAMIA: 'the screech owl [night
monster] shall also rest there'. A lamia was a witch or
demon supposed to suck the blood of children. The Vulgate
Latin for this verse runs: 'Et occurent daemonia onocen-
tauris, et pilosus clamabit alter ad alterum: ibi cubavit
lamia, et invenit sibi requiem.' The inscription is not in
capitals in the MS.

THE UNCOMMON PRAYER-BOOK

228 *Title*: first published in the *Atlantic Monthly*, 127, 6 (June 1921), 756–65; reprinted in WTC (1925). *MS*: sold at Sotheby's, November 1936, to Owen Hugh Smith; now at Eton College. *Text*: MS collated with printed versions.

the Leventhorp house: MS. Printed versions have 'Leventhorp House', which is rather different.

Gaulsford . . . Swan Hotel . . . valley of the Tent: the general location is clearly the valley of the Teme in what is now Hereford and Worcester. The Swan is perhaps based on the Swan at Tenbury Wells (where MRJ stayed in 1932, but he may well have known it previously). The Stanfords have their counterparts in Stanford on Teme and Stanford Bridge. The general area was familiar to MRJ: his brother Sydney had been Headmaster of Malvern from 1897 to 1914, and his sister Grace moved to nearby Presteigne in Radnorshire from Livermere in 1916.

versicles and responses: short sentences said or sung alternately by priest and congregation.

230 *Gregory singin'*: Gregorian chanting, also known as plain chant or plain song; named after Pope Gregory I.

da capo: (music) 'repeated from the beginning'.

231 *the Plague-year*: 1664–5.

the Triumph of Loyalty and the Defeat of Sedition: i.e. the Restoration of Charles II in May 1660.

Cromwell, Ireton, Bradshaw, Peters, and the rest: Oliver Cromwell (1599–1658), Henry Ireton (1611–51), John Bradshaw (1602–59), Hugh Peters (1598–1660)—all indicted for the regicide of Charles I.

Lady Sadleir: Lady Anne Sadleir, a fanatical royalist and donor of the Trinity Apocalypse, part of the western manuscript collection of Trinity College, Cambridge, which MRJ had begun systematically cataloguing in 1897. He also dealt with this MS in a facsimile edition published for the Roxburghe Club in 1909 and in his 1927 Schweich Lectures to the British Academy, published as *The Apocalypse in Art* (1931).

Oliver Cromwell's grave: Cromwell died on 3 September

1658. He was first buried in Westminster Abbey, but after the Restoration in 1660 his body was dug up, gibbeted at Tyburn, and afterwards buried there.

232   *Abbey Dore . . . Lord Scudamore's work*: Abbey Dore, Herefordshire, a Cistercian foundation, was one of MRJ's favourite churches. He called it 'one of the most surprising and delightful of all the places I have to write about' in his book *Abbeys* (1925). Lord Scudamore was 'an enthusiastic churchman of the Laudian type' who in 1633 restored the transepts and choir of the abbey church. The restored church was reconsecrated in 1634.

   one of the Dallams: Thomas Dallam (*fl.* 1615) and his son Robert (1602–65), organ builders. Thomas was responsible for the organ at King's (1606).

233   *Psalm cix . . . Deus laudem*: CGS has, incorrectly, *Deus laudum*. The psalm ('Hold thy tongue, O God of my praise') is indeed savage.

236   *Homberger*: Homberger/Poschwitz is the only deliberately Jewish character in MRJ's fiction and is painted in decidedly uncomplimentary terms.

A NEIGHBOUR'S LANDMARK

244   *Title*: first published in WTC (1925). The title is a quotation from the Commination in the Book of Common Prayer: 'Cursed is he that removeth his neighbour's landmark'. *MS*: untraced. *Text*: CGS.

   'The Stricken Years' . . . Times Literary Supplement: apparently, a fictional article.

246   *'That which walks . . . why it cries'*: a couplet praised by A. E. Housman as being 'good poetry'.

248   *Birket Foster*: Myles Birket Foster (1825–99), English painter and illustrator who specialized in roadside and woodland landscapes with rustic figures.

249   *'With no language but a cry'*: from Tennyson's *In Memoriam*.

254   *Scott's Glenfinlas*: the ballad 'Glenfinlas, or Lord Ronald's Coronach' by Sir Walter Scott, which appeared in M. G. ('Monk') Lewis's *Tales of Wonder* (1801). MRJ thought that 'Glenfinlas' and 'Scott's 'The Eve of St John' 'must

always rank as fine ghost stories' ('Some Remarks on Ghost Stories': see p. 343).

255   *the State Trials*: these, first issued in 1809, formed a favourite part of MRJ's recreational reading. The cream of the trials, in his opinion, were to be found for the years 1649–1700, in particular the period of the Popish Plot (drawn on in 'The Rose Garden': see p. 319), the reign of James II, and the years immediately following the Revolution. He especially relished those in which Judge Jeffreys figured. Amongst these 'The Lady Ivie's Trial for a great part of Shadwell' was a particular favourite. He recommended the State Trials because 'in them alone . . . do we find the unadorned common speech of Englishmen'. His own pastiche of a State Trial under Judge Jeffreys occurs in 'Martin's Close' (*MGSA*, 1911).

   the Lady Ivy . . . Theodosia Bryan: a historical character, tried before Judge Jeffreys for forging land claims (see previous note). MRJ noted that she 'seems to answer very completely to the French designation of a *triste personage*'.

256   [*Thanks to the researches . . . responsible*]: this paragraph was added to the *CGS* reprint of the story and does not appear in WTC. It is not an invented reference. MRJ had suggested to Sir John Fox that the trial of Lady Ivie should be reissued and it duly appeared in 1929, with a Preface by MRJ.

A WARNING TO THE CURIOUS

257   *Title*: first published in the *London Mercury*, XII, 70 (Aug. 1925), 354–65. Reprinted in WTC (1925). MS: sold at Sotheby's, November 1936, to Elkin Matthews; untraced. *Text*: CGS (1931).

   Seaburgh: Aldeburgh, Suffolk, where MRJ's paternal grandmother had lived and where his brothers went to school. He was often there until his grandmother died in 1870. ('The first painted window ever I saw is in the church here,' he wrote from Aldeburgh in April 1921. 'The first organ I heard is likewise here and the first anthem performed I know not on what occasion caused me to burst into tears of apprehension and be led from the sacred edifice.') He returned to Aldeburgh regularly in later life, staying at the White Lion. See *Suffolk and Norfolk*, pp. 102–4: ' "Sung by Crabbe and figuring in Wilkie Collins's *No Name*, [Aldeburgh] has a special charm for those who, like myself, have known it from childhood, but I don't find it easy to put that charm into words.'

259 *Froston*: probably Theberton, where the three crowns are conspicuous.

261 *in 1687 . . . dug up at Rendlesham*: Rendelsham was the site of a Saxon palace. A silver crown, reputed to have been Redwald's, was indeed dug up at this date 'and (it is painful to relate) was melted down almost at once, so that we know nothing of its quality' (*Suffolk and Norfolk*, p. 11).

the war of 1870 . . . the South African War: the Franco-Prussian war of 1870–1 and the second Boer War of 1899–1902.

267 *Paschal moon*: Easter moon.

268 *as Christian did through that Valley*: Bunyan, *Pilgrim's Progress*; cf. note to ' "Oh, Whistle, and I'll Come to You, My Lad" ', p. 313.

RATS

275 *Title*: first published in *At Random*, an emphemeral 'Edited by present Etonians' that appeared on Saturday 23 March 1929, pp. 12–14; reprinted in Cynthia Asquith's anthology *Shudders* (1929) and in *CGS* (1931). MS: untraced. *Text*: CGS.

'And if you was to walk . . . under 'em': from Dickens's Christmas story 'Tom Tiddler's Ground' (*All the Year Round*, 1861).

276 *Orlando Whistlecraft . . . 'Charming Year'*: Orlando Whistlecraft was the pseudonymous author of *The Magnificent and Notably Hot Summer of 1846* (1846), *The Weather Record of 1856* (1857), *The Weather Almanack* (1856, etc.), amongst other works on climate and meteorology.

Thetford Heath: cf. *Suffolk and Norfolk*, p. 66: 'Thetford I will not treat of now, only pausing to note that not far from the Bury road, on the west side, you may catch sight of a block of stone on the heath which I have always taken to be the base of a gibbet: certainly the locality would have suited highwaymen.'

THE EXPERIMENT

281 *Title*: first published in the *Morning Post*, 31 December 1930. Not in *CGS*. *MS*: untraced. *Text*: *Morning Post*.

284 *good Bishop Moore*: undoubtedly John Moore (1646–1714), bishop successively of Norwich and Ely and a Fellow of Clare College, Cambridge. His famous library was bought by George I and presented to the University Library at Cambridge.

THE MALICE OF INANIMATE OBJECTS

288 *Title*: first published in the first number of *The Masquerade*, an Eton magazine, for June 1933 (29–32). The title appears in the incomplete list of his writings, written at the back of an interleaved Greek Testament that also served as a rudimentary diary, MRJ prepared to help A. F. Scholfield in the compilation of the *Elenchus* (see Select Bibliography). The story was reprinted, with an introduction by the present editor, in *Ghosts and Scholars* 6 (1984), 1–5. *MS*: in private hands. *Text*: *The Masquerade*.

A VIGNETTE

293 *Title*: first published in the *London Mercury*, 35 (Nov. 1936), 18–22, after MRJ's death. A headnote by the Editor, R. A. Scott-James, describes how MRJ's friend Owen Hugh Smith had asked him 'to try and recapture the mood in which he wrote *Ghost Stories of an Antiquary*' and to supply something suitable for the Christmas number of the magazine. The MS of 'A Vignette', written on lined foolscap, was sent to the *Mercury* on 12 December 1935 with a covering note:

I am ill satisfied with what I enclose. It comes late and is short and ill written. There have been a good many events conspiring to keep it back, besides a growing inability. So pray don't use it unless it has some quality I do not see in it.

I send it because I was enjoined to do something by Mr Owen Hugh Smith.

For the possible biographical implications of the story see Introduction, p. xxix. MS: untraced. *Text: London Mercury.*

the spacious garden of a country rectory: the rectory at Livermere, near Bury St Edmunds in Suffolk, James's childhood home. For a description of the rectory as James knew it see Lubbock, *Memoir*, and also MRJ's *Suffolk and Norfolk* (1930), in which he wrote: 'Livermere Hall is gone, and many oaks in its park are cut down . . . But village and park have some beauties left.'

the Hall: the seventeenth-century Livermere Hall was owned by MRJ's 'Cousin Jane'—Jane Anne Broke, who married James St Vincent, 4th Baron de Saumarez, in 1882. She was the stepdaughter of William Horton, MRJ's uncle, and inherited Livermere Hall in 1855. It was through her that Herbert James had been offered the Livermere living. The Hall was demolished in 1923.

294   '*gain-giving*': misgiving; *Hamlet*, v.ii.227.

      '*the hidea of such a thing!*': a phrase used by Sarah Holder, a family servant.

296   *parts of a novel*: J. S. Le Fanu's *The House by the Churchyard* (by 'Charles de Cresseron'), serialized in the *Dublin University Magazine*, 1861–3. The quotation 'the aerial image of the old house, with its peculiar malign, scared, and skulking aspect' had a particular fascination for MRJ and was referred to in his 1929 *Bookman* article on ghost stories (see p. 346). On both occasions 'scared' is misquoted as 'sacred'.

APPENDIX

M. R. JAMES ON GHOST STORIES

(i) from the Preface to *Ghost Stories of an Antiquary* (1904)

I WROTE these stories at long intervals, and most of them were read to patient friends, usually at the season of Christmas. One of these friends [James McBryde] offered to illustrate them, and it was agreed that, if he would do that, I would consider the question of publishing them. Four pictures he completed, which will be found in this volume, and then, very quickly and unexpectedly, he was taken away. This is the reason why the greater part of the stories are not provided with illustrations. Those who knew the artist will understand how much I wished to give a permanent form even to a fragment of his work; others will appreciate the fact that here a remembrance is made of one in whom many friendships centred. The stories themselves do not make any very exalted claim. If any of them succeed in causing their readers to feel pleasantly uncomfortable when walking along a solitary road at nightfall, or sitting over a dying fire in the small hours, my purpose in writing them will have been attained.

(ii) from the Preface to *More Ghost Stories of an Antiquary* (1911)

Some years ago I promised to publish a second volume of ghost stories when a sufficient number of them should have been accumulated. That time has arrived, and here is the volume. It is, perhaps, unnecessary to warn the critic that in evolving the stories I have not been possessed by that austere sense of the responsibility of authorship which is demanded of the writer of fiction in this generation; or that I have not sought to embody in them any well-considered scheme of 'psychical' theory. To be sure, I have my ideas as to how a ghost story ought to be laid out if it is to be effective. I think that, as a rule, the setting should be fairly familiar and the majority of the characters and their talk such as you may meet or hear any day. A ghost story of which the scene is laid in the twelfth or thirteenth century may succeed in being romantic or poetical: it will never put the reader into the position of saying to himself, 'If I'm not very careful, something of this kind may happen to me!' Another requisite, in my opinion, is that the ghost should be malevolent or odious: amiable and helpful apparitions are all very well in fairy tales or in local legends, but I have no use for them in a fictitious ghost story. Again, I feel that the technical terms of 'occultism', if they are not very carefully handled, tend to put the mere ghost story (which is all that I am attempting) upon a quasi-scientific plane, and to call into play faculties quite other than the imaginative. I am well aware that mine is a nineteenth- (and not a twentieth-) century conception of this class of tale; but were not the prototypes of all the best ghost stories written in the sixties and seventies?

However, I cannot claim to have been guided by any very strict rules. My stories have been produced (with one exception) at successive Christmas seasons. If they serve to amuse some readers at the Christmas-time that is coming—or at any time whatever—they will justify my action in publishing them.

(iii) from the Prologue to J. S. Le Fanu, *Madam Crowl's Ghost* (1923)

[Le Fanu] stands absolutely in the first rank as a writer of ghost stories. That is my deliberate verdict, after reading all the supernatural tales I have been able to get hold of. Nobody sets the scene better than he, nobody touches in the effective detail more deftly. I do not think it is merely the fact of my being past middle age that leads me to regard the leisureliness of his style as a merit; for I am by no means inappreciative of the more modern efforts in this branch of fiction. No, it has to be recognized, I am sure, that the ghost story is in itself a slightly old-fashioned form; it needs some deliberateness in the telling: we listen to it the more readily if the narrator poses as elderly, or throws back his experience to 'some thirty years ago'.

(iv) from the Introduction to V. H. Collins (ed.), *Ghosts and Marvels* (Oxford, 1924)

Often have I been asked to formulate my views about ghost stories and tales of the marvellous, the mysterious, the supernatural. Never have I been able to find out whether I had any views that could be formulated. The truth is, I suspect, that the *genre* is too small and special to bear the imposition of far-reaching principles. Widen the question, and ask what governs the construction of short stories in general, and a great deal might be said, and has been said. There are, of course, instances of whole novels in which the supernatural governs the plot; but among them are few successes. The ghost story is, at its best, only a particular sort of short story, and is subject to the same broad rules as the whole mass of them. Those rules, I imagine, no writer ever consciously follows. In fact, it is absurd to talk of them as rules; they are qualities which have been observed to accompany success.

Some such qualities I have noted, and while I cannot undertake to write about broad principles, something more concrete is capable of being recorded. Well, then: two ingredients most valuable in the concocting of a ghost story are, to me, the atmosphere and the nicely managed crescendo. I assume, of course, that the writer will have got his central idea before he undertakes the story at all. Let us, then, be introduced to the actors in a placid way; let us see them going about their ordinary business, undisturbed by forebodings, pleased with their surroundings; and into this calm environment let the ominous thing put out its head, unobtrusively at first, and then more insistently, until it holds the stage. It is not amiss sometimes to leave a loophole for a natural explanation; but, I would say, let the loophole be so narrow as not to be quite practicable. Then, for the setting. The detective story cannot be too much up-to-date: the motor, the telephone, the aeroplane, the newest slang, are all in place there. For the ghost story a slight haze of distance is desirable. 'Thirty years ago', 'Not long before the war', are very proper openings. If a really remote date be chosen, there is more than one way of bringing the reader in contact with it. The finding of documents about it can be made plausible; or you may begin with your apparition and go back over the years to tell the cause of it; or (as in 'Schalken the Painter') you may set the scene directly in the desired epoch, which I think is hardest to do with success. On the whole (though not a few instances might be quoted against me) I think that a setting so modern that the ordinary reader can judge of its naturalness for himself is preferable to anything antique. For some degree of actuality is the charm of the best ghost stories; not a very insistent actuality, but one strong enough to allow the reader to identify himself with the patient; while it is almost inevitable that the reader of an antique story should fall into the position of the mere spectator.

(v) 'Stories I Have Tried to Write', first published in *The Touch-stone*, 2 (30 Nov. 1929), 46-7; reprinted in *The Collected Ghost Stories of M. R. James* (1931), 643-7

I have neither much experience nor much perseverance in the writing of stories—I am thinking exclusively of ghost stories, for I never cared to try any other kind—and it has amused me sometimes to think of the stories which have crossed my mind from time to time and never materialized properly. Never properly: for some of them I have actually written down, and they repose in a drawer somewhere. To borrow Sir Walter Scott's most frequent quotation, 'Look on (them) again I dare not.' They were not good enough. Yet some of them had ideas in them which refused to blossom in the surroundings I had de-vised for them, but perhaps came up in other forms in stories that did get as far as print. Let me recall them for the benefit (so to style it) of somebody else.

There was the story of a man travelling in a train in France. Facing him sat a typical Frenchwoman of mature years, with the usual moustache and a very confirmed countenance. He had nothing to read but an antiquated novel he had bought for its binding—*Madame de Lichtenstein* it was called. Tired of look-ing out of the window and studying his *vis-à-vis*, he began drowsily turning the pages, and paused at a conversation be-tween two of the characters. They were discussing an acquain-tance, a woman who lived in a largish house at Marcilly-le-Hayer. The house was described, and—here we were coming to a point—the mysterious disappearance of the woman's husband. Her name was mentioned, and my reader couldn't help thinking he knew it in some other connexion. Just then the train stopped at a country station, the traveller, with a start, woke up from a doze—the book open in his hand—the woman opposite him got out, and on the label of her bag he read the name that had seemed to be in his novel. Well, he went on to Troyes, and from there he made excursions, and one of these took him—at lunch-time—to—yes, to Marcilly-le-Hayer. The hotel in the Grande Place faced a three-gabled house of some pretensions. Out of it came a well-dressed woman *whom he had seen before*.

Conversation with the waiter. Yes, the lady was a widow, or so it was believed. At any rate nobody knew what had become of her husband. Here I think we broke down. Of course, there was no such conversation in the novel as the traveller thought he had read.

Then there was quite a long one about two undergraduates spending Christmas in a country house that belonged to one of them. An uncle, next heir to the estate, lived near. Plausible and learned Roman priest, living with the uncle, makes himself agreeable to the young men. Dark walks home at night after dining with the uncle. Curious disturbances as they pass through the shrubberies. Strange, shapeless tracks in the snow round the house, observed in the morning. Efforts to lure away the companion and isolate the proprietor and get him to come out after dark. Ultimate defeat and death of the priest, upon whom the Familiar, baulked of another victim, turns.

Also the story of two students of King's College, Cambridge, in the sixteenth century (who were, in fact, expelled thence for magical practices), and their nocturnal expedition to a witch at Fenstanton, and of how, at the turning to Lolworth, on the Huntingdon road, they met a company leading an unwilling figure whom they seemed to know. And of how, on arriving at Fenstanton, they learned of the witch's death, and of what they saw seated upon her newly-dug grave.

These were some of the tales which got as far as the stage of being written down, at least in part. There were others that flitted across the mind from time to time, but never really took shape. The man, for instance (naturally a man with *something* on his mind), who, sitting in his study one evening, was startled by a slight sound, turned hastily, and saw a certain dead face looking out from between the window curtains: a dead face, but with living eyes. He made a dash at the curtains and tore them apart. A pasteboard mask fell to the floor. But there was no one there, and the eyes of the mask were but eyeholes. What was to be done about that?

There is the touch on the shoulder that comes when you are walking quickly homewards in the dark hours, full of anticipation of the warm room and bright fire, and when you pull up, startled, what face or no-face do you see?

Similarly, when Mr Badman had decided to settle the hash of Mr Goodman and had picked out just the right thicket by the roadside from which to fire at him, how came it exactly that when Mr Goodman and his unexpected friend actually did pass, they found Mr Badman weltering in the road? He was able to tell them something of what he had found waiting for him— even beckoning to him—in the thicket: enough to prevent them from looking into it themselves. There are possibilities here, but the labour of constructing the proper setting has been beyond me.

There may be possibilities, too, in the Christmas cracker, if the right people pull it, and if the motto which they find inside has the right message on it. They will probably leave the party early, pleading indisposition; but very likely a *previous engagement of long standing* would be the more truthful excuse.

In parenthesis, many common objects may be made the vehicles of retribution, and where retribution is not called for, of malice. Be careful how you handle the packet you pick up in the carriage-drive, particularly if it contains nail-parings and hair. Do not, in any case, bring it into the house. It may not be alone . . . (Dots are believed by many writers of our day to be a good substitute for effective writing. They are certainly an easy one. Let us have a few more . . . . . .)

Late on Monday night a toad came into my study: and, though nothing has so far seemed to link itself with this appearance, I feel that it may not be quite prudent to brood over topics which may open the interior eye to the presence of more formidable visitants. Enough said.

(vi) 'Some Remarks on Ghost Stories', *The Bookman* (December 1929), 169–172

Very nearly all the ghost stories of old times claim to be true narratives of remarkable occurrences. At the outset I must make it clear that with these—be they ancient, medieval or post-medieval—I have nothing to do, any more than I have with those chronicled in our own days. I am concerned with a branch of fiction; not a large branch, if you look at the rest of the tree, but one which has been astonishingly fertile in the last thirty years. The avowedly fictitious ghost story is my subject, and that being understood I can proceed.

In the year 1854 George Borrow narrated to an audience of Welshmen, 'in the tavern of Gutter Vawr, in the county of Glamorgan', what he asserted to be 'decidedly the best ghost story in the world'. You may read this story either in English,

in Knapp's notes to *Wild Wales*, or in Spanish, in a recent
edition with excellent pictures (*Las Aventuras de Pánfilo*). The
source is Lope de Vega's *El Peregrino en su patria*, published in
1604. You will find it a remarkably interesting specimen of a
tale of terror written in Shakespeare's lifetime, but I shall be
surprised if you agree with Borrow's estimate of it. It is nothing
but an account of a series of nightmares experienced by a
wanderer who lodges for a night in a 'hospital', which had been
deserted because of hauntings. The ghosts come in crowds and
play tricks with the victim's bed. They quarrel over cards, they
squirt water at the man, they throw torches about the room.
Finally they steal his clothes and disappear; but next morning
the clothes are where he put them when he went to bed. In
fact they are rather goblins than ghosts.

Still, here you have a story written with the sole object of
inspiring a pleasing terror in the reader; and as I think, that is
the true aim of the ghost story.

As far as I know, nearly two hundred years pass before you
find the literary ghost story attempted again. Ghosts of course
figure on the stage, but we must leave them out of consideration. Ghosts are the subject of quasi-scientific research in this
country at the hands of Glanville, Beaumont and others; but
these collectors are out to prove theories of the future life and
the spiritual world. Improving treatises, with illustrative instances, are written on the Continent, as by Lavater. All these,
if they do afford what our ancestors called amusement (Dr
Johnson decreed that *Coriolanus* was 'amusing'), do so by a side-
wind. *The Castle of Otranto* is perhaps the progenitor of the
ghost story as a literary genre, and I fear that it is merely
amusing in the modern sense. Then we come to Mrs Radcliffe,
whose ghosts are far better of their kind, but with exasperating
timidity are all explained away; and to Monk Lewis, who in the
book which gives him his nickname is odious and horrible
without being impressive. But Monk Lewis was responsible for
better things than he could produce himself. It was under his
auspices that Scott's verse first saw the light: among the *Tales
of Terror and Wonder* are not only some of his translations,
but 'Glenfinlas' and the 'Eve of St John', which must always
rank as fine ghost stories. The form into which he cast them
was that of the ballads which he loved and collected, and we
must not forget that the ballad is in the direct line of ancestry
of the ghost story. Think of 'Clerk Saunders', 'Young Benjie', the

'Wife of Usher's Well'. I am tempted to enlarge on the *Tales of Terror*, for the most part supremely absurd, where Lewis holds the pen, and jigs along with such stanzas as:

> All present then uttered a terrified shout;
> 　All turned with disgust from the scene.
> The worms they crept in, and the worms they crept out,
> And sported his eyes and his temples about,
> 　While the spectre addressed Imogene.

But proportion must be observed.

If I were writing generally of horrific books which include supernatural appearances, I should be obliged to include Maturin's *Melmoth*, and doubtless imitations of it which I know nothing of. But *Melmoth* is a long—a cruelly long—book, and we must keep our eye on the short prose ghost story in the first place. If Scott is not the creator of this, it is to him that we owe two classical specimens—'Wandering Willie's Tale' and the 'Tapestried Chamber'. The former we know is an episode in a novel; anyone who searches the novels of succeeding years will certainly find (as we, alas, find in *Pickwick* and *Nicholas Nickleby*!) stories of this type foisted in; and possibly some of them may be good enough to deserve reprinting. But the real happy hunting ground, the proper habitat of our game is the magazine, the annual, the periodical publication destined to amuse the family circle. They came up thick and fast, the magazines, in the thirties and forties, and many died young. I do not, having myself sampled the task, envy the devoted one who sets out to examine the files, but it is not rash to promise him a measure of success. He will find ghost stories; but of what sort? Charles Dickens will tell us. In a paper from *Household Words*, which will be found among *Christmas Stories* under the name of 'A Christmas Tree' (I reckon it among the best of Dickens's occasional writings), that great man takes occasion to run through the plots of the typical ghost stories of his time. As he remarks, they are 'reducible to a very few general types and classes; for ghosts have little originality, and "walk" in a beaten track.' He gives us at some length the experience of the nobleman and the ghost of the beautiful young house-keeper who drowned herself in the park two hundred years before; and, more cursorily, the indelible bloodstain, the door that will not shut, the clock that strikes thirteen, the phantom coach, the compact to appear after death, the girl who meets her double, the cousin who is seen at the moment of his death far away in India, the maiden lady who 'really did see the Orphan Boy'. With such things as these we are still familiar. But we have rather forgotten—and I for my part have seldom met—those with which he ends his survey: 'Legion is the name of the German castles where we sit up alone to meet the spectre —where we are shown into a room made comparatively cheerful for our reception' (more detail, excellent of its kind, follows), 'and where, about the small hours of the night, we come into the knowledge of divers supernatural mysteries. Legion is the name of the haunted German students, in whose society we draw yet nearer to the fire, while the schoolboy in the corner opens his eyes wide and round, and flies off the footstool he has chosen for his seat, when the door accidentally blows open.'

As I have said, this German stratum of ghost stories is one of which I know little; but I am confident that the searcher of magazines will penetrate to it. Examples of the other types will accrue, especially when he reaches the era of Christmas Numbers, inaugurated by Dickens himself. His Christmas *Numbers* are not to be confused with his Christmas *Books*, though the latter led on to the former. Ghosts are not absent from these, but I do not call the *Christmas Carol* a ghost story proper; while I do assign that name to the stories of the Signalman and the Jury-man (in 'Mugby Junction' and 'Dr Marigold').

These were written in 1865 and 1866, and nobody can deny that they conform to the modern idea of the ghost story. The setting and the personages are those of the writer's own day; they have nothing antique about them. Now this mode is not absolutely essential to success, but it is characteristic of the majority of successful stories: the belted knight who meets the spectre in the vaulted chamber and has to say 'By my halidom', or words to that effect, has little actuality about him. Anything, we feel, might have happened in the fifteenth century. No; the seer of ghosts must talk something like me, and be dressed, if not in my fashion, yet not too much like a man in a pageant, if he is to enlist my sympathy. Wardour Street has no business here.

If Dickens's ghost stories are good and of the right complexion, they are not the best that were written in his day. The palm must I think be assigned to J. S. Le Fanu, whose stories of 'The Watcher' (or 'The Familiar'), 'Mr Justice Harbottle', 'Carmilla', are unsurpassed, while 'Schalken the Painter',

'Squire Toby's Will', the haunted house in 'The House by the Churchyard', 'Dickon the Devil', 'Madam Crowl's Ghost', run them very close. Is it the blend of French and Irish in Le Fanu's descent and surroundings that gives him the knack of infusing ominousness into his atmosphere? He is anyhow an artist in words; who else could have hit on the epithets in this sentence: 'The aerial image of the old house for a moment stood before her, with its peculiar malign, scared and skulking aspect.' Other famous stories of Le Fanu there are which are not quite ghost stories—'Green Tea' and 'The Room in the Dragon Volant'; and yet another, 'The Haunted Baronet', not famous, not even known but to a few, contains some admirable touches, but somehow lacks proportion. Upon mature consideration, I do not think that there are better ghost stories anywhere than the best of Le Fanu's; and among these I should give the first place to 'The Familiar' (*alias* 'The Watcher').

Other famous novelists of those days tried their hand—Bulwer Lytton for one. Nobody is permitted to write about ghost stories without mentioning 'The Haunters and the Haunted'. To my mind it is spoilt by the conclusion; the Cagliostro element (forgive an inaccuracy) is alien. It comes in with far better effect (though in a burlesque guise) in Thackeray's one attempt in this direction—'The Notch in the Axe', in the *Roundabout Papers*. This to be sure begins by being a skit partly on Dumas, partly on Lytton; but as Thackeray warmed to his work he got interested in the story and, as he says, was quite sorry to part with Pinto in the end. We have to reckon too with Wilkie Collins. *The Haunted Hotel*, a short novel, is by no means ineffective; grisly enough, almost, for the modern American taste.

Rhoda Broughton, Mrs Riddell, Mrs Henry Wood, Mrs Oliphant—all these have some sufficiently absorbing stories to their credit. I own to reading not infrequently 'Featherston's Story' in the fifth series of *Johnny Ludlow*, to delighting in its domestic flavour and finding its ghost very convincing. (*Johnny Ludlow*, some young persons may not know, is by Mrs Henry Wood.) The religious ghost story, as it may be called, was never done better than by Mrs Oliphant in 'The Open Door' and 'A Beleaguered City'; though there is a competitor, and a strong one, in Le Fanu's 'Mysterious Lodger'.

Here I am conscious of a gap; my readers will have been conscious of many previous gaps. My memory does in fact slip on from Mrs Oliphant to Marion Crawford and his horrid story of

'The Upper Berth', which (with 'The Screaming Skull' some distance behind) is the best in his collection of *Uncanny Tales*, and stands high among ghost stories in general.

That was I believe written in the late eighties. In the early nineties comes the deluge, the deluge of the illustrated monthly magazines, and it is no longer possible to keep pace with the output either of single stories or of volumes of collected ones. Never was the flow more copious than it is today, and it is only by chance that one comes across any given example. So nothing beyond scattering and general remarks can be offered. Some whole novels there have been which depend for all or part of their interest on ghostly matter. There is *Dracula*, which suffers by excess. (I fancy, by the way, that it must be based on a story in the fourth volume of Chambers's *Repository*, issued in the fifties.) There is *Alice-for-Short* [by W. de Morgan, 1907], in which I never cease to admire the skill with which the ghost is woven into the web of the tale. But that is a very rare feat.

Among the collections of short stories, E. F. Benson's three volumes rank high, though to my mind he sins occasionally by stepping over the line of legitimate horridness. He is however blameless in this aspect as compared with some Americans, who compile volumes called *Not At Night* and the like. These are merely nauseating, and it is very easy to be nauseating. I, *moi qui vous parle*, could undertake to make a reader physically sick, if I chose to think and write in terms of the Grand Guignol. The authors of the stories I have in mind tread, as they believe, in the steps of Edgar Allan Poe and Ambrose Bierce (himself sometimes unpardonable), but they do not possess the force of either.

Reticence may be an elderly doctrine to preach, yet from the artistic point of view I am sure it is a sound one. Reticence conduces to effect, blatancy ruins it, and there is much blatancy in a lot of recent stories. They drag in sex too, which is a fatal mistake; sex is tiresome enough in the novels; in a ghost story, or as the backbone of a ghost story, I have no patience with it.

At the same time don't let us be mild and drab. Malevolence and terror, the glare of evil faces, 'the stony grin of unearthly malice', pursuing forms in darkness, and 'long-drawn, distant screams', are all in place, and so is a modicum of blood, shed with deliberation and carefully husbanded; the weltering and wallowing that I too often encounter merely recall the methods of M. G. Lewis.

Clearly it is out of the question for me to begin upon a series of 'short notices' of recent collections; but an illustrative instance or two will be to the point. A. M. Burrage, in *Some Ghost Stories*, keeps on the right side of the line, and if about half of his ghosts are amiable, the rest have their terrors, and no mean ones. H. R. Wakefield, in *They Return at Evening* (a good title) gives us a mixed bag, from which I should remove one or two that leave a nasty taste. Among the residue are some admirable pieces, very inventive. Going back a few years I light on Mrs Everett's *The Death Mask*, of a rather quieter tone on the whole, but with some excellently conceived stories. Hugh Benson's *Light Invisible* and *Mirror of Shalott* are too ecclesiastical. K. and Hesketh Prichard's 'Flaxman Low' is most ingenious and successful, but rather over-technically 'occult'. It seems impertinent to apply the same criticism to Algernon Blackwood, but 'John Silence' is surely open to it. Mr Elliott O'Donnell's multitudinous volumes I do not know whether to class as narratives of fact or exercises in fiction. I hope they may be of the latter sort, for life in a world managed by his gods and infested by his demons seems a risky business.

So I might go on through a long list of authors; but the remarks one can make in an article of this compass can hardly be illuminating. The reading of many ghost stories has shown me that the greatest successes have been scored by the authors who can make us envisage a definite time and place, and give us plenty of clear-cut and matter-of-fact detail, but who, when the climax is reached, allow us to be just a little in the dark as to the working of their machinery. We do not want to see the bones of their theory about the supernatural.

All this while I have confined myself almost entirely to the English ghost story. The fact is that either there are not many good stories by foreign writers, or (more probably) my ignorance has veiled them from me. But I should feel myself ungrateful if I did not pay a tribute to the supernatural tales of Erckmann–Chatrian. The blend of French with German in them, comparable to the French–Irish blend in Le Fanu, has produced some quite first-class romance of this kind. Among longer stories, 'La Maison Forestière' (and, if you will, 'Hugues le Loup'); among shorter ones 'Le Blanc et le Noir', 'Le Rêve du Cousin Elof' and 'L'Œil Invisible' have for years delighted and alarmed me. It is high time that they were made more accessible than they are.

There need not be any peroration to a series of rather disjointed reflections. I will only ask the reader to believe that,
though I have not hitherto mentioned it, I have read *The Turn
of the Screw.*

(vii) 'Ghosts—Treat Them Gently!', *Evening News* (17 April
1931)

What first interested me in ghosts? This I can tell you quite
definitely. In my childhood I chanced to see a toy Punch and
Judy set, with figures cut out in cardboard. One of these was
The Ghost. It was a tall figure habited in white with an unnaturally long and narrow head, also surrounded with white,
and a dismal visage.

Upon this my conceptions of a ghost were based, and for
years it permeated my dreams.

Other questions—why I like ghost stories, or what are the
best, or why they are the best, or a recipe for writing such
things—I have never found it easy to be so positive about.
Clearly, however, the public likes them. The recrudescence of
ghost stories in recent years is notable: it corresponds, of course,
with the vogue of the detective tale.

The ghost story can be supremely excellent in its kind, or
it may be deplorable. Like other things, it may err by excess or
defect. Bram Stoker's *Dracula* is a book with very good ideas
in it, but—to be vulgar—the butter is spread far too thick.
Excess is the fault here: to give an example of erring by defect
is difficult, because the stories that err in that way leave no
impression on the memory.

I am speaking of the literary ghost story here. The story that
claims to be 'veridical' (in the language of the Society of
Psychical Research) is a very different affair. It will probably
be quite brief, and will conform to some one of several familiar
types. This is but reasonable, for, if there be ghosts—as I am
quite prepared to believe—the true ghost story need do no more
than illustrate their normal habits (if normal is the right word),
and may be as mild as milk.

The literary ghost, on the other hand, has to justify his
existence by some startling demonstration, or, short of that,
must be furnished with a background that will throw him into
full relief and make him the central feature.

Since the things which the ghost can effectively do are very limited in number, ranging about death and madness and the discovery of secrets, the setting seems to me all-important, since in it there is the greatest opportunity for variety.

It is upon this and upon the first glimmer of the appearance of the supernatural that pains must be lavished. But we need not, we should not, use all the colours in the box. In the infancy of the art we needed the haunted castle on a beetling rock to put us in the right frame: the tendency is not yet extinct, for I have but just read a story with a mysterious mansion on a desolate height in Cornwall and a gentleman practising the worst sort of magic. How often, too, have ruinous old houses been described or shown to me as fit scenes for stories!

'Can't you imagine some old monk or friar wandering about this long gallery?' No, I can't.

I know Harrison Ainsworth could: *The Lancashire Witches* teems with Cistercians and what he calls votaresses in mouldering vestments, who glide about passages to very little purpose. But these fail to impress. Not that I have not a soft corner in my heart for *The Lancashire Witches*, which—ridiculous as much of it is—has distinct merits as a story.

It cannot be said too often that the more remote in time the ghost is the harder it is to make him effective, always supposing him to be the ghost of a dead person. Elementals and such-like do not come under this rule.

Roughly speaking, the ghost should be a contemporary of the seer. Such was the elder Hamlet and such Jacob Marley. The latter I cite with confidence and in despite of critics, for, whatever may be urged against some parts of A *Christmas Carol*, it is, I hold, undeniable that the introduction, the advent, of Jacob Marley is tremendously effective.

And be it observed that the setting in both these classic examples is contemporary and even ordinary. The ramparts of the Kronborg and the chambers of Ebenezer Scrooge were, to those who frequented them, features of every-day life.

But there are exceptions to every rule. An ancient haunting can be made terrible and can be invested with actuality, but it will tax your best endeavours to forge the links between past and present in a satisfying way. And in any case there must be ordinary level-headed modern persons—Horatios—on the scene, such as the detective needs his Watson or his Hastings to play the part of the lay observer.

Setting or environment, then, is to me a principal point, and the more readily appreciable the setting is to the ordinary reader the better. The other essential is that our ghost should make himself felt by gradual stirrings diffusing an atmosphere of uneasiness before the final flash or stab of horror.

Must there be horror? you ask. I think so. There are but two really good ghost stories I know in the language wherein the elements of beauty and pity dominate terror. They are Lanoe Falconer's 'Cecilia de Noel' and Mrs Oliphant's 'The Open Door'. In both there are moments of horror; but in both we end by saying with Hamlet: 'Alas, poor ghost!' Perhaps my limit of two stories is overstrict; but that these two are by very much the best of their kind I do not doubt.

On the whole, then, I say you must have horror and also malevolence. Not less necessary, however, is reticence. There is a series of books I have read, I think American in origin, called *Not at Night* (and with other like titles), which sin glaringly against this law. They have no other aim than that of Mr Wardle's Fat Boy.

Of course, all writers of ghost stories do desire to make their readers' flesh creep; but these are shameless in their attempts. They are unbelievably crude and sudden, and they wallow in corruption. And if there is a theme that ought to be kept out of the ghost story, it is that of the charnel house. That and sex, wherein I do not say that these *Not at Night* books deal, but certainly other recent writers do, and in so doing spoil the whole business.

To return from the faults of ghost stories to their excellence. Who, do I think, has best realized their possibilities? I have no hesitation in saying that it is Joseph Sheridan Le Fanu. In the volume called *In a Glass Darkly* are four stories of paramount excellence, 'Green Tea', 'The Familiar', 'Mr Justice Harbottle', and 'Carmilla'. All of these conform to my requirements: the settings are quite different, but all *seen* by the writer; the approaches of the supernatural nicely graduated; the climax adequate. Le Fanu was a scholar and poet, and these tales show him as such. It is true that he died as long ago as 1873, but there is wonderfully little that is obsolete in his manner.

Of living writers I have some hesitation in speaking, but on any list that I was forced to compile the names of E. F. Benson, Blackwood, Burrage, De la Mare and Wakefield would find a place.

But, although the subject has its fascinations, I see no use in being pontifical about it. These stories are meant to please and amuse us. If they do so, well; but, if not, let us relegate them to the top shelf and say no more about it.

JANE AUSTEN	Catharine and Other Writings
	Emma
	Mansfield Park
	Northanger Abbey, Lady Susan, The Watsons, and Sanditon
	Persuasion
	Pride and Prejudice
	Sense and Sensibility
ANNE BRONTË	Agnes Grey
	The Tenant of Wildfell Hall
CHARLOTTE BRONTË	Jane Eyre
	The Professor
	Shirley
	Villette
EMILY BRONTË	Wuthering Heights
WILKIE COLLINS	The Moonstone
	No Name
	The Woman in White
CHARLES DARWIN	The Origin of Species
CHARLES DICKENS	The Adventures of Oliver Twist
	Bleak House
	David Copperfield
	Great Expectations
	Hard Times
	Little Dorrit
	Martin Chuzzlewit
	Nicholas Nickleby
	The Old Curiosity Shop
	Our Mutual Friend
	The Pickwick Papers
	A Tale of Two Cities

ANTHONY TROLLOPE

An Autobiography

Ayala's Angel

Barchester Towers

The Belton Estate

The Bertrams

Can You Forgive Her?

The Claverings

Cousin Henry

Doctor Thorne

Doctor Wortle's School

The Duke's Children

Early Short Stories

The Eustace Diamonds

An Eye for an Eye

Framley Parsonage

He Knew He Was Right

Lady Anna

The Last Chronicle of Barset

Later Short Stories

Miss Mackenzie

Mr Scarborough's Family

Orley Farm

Phineas Finn

Phineas Redux

The Prime Minister

Rachel Ray

The Small House at Allington

La Vendée

The Warden

The Way We Live Now

THE OXFORD SHERLOCK HOLMES

ARTHUR CONAN DOYLE
The Adventures of Sherlock Holmes
The Case-Book of Sherlock Holmes
His Last Bow
The Hound of the Baskervilles
The Memoirs of Sherlock Holmes
The Return of Sherlock Holmes
The Valley of Fear
Sherlock Holmes Stories
The Sign of the Four
A Study in Scarlet

*The
Oxford
World's
Classics
Website*

www.worldsclassics.co.uk

- Information about new titles
- Explore the full range of Oxford World's Classics
- Links to other literary sites and the main OUP webpage
- Imaginative competitions, with bookish prizes
- Peruse *Compass*, the Oxford World's Classics magazine
- Articles by editors
- Extracts from Introductions
- A forum for discussion and feedback on the series
- Special information for teachers and lecturers

www.worldsclassics.co.uk

American Literature

British and Irish Literature

Children's Literature

Classics and Ancient Literature

Colonial Literature

Eastern Literature

European Literature

History

Medieval Literature

Oxford English Drama

Poetry

Philosophy

Politics

Religion

The Oxford Shakespeare

A complete list of Oxford Paperbacks, including Oxford World's Classics, OPUS, Past Masters, Oxford Authors, Oxford Shakespeare, Oxford Drama, and Oxford Paperback Reference, is available in the UK from the Academic Division Publicity Department, Oxford University Press, Great Clarendon Street, Oxford OX2 6DP.

In the USA, complete lists are available from the Paperbacks Marketing Manager, Oxford University Press, 198 Madison Avenue, New York, NY 10016.

Oxford Paperbacks are available from all good bookshops. In case of difficulty, customers in the UK can order direct from Oxford University Press Bookshop, Freepost, 116 High Street, Oxford OX1 4BR, enclosing full payment. Please add 10 per cent of published price for postage and packing.